THE
CONTROVERSIAL
MAYAN QUEEN

THE CONTROVERSIAL MAYAN QUEEN

Sak K'uk of Palenque

Born 584 CE – Acceded 612 CE – Died 640 CE

LEONIDE MARTIN

Mists of Palenque Series Book 2

Made for Success
P.O. Box 1775
Issaquah, WA 98027

The Controversial Mayan Queen: Sak K'uk of Palenque

Library of Congress Cataloging-in-Publication data

Martin, Leonide
    The Controversial Mayan Queen: Sak K'uk of Palenque.
    Mists of Palenque Book 2
    p. cm.
    ISBN: 978-1-61339-881-4 (pbk.)
    LCCN: 2016913875

To contact the publisher,
please email service@MadeforSuccess.net or call +1 425 657 0300.

Made for Wonder is an imprint of Made for Success Publishing.

Printed in the United States of America

CONTENTS

List of Characters and Places

Sak K'uk – Characters   (*historical person)

<u>Royal Family of Lakam Ha</u>
*Sak K'uk** – Acting ruler of Lakam Ha 612-615 CE, mother of Janaab Pakal
*Kan Mo' Hix** – husband of Sak K'uk
*K'inich Janaab Pakal** – son of Sak K'uk and Kan Mo' Hix
*Hun Pakal** – father of Sak K'uk
*Aj Ne Ohl Mat** – brother of Sak K'uk, ruler of Lakam Ha 605-612 CE
Yaxun Xul – father of Kan Mo' Hix
Hohmay – wife of Aj Ne Ohl Mat
Muwaan Mat – Primordial Mother Goddess, named ruler of Lakam Ha 612-615 CE

<u>Main Courtiers/Warriors of Lakam Ha</u>
Chakab – older Nakom (warrior chief) of Lakam Ha
Oaxac Ok – distant cousin of Sak K'uk
Ch'amak – distant cousin of Sak K'uk
Uc Ayin – courtier, musician, artist of Lakam Ha
*Yax Chan** – young architect of Lakam Ha
K'anal – scribe of Lakam Ha
Ikim – potter of ceramics at Lakam Ha

<u>Priests/Priestesses</u>
Pasah Chan – High Priest of Lakam Ha
Kab' – wife of Pasah Chan
Ah K'uch – old calendar priest
Usin Ch'ob – High Priestess of Lakam Ha

Other Lakam Ha Nobles
Tunsel – Pakal's nursemaid
Kitam – noble opponent to Bahlam dynasty in Lakam Ha
Pax Koh – noble opponent to Bahlam dynasty in Lakam Ha
Yonil – beautiful young noble woman of Lakam Ha, in love with Pakal
Tulix – young noble woman of Lakam Ha
Muyal – young noble woman of Lakam Ha

Usihwitz Characters
Ek Chuuah – vengeful noble exiled from Lakam Ha, leader of attack plot
Yax Chapat – son of Ek Chuuah
Yahau Chan Muwaan I* – ruler of Usihwitz 603 - ? CE

Kan Characters
Yuknoom Ti' Chan* – ruler of Kan 619-? CE
Tajoom Uk'ab K'ak* – ruler of Kan 622-630 CE
Uneh Chan* – ruler of Kan 579-611 CE
Tajoom – High Priest of Kan
Wamaw Took – Nakom (warrior chief) of Kan

Characters from other cities
Zotz (Bat) Dynasty – displaced Kan Dynasty from Uxte'tun
Manik – sister of Uc Ayin, lives in Sak Tz'i
Ho' Tok – visiting trader from Nab'nahotot

Ancestors
U K'ix Kan – quasi-human being created by Triad Deities, lived hundreds of years, brought forth first truly human ancestor of Bahlam Dynasty (K'uk Bahlam I)
K'uk Bahlam I* – first historic ruler of Lakam Ha 431-435 CE, founder of Bahlam Dynasty
Muwaan Mat – Primordial Mother Goddess, mother of Triad Deities
Kan Bahlam I* – grandfather of Sak K'uk, ruler of Lakam Ha 572-583 CE
Yohl Ik'nal* – mother of Sak K'uk, ruler of Lakam Ha 583-604 CE

Cities and Polities

<u>Ancestral Places</u>
Matawiil – mythohistoric origin lands at Six Sky Place
Toktan – ancestral city of K'uk Bahlam I, founder of Lakam Ha dynasty
Nakbe – (El Mirador), called Chatan Uinik – Second Center of Humans
Petén – lowlands area in north Guatemala, densely populated with Maya sites

<u>B'aakal Polity and Allies</u>
B'aakal – "Kingdom of the Bone," polity governed by Lakam Ha (Palenque)
Lakam Ha – (Palenque) "Big Waters," major city of B'aakal polity, May Ku
Popo' – (Tonina) in B'aakal polity, linked to Lakam Ha by royal marriage
Yokib – (Piedras Negras) in B'aakal polity, later allied with Kan
Wa-Mut – (Wa-Bird, Santa Elena) in B'aakal polity
Nututun – City on Chakamax River, near Lakam Ha
Sak Tz'i – (White Dog) in B'aakal polity, later allied with Kan
Anaay Te – (Anayte) in B'aakal polity
B'aak – (Tortuguero) in B'aakal polity
Mutul – (Tikal) great city of southern region, ally of Lakam Ha, enemy of Kan
Nab'nahotot – (Comalcalco) city on coast of Great North Sea (Gulf of Mexico)
Oxwitik – (Copan) southern city allied with Lakam Ha by marriage

<u>Ka'an Polity and Allies</u>
Ka'an – "Kingdom of the Snake," polity governed by Kan
Kan – refers to residence city of Kan (Snake) Dynasty
Uxte'tun – (Kalakmul) early home city of Kan Dynasty, usurped by Zotz (Bat)
    Dynasty
Dzibanche – home city of Kan dynasty (circa 400-600 CE)
Pakab – (Pomona, Pia) in Ka'an polity, joined Usihwitz in raid on Lakam Ha
Pa'chan – (Yaxchilan) in Ka'an polity
Waka' – (El Peru) ally of Kan, enemy of Mutul

<u>Coastal, Trading, and Yukatek Cities</u>
Yalamha – coastal trading city on long peninsula (Ambergris Caye)
Xpuhil – City near Wukhalal Lagoon
Kuhunlich – City near Wukhalal Lagoon
Becan – City near Wukhalal Lagoon

Cities that switched allegiance
Uxwitza – (Caracol) allied with Mutul, later with Kan
B'uuk – (Las Alacranes) city where Kan installed puppet ruler
Nahokan – (Quirigua) southern city, ally of Oxwitik
Tan-nal – (Seibal) southern city, ally of Maxam
Imix-ha – (Dos Pilas) southern city, ally of Tan-nal and Kan
Maxam/Saal – (Naranjo) southern city, initially offshoot of Mutul, then ally of Kan
Kan Witz-nal – (Ucanal) southern city, ally of Kan and Tan-nal, former Mutul ally
Usihwitz – (Bonampak) in B'aakal polity, later enemy of Lakam Ha, allied with Kan

Places and Rivers

K'uk Lakam Witz – Fiery Water Mountain, sacred mountain of Lakam Ha
Nab'nah – Great North Sea (Gulf of Mexico)
K'ak-nab – Great East Sea (Gulf of Honduras, Caribbean Sea)
Wukhalal – lagoon of seven colors (Bacalar Lagoon)
K'umaxha – Sacred Monkey River (Usumacinta River), largest river in region, crosses plains north of Lakam Ha, empties into Gulf of Mexico
Michol – river on plains northwest of Lakam Ha, flows below city plateau
Chakamax – river flowing into K'umaxha, southeast of Lakam Ha
Tulixha – large river (Tulija River) flowing near B'aak
Chih Ha – subsidiary river (Chinal River) flows into Tulixha
B'ub'ulha – western river (Rio Grijalva) flowing into Gulf of Mexico near Nab'nahotot
Pokolha – southern river (Rio Motagua) by Nahokan, near Oxwitik

Small rivers flowing across Lakam Ha ridges
Kisiin – Diablo River
Bisik – Picota River
Tun Pitz – Piedras Bolas
Ixha – Motiepa River
Otolum – Otolum River
Sutzha – Murcielagos River
Balunte – Balunte River
Ach' – Ach' River

Maya Deities

Hunab K'u (Hun Ahb K'u) – Supreme Creator Being, giver of movement and measure

Muwaan Mat (Duck Hawk, Cormorant) – Primordial Mother Goddess, mother of B'aakal Triad

Hun Ahau (One Lord) – First born of Triad, Celestial Realm

Mah Kinah Ahau (Underworld Sun Lord) – Second born of Triad, Underworld Realm, Jaguar Sun, Underworld Sun-Moon, Waterlily Jaguar

Unen K'awill (Infant Powerful One) – Third born of Triad, Earthly Realm, Baby Jaguar, patron of royal bloodlines, lightning in forehead, often has one snake-foot

Ahauob (Lords) of the First Sky:
  B'olon Chan Yoch'ok'in (Sky That Enters the Sun) – 9 Sky Place
  Waklahun Ch'ok'in (Emergent Young Sun) – 16 Sky Place
  B'olon Tz'ak Ahau (Conjuring Lord) – 9 Sky Place

Ix Chel – Earth Mother Goddess, healer, midwife, weaver of life, fertility and abundance, commands snake energies, waters and fluids, Lady Rainbow

Hun Hunahpu – Maize God, First Father, resurrected by Hero Twins, ancestor of Mayas

Yum K'ax – Young Maize God, foliated god of growing corn, resurrected Hun Hunahpu

Wuqub' Kaquix – Seven Macaw, false deity of polestar, defeated by Hero Twins

Hun Ahau – (Hunahpu), first Hero Twin

Yax Bahlam – (Xbalanque), second Hero Twin

Wakah Chan Te – Jeweled Sky Tree, connects the three dimensions (roots-Underworld, trunk-Middleworld, branches-Upperworld)

Xibalba – Underworld, realm of the Lords of Death

Xmucane – Grandmother Deity of Maya People, Heart of Earth

Xpiyakok – Grandfather Deity of Maya People

Bacabs – Lords of the Four Directions, Hold up the Sky

Ahau Kinh – Lord Time

Itzamna – Sky Bar Deity, Magician of Water-Sacred Itz, Teacher-Builder

K'ukulkan – "Feathered Serpent" God of Transformation

Witz Monster – Cave openings to Underworld depicted as fanged monster mask

Titles

Ahau – Lord
Ixik – Lady
Ix – honorable way to address women
Ah – honorable way to address men
K'uhul Ahau – Divine/Holy Lord
K'uhul Ixik – Divine/Holy Lady
Ah K'in – Solar Priest
Ah K'inob – pleural of Solar Priest
Ix K'in – Solar Priestess
Ix K'inob – pleural of Solar Priestess
Halach Uinik – True Human
Yum – Master
Nakom – War Chief
Sahal – ruler of subsidiary city
Ah Kuch Kab – head of village (Kuchte'el)
Chilam – spokesperson, prophet
Batab – town governor, local leader from noble lineage
Kalomte – K'uhul Ahau ruling several cities, used often at Mutul and Oxwitik
May Ku – seat of the *may* cycle (260 tuns, 256 solar years), dominant city of region
Yahau – His Lord (high subordinate noble)
Yahau K'ak – His Lord of Fire (high ceremonial-military noble)
Ba-ch'ok – heir designate
Juntan – precious one, signifies relationship between mother and child as well as between deities and ahau, also translated "beloved of"

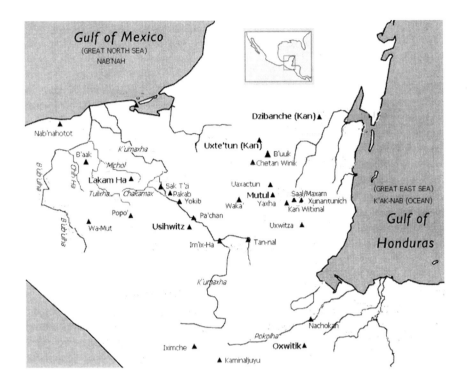

Central and Southern Maya Regions in
Middle Classic Period (500-800 CE)

Names of cities, rivers and seas are the ones used in this book. Most are known Classic Period names; some have been created for the story. Many other cities existed but are omitted for simplicity.

Inset map shows the location of Maya Regions in southern Mexico, Yucatan Peninsula and Central America.

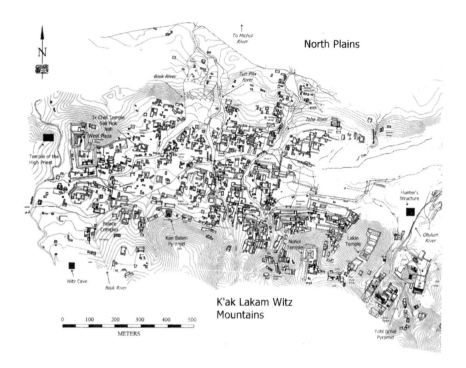

Lakam Ha (Palenque) Western and Central Areas
Older Sections of Settlement circa (500-600 CE)

Dark boxes are fictional structures added for the story. Structures important to the story are labeled. This does not signify that these structures were actually used for purposes described in the story. The city extends further east, but these sections were built later.

Based upon maps from The Palenque Mapping Project, Edwin Barnhart, 1999.

A FAMSI-sponsored project. Used with permission of Edwin Barnhart.

The Rabbit Scribe

"On the back of the ninth katun, god was lost; ahau was lost. She could not adorn the Gods of the First Sky. . . On the back of the 3 Ahau Katun, Ix Muwaan Mat could not give their offerings."

> **Temple of the Inscriptions**, dedicated to K'inich Janaab Pakal
> Completed by his son Kan Bahlam II, circa 9.12.11.12.10 (c. 684 CE)
> Based on translation by Gerardo Aldana, *The Apotheosis of Janaab' Pakal*, University of Colorado Press, 2007

"Today, in the immediate wake of the nearly complete decipherment of Maya hieroglyphs, much of our information about Maya history, beliefs, and experience comes directly from the Maya themselves, through the writings they left behind in books, on monuments, on tablets, and in many other media."

> David Stuart & George Stuart, *Palenque: Eternal City of the Maya*
> Thames & Hudson Ltd., London, 2008

SAK K'UK—I

BAKTUN 9 KATUN 8 TUN 12 (606 CE—607 CE)

1

PAKAL'S NURSEMAID WAS worried. Creases marred her smooth forehead, her lips drawn tight as a purse-string. She scurried through long corridors, eyes darting to every door and scanning the small chambers within. Crossing the inside patio, she quickly assessed each corner and glanced behind benches and plants.

Not yet two solar years old and the child was a master of escape. How far could his toddler's legs carry him? Her mistress would be most annoyed that he once again eluded supervision. Or much worse if any harm came to him.

Her search of Sak K'uk's quarters in the palace was fruitless. She enlisted help from other attendants, but none could locate the child. The sun was near zenith, its intense brightness almost blinding when reflected off white stucco walls and plazas. There was nothing to do but report Pakal's absence and muster a larger search.

Trembling and bowing low to the ground, Tunsel approached Sak K'uk, whose temper was well known among her attendants.

"My Lady, much is it my sorrow to report we cannot find your son, the sun-blessed Pakal."

Sak K'uk's face was stony, her voice hard.

"So it is, yet another time, you have failed in your duties. What is so difficult in knowing the whereabouts of a child? Find him at once, or I shall dismiss you this day." She signaled to the palace guard standing nearby. "Summon several men and search the entire palace complex. Bring Pakal to me as soon as you find him."

Tunsel and the guard rushed away and Sak K'uk dropped onto a stone bench. Tears smarted her eyes and she blinked them away, loath to reveal any weakness. But she was concerned, not just about her son's safety but her own abilities as a mother. Though the depth of her love for Pakal surprised her, mothering did not come naturally. She was not mesmerized by babies as were other women, she did not enjoy their nonsense babbles and disliked the drooling and feeding and toileting that seemed to go on endlessly. Those functions she gladly relinquished to nursemaids.

Any good mother should know where her children were, however. Simply because supervision was delegated to nursemaids did not absolve her of responsibility.

She would rather be in the Popol Nah, Council House, discussing Lakam Ha governance with leaders and interrogating messengers about happenings in the B'aakal polity. Especially so, since her brother was proving an ineffective ruler. She never respected Aj Ne Ohl Mat despite his attempts at leadership; his mind did not grasp political subtleties and he had little skill in the art of influence and intimidation. Only the abilities of her father and husband that kept the ahauob in line and the city functioning. She kept away from the Council House because she might lose control of her tongue and berate her brother in front of his courtiers.

The sun began its afternoon descent as Tunsel conferred impatiently with guards and palace attendants. None had seen the child despite repeated searching within the palace complex. They agreed to widen the search to nearby complexes and walkways. The nursemaid was frantic, gripped by fear for her charge and also herself. Dismissal from service to the ruler's sister would bring shame upon her family. Their standing would fall in status-conscious Maya culture, reducing opportunity for lucrative positions and advantageous marriages. Tunsel came from minor nobility, and her palace affiliations were much prized by her parents.

"Where can the boy be?" she moaned to herself, reviewing where she last saw him and what he was doing. It was at the edge of the patio adjoining his quarters, and he was throwing handfuls of dust into a beam of sunlight breaking through slots in the roofcomb. She left briefly to fetch a cloth for cleaning his hands, and upon returning he was gone.

The sun! Suddenly her mind was sharply focused. Pakal loved the sun; he sought it and often danced in sunbeams. In fact, his first word was *"k'in"* as the Maya called the sun. He must be in search of the sun, trying to get closer. That meant climbing a hill or temple pyramid. Someone would see him climbing a pyramid, but brush on a hill would easily conceal his small form.

Her legs pummeled as she raced toward the nearest hill, rising just west of the palace complex, the beginning of foothills that soon soared to cresting heights. Racing through the west plaza and crossing the footbridge spanning the Bisik River, Tunsel marveled that no one sighted the child on his excursion. Though his legs were long for his age, it was surprising that he could cover this distance. How she knew with such certainty that he took this path she did not question.

She sighted the trail wending across the hill, but saw no small form along its path. Sandals crunching on pebbles, Tunsel bounded up the trail with pounding heart. She gasped for breath, cursing her laziness from soft palace life. That life she would soon lose or perhaps all life if she did not find Pakal soon. The hill summit was just ahead and she called inwardly for the goddess Ix Chel's largesse.

Please let the boy be there!

Salty sweat mingled with tears as she ascended the final rise and spotted the boy. He was standing on a small boulder, arms lifted to the sun, singing in a high sweet voice. She rushed up and grabbed him into her arms. The surprised boy thrashed momentarily then relaxed into her embrace as she dropped to the ground. He reached to wipe away her tears and smeared her dusty face.

"Tunsel cry?"

"Tunsel happy Pakal is safe. Can we go home now?"

He studied her face solemnly and nodded. Then he turned his face toward the sun and burst into a huge smile. His almond eyes shone and he pointed at the sun.

"K'in Ahau. K'in Ahau loves Pakal."

"Yes, and Pakal loves his Father Sun." Tunsel in turn studied Pakal's face. "You are k'inich, sun-faced. We must call you K'inich Janaab Pakal. That is perfect, let us tell your mother and perhaps she will forgive us."

"Mother wants Pakal now?"

"Yes, let us go home now. Your mother waits. I will carry you; your legs must be tired from such a long climb." Rising with renewed vigor, Tunsel held the child tightly as she descended, silently thanking Ix Chel and resolving to never let Pakal escape her sight again.

Torchlight flickered from walls of the dining chamber in Sak K'uk's quarters. Dusk settled over the plateau of many waters as attendants served bowls of bean and squash stew seasoned with peppers and green herbs. Only two dined this evening with Sak K'uk, her father and husband. She regaled them with Pakal's latest adventure, his quest to reach K'in Ahau-Sun Lord on the hilltop.

"Tunsel conferred a new title on him, calling him k'inich, sun-faced. The cadence of this pleases me—K'inich Janaab Pakal."

"It is most fitting for the royal ahau of Lakam Ha," Hun Pakal said.

"So it is. We are descended from Hun Ahau, the son of the Sun Lord who we also call K'in Bahlam, the Sun Jaguar. The Bahlam family and the Sun are inseparable." She smiled at her father, while noticing how he had aged since her mother's death. Strange that only two years could reap such havoc; but he and Yohl Ik'nal had been exceptionally close and he missed her terribly.

"You should dismiss that girl," Kan Mo' Hix opined. "Tunsel does not watch Pakal closely enough; the boy is always running off. It makes me concerned."

"Hmmm," murmured Sak K'uk. She dipped maize cake into her bowl of stew and chewed thoughtfully. She disliked contradicting her husband; they had enough issues already ripe for conflict, but she had decided to retain Pakal's nursemaid.

"That I have considered," she replied. "Pakal is very fond of her. Think on it, I must." Quickly changing the subject, she asked her husband: "What transpired in Council today?"

"More debate over extracting tribute from Usihwitz. That testy contingent of our ahauob cannot let go of our defeat in the ballgame. This sully on the reputation of Lakam Ha seems more important than our prosperity and peaceful life. And Aj Ne Ohl Mat does little to deflect their criticisms; I doubt he has one creative political thought, devoting all his talents to poetry and music." Disdain fairly dripped from Kan Mo' Hix' voice and his hand sign conveyed dismissal.

"Peace and prosperity indeed are the problem," observed Hun Pakal. "They are bored; they have not enough to occupy their small minds. Warriors want to ply their skills in more than flower wars or ballgames. Some ahauob thrive on conflict; their lives lack spice without it."

"Aj Ne cannot manage this situation," Sak K'uk said flatly. In her heart she believed she could, but her brother was ruler.

"We must find ways to divert this wave of discontent," said Hun Pakal.

"Is not the artist Uc Ayin among the circle of opposition? And also frequent courtier in Aj Ne's artistic gatherings?"

Sak K'uk's eyes caught her fathers' in unspoken caution. They knew the questionable role Uc Ayin had played in Usihwitz' unsuccessful raid several years earlier. Only by leaving the city had he escaped death.

"Uc Ayin could be a source, yes, if we can obtain his cooperation, for he does move among camps," said Kan Mo' Hix.

"If he can be trusted," Hun Pakal noted.

"He rides the winds of advantage. I will cultivate him; that will be flattering. He did spend much time in my father's house but comes less often now that the ruler includes him as a fellow artist. What need have we of artists as leaders? Warriors, men trained in skills of strategic attack and managing resources make the best rulers." Kan Mo' Hix gestured toward Hun Pakal. "You or I would be a better ruler for Lakam Ha. This designation of Aj Ne Ohl Mat as heir, his selection for succession was a mistake. Not to imply disrespect for our late ruler, your honored mother." He nodded toward Sak K'uk.

It took great determination for Sak K'uk to withhold her caustic remarks. She chewed a piece of maize cake furiously. Kan Mo' Hix was oblivious to both the embedded insult and exposure of ambition in his remarks. It was becoming apparent that her husband aspired to rulership.

Fine ruler he would make, she thought, *with such lack of diplomacy.*

Hun Pakal's face was clouded, but he said nothing.

Their meal finished with cups of cocoa laced with chile. They agreed to meet again once Kan Mo' Hix obtained information about the opposition's objectives. He left first, bowing and touching fingertips with Sak K'uk in a gesture of affection. She responded as expected, reaching toward his fingers with hers and smiling, though her true feelings dictated a slap.

When her husband disappeared through the door drape, she sank down with a sigh.

"Often it is, he is insufferable," she whispered to her father.

"Insufferably ambitious. That he would make an admirable ruler, I doubt. This situation we have is not good. Aj Ne is weak and distracted, discontent is mounting, and Pakal is years away from being capable of acceding. Were it not so disruptive, I might even support the idea of Kan Mo' Hix as ruler."

"Father, this is not wise. He would bring difficulties to us, for he is rash and lacks judgment. He is too reactive about the Usihwitz situation. Can you imagine him spreading the cloak of reason and calmness over our nobles?"

"Ah, no . . . he would create quite the opposite effect. There is trouble gathering in our recalcitrant subordinate city, however. Never believe that Ek Chuuah is finished with his lust for revenge. It is certain he has used these years to perfect his plans, even if the defeat he suffered in the first raid diminished his status in Usihwitz. Would that our intelligence was better."

"Lack of information about neighboring cities is a major detriment," agreed Sak K'uk. "We cannot be prepared without some knowledge of hostile intentions. It appears we must work with the leadership situation we now have, faulty as it may be. Can we not give more support to Aj Ne?"

"Perhaps we can. I will again try to interest him in court rituals and council strategy, though he shows little aptitude. Your mother was a master at courtly arts; it is regretful that he inherited so little of it from her."

Hun Pakal cast his eyes down, but not before his daughter caught the shadows of sadness in their depths. After a few moments, he said wistfully: "The poetry of Aj Ne is quite good, think you not?"

Sak K'uk placed a hand on her father's shoulder.

"Mother was a great ruler. I also miss her presence, her strength and vision, so much. Yes, Aj Ne does write poetry well."

They sat in silence, sipping cacao. Sak K'uk cared little for her brother's poetry, but she yearned to give comfort to her father, some acknowledgement of his son's value.

"You are intelligent and determined." Hun Pakal simply stated facts with no hint of flattery. "Perhaps you can improve your husband's judgment and hone his leadership abilities."

Caught by surprise, Sak K'uk laughed aloud. Seeing that her father was serious, she conceded: "So it might be possible. Yes, I will try applying my intelligence to this daunting task."

They embraced warmly and Hun Pakal left. Sak K'uk reflected on how different her parents' marriage was than her own. By custom, Maya nobles each had private sleeping chambers and different sets of attendants. Her parents, however, slept together more often than not. Their closeness was remarkable, something she admired but did not understand. In her own marriage, Kan Mo' Hix visited her sleeping pallet often enough but never stayed with her through the night. She enjoyed the physical contact, but could easily remain alone for long periods. It was not correct timing for them to conceive another child, and she was taking herbs to prevent pregnancy, so frequent intercourse was not necessary.

The Maya were sexually continent people. They viewed male and female sexual union as a sacred act, one that combined powerful creative energies and augmented inner spiritual processes. It was undertaken consciously and deliberately, treated with honor and respect. To overindulge sexually was to squander one's life force, the *itz* that permeated all existence with sacred essence.

Sak K'uk was not troubled that her husband might lie with other women. This was not common practice among Maya ahauob, especially those in the highest positions. He was too focused on building personal power to waste any on such frivolities. She was troubled about his ambitions, his self-focused perspectives that fell short of true dedication to the welfare of the B'aakal polity and Bahlam dynasty.

Her thoughts returned to her wandering son. He was already precocious, walking and speaking early, exuding a magical presence that entranced those around him. Everyone basked in the radiance of his loving nature, kind and comforting. He certainly exhibited qualities of Yohl Ik'nal, his visionary grandmother, including the ability to elude attendants and explore other dimensions. Tunsel said he was communing with the sun on the hilltop; often he related to this deity as though he were actually the son of K'in Ahau.

As indeed he is, she mused.

Sak K'uk often brought Pakal with her on visits to the underground chamber, the most sacred shrine of Lakam Ha, the Sak Nuk Nah or "White Skin House." When he had just passed his third solar year, she visited the shrine to honor her grandfather Kan Bahlam's voyage to the celestial realms. Seated on the altar-throne in the hidden sanctum, she meditated with closed eyes while Pakal sat on a mat at her feet. After a short time of silence, the boy's gleeful giggles interrupted her reverie. Too curious to concentrate, Sak K'uk peeked under lowered eyelids at her son.

Pakal was dancing in small circles, waving his hands furiously in the air. He lunged and swatted with one hand, then the other, and burst into a ripple of laughter. Next he jumped backward, danced in more circles, and repeated the gestures.

Sak K'uk could not contain her curiosity.

"What are you doing, Pakal?"

He glanced at her, but continued his movements.

"See, mother, see!" he exclaimed, pointing into the air at his chest level.

She focused where he pointed but saw nothing except wavering torchlight.

"Dearest, I do not see anything. What do you see?"

"The Baby Jaguar, see he plays with me."

"The Baby Jaguar? Unan K'awiil in his baby jaguar form?"

"Yes, yes, do you see him? His paws, he paws at me, I jump away." Pakal swatted again in the air and laughed. "He will not get me, I am fast!"

Sak K'uk frowned, squinting to bring ephemeral forms into sharper contrast, but was unable to see her son's playmate.

"Much to my regret, I cannot see the Baby Jaguar."

Pakal stopped his movements and stared at his mother, his surprised eyes conveying confusion.

"You cannot see him? He is here . . . Oh, he has gone! Mother, you made Baby Jaguar go away!"

"Truly I am sorry, dearest," she enjoined. "What did he look like?"

"Like Baby Jaguar!" Pakal said with annoyance, then softened and hugged his mother. "He has black spots, many spots, he lies on his back and waves his paws and wiggles his tail. He smiled at me, I saw his little fangs, but he was careful not to bite. He wants to play. He is very cute. I am sorry you cannot see him."

"Perhaps I will see him the next time he comes to play with you. Does he come often?"

"Yes, often when we are in the White Skin House. First he watched me; today he played the most ever. Can we come here tomorrow? I want to play with Baby Jaguar."

"Of course, my love. We can come very often."

Sak K'uk was eager to discuss Pakal's experience with the High Priest. To her knowledge, never before had such a young child with no training been visited by a Triad God, much less been able to clearly see and interact with the deity.

2

Pasah Chan, High Priest of Lakam Ha, contemplated the significance of what Sak K'uk told him about her son. Although holding the exalted office as head of his city's priesthood for less than five solar years, his lengthy preparation in calendric and occult arts and the rigorous selection process leading up to his nomination gave him confidence in his spiritual leadership. He searched his memory for similar scenarios in which very young children demonstrated unusual psychic and inter-dimensional abilities, but could not recall anything similar. Of course, Pakal's grandmother Yohl Ik'nal was known for her skills at journeying since her middle youth and for her prowess as a seer later in life. As ruler she clearly embodied the Triad Gods in rituals and communicated with various deities. But at such an early age, to become playmate to Unen K'awiil? Of this, he had never heard.

Tall for a Maya with sinewy limbs and slender frame, Pasah Chan came from a minor noble family fortunate enough to cultivate favor with the former High Priest Wak Batz. Through gifts and tribute that stretched the family's resources, the eldest son gained admittance into priestly training. There he excelled, using his keen memory and natural intelligence to advance in studies. His aptitude for ruthless competition played no small role in his progress, and he became the old High Priest's favorite acolyte. Partly through admiration for his command of esoteric knowledge, and partly due to his intimidating personality, the Council of Priests nominated Pasah Chan upon the passing of Wak Batz. He underwent the series of trials required of High Priest candidates to demonstrate his mastery over emotions, body functions, elements of nature, and spirit world assistants. In all tests he exceeded expectations.

The face of Pasah Chan resembled a bird of prey. Beaked nose overshadowed thin lips drawn tight against jutting cheekbones, half-lidded eyes held the penetrating glare of a hawk. Over his small-domed crown, dark hair crested from his narrow forehead pushed upward by a feathered band with a long braid falling down his back. Although the crest was intended to mimic the elongated skulls of high-ranked elites, it did not conceal his defect. His parents had failed to apply the headboards used to elongate the skull properly during his infancy. Of this defect, he was quite self-conscious.

His eyes narrowed into slits as he concentrated. Again he reviewed his conversation with Sak K'uk and her father, Hun Pakal.

"Surely this means Pakal is favored by Unen K'awiil, perhaps destined for rulership?" Sak K'uk tried to keep her voice tentative, but Pasah Chan could sense her conviction.

"The Baby Jaguar, designator of royal lineage, would not appear to such a young child were it not significant," added Hun Pakal.

"Perhaps, perhaps," Pasah Chan murmured, rubbing his chin. "Yes, it is most unusual, and the child is advanced for his age. Yes, this bears contemplation, to discern the hidden meanings and the intentions of the deity. I must reflect, seek precedence and spiritual guidance."

Sak K'uk persisted.

"Would it not seem an indication to begin Pakal's training early? His abilities are unfolding naturally; these must be shaped by adepts in the priesthood so the proper skills are developed."

"And to keep him safe," said Hun Pakal, thinking of Yohl Ik'nal's untutored travels and the risks involved.

"Indeed, indeed, these are important considerations," the High Priest replied. "It is highly irregular for a child not yet attained of four tuns to enter shamanic training, when the normal age for elite boys is seven tuns. His abilities are unusual, of course, and this brings other elements into the situation. As you both note, his safety is a concern. And he is of ruling lineage with no heir yet born to the ruler, although that might change soon."

Sak K'uk and Hun Pakal exchanged surprised glances. Pasah Chan gloated that he possessed information the two royals did not have. Just two days ago the Chief Priestess of Ix Chel informed him that Aj Ne Ohl Mat's wife Hohmay was pregnant. After years of barrenness, the arts of the healing priestesses had finally succeeded in bringing about a conception. It was a precarious pregnancy founded on extreme measures, secrets the healers would not reveal. They had great concern over the outcome and planned ceaseless surveillance of Hohmay and a rigid protocol of diet, herbs, spiritual ritual and careful activity.

"The Ix Chel priestesses have assisted Hohmay to conceive." Pasah Chan allowed the words to roll from his tongue deliciously, savoring their impact.

Sak K'uk could not conceal her shock. Hun Pakal looked crestfallen.

"Only two days ago was I informed of this momentous event," continued the High Priest. "As you can imagine, the Ix Chel priestesses will be at her side every moment, and continue to apply their skills to support the pregnancy."

"Ix Chel be praised," Sak K'uk managed to mutter. "Truly her priestesses are exceptionally skilled, may all go well."

"When is the child to be born?" asked Hun Pakal.

"In seven moons."

"Should all go well. Truly remarkable. Yet the child may be a girl, leaving Pakal the more logical choice," Hun Pakal observed.

"Given the great difficulty Hohmay had conceiving, perhaps it was impossible to follow all procedures to assure the child's gender," Pasah Chan admitted. "Although the Ix Chel priestesses do believe the child conceived is male."

"But they are not certain," suggested Sak K'uk.

"That is true. We will see; there is much that must pass until the pregnancy is culminated. Concerning Pakal, I will reflect upon his early entry into training."

"This we deeply appreciate," said Sak K'uk. Eyes bright with intense passion, she directed a piercing look at the High Priest.

"Pakal is destined for greatness. I have been given many signs of this and have no doubt of its truth. My mother Yohl Ik'nal also envisioned Pakal bringing Lakam Ha to its zenith. He must be trained soon."

Pasah Chan blinked, bringing himself into the present. That look in Sak K'uk's eyes had shaken him, and her mother's visions were always to be taken seriously. Was Pakal destined to rule Lakam Ha, to bring forth its apogee?

The High Priest intended to become even more important than his position demanded. He wanted to be the most powerful man in Lakam Ha, the shaper of its course, the master of rulers. Watching the current ruler Aj Ne Ohl Mat, observing the weakness of his leadership and his passive personality, gave Pasah Chan reassurance. He could easily influence and control this ruler, and most likely his progeny. The Council was divided and contentious; they could be manipulated and one contingent played against the other. Should rulership remain in this line, his goals were as good as accomplished.

But rulership in Sak K'uk's lineage was another issue. Already Hun Pakal and Kan Mo' Hix aggregated a strong group of supporters, ready to follow their leadership. Rumors circulated that Kan Mo' Hix should be made ruler. He would certainly bring a stronger hand to leadership, but his impulsiveness might spark serious disruptions. Just how far the opposition group would go was an unknown. Civil strife and possible internal battle were unappealing possibilities.

If it was true that Pakal was destined for greatness, for rulership, then Pasah Chan was cultivating the wrong branch of the family. Maybe Hohmay would bear a son to keep succession in their line, but that was far from certain. He doubted the pregnancy would end successfully. If Pakal did become heir, and if he trained the boy from an early age, his opportunity for influence would be immense.

His brows knitted, Pasah Chan struggled to remember ephemeral images from ancient codices written in early forms of the Mayan language. Was there some distant prophecy about a great ruler, one whose mission was to guide his people to remember their celestial mandate, to inspire art and architecture that reflected cosmic harmony, to spark a creative vortex that would draw admiration from all parts of the world? Just beyond the fringes of memory some tantalizing fragments danced, but remained elusive. He must consult with the elderly priest who was the most revered codex expert.

The High Priest ascended the temple plaza as the sun caressed verdant peaks of the western mountains, sliding toward the distant great waters. Although the afternoon was warm, the old priest sat bundled in his blanket, cross-legged upon a low wall bench flanking the plaza. From this uppermost plaza of the High Priest's Temple, a spectacular view spread below. Hazy plains rolled toward the horizon, patches of green mingling with golden fields of maize and olive leafed orchards. Like a traveling serpent, the Michol River curled across the plains, as towering trees that lined the river trailed lianas in its turbid waters. A few canoes plied the swift currents, hugging the banks as pilots propelled them with long poles.

The old man seemed oblivious of his visitor, eyes closed and head nodding in the sunlight. Pasah Chan noted the deeply wrinkled face, each crease representing cycles of time. Surely the old man had passed 104 tuns, twice the 52-tun age of elders. It was said that when 104 tuns were attained, humans had completed all the cycles of life and became living repositories of history and wisdom. Young people would sit in their hallowed presence to reflect upon time's passages and the phases of earthly and celestial life. Simply to touch their wrinkled faces and hands was to receive blessings and attain deeper understandings.

Pasah Chan cleared his throat noisily. Slowly the old man turned toward him, watery eyes blinking and toothless mouth opening. His corneas were clouded and whitened. He tilted his head to obtain a better view of this visitor, wrinkled lips pursing and popping like a gasping fish. His thin, clawed hands picked tremulously at the blanket.

"Greetings of the afternoon, Ah K'uch, Honored Ancient One," said Pasah Chan. "It is good to enjoy Father Sun's warmth, is it not?"

"K'in Ahau is good, he warms my old bones," replied Ah K'uch in a high, reedy voice. "Greetings to you, Pasah Chan, High Priest. How passes your day?"

"It is well, and I am happy to be with you again. May I join you?"

Ah K'uch nodded and gestured to the bench beside him. Moving his clouded gaze to the view below, he gave a gummy smile.

"Such beauty does Hun Ahb K'u, the Infinite Creator of All give to this world. So shall I miss it, when I traverse the sky in the Celestial Canoe."

"Let us hope that is yet far in the future."

"Ah, hah," the old man chuckled. "Not so far, not so far."

Both men fell silent, each contemplating their destinies and life's temporality.

"There is a task you might yet do, something of great importance to our city's future." The High Priest spoke softly but with crisp enunciation. "It is something that means much to me. A personal favor."

Ah K'uch tilted his head back, looking upward into the young priest's face.

"What would you have me do?"

"Search among ancient codices for a prophecy for Lakam Ha. A prophecy for these current times, about a great leader who is destined to bring Lakam Ha to its highest point. It is likely that the leader would also be the ruler, one yet to come, but soon."

"Why do you ask me? You are a codex expert yourself, you could do that search." Ah K'uch shrugged and wagged his head. "Here am I, a very old man. My wits are not as sharp as yours. My eyes are failing me. My limbs are frail and weak."

"Your knowledge of codices far surpasses that of any priest, myself included," Pasah Chan replied. "You say your wits are not so sharp, but your memory is boundless. It is such that should you command it, focus your mind, set your intention, that you can remember which among the thousands of codices speaks of this prophecy. I vaguely recall some prophecy concerning Lakam Ha's destiny, but would spend countless days in fruitless searching. You can summon it to mind, scanning your memory."

"Ah, perhaps that is so. Might not it take me countless days also? I have fewer days to count than you." Enjoying his own humor, Ah K'uch chuckled.

Pasah Chan smiled, giving the hand sign for losing a point.

Time passed as the men sat in silence. The sun hovered at the mountain's edge, sending golden beams across the plaza. Birds called in the forests, jostling for position among branches. Pasah Chan sighed, resigning himself to doing the search. It would take a long time, and Sak K'uk would keep pressing him to train Pakal. He had hoped to get the information quickly upon which to base his decision.

"I will do it." The old priest's reedy treble startled Pasah Chan.

"Something to amuse my old mind before I join the ancestors. Yes, I know where to begin. It is a good thing, High Priest, that you reminded me of my memory." He coughed and chuckled simultaneously while the younger man bowed and smiled.

A special chamber in the Temple of the High Priest was devoted to housing the codices. It was the uppermost chamber of the temple school, chosen to receive maximum light and air. The school was a two-tiered square building opening into a secluded courtyard. On the lower level were numerous classrooms; the upper held small chambers for meditation. The entire western-facing side of the upper level was a series of interconnected rooms with stone shelves lining the walls. These shelves held thousands of codices, the heritage of untold years of scribal work reaching far into Lakam Ha's mythohistoric past. The codices held the arcane knowledge of the Maya; astronomy, astrology, divination, sacred geometry, numerology, healing arts and herbalism, calendars, alchemical recipes, history of dynasties and rulers, tales of Gods and ancestors, philosophy, language, arts and music. It was an unparalleled library, a hidden font of wisdom from ancient times.

Each codex was made of bark paper in long strips, folded like an accordion that fanned out when extended. The Maya harvested inner layers of bark from the wild fig tree, soaked and boiled it in maize water treated with lime or ash. Then the bark was rinsed and pliable strips were laid out on a wooden board. The first layer was lengthwise and the next was crosswise. The damp bark was pounded with a hafted stone beater into a continuous sheet of paper, some as long as three arm's length. After drying in the sun, the paper was peeled off the wooden board and smoothed with a stone. Since the bark was never made into a pulp, it retained a fibrous texture that was not smooth enough for Maya scribes to write easily. They covered the paper with a thin layer of plaster before writing on it.

Natural dyes were prepared in many colors; black, red and yellow were much favored though blue and green also were used. The particularly lovely shade of Maya blue was made from indigo fused with palygorskite by the heat of burning copal incense in ceremonial bowls. Scribes used quills from bird feathers or a wooden stylus, dipping them in dyes held in seashells or conches. The monkey scribe or rabbit scribe was the animal uay—companions who represented the sacred art of glyphic writing, recording numbers and drawing pictures that filled the codices.

Ah K'uch sat on a raised platform covered with a woven mat. A rectangular wooden box served to elevate and display unfolded codices as he examined them. Positioned next to a window opening toward the west, he took full advantage of sunlight to improve his ability to see. Beside him sat three assistants, acolytes assigned to fetch and shelve codices and explain images he had difficulty making out. They also plied the old priest with warm cacao drinks and maize cakes to keep up his energy.

It was his third day of work, and he was beginning to wonder if his memory had failed him. After examining over 30 ancient codices, he had not found the one containing the Lakam Ha prophecy. He was certain there was such a prophecy, he clearly recalled having read it in his youth, but could not remember all the details.

This called for different tactics.

"I will sleep now," he announced to his assistants.

They were perplexed, for they knew he was on a time-sensitive assignment.

"Master, is not your intent to find the codex today? Very soon, is that not important?" asked one young acolyte.

"You are correct, that is my intent," replied Ah K'uch. "My methods may seem strange to you. Now I am called to sleep, to dream and to remember in the dreamtime. In this way shall the codex come to me."

Obediently, the acolytes prepared a pallet for the old priest in a darker corner of the chamber. Sighing, he reclined his achy body and soon was snoring loudly.

Patiently the assistants sat in vigil as the old man slept. The sun crossed overhead and began its afternoon descent, bright squares of light forming through windows and moving slowing across the floor. After a series of snorts that interrupted throaty snores, the old priest woke, blinked furiously, wiped his watering eyes, and sat up.

His voice gurgled, requiring some coughing to clear his throat.

"Bring me the codex on the farthest shelf to the west; it is low and close to the floor. It is called the Noh Ek Almanac of Baktun 8 Katun 18. Be careful! Handle it gently, it is very ancient. From the times of our venerated lineage founder, Holy Ancestor K'uk Bahlam."

As the assistants scrambled to retrieve the codex, Ah K'uch groaned and lurched to his feet, limping slowly to his scribe platform. Stretching and sighing, he sat cross-legged and reached to receive the dusty codex from his assistant. Spreading it and gently turning the flaps, he scanned through pages of Noh Ek (Venus) almanacs with neat rows of day and month signs, dot-and-bar numbers, and pictures of deities. Columns of glyphs along page edges or across the top added further information.

"Ah!" he exclaimed, bony finger tracing a glyph column that accompanied numbers and images. The three assistants crowded around, straining to see. They could not decipher the antiquated glyphic forms, though the numbers and deity images were familiar.

"What does it say, master?" asked one assistant.

"Bring writing materials, copy this down as I read," ordered Ah K'uch.

As soon as the assistant scribe was set up with new bark paper, quill pen and dye, the old priest read slowly.

"Dawn counts the drumbeats,
counts the Katuns, the bundles of stones.
Dawn counts the guardian spirit of the sun-eyed torch
at the center of the sun, the Sun Eyed Lord of the Shield.
The sun-eyed torch at 12th Sky Place, B'aak.

"When T'zek falls in the Waters of the Night.
Baktuns make 1, Katuns make 10, Tuns make 9 at Toktan,
Place of Clouds and Many Waters.
The Celestial Twins sit upon the Earth-Sky Band.
Noh Ek the "Great Star" shines, the False Sun,
begins the Count of Days of the Sun Passer, Noh Ek.

"Lady Moon—Ix Uc ascends in Uo, 8th Sky Place.
She dangles below her K'awiil Ek and Chak Ek,
above the Waters of the Night.
And the Katun Lord, he of the mirror scepter, K'awiil Ek,
turns around at the heart of 8th Sky Place.
It happens, it is done.
The Sun Eyed Lord of the Shield,
he touches the earth, the 8 Ahau Lord,
And the white paper headband is handed over to him.
And great things come to the Place of Clouds and Many Waters.
So is it written upon the sky, so is it written upon the earth."

As soon as the dyes dried upon the new codex, Ah K'uch had his assistants bundle it together with the ancient codex in soft white blankets. To their disappointment, the old priest gathered up the bundle himself and carried it to the chambers of the High Priest. Although he had translated the archaic glyphs into current language, and this they had carefully written in modern glyphs, they did not understand the arcane imagery. Nor were they likely to be told the meanings, for this appeared to be meant for the High Priest alone. Only so much were acolytes given to understand.

Pasah Chan sat alert and eager as the old priest displayed the two screen-fold codices, one still smelling of new dyes and the other musty and discolored with age. First, Ah K'uch read the translation and then the High Priest re-read the glyphs himself. He looked over the ancient codex, understanding most of the glyphs, checking the translation. All appeared accurate, as best he could ascertain.

"Much here relates to the stars and zodiac," he said. "When was the original codex written?"

"In Baktun 8 Katun 18 (397 CE), in the time of Holy Ancestor K'uk Bahlam. Our revered lineage founder was born in that Katun, and acceded when he had attained 20 solar years in the next Katun. He must have been a child when it was written," Ah K'uch remarked.

"Let us examine these verses together. They begin with dawn and a count of Katuns that relate to the sun and some being 'at the center of the sun' called Sun Eyed Lord of the Shield. K'in Ahau, Sun Lord, is not called this way," observed Pasah Chan.

"See the use of 'Lord of the Shield' that calls to mind young Pakal's name, which is shield. But 'sun-faced'? What make you of that?"

The High Priest pondered for a few moments, and then his eyes lit up.

"Know you that the household of Pakal often calls him 'k'inich' or sun-faced?" he exclaimed. "This I learned only recently. It appears his nursemaid gave him that appellation because he loves to lift his face to the sun. The boy seeks the sun; there was an incident where he wandered away from home all alone, and she found him sitting on a high rocky outcropping gazing at the sun."

"K'inich Ahau Pakal, Sun-faced Lord of the Shield," repeated the old priest. "But the boy's other name is Janaab."

"Is that not an old-fashioned way of saying Lord, Ahau?"

"Why, so it is!" chimed Ah K'uch, chuckling. "K'inich Janaab Pakal. Your memory is better than mine."

"That I doubt," Pasah Chan smiled. "You found the codex from memory. Let me see. This Sun Eyed Lord of the Shield is guardian spirit of the sun when it rises at dawn at 12 Sky Place of B'aak. That is the twelfth zodiac sign, B'aak the skeleton."

"That is so. It is occurring when the zodiac sign T'zek, the scorpion, falls below the horizon. Then we have a distance number placing this event in the future, 1 Baktun, 10 Katuns and 9 Tuns from when the codex was written. At Toktan, the earlier name given Lakam Ha. Can you calculate this future date quickly? My mind is too weak for such calculations without figuring the numbers on paper." The old priest chuckled.

Pasah Chan closed his eyes and ran the numbers internally. He had trained many hours to perfect this skill that required manipulating 5 sets of numbers in base 20. Since the Maya used zero, their count was from 0 to 19, except in the second lowest position when the highest count was 18 (0 to 17). When the k'in (day) count reached 19, then the uinal (month) advanced by one. When the uinal reached 18, then the tun (year) advanced by one. When the tun reached 19, then the katun (20-tun period) advanced by one, and when the katun reached 19, then the baktun (400-tun period) advanced by one.

Now he was required to subtract, and the mental gyrations were demanding. Soon he worked it out, and again his eyes lit with excitement.

"Although we do not have the exact day and month, the other future time positions arrive at Baktun 9 Katun 8 Tun 9, which matches when Pakal was born. I can check the exact day and month using the other astronomic clues. They are quite precise. The Celestial Twins, Noh Ek (Venus) and Xux Ek (Mercury) are close to the horizon when Noh Ek appears as Eveningstar. This begins a new Noh Ek cycle that initiates the count of days until he becomes Sun Passer as Morningstar. The Moon rises in the eighth zodiac sign of Uo (frog), and below her in a line are K'awiil Ek (Jupiter) and Chak Ek (Mars). They are just above the western horizon at dusk. K'awiil Ek is resuming his forward motion after being still."

"Ah, there we have it. The Sun Eyed Lord of the Shield, young K'inich Janaab Pakal, is born, he touches the earth. Was he not born on the day 8 Ahau?"

"It is so. And he will receive the white paper headband of rulership. The verses finish by saying this brings great things to Toktan, our city Lakam Ha."

Both priests settled into silent contemplation, each pursuing his thoughts. Ah K'uch was pleased that his service to the High Priest was so successful; gratified that in his waning years he could still accomplish something significant. Pasah Chan was astonished at the clarity of the ancient prophecy, and its congruence with everything Sak K'uk and her mother Yohl Ik'nal had envisioned. He felt certain that when he checked the records of the sky's configuration on the date of Pakal's birth, he would find exactly the astronomical pattern the codex described.

"May I ask, honored High Priest, what you will do with this information?" Ah K'uch was curious. "Needless to say, this information shall I keep solely to myself."

Pasah Chan smiled warmly at the aged man, sincerely appreciative of his help.

"It is you who are the honored one, Elder Priest, for your exceptional work. This shall I do: I will take the boy Pakal into training early to become a shaman-ruler."

The old priest nodded and chuckled.

"It is fitting. Now have I one request for you. Allow me to also teach the boy, while I have yet the mind and strength. For he should know the antiquated language of our forebears and study their prophetic codices."

"It is done."

SAK K'UK—II

BAKTUN 9 KATUN 8 TUN 14 (608 CE—609 CE)

1

THE PROW OF the long canoe sliced through still water, leaving a frothy wake in the green lagoon. Distant roars of waves crashing against the seaward side of the barrier reef drifted over the flat grassy peninsula punctuated by brackish ponds. Seagulls circled and cried, seeking easy prey in disturbed waters. The canoe, carved from a single tall tree, was the length of eight men and nearly as wide as two men. It required six paddlers and could carry 20 passengers in addition to cargo. These long canoes were used by coastal traders to navigate the Great East Sea that spread past horizons to the east and north, called K'ak-nab.

Most of the forward portion was filled with bundles, trade goods intended for elite nobles of the Ka'an polity. From inland came corn and cacao, pottery, jade, obsidian and grinding stones of volcanic basalt. From the coast came conches, shells, stingray spines and spondylus, the highly valued spiny red oyster shell. Salt was a commodity needed by everyone, harvested from shallow ponds along the length of the peninsula.

In the aft portion, several passengers crouched, taking advantage of the swift canoe to shorten their journeys. Travel by waterways was much quicker than overland through dense jungles. Many rivers coursed from western mountain ranges toward the K'ak-nab. The canoe's captain showed his passengers a canal recently cut through the shortest portion of the north peninsula. This, he explained, gave canoes access from the lagoon to the sea at a point above the dangerous barrier reef where many boats with valuable cargo were lost.

Two passengers watched with particular interest as they passed the mouth of the narrow canal, where low-growing mangroves dipped skinny roots into the water.

"These must be cut back often," the canoe captain remarked.

"A great work, this canal," replied the older passenger. He shifted position to straighten his right leg that became achy from an old injury when he kept it flexed too long.

"Go you frequently upon the Great East Sea?" asked the younger. "How far north have you gone?"

"There have I journeyed past Cuzamil, the large island of the upper east coast," said the captain, "but not into the Nab'nah, the Great North Sea. That I desire to do, Gods willing, but it is a very long voyage. This boat I take upon the K'ak-nab three or four times each tun to settlements near the large island. Most of my trips are past the peninsula into the Chetumal and Wukhalal lagoons, to the many cities in the region."

"When do we arrive at the Wukhalal shore near Dzibanche?" asked the older man.

The captain lifted his bronzed and weathered face toward the sun, now nearly overhead. He checked landmarks, subtle coastal features that appeared all the same to untrained eyes.

"By dusk we shall arrive there," he said. "We will camp overnight before starting the land journey, for that will require most of the day. Many bundles of fine goods have I for the Lords of Kan, and they reward me richly for such luxuries."

"The Kan dynasty prospers, so you say. Of this, I am pleased to hear."

"Seek you dispensation from the Kan Lords?"

"Dispensation of a certain type. Not their wealth, but their power."

"Ah, powerful indeed is the snake of Kan. Under the leadership of Uneh Chan, Ka'an K'uhul Ahau, their influence has spread from Uxwitza in the south to cities along the K'umaxha—Sacred Monkey River in the west. Only Zotz, the Bat dynasty of Uxte'tun, thwarts their dominance of the eastern lowlands."

"Indeed. Let us speak more of this later."

Ek Chuuah's eyes caught those of his son, Yax Chapat. They traveled together on a mission that involved both the Kan and Zotz dynasties, but it was ultimately targeted at the Bahlam dynasty of B'aakal. Slight lowering of the father's eyelids was signal enough for the son to remain silent on this subject.

Calls from the front rowers summoned the captain forward to assess passage through sandbars, which shifted with every voyage. Ek Chuuah leaned against the smooth canoe sides and rubbed the back of his knee. His fingers moved across a wide scar, feeling again the knotted hamstring that still caused him to limp after so many years. Bitterness surged as he recalled that distant Flower War where this injury changed his life. The deep and serious cut delivered by the seasoned Usihwitz warrior, in violation of the sacred rules given by the Gods, was no accident. He had not a shred of doubt that Kan Bahlam had masterminded the wounding to remove him from Lakam Ha and dismantle the core of opposition. His grudge was not against the warrior, but against his former K'uhul Ahau and descendants.

Above all, Ek Chuuah wanted justice. It was intrinsically wrong, deliberately flaunting the Triad Deities and their laws meant to control base motives of humans. Yet no divine retaliation had fallen upon Kan Bahlam, and his dynasty continued through his daughter Yohl Ik'nal and now grandson Aj Ne Ohl Mat. How had justice been served? He admitted that his life in Usihwitz was successful, that he had attained a high level of power and respect in his adopted city. But not high enough. He coveted the throne, now for his son. Yahau Chan Muwaan, the current ruler of Usihwitz, had been placed in office only a year ago by the influence of the Pa'chan ruler, probably following orders given by Kan ruler Uneh Chan. Pa'chan had long been allied with Kan and did their bidding.

Yahau Chan Muwaan was not a legitimate ruler, in Ek Chuuah's estimation. The new ruler was of a different patrilineage than preceding ruler Joy Bahlam, whose young son died under questionable circumstances. The true ruling lineage continued through the daughter, recently married to Yax Chapat.

The irony did not escape Ek Chuuah. It was a parallel situation to the accession of Yohl Ik'nal. That woman, who so enraged him, now served as a model for his own son's access to power. They would learn from her example, use strategy and manipulation to strengthen their family's position and establish their dynasty. No woman would rule in Usihwitz, he vowed. Yax Chapat would become co-regent and soon take over rulership. This trip to Kan was a large part of the strategy. Ek Chuuah sought assistance from Kan for another attack on Lakam Ha, this time carefully planned to bring about destruction and humiliation. Such an impressive victory would boost his family's standing, bring booty to his city and enable his forces to unseat Yahau Chan Muwaan and place his own son on the throne.

Long had Ek Chuuah contemplated a decisive victory over Lakam Ha, an axing or chopping event to destroy the very heart of his former city. His dismay over the Triad Deities' disregard of sacred justice in the Flower War set the framework for his scheme. In Usihwitz, especially after the city broke alliance with Lakam Ha and strengthened ties to Kan, the Triad Deities lost respect. Spiritual focus shifted to K'in Ahau the Father of the Triad. Feeling the hold of the Triad Deities on him dissipating, Ek Chuuah conjured an image of desecrating the most sacred shrine in Lakam Ha, the Sak Nuk Nah—White Skin House. Damaging this link to the Triad Deities and razing the city would indeed "chop down" Lakam Ha.

In that would be justice—and revenge.

Clouds low in the western sky glowed pink and gold with the sun's final rays. Wukhalal, lagoon of seven colors, faded from turquoise to pale green to milky white closer to shore. The setting sun cast golden glints across placid waters. The long canoe closed in on the curving shoreline, paddlers seeking coves with muddy sand beaches between clusters of reeds on which to ground the hull. Finding one to his liking, the captain ordered rowers to jump into shallow water and pull the canoe far enough on shore to stabilize it. Passengers and crew disembarked and set up camp in a grassy meadow bordered by scrubby trees. They found an "eye of water" nearby, small springs bubbling sweet water to surface through the limestone plateau. Fish caught during the voyage were soon roasting over spits, savored by travelers along with maize cakes and fresh wild papayas.

After the meal, Ek Chuuah drew the captain into conversation. Yax Chapat listened attentively, his bright eyes taking in every gesture and voice tone. He knew this trip was training him for leadership and he shared his father's ambition to become ruler of Usihwitz.

"Your family has traded along this coast for generations, yes?" Ek Chuuah asked.

"Yes, many generations," the captain replied. "Our people have lived on the peninsula since the town of Yalamha was founded over 2 baktuns ago (about 789 years). The largesse of the sea and prosperous trade along the coast has brought us abundance. It is a good life."

"So must it be. Know you of the region's history? Your trade brings opportunities to speak with leaders and rulers, those who shape their cities and people."

"In this, I have much interest. What would you know?"

"The relations between the Kan and Zotz dynasties, their cities and influences. To have more knowledge will help me when I meet with Uneh Chan." Ek Chuuah smiled and bowed in deference, gesturing the captain to continue.

"The house of the snake, Kan dynasty, is most ancient. Their family goes back to the greatest city in the lowlands, the famed and magnificent Nakbe, the Chatan Winik city, called the 'Second Center of Humans.' Rising in splendor above a sea of trees, temples larger and grander than any built since, Nakbe commanded the entire region. Then came time to leave, the ahauob and people went away from their grand city for the Gods ordained it. This I do not understand, but the ways of Gods are obscure to men. Families from Nakbe went to other locations in the lowlands, found suitable conditions and built many other cities: Xpuhil, Kuhunlich, Becan, Dzibanche, Uxte'tun. Perhaps Uxte'tun is the oldest, more ancient than my town of Yalamha. There great pyramids, huge complexes were built to remind them of Nakbe, but none as large as the mother city. It is said, by scribes and sages, that the Kan family founded Uxte'tun. They resided there many generations and spread their influence in the region. But then came the Bat people."

The captain paused, relishing the attention of the two Usihwitz ahauob. Ek Chuuah reached into his pouch and removed cigars of dried and rolled tobacco leaves. Passing them to the captain and Yax Chapat, he used a dry branch to catch the campfire flames and lighted the cigars. The men puffed in silence, savoring the aromatic fumes curling through their nostrils and creating an astringent taste. Tobacco smoke also kept the large and bloodthirsty lagoon mosquitoes at bay.

"These are good," the captain observed. "Where do you obtain the leaves?"

"Near Usihwitz, in the higher hills," Ek Chuuah said. "If you visit our city, I can show you the fields."

"Ah, your city is so far inland," the captain bemoaned. "Too much overland travel. It will not suit my trade; there are not connecting rivers. Such good tobacco. . . perhaps I could send an envoy."

"Perhaps. You were saying the Bat people came?"

"Ah, the Bat people." The captain pulled thoughtfully on his cigar, blowing smoke rings. "Where did the Bat people come from? No one knows. They were not from Nakbe, not from this region. Perhaps from the north? It remains mysterious. They are a strong and determined people, war-like, ever ready to fight. They entered Uxte'tun and evicted the Kan family, though the battle was fierce. Then they defaced the Kan monuments, removed the Kan family history, and replaced it with their names. Kan has never gotten over this insult, yet they have not felt powerful enough to assault the Zotz rulers. Kan left and established the dynasty at Dzibanche, where they now reside."

"When did that happen? Kan has expanded its influence in my lifetime, delivered a remarkable defeat to Mutul and courted alliances among K'umaxha River cities."

"Less than a baktun ago (394 years), perhaps four or five generations' span. As you say, Kan has expanded its power. Many cities bowed to Kan influence and had their rulers installed by them, or had katun ceremonies overseen by Kan lords. Uneh Chan is experienced and ambitious; he will seek more glory and tribute to fatten his coffers."

Ek Chuuah smiled inwardly; that suited his plan perfectly.

"Do you trade with Uxte'tun?" Yax Chapat asked.

"Very little. Their ways are too foreign, I trust them not. All my goods are quickly taken up by ahauob in Dzibanche and other cities in the region."

"Of Kan ruler Uneh Chan I would know more," Ek Chuuah said. "You trade with him often; you are clever in obtaining the best value for your goods. Yours is a keen appraisal of motives and desires, most important for successful trading. Has Uneh Chan any qualities that one should note?"

"Ah, yes." The captain basked in praise that he considered well deserved. Savoring the moment, he puffed his cigar and contemplated. "Of Uneh Chan will I say, a quality well worth noting, that he is a handsome man and vain of his appearance. This trait makes my work easy, flattery being a staple of my occupation. Ha!"

The men all chuckled. All Maya elite practiced body adornment with jewelry and costume, and rulers felt compelled to outshine their ahauob.

"This can I use to advantage," said Ek Chuuah.

"Perhaps even more so with an impressive gift. Yes, I have just the thing, a rare turquoise jade pectoral pendant, carved with K'in Ahau's face, set in strands of spondylus beads so red as to drip like sacred blood after penis-piercing rituals. The perfect gift to express his royal status." The captain smiled broadly, pleased at this trade opportunity. "Let me show you, it is very fine work."

Another round of cigars and the best part of Ek Chuuah's cacao pods were required to complete the deal. He carefully folded the heavy pendant in thick cloths and slept with it close to his side. It was a gift worthy of the Gods.

Dzibanche nestled in park-like meadows, long expanses of grass bordered by stately mahogany trees and white flowering willows. Palmettos rustled and thin stemmed Sabal palms waved starburst leaves in the gentle breeze. Golden ferns peeped out from dense stands of logwood trees above undergrowth of kopte bushes with red flowers, some forming small fruit. The city was large with impressive pyramids rising above multiple plazas, some connected by raised platforms. Houses of nobles clustered in complexes around the periphery with the palace situated at the eastern side. Signs of recent building activity abounded, several structures were in process, and workers toiled placing large stones and mixing plaster. Plazas buzzed with activity as richly attired ahauob shopped, visited and promenaded among artisans, farmers, traders, and musicians plying their trades.

The impression given to the visitors from Usihwitz was one of prosperity and expansion. They passed the area where their captain was already spreading his wares on blankets as nobles crowded around. He waved cheerfully and gestured greetings, but was too occupied for a visit. The Usihwitz nobles were en route to the palace for an audience with Ka'an K'uhul Ahau, Uneh Chan, and did not tarry. The palace sat atop a four-tiered platform accessed by wide stairs, upon which warriors stood in light cotton armor, holding long spears. Such military display rarely occurred in the K'umaxha River cities, and it signaled a different mind-set, one of deliberate muscle flexing to impress or intimidate.

Ek Chuuah took note of this, for it fit his purposes. He knew the Kan rulers were aggressive and intent upon spreading their influence, and he planned on cultivating these traits. His fingers squeezed the bundle containing the magnificent pendant, relishing its bulk and weight.

At the top of the stairs, the Royal Steward greeted the visitors and guided them through narrow corridors with high corbelled arches into a waiting chamber. It faced a quiet inner courtyard where a few nobles stood in conversation. After a considerable wait, the visitors were summoned to the ruler's throne room. Long and narrow, the throne room also opened to the inner courtyard, rising above it atop a flight of broad stairs. The nobles glanced upward and watched curiously. More warriors stood on the stairs.

The throne was supported by a Witz Monster mask with a sky bar along its upper edge, ending in two serpent heads. This signified that the ruler sat in the sky, the Upperworld, above a cave giving access to the Underworld through a witz or sacred mountain. Serpent heads on either end formed the Celestial Serpent, as the Milky Way was known, indicating the ruler's command of cosmic forces. In a double word play, the serpent heads also represented the glyph for Kan, the snake dynasty.

Uneh Chan sat with one knee folded beneath the other leg that dangled over the edge of the throne in the Maya ruler's typical throne posture. He was of middle age, his body strong and well-muscled, his face sculpted perfection of Maya elite: tilted almond eyes, straight nose proceeding without dip to the forehead of his elongated skull, high cheeks and full chiseled lips, defined chin and powerful jaw line. Dancing upon his head was an elaborate headdress of feathers, jade and beads with K'awill and K'in Ahau images, and the Kan serpent glyph sat prominently over his brow. Only a richly beaded neck collar covered his upper chest, and his short skirt sported the woven mat pattern of rulers accented by a colorful loincloth. Heavy jewelry of jade and stones adorned his wrists and ankles, and he wore large earspools.

Ek Chuuah and Yax Chapat sank to their knees and bowed deeply, right hand clasping left shoulder. They remained still until the ruler called them to approach, and then wriggled forward on their knees until they reached the mats at the foot of the throne. Finally able to look up directly at the ruler, Ek Chuuah was gratified that the captain's assessment rung true. In the subtle lift of his chin, the haughty stare down his long straight nose, the outward thrust of hard pectoral muscles, the Kan ruler revealed vanity. He also displayed supreme confidence; more than Ek Chuuah thought was merited in light of the captain's story about the Bat dynasty take-over. This would be added fuel for the fire that Ek Chuuah intended to ignite.

After courtly formalities of greeting, the ruler inquired as to the purpose of their visit. Ek Chuuah's eyes swept the throne room, noting the presence of the Royal Steward, the ruler's scribe, and three other well-attired nobles whom he took to be main advisors or courtiers. One appeared to be a Nakom or war chief from his burly form and multiple scars, and the large obsidian dagger hanging from his waistband.

"Long has it been my desire to pay homage to the ruler of mighty Kan," said Ek Chuuah. "In the associations between our cities, I have met some of your warriors and nobles, wise and strong men, much admired in Usihwitz. The prowess of Kan commands great respect; many are the seatings of sahals and oversights of ceremonies in cities under the dominion of Kan's leaders. In honor of these accomplishments, and to acknowledge the recent accession of the new ruler of Ka'an polity, Uneh Chan the Holy Lord of Ka'an, do my son and I travel this great distance."

Uneh Chan nodded, making the feathers of his headdress bobble gracefully, and gestured his acceptance of these compliments. His advisors maintained neutral faces.

"Much is it our pleasure to receive your acknowledgements," he drawled. "This night shall you join us in a feast, that you may enjoy the delights of these bountiful lands."

"Our hearts burst with gratitude, Holy Lord. It is clear that your prowess is matched by your generosity. Greatly shall we anticipate this wondrous feast. In humble thanks, I should wish to offer you our gift, a symbol of our deep appreciation and respect."

Ek Chuuah lifted the pendant bundle and offered it to the ruler. The Royal Steward moved quickly, taking the bundle and holding it level with the ruler's chest. At the ruler's gesture, the Royal Steward unwrapped the cloth and held up the pectoral in its shining magnificence. Light rippled over the red spondylus beads, glinted from bronze disks and illuminated the turquoise jade face of K'in Ahau. All eyes were riveted upon the unusual piece of jewelry.

"For the Holy Lord whose perfection of form reflects truly his divine nature, a pectoral pendant whose maker was surely inspired by the deities themselves. May it be a fitting complement to that Sacred One who is, in himself, already perfectly complete."

A smile flitted across Uneh Chan's lips and his eyes sparked. Not only was the pectoral exquisite, the giver's words were the epitome of courtly Maya speech. Beauty and eloquence pleased the ruler. He gestured for the Royal Steward to remove his neck collar and hang the pendant. Murmurs of praise accompanied this exchange as the ruler turned, showing the pectoral pendant to his advisors. His fingers caressed the jade, and he nodded toward Ek Chuuah.

"This holds much beauty and power," said Uneh Chan. "You have done well."

The atmosphere relaxed and the Royal Steward called for refreshments; fruit juices lightly fermented. The ruler inquired about conditions in Usihwitz following the seating of Yahau Chan Muwaan, done under the auspices of Kan. Ek Chuuah related that the city was content with this choice, avoiding mention of his real views and ultimate ambitions. What did trouble his city, he added, was the treachery of Lakam Ha and the continued threat that they might reassert their dominance.

"What is needed is a decisive defeat of Lakam Ha, a chopping down event," he finished.

"Memory does serve me that your last raid on Lakam Ha was unsuccessful," observed Uneh Chan. "Why would another attack now fare better?"

"Leadership at Lakam Ha has changed and is no longer strong," replied Ek Chuuah. "You are aware that Aj Ne Ohl Mat is ineffective, that much discontent rumbles in Lakam Ha about rectifying their loss in the ball game with us, and restitution for our raid. In essence, governance is done by the ruler's father, Hun Pakal, and brother-in-law, Kan Mo' Hix. Without full authority, however, they are unable to dispel dissent. It is a charged situation, ripe for exploitation."

"The real reason why our raid failed was the seer ability of Yohl Ik'nal," Yax Chapat added. "She foresaw the attack, knew who in her city were involved, allowed Lakam Ha forces to prepare. Without her ability, our raid would have succeeded."

The young man's passion was obvious, though he had been only a child then and could not take part in the raid. His wounded pride over his father's humiliation still smarted.

"So have I heard, this woman ruler had great powers as a seer," said Uneh Chan. "Does she not have a daughter? Might it be that the daughter also possesses such abilities?"

"Yes, there is a daughter, Sak K'uk. From all I can discern, she does not have many abilities as a seer," replied Ek Chuuah. "Her temperament is impatient and hot-headed, she has not the depth of shamanic training as her mother, nor the natural visionary capacity."

"Ummm. Then there is a different situation in Lakam Ha."

"Yes, and Lakam Ha could become another gem in the headdress of Kan. A gem ripe for collecting, should we join forces. I have warriors ready for this attack, but our forces alone are not enough. We need the strength of Kan, of your skilled warriors, to accomplish it. Lakam Ha is prosperous, full of tribute. Kan could gain much in this mission." Ek Chuuah was at his most persuasive, dark face alive with enthusiasm.

Uneh Chan stroked his new pectoral and contemplated. He turned to his Nakom.

"Wamaw Took, what think you?"

The war chief came forward and stood next to the throne. He asked a few questions about Ek Chuuah's forces and his estimation of Lakam Ha's defenses.

"It could be done," he said shortly. "Have we enough reason?"

"More reason than glory and bounty can I give you," interjected Ek Chuuah. "There resides in your fair land blight, one that has thwarted the greatness of Kan. I speak of the usurpers, the foreigners of the Zotz dynasty who infamously took the great city of Uxte'tun from the Kan dynasty. In this is the same injustice that casts dark shadows upon Usihwitz; one who is undeserving takes power from the righteous rulers. Such injustice cannot be allowed to prevail."

Uneh Chan's body tensed and Wamaw Took bristled. Suspense crackled in the atmosphere, for none expected Ek Chuuah to focus upon this source of Kan's shame.

"We can bring justice to both our cities," he continued, voice resonant and compelling. "After we join forces to defeat Lakam Ha, bolstered by our certain victory, we will turn our wrath toward the Bat dynasty and drive them from Uxte'tun."

Silence hovered, suspended like electric charges before a thunderstorm. Uneh Chan's eyes blazed with the fire of revenge. No greater act could a Kan ruler achieve than to restore their dynasty's heritage city, the most splendid accomplishment in their legacy of power. He yearned for restitution; now he was beginning to believe it was possible.

"You foresee certain victory over Lakam Ha?" His clipped tone shot a challenge toward Ek Chuuah.

"My plan is carefully developed. This attack have I studied for many years. Properly executed, it cannot fail." Ek Chuuah focused his energies to radiate full confidence.

The Kan ruler studied his visitor with calculating eyes, reading the man's deep passion and utter dedication to revenge. These were emotions Uneh Chan shared and understood. In that moment, an alliance of spirit was forged.

"The Gods have spoken through you, Ek Chuuah," he said slowly. "This we can do together. The plan must be examined carefully. We will consult with Wamaw Took and our High Priest Tajoom, to determine how Lakam Ha can be chopped down in the most devastating way. This victory will empower our warriors; inspire their courage and strength. Next shall we take down the Bat dynasty."

Torches cast leaping shadows upstairs ascending the highest pyramid temple in Dzibanche. Towering Chaak masks on both sides were bathed in red hues. The storm deity grimaced and leered, huge mouth gaping wide, single long barbel fang protruding, bulging eyes staring through hooked pupils, snout upturned, shell earspools dancing. Above the Chaak mask twin towers flanked the upper stairs, glowing sunset orange. Set back on the top platform was a square structure with the Witz Monster mask framing its entrance. Heavy brows curled into sky spirals, square eyes held sun crosses, hooked nose sat close upon a row of squared teeth stretching across the upper doorway, fanged jaws wrapped around the sides.

The pyramid was a mountain, and at its summit was a cave for entering the mysterious Underworld realms. No mountain caves were found in the flat lands near the coast, though there were many watery caverns that networked underground rivers and sinkholes called tzo'not. The pyramid mountain with its Witz Monster provided the Maya access; these were sacred structures that contained the essential energies of their topographical counterparts. Behind the cave door was the sanctum where ancestors, Gods and enchantments were conjured.

The work undertaken this evening by Dzibanche High Priest Tajoom required a mountain cave ritual. The spells he intended to invoke were only possible using the powers of the Death Lords, whose Underground realm of Xibalba was entered by going deep within caves. The Ka'an K'uhul Ahau and his Nakom, Wamaw Took, with the two visitors from Usihwitz, participated in this ritual as key parties to the actions being conjured.

Their objective was inducing the Death Lords to inject their forces into human actions that would chop down Lakam Ha, destroy the city's most sacred shrine, and collapse the portal it held to the Gods and ancestors.

This plan was finalized through a series of discussions. Ek Chuuah described his idea that the greatest injury to Lakam Ha would be desecrating the Sak Nuk Nah—White Skin House shrine. Uneh Chan added that taking the ruler and his father captives would shatter leadership and bring chaos to the city. Wamaw Took insisted that decisive battle in which most of Lakam Ha's warriors were killed was the best way to defeat them. Yax Chapat agreed that such a defeat was necessary, but noted the valor of Lakam Ha warriors and resilience of leadership after earlier attacks.

"To take Lakam Ha and the Bahlam dynasty down, we must strike them at the core, that source from which they draw identity and sustenance," said Tajoom. "Ek Chuuah has struck upon what forms that core, their special relationship to the B'aakal Triad Deities. Because Lakam Ha rulers satisfy these deities with rituals and gifts, the deities protect them. Their communications are perfect, their ceremonies are proper, and the deities are pleased. It is this relationship that we must break."

"Just as I propose," said Ek Chuuah. "We must desecrate their most sacred shrine, the Sak Nuk Nah."

"To desecrate the shrine is essential, but not sufficient. They can build a new shrine, recreate the White Skin House, and make appeasements to the Triad Deities. Something more is needed," Tajoom brooded.

"How can we permanently damage their relationship with the Triad?" asked Yax Chapat.

Tajoom looked at the young man with increased respect. The High Priest's deep-set eyes that burrowed under sharp cheeks began to glow like coals; his thin lips drew tight over teeth filed into sharp points. Creases deepened as he concentrated, carving grooves over grizzled brows. Sucking in hissing breaths, he exhaled "haaaa" through an open throat several times. His eyes rolled upward with fluttering lids. The other men watched in silent fascination as the shaman-priest went into a trance.

Wamaw Took prepared to catch Tajoom should he fall, but the slender man stood straight as a spear shaft. After several moments, Tajoom opened his eyes and looked at each man intently. When he spoke, his words escaped in breathy hisses.

"It has been shown to me, thanks be to great Chaak, creator of storms and destruction. It is clear what will destroy Lakam Ha. We must shatter the portal they have built to the Triad Deities using the energies of the Sak Nuk Nah. No ordinary desecration, no mere physical destruction, can accomplish this. With the assistance of the Lords of Xibalba, the Death Lords, I will conjure a dark spell; place a curse upon this portal that will take it down. When the portal is broken, the rulers will no longer be able to communicate with and satisfy the deities. The power of Lakam Ha will be ended."

A smile of gratification curled Yax Chapat's lips.

The four men fasted and remained in seclusion for two days, preparing inwardly by cleansing and contemplation. The High Priest chanted and prayed in addition, forming strong mental links to the Death Lords. At dusk on the second day, the men ascended the stairs of the pyramid to meet the High Priest at the entrance into the sacred cave, the toothed and fanged jaws of the Witz Monster mask. Steady drumbeats accompanied their ascent, played by assistant priests in the slow rhythm of interments for those entering the Underworld. Tajoom held a smoking censer and encircled the four men with copal fumes, the final act of energetic cleansing. In order of rank, they followed him through the gaping mouth and into the sacred mountain cave.

A round altar was set in the center of the cave, carved with glyphs of prayers and conjuring images. Wall sconce torches cast eerie flickering shapes against wall murals of deities, who appeared to gesticulate and leer. In the altar center sat a human size crystal skull of smoky quartz. Deep empty sockets gazed at the entering men as it greeted them with the toothy grin of death. Images sparked across its domed skull, and mysterious occlusions within the crystalline matrix swarmed. The skull was alert, waiting, anticipating. It was eager to be fed.

The High Priest and four men walked four times around the altar. Drums and chants by assistant priests kept an insistent rhythm. At four stations around the altar, other assistants sat holding baskets filled with bark paper and sharp stingray spines. The four men settled onto low stone seats at each station and attendants placed a basket between the thighs of each. They had made a covenant to perform bloodletting, a required part of the spell the High Priest would conjure. This action produced *itz*, the sticky, slippery substance that carried *ch'ulel*, essential life force energy.

The most powerful itz came from blood. The most sacred human itz flowed through blood from tongue, ear lobes and penis. For the evening's work, blood was necessary from the penis, for this was how men merged with Gods to become creators, to materialize things into existence, to perform world-making tasks. This produced sympathetic magic, replicating supernatural forces of creation to manifest events on earth. The men became manifestations of the original deity bloodletters that brought creation into being from the energy fields of the Upperworld.

The men wore little, only plumed headdresses and short skirts that opened in front to reveal their genitals. They repeated a series of chants led by the High Priest, the mysterious language of an abyss beyond the reach of finite minds, plummeting to the depths of the Underworld. The drums reached crescendo as the men grasped stingray spines, razor-sharp spikes of self-sacrifice, and raised them high above their heads. The drums ceased. In unison, their heads snapped back and feathers of the plumed headdresses shuddered as they plunged the spines through their penises.

Yax Chapat hesitated momentarily, for this was his first bloodletting. Though prepared mentally and in altered consciousness from analgesic substances, he instinctively recoiled at the self-inflicted suffering. Grimacing, he forcefully willed his hand to deliver one stab. Pain electrified his body as he went rigid and could not plunge the spike again. It was sufficient, however. A steady stream of bright red itz dripped from his penis onto the bark paper, soaking it quickly.

The other three men, more experienced or perhaps having taken greater amounts of analgesic, continued making several stabs and drenched their bark paper with blood. Attendants set fire to the paper and clouds of smoke billowed upward, swirling and undulating in the wavering light. They used some blood-saturated strips to wipe the teeth and eye sockets of the crystal skull. Streaks of sticky itz formed oozing patterns on its glistening surface, feeding it ch'ulel, life force essence.

As the four men sat straight and silent, shocked and numbed as their creative power dripped to feed the crystal skull and invoke forces of manifestation, the drums struck a soft cadence and the High Priest spoke.

"Here it is, here we are.
Now we enter the Dark House, the road to Xibalba.
Open are its doors, wide spread is the cave mouth.
We descend, we fall into the depths
We go down the face of a cliff
We cross through the change of canyons
Across Pus River and Blood River
Past thronging birds grasping at us with talons
Past snakes and scorpions biting and snapping claws
Past bats and mosquitoes and owls that screech and bite
To the crossroads, but we know the roads.
Not the Red Road, the White Road, the Green Road,
But the Black Road, the road to your inner sanctum
Oh, you Lords of Death.
Here am I, you know me, I am Tajoom, High Priest of Dzibanche.
These three men are my companions, they are with me
And they have given their sacred itz in tribute to you.
Soon you will be fed more, my sacred itz will be added
To call you forth, to make our request.
I am Tajoom, High Priest of Dzibanche
And I know some things.
I know your names, I can name you and call you:
Come, One Death
Come, Seven Death
Come, Scab Stripper
Come, Blood Gatherer

51

Come, Demon of Pus
Come, Demon of Jaundice
Come, Bone Scepter
Come, Skull Scepter
Come, Wing
Come, Packstrap
Come, Bloody Teeth
Come, Bloody Claws."

The High Priest named each Death Lord. All of their identities were accounted for, every one of their names spoken rightly, there was not a single name missed. He met their requirements, no name was omitted, and all names were called correctly.

Tajoom continued chanting their names, while he took an ornately carved obsidian blade crowned with shimmering quetzal feathers from his attendant's basket. The attendant draped around the priest's shoulders a long boa constrictor skin, patterned with black scrolls bordering white and tan patches. Tajoom began to dance, a measured hip-swaying toe-heel strut, weaving his arms in sinuous motions making the snakeskin appear alive. Slowly he circled the altar, touching each of the three men on the chest with the snake head, while making hissing sounds.

When he completed the circle, drums broke into frantic thumping. Eyes half closed in ritual ecstasy, Tajoom made multiple slashes on his inner thighs with the sharp obsidian blade. Then he burst into energetic leaps and bows, brandishing the bloody knife in one hand and the snake head in the other. His chest was bare except for a glimmering neck collar of white shells and clear beads that caught firelight and exploded it into a kaleidoscope of rainbow colors. His tall headdress of red macaw and black crow feathers swayed and swooped like birds on wild dashes through fire-lit jungles. He wore a special skirt made of knee-length strips of white cloth. Twirling madly, he caused the strips to flap against his bleeding thighs and scatter droplets of blood over the crystal skull. Blood splattered against the seated men and attendants also, but they remained motionless in strict concentration. Soon the skull was drenched in blood, the floor full of rivulets and the wall murals partly obscured.

The High Priest performed the bloody dance for an interminable time, finally sinking to his knees in exhaustion and faintness. The drums fell silent. Attendants stoked incense burners and more pungent copal smoke poured into the cave. All was in complete stillness, in bated silence.

Yax Chapat squinted into the smoky room without moving his head. His eyes darted back and forth, seeking the ominous presence that he could feel. Swirling smoke thickened and dissipated, hinting of forms yet unseen. Suddenly a chill shot up his spine and he trembled involuntarily. Hairs lifted along his arms and neck, his throat went completely dry and he could not blink, though he wanted to close his eyes. A horrid stench filled the room, something rotten and decayed and utterly evil.

Tajoom revived with the putrid smell, lifting his head and signaling attendants to help him stand. Once upright, the thin man seemed possessed by uncanny energy, pushed attendants away and began the toe-heel strut.

"Welcome, One Death, welcome Seven Death," he said. "Your minion in the Middleworld, your son in dark magic, I myself Tajoom welcome you. Here are my friends, my companions, and we all welcome you. We bow to the power of the Underworld Lords."

All present clasped right hand to left shoulder and bowed.

Tajoom lifted obsidian knife in one hand and snake head in the other. His dance became more animated and he lifted one foot above the other knee, high-stepping and cackling with glee. Stench and awesome power expanded and filled the room. Attendants shrank back against the walls, but the three men sat upright.

Yax Chapat gasped and fought against coughing. Through tearing eyes he watched shadowy forms take shape in the smoke, two creatures that danced in mirror image of Tajoom. They were tall with skinny arms and legs, and rotund bellies. As his vision cleared, he shuddered to recognize the Death Lords. Legs made of fleshless bones, joints protruding, bloated bellies holding death's decomposition, bony fingers with claw-like nails, skeletal spines holding up skulls with jagged teeth and bulging eyeballs.

The Death Lords grinned and leered, wiggling fingers toward the seated men as they danced around the altar. Wisps of copal smoke formed bracelets around their ankles and wrists; a supernatural torch glowed from the backs of their skulls. They did not speak, but words took shape in Tajoom's mind and he understood their communications.

"Why do you summon us, Tajoom, High Priest of Dzibanche?"

"For your powers. For your skills in destruction."

"You have made appropriate sacrifice and called us properly. You may request our powers and skills."

"Into this crystal skull, place a spell that will break the portal in the Sak Nuk Nah of Lakam Ha, the portal that connects the ahauob with the Triad Deities. This is my request. Give to me and these three men who are my companions, the secret chant that will release the spell when the skull is brought into the Sak Nuk Nah."

"Thus have you requested, thus shall we do, with the help of Wing."

Immediately a huge bat swept through the room, uttering blood-chilling shrieks and intensifying the stench with droppings that spattered onto the floor, the seated men and the crystal skull. Yax Chapat tried not to flinch but could not help himself as acidic bat feces splattered on his head and dripped down his face. The bat made another round and seemed to deliberately unload feces on him again, just for spite. Wing then landed behind the two Death Lords and blinked its startling round eyes at the men.

"All is done, all is set, the spell is cast, the skull is empowered," One Death communicated to Tajoom.

"May you reveal to me the chant to release the spell?" asked the High Priest.

"This must be said to bring about the destruction that is your purpose:

Mixekuchu kib' ronojel Xibalba	All the Xibalbans have gathered together
Are k'u retal wa chi qak'ux	Here is the sign in our hearts
Chojim ab'aj kamik qe b'ak.	Their instrument for death will be a skull."

Tajoom bowed deeply and thanked the Death Lords. He repeated the chant several times in his mind to commit the words to memory. With no further communication, the Underworld denizens began to dematerialize, their forms becoming wispy and transparent until they vanished. The priest sealed the ritual by circling again four times, tapping the three men on the chest at each round and chanting release phrases. Removing the snakeskin, he draped it over the blood and guano-coated skull and signaled for his attendant to place them all inside a woven pouch.

Attendants supported the exhausted men to chambers behind the temple-cave where they were bathed and wrapped in cotton blankets to sleep. The High Priest and the crystal skull were ritually bathed in a separate chamber, and taken to a pallet to sleep beside each other. Later Tajoom taught the three men the Xibalban's chant. Any one of the four men could release the spell using this chant while gazing into the eye sockets of the crystal skull. They must not speak it aloud until the skull was in place inside the Sak Nuk Nah of Lakam Ha.

2

The young deer lifted his white-tipped chin from the tender grass shoots. Sunlight filtered through the forest canopy, dappling the deer's grayish brown coat. Small antlers sprouted from his forehead; it would be two more seasons before they were mature. At the forest edge, trees were widely spaced allowing ferns, grasses and fruiting shrubs to flourish and provide nourishing forage.

His moist black nose sniffed the humid air as his large, funnel-shaped ears rotated back and forth seeking unusual sounds. Only the buzzing of insects and twitters of birds floated on the hushed forest air. The deer's stubby white tail was half-raised; he would flash it just before bolting from danger. He could detect nothing threatening.

But he knew something was watching him.

The young buck was alone. He had been banished as a yearling when his mother gave birth to another fawn and she kicked and butted him from her range. He followed at the edge of her path for a while, but eventually gave up and ranged on his own. At times, he cautiously grouped with other yearlings as they avoided the range of mature bucks.

Flicking his tail against flies, he rotated his large ears again, stamped his front foot then resumed grazing. After a few nibbles, he raised his head and looked from side to side. Though he could detect nothing, instinctively he sensed a presence. Something was drawing him, summoning him toward it. Something calm, quiet, peaceful. The deer walked toward a cluster of brush and peered inside. His eyes met another pair of eyes, dark as pools of obsidian and radiant as the night sun. Eyes of kindness and compassion, eyes of appreciation and admiration.

Unafraid, the young deer gazed at the brown-skinned creature seated on a cushion of leaves behind the shrubs. He did not recognize it among forest creatures, but it posed no threat and sat only as tall as his shoulder. Moving closer, he caught an unfamiliar scent and froze, tail raised in alarm. The creature made soft sounds, not unlike the deer's mother once made to call him. Curious again, the deer relaxed and stepped closer. Time passed in complete stillness as they regarded each other.

Very slowly, in a fluid motion, the brown-skinned creature moved an arm upward and offered juicy Ramon berries. The delicious sweet smell of the forest delicacy beckoned the deer. Undecided, the deer glanced around and stamped his foot, flicking his tail repeatedly. More soothing sounds reassured him and he reached his wet muzzle to quickly gobble up the berries. Then he suddenly whirled, bounded a short distance and stopped to gaze back over his shoulder, still licking berry juice from his lips. After advancing to take berry treats several more times and then retreating, the deer felt satisfied and slowly walked off into the forest.

Pakal closed his eyes and recalled the High Priest's teachings about how animals conserved cultivated and utilized energies. The deer was a frequent example.

"Observe, Pakal, how the deer conserves energy when sleeping," said Pasah Chan, High Priest of Lakam Ha. "When he sleeps, the deer curls his body, tucks his head next to his side and places a hoof against his anal opening. This closes off the two portals in the head and spinal base where energy enters and leaves the body. He avoids losing vital energy this way. In humans, we use the technique of fixing closed eyes at the psychic center located between the eyebrows, filling the lungs to close the diaphragm and contracting the anal muscles to close the spinal portal. Doing this during meditation conserves our energy and balances the portals at the crown and base of the spine."

Meditation brought the mind and body into perfect harmony, using breath and focus. When completely harmonious, one emanated peacefulness that put all other creatures at ease. Then animals would approach with no fear or aggression.

Pakal smiled inwardly. His mentor's teachings had proven true; today's experience with the young deer affirmed it. There were other important uses of energy to be learned from observing deer, the High Priest had told him.

"When the deer runs across the fields," said Pasah Chan, "he takes leaps and appears to float, his hooves barely touching the ground. Deer can leap over high bushes and across wide streams. What makes them so light, so able to float? It is because they can move their energy upward. When the deer runs, all his energy is in his extremities: the hoofs, tail and horns. Deer are very powerful. Through closing portals of the body, they maintain internal energy and circulate it where needed. Thus, they can send great energy to extremities to allow leaping with ease and grace."

Likewise, animals such as the jaguar had special abilities to move energy downward. The jaguar symbolized force captured in bones and tendons. It was relaxed, agile, and unconcerned. Every movement in its life was done without striving, lightly and softly, never awkwardly. Moving its energy downward, the jaguar used relaxed power and flexible joints, never forcing its actions or becoming exhausted.

"This ruling lord of animals has the most resistant bones, so strong that powder of its bones is powerful medicine. When descending mountains and heights, use the relaxed force of the jaguar to control your descent; when climbing high use the deer's power to ascend without effort," advised Pasah Chan. "Meditation will give you control of both these energetic forces, to enter deeply relaxed and highly concentrated states."

Pakal learned many ways to meditate. He studied the fundamental principles of breath control, use of *Ik* or wind. To absorb energy from his surroundings, he would inhale sucking in the lower abdomen, and exhale while relaxing the abdomen. Upon inhalation, he inflated all his muscles by filling them with bubbles of light. These bubbles infused vital energy until he felt tickling heat running all through his body. When this tickling heat coursed through his veins, it was called "lightning in the blood" and signaled the presence of truth and healing powers.

He learned postures called *K'u* to regulate and control the direction of energy, accompanied by hand signs that added finesse to his purpose. With these postures and gestures, he could draw down the energy of Father Sun, command the elements, manifest things in the Middleworld, enter trance states that brought him to other times and places, send blessings or healing energies, harmonize with creative impulses from the cosmic center, call forth the presence of other beings, and initiate life cycle processes of birth, death and rebirth.

Among the first shamanic powers mastered by young Pakal was calling the wind. Doing this required a perfectly calm day when no breath of air stirred. After preparing through meditation and concentration of energy, Pakal stood on a hilltop where a few trees dangled their leaves listlessly. To the east, the hill sloped down toward the plains. Pakal intended to call the wind from the east, the direction from which it usually originated during this dry season. Closing his eyes and focusing one-pointedly upon the wind, Pakal chanted an invocation.

"Come, Honored Ik', natural force filling the universe.
Ik' that exists in all things from the greatest to the smallest.
We find you in the sky, upon the land and in all living things.
Knowing you, we are in harmony with nature.
Come, Honored Ik', blow across this hill.
I, Pakal, summon you."

With eyes closed, Pakal began slow arm movements forming a circle from east to west. His hands cupped into the summoning gesture, fingers together and thumbs pressed against the edge of his palms. In rhythm with the arm circles, he moved his cupped fingers as if to grasp the wind and pull it toward the west. He added a swooshing sound by blowing softly out through pursed lips.

After some moments, Pakal felt a wisp of hair stirring against his sweaty neck. Opening his eyes, he intensified his motions and sounds. He watched the hanging leaves, which soon began to rustle and sway. In one final motion, he breathed out gratitude to the wind, Ik'. Gusts wafted across the hill making the leaves dance riotously and cooling his neck.

Summoning the rain was more difficult and complex. It required the Ch'a Chaak ceremony involving four young boys and several assistants to construct the altar, build the fire pit, make sacred breads and bring a sacrifice. During the dry season, Pasah Chan determined that Pakal was ready and arranged the ceremony. A wooden altar was built, held together by sapling poles and vines, and a fire pit dug nearby. Women of the assistants' families ground corn into maize dough of various colors to cook in the fire pit, for the sacred breads must be layered like the three worlds. Ocellated turkeys were ritually killed and their meat prepared for the fire pit, and honey wine was brought to add to the altar.

After three days of prayers and preparation, the group converged at the altar site located at the edge of cornfields on the plain below Lakam Ha. They lit logs in the fire pit early in the morning, and when these became glowing coals, they placed the turkey meat wrapped in banana leaves into the pit and covered this with a thin layer of rocks. A flat stone was placed on top for cooking the maize cakes later.

When Pasah Chan judged the time was right, he lit copal incense and called all present to begin the ceremony. The four boys crouched beside the four poles of the altar, while the assistants stood nearby. As pungent copal smoke billowed, Pakal came forward to take the censer and conduct the ceremony. For a moment, his eyes locked with those of the High Priest. Insecurity flashed across Pakal's dark eyes. He was the youngest acolyte to ever perform the Ch'a Chaak, having passed only seven solar years. Pasah Chan kept his gaze opaque; this would be a real test of the boy's abilities.

Inhaling deeply, Pakal focused inward and breathed to absorb energy. Determination welled upward, filling his body with tickling heat. Holding the censer firmly, he raised his voice in the Chaak chant and began moving counterclockwise around the altar. At first, the chant seemed stuck in his throat and came out in quavering notes. Pakal swallowed and cleared his throat, eyes darting toward his teacher. Pasah Chan stood rigidly, aloof and distant, gazing across the cornfields.

Pitching his voice into a higher octave to show proper respect, Pakal chanted clearly to Lord Chaak, the rain god, calling for his assistance to bring rain from the cloudless sky.

"Ch'a Chaak, Ceremony to Bring the Rain, let us call, let us seek,
Lord Chaak, Thunderstorm-Lightning of Four Directions,
Green Thunderstorm of Fifth Direction,
Carrier of Rain Clouds upon his back.
Here he is at the first corner; White Thunderstorm, a turkey is his offering.
Here he is where the day ends, Black Thunderstorm, the blood of a tree, sacred copal is his offering.
Here he is at the Great Door, Yellow Thunderstorm, drumming is his offering.
Here he is where the day begins, Red Thunderstorm, fire is his offering.
Perhaps Thunderstorm is there on the green earth, Green Thunderstorm, dripping water through his fingers on top of sprouting corn.
Perhaps Thunderstorm is there, nesting in the sky, growing fruit in the sky.
Perhaps Thunderstorm is there, compressing the air with his hands on a mountaintop.
Perhaps he really is there, stopping to rest on Thunderstorm Mountain.
Lord Chaak, Thunderstorm, is there under the sky and the rain comes day and night.
Lord Chaak, Thunderstorm, is stooping as he goes along.
The rain has arrived."

Pakal circled the men and boys each in turn, gesturing them to begin their performances. The four men made roaring sounds of thunder with their voices, *ruum-ruum-ruum,* clapping small wooden mallets together, beating wooden drums and sprinkling water from gourds onto the boys who crouched beside the poles. The four boys enacted frogs awakened by the rainstorm, croaking the frog call *uuoo-uuoo.* They imitated insects of the night by chirping, made hoots of owls and high-pitched bat squeaks. All these sounds were amplified when the land and forests were saturated with wetness. Their performance replicated the earth and sky during rainstorms.

Pakal approached the altar and grasped a sapling pole, shaking it as wind would shake the thatch roof of houses. He signaled for assistants to bring offerings and the men carefully removed maize cakes and banana leaf wrapped meat from the fire pit. As the offerings were placed on the altar, Pakal chanted and again called Lord Chaak to bring rain. Eyes open only a slit he raised his face to the sky and lifted his arms, cupping hands into the summoning gesture. After several repetitions, Pakal dropped his arms into the gesture for bringing forth or birthing. Both upper arms were held close against his sides, left hand lifted to shoulder height and right hand extended below waist, both open palms facing outward. With the left hand he drew the creative power of Lord Chaak down from the sky; with the right hand he birthed Chaak's storm power into the Middleworld. Holding this gesture, Pakal fell into a trance, communing directly with the rain and storm deity.

All activity around the altar ceased. The participants waited, anxiously glancing skyward. Pasah Chan held his breath, for this was a critical moment. Had the boy made successful supplication; was his power enough that Lord Chaak would respond?

The late afternoon air hung heavy and still, expectant, infused with tension. For what seemed an eternity, nothing stirred. Suddenly from a distance came the deep rumble of thunder. A cool wind slid across the plains and rustled leaves on the altar vines. White clouds formed above the eastern horizon, skittering rapidly over the plains and boiling into dark-bellied heralds of rain. As the clouds passed over the ceremonial altar, fat raindrops spattered the ground and hissed on the fire pit coals. All lifted their faces and smiled as cooling droplets trickled on warm skin. In particular, Pasah Chan smiled wryly to himself. This boy was truly extraordinary.

The rain was light and short, the clouds quickly dissipated. But, Pakal had successfully called the rain; he petitioned correctly and Lord Chaak responded. Pasah Chan bowed and clasped his shoulder in acknowledgement, then invited all to partake of the altar offerings in celebration.

Pasah Chan instructed Pakal on the cyclic essence of reality.

"All in nature is a cycle. The pathways of the sun, the journey of the moon in the sky, the life of flowers. All life follows the seasons of the year. When the flowers open, the birds unite to procreate. In the heat of summer, they raise their young and prepare them to survive the chilling rains or migrate to warmer lands. Every year, Pakal, you must be attentive and follow the seasons of your life. Now you are in the season of flowering, a young bud just opening. As you grow, your force will increase. When the summer of your life arrives, you will be strong, vigorous. Cultivate your interests in this time, explore everything to satisfy your desires but do so with moderation and within moral boundaries. Conquer and defeat that which is evil, push forward toward the good.

"When the winds arrive and leaves fall to coat the forest floor, youth recedes and you come to the horizon of your life. You will then plan the remainder of life and the route to take. Then will appear the consequences of your past actions, so choose those actions well. It will be time to slow the pace of life, to make more tranquil its rhythms. It will be time to teach others, to transmit what you hold in your heart and mind. This leads into the time to prepare for your leaving.

"Finally will arrive the days of cold and snow, the closing of the cycle. Your hair whitens and your step slows. Be tranquil and at peace. Meditate and contemplate the significance of your life. In this time, prepare for physical death. It brings close the time of liberating your spirit when you will show to your people the continued cycle of being. Many are afraid of death, but death is merely transformation. Life does not cease, it only changes, like the butterfly transforms within its cocoon. Those too attached to life cannot imagine the wonder that awaits.

"You cannot be in the temple and the forest simultaneously. You cannot wear two sets of clothes at the same time. The shell that is your body remains upon the earth, to make you lighter for a grander reality. The body shell you can use, break and destroy. But the spirit is indestructible. Go forth in this knowledge that you have a marvelous destiny in the dwelling of the immortals.

"Those afraid of death have much hidden from them. You have great wisdom to give our people; remember to use your powers to serve others. You must overcome all obstacles, including both self-aggrandizement and all personal fears. Become the master of your body and mind."

Pakal learned to control his thoughts and feelings, to regulate the activity of his body and mind. The latter presented the greatest challenge, for the mind was a trickster always finding ways to circumvent his techniques. He became the observer of his mental landscape, watched beliefs, fears, and emotions play out without reacting or grasping. These wafted across his awareness and dissipated, rose and fell, ultimately resolving into nothingness. He focused until his mind became empty, a clear field of calmness, and entered the blissful state of pure awareness. He simply *was*.

3

Pakal's long legs took two steps at a time as he bounded up the tiered stairways leading to the Temple of the High Priest. He was late for his favorite lesson, studying Mayan hieroglyphs inscribed in fan-folded codices with the old calendar priest Ah K'uch. Wending his way through vaulted hallways and across the wide central plaza, he quickly ascended the final set of stairs and entered the western chamber that held thousands of codices. Passing through several interconnected rooms, he found the old priest seated on his raised platform with a codex in place on the wooden display box.

Pakal bowed deeply, clasping left shoulder with right hand.

"It is my regret to be late, honored Ah K'uch. Now am I before you for teachings."

Ah K'uch turned his cloudy owl-like eyes toward the boy, wrinkled lips held tight. He paused just long enough to make Pakal uncomfortable, and then gave a toothless grin. The boy relaxed and smiled back.

"The young are always busy." Ah K'uch's voice was high and reedy but conveyed an ease of command that Pakal instinctively recognized. He intended to develop that quality in his voice as it matured.

"The old, as am I, never busy themselves but savor each moment life still gives them." Ah K'uch appeared wrapped in deep contemplation. Pakal stood respectfully and waited until the old priest spoke again.

"Let us resume study of this divinatory almanac based on the original hearthstone event. Do you remember when this calendar began?"

"At our last session you said it began at the end of the previous count of thirteen bundles when the hearthstone stars rose at midnight and reached the middle of the sky at dawn," Pakal replied eagerly and with perfect recall.

"It is as you say." Ah K'uch was pleased with the boy's memory. "And which are the hearthstone stars?"

"They are the three stars dangling below the feet of the peccary constellation, *Am Kitam*," Pakal replied without hesitation. "The three stars are called *osh-lot*, three together and their names are *Tunsel*—little woodpecker (Rigel), *Mehem Ek*—Semen Star (Alnitak), and *Hun Rakan*—One Leg (Saiph)."

"Ah, yes, that is so. You have remembered well. Now let us consider the infinite structure of the Long Count calendar. On what date did the current creation begin?"

"On 4 Ahau 8 Kumk'u, the birth of the Fourth Sun and creation of the True People, Halach Uinik." This date combined the day number from the 1—13 numeric Tzolk'in calendar, the day name of the 20-day uinal (month), and the numeric sequence of the day within one of the 18 months.

"Yes, that date marked the end of the previous age, when the 13 bundles were completed. And now tell me how to calculate 13 bundles."

Pakal frowned, drawing his eyebrows together as he concentrated and tried running mental calculations. The mathematical poetics of the Maya 13 x 20 = 260 day Tzolk'in—sacred calendar interacting with the 18 x 20 = 360 day Haab—seasonal calendar intrigued him and he worked hard to commit these to memory. The 13 bundles were the baktun count, made up of 20 katuns, and the katun count was comprised of 20 stones or tuns, the year count. He understood that 18 uinals of 20 days made up one tun, and one tun was 360 days or kins. He also knew that the solar year was 365 days plus a few hours, but the Maya preferred the elegant numerology and sacred symbolism of 260 x 360. But beyond the count of baktuns, he was lost. Then he shrugged and lowered his eyes, admitting his confusion.

"Further I do not understand, Master. From Pasah Chan, I learned how to count with the dot and bar system, where a dot is one and a bar is five. It is a 20-base system, with increments at each level of 20 times the previous number. From the lowest position up to the fifth there are increasing numbers. First level equals one, second level equals 20, third level equals 400, fourth level equals 8000, and fifth level equals 160,000.

"But you taught me that the calendars are counted differently. Each day has the value of one at the first level, but at the second level of the uinal the increment is only 18. That brings the tun at the third level to 360 days. Then the system reverts back to 20-base so there are 20 tuns to make one katun of 7,200 days. The baktuns are formed by the count of 20 katuns for each baktun, to complete the baktun count at 144,000 days. But when baktuns become 13, the calendar makes a great shift and all five levels return to zero. This is said to signify completion of an era, the time when a new Sun is born. What happens with the remaining baktuns up to a count of 20? Why do not baktuns follow the same pattern as the other levels of the count?"

"Ah, this is part of the mystery and magic of calendars. Can you be more than one thing at the same time? Are you not both a boy and a son? Can a jaguar be beautiful and dangerous and loving of its cubs? Do not limit your mind to believe there is only one explanation, a single quality, an exclusive meaning given to the wondrous creations of the Gods. Time is divine. It flows eternally without beginning or end. Nothing exists without time, and space is the platform on which the divine expressions of time play out. Deities acting within different spaces are the changing faces of time. You have studied the face glyphs for numbers, and the face glyphs for the five levels of the Long Count. Those are our artist's depictions of the Gods of numbers and time. But consider this mystery: the numbers and measures of time are Gods themselves. Gods have will and volition, they choose to create and craft their manifestations in our world. Do you understand?"

Pakal was not sure he did understand but made an attempt.

"The calendar can be different things, or can be understood in more than one way. There can be a progression to the next level at Baktun 13 and different progressions at other levels. The mathematic counts can use 20-base while calendar counts use different bases. It is all dreamt in the imagination of the Gods. Is this understanding correct?"

"Excellent! The Long Count calendar allows you to express an infinitely large number by writing a long string of 13s continuing in positions above the fifth level. Now recite to me what that count would say."

"Zero kin, zero uinal, zero tun, zero katun, 13 baktun, then 13—13—13—13—13—13— for as long as you wanted?"

"It is so. And if you wanted to express a specific and accurate amount of time that has elapsed since the last creation began, how would you say it?"

"You would recite the exact numbers for each of the five positions, such as 6 kins, 14 uinals, 2 tuns, 9 katuns, 10 baktuns. But what happens after you reach 13 baktuns?"

"Then you must use higher value positions, new Gods of Time. These do exist but most calendar keepers do not know them. Not all minds can grasp such large time periods and in practical use these greatly exceed many human lifetimes. Now comes important and occult information, not taught to many. I shall tell you some of their names. Above the baktun comes piktun, above that comes kalabtun, then kinchiltun and then alautun. When next you come, I will show you the codex with their god face glyphs. Can you imagine how immense the day count would be if continued through the alautun?"

Pakal reflected upon the endless possibilities of numbers and calendars. His mind swirled and tumbled with numbers beyond expressing. He shook his head.

"This is impossible to imagine. You would multiply 144,000 days by 20 to get 1,872,000 days, then multiply that by 13 and the result by 13 and that result by 13 and . . . oh, the number of days is beyond calculation!"

"Just so. The Long Count goes back to the very beginning of time when no one was present to do the counting that led to the original placement of the hearthstones. So for practical purposes, we counted backward from a later date during the early times of our people to establish 4 Ahau 8 Kumk'u as the seating of the hearthstones for the current Sun. So we say the new creation began on completion of the 13 bundles."

Pakal scrutinized the old priest's wrinkled face. Ah K'uch waited patiently to see where his pupil's mind was going.

"The lifetime of a man is 3 katuns, so has Pasah Chan taught me," the boy began. "Three katuns equals 60 tuns, the time in which Father Sun completes his journey from south to north 59 times in the solar year. Yet a single baktun is 360 tuns, more than six lifetimes. It is not surprising that few people trouble themselves to think beyond a baktun."

"That is so. Few are the 5 Katun Lords, rulers who live beyond 80 tuns."

"Honored Elder, have you attained to Katun 5?"

Ah K'uch chuckled and nodded, touching his copious wrinkles.

"So testifies my face. Perhaps I shall see Katun 6, should the Gods be willing. But let us return to your lesson on the divinatory almanac. Come sit here beside me."

Pakal climbed onto the raised platform and sat beside the old priest. Settling on the mat cross-legged, he was now able to see the fan-folded codex with its colorful glyphs, drawings and dot-and-bar numbers. Ah K'uch pointed to a complex drawing of a woman with an intricate headdress seated on a raised dais receiving offerings.

"Here we have *Ix K'in Sutnal*, she of the sun's place of return. She is the Lady of the House in the constellation of *Itzam Huh*—Iguana. This is one of 13 constellations of our zodiac, whose stars are situated at the autumnal equinox, the place where the sun comes around again when day and night are equal. In this depiction, she sits on her throne made of the Star Band, the vault of the sky. Her headdress has the face of the iguana, its breath curling upward from elongated nose, its back fin fanned out above her shoulders. In one hand she receives offerings of food, drink in a vase, and a smoking censer. The other hand rests by her side, fingers pointing behind her."

The boy studied the drawing carefully, identifying all the elements mentioned by the old priest. Several other drawings and glyphs were nearby and the priest pointed to them.

"These two drawings are the spirit uay of the Lady of the House; they are frogs. See that one frog appears to be swallowing the sun. This signifies that the sun has entered the part of the sky occupied by the constellation Itzam Huh. The other frog is facing downward and raindrops are pouring from its body. This depicts the onset of rains as the rainy season begins in our locale at autumnal equinox. Soon will be time for planting corn.

"There is another very important message in these figures when we study the calendar glyphs next to them. This codex makes predictions about astronomical events that will take place a long time in the future. Here in this group of glyphs are interval numbers projecting to the end of the current creation, when Baktun 13 will be completed and the Long Count will reset to all zeros. This will be on the date 4 Ahau 3 Kank'in (December 21, 2012). The 260-day sacred calendar will stand at the same place it did when the hearthstones of the Fourth Sun were set in place, but the solar calendar will be in another uinal, Kank'in instead of Kumk'u. Then the sun will be in the middle of the Milky Way passing by the constellation *T'zek*—Scorpion, and the three hearthstones of Am Kitam—Peccary will rise at dusk and reach meridian at midnight."

"So will begin the Fifth Sun," Pakal concluded.

"It is so!" Ah K'uch beamed happily at his student. "At that time, the Lady of the House will soar at meridian as the dawn comes. The divinatory pronouncement of this stellar configuration is that the new era will have a feminine character. This will be a good time for planting, for creating anew, and for new beginnings."

4

The small group of noble women continued their chatter as an attendant escorted them through an arched portico leading back to the palace entrance. Red and yellow borders of their bright white huipils swished as they walked, jewelry clinked at wrists and dangled from elaborate braids piled atop their heads. Heavy earspools and neck collars of jade, turquoise and serpentine completed their everyday attire when in attendance to royalty in the palace.

In the reception chamber of the ruler's sister, they played board games with colored beans and gambled using bone dice marked with the Maya dot-and-bar numbering system. Frequently they worked together weaving fine patterns on cotton fabric, using backstrap looms. Today's activities had focused on painting dried gourds in delicate designs, each woman trying to outdo the others with creative images of family, ancestors or deities. Their normal time was cut short, however, and many had to leave work unfinished.

Alone in the reception chamber, the ruler's sister, Sak K'uk, brushed a strand of hair away from her face absently. She held a round, hollow gourd carefully by its upper rim where the top was cut away. Turning it slowly with care not to touch the wet paint, she evaluated her handiwork. Two women danced in unison, arms outstretched and fingers upward, feet following the heel-toe pattern. Their elaborate costumes identified them as royalty. Around the other side of the gourd, monkey and macaw musicians played drums, rattles, and clay flutes. Twining vines circling the entire gourd formed borders above and below the scene, sprouting lilies and pads.

Only a few more dabs of paint were needed. Sak K'uk wanted to finish her work and set it on a circular stand of twisted reeds to dry. Surely she had enough time before her visitor arrived. With a sigh, she reached for the tiny feather brush, dipped it in blue dye and added deft strokes to the macaw's feathers.

She had dismissed her group of women courtiers early because of the visitor. Why had her sister-in-law Hohmay requested a private audience? This both annoyed and troubled her.

Sak K'uk and Hohmay were not close and infrequently saw each other. There was an underlying tension between them, due in no small part to Sak K'uk's frequent criticism of her brother's performance as ruler of Lakam Ha. In recent months, Aj Ne Ohl Mat seemed more withdrawn and presided less often in the Popol Nah—Council House. When the ruler was absent, their father Hun Pakal assumed the throne position. Or worse, Sak K'uk's ambitious husband Kan Mo' Hix took the leadership bench. Although she deliberately stayed away from this governing council, she was acutely aware of the dissonance and discord simmering among the ahauob.

Finally satisfied that the gourd painting was completed, Sak K'uk set it upon the reed stand and rose to wash her paint-stained fingers, summoning an attendant with a hand gesture. As she finished drying her hands, footsteps in the hall alerted her to the visitor's arrival.

"Here comes Ixik Ahau, the Holy Lady Hohmay," intoned the steward.

"Ma'alo K'in—good day," said Sak K'uk.

"May this day be well for you," replied Hohmay.

Sak K'uk dismissed her steward with a small hand wave and signaled Hohmay to be seated on nearby mats. As they settled down, Sak K'uk was struck at her sister-in-law's thinness, bordering on emaciation. Despite the best efforts of

Hohmay's face painter, dark circles accentuated both eyes and the very skin of her face seemed to hang listlessly from high cheekbones. Her lips were drawn tight and thin over teeth too large for her delicate face. The flatness of her stomach proclaimed her conceptive failures.

Hohmay had never recovered from her last miscarriage. The pregnancy was difficult and the ministrations of Ix Chel priestesses could not control her nausea. She steadily lost weight and strength as the pregnancy sucked life force from her body. Then the miscarriage at six moons with ensuing hemorrhage sapped the *ix* from her very blood stream, leaving her pale and wan. Worst of all was the emotional trauma, the loss of yet another potential heir, this one a tiny and perfectly formed boy whose immature lungs failed within moments of birth. Hohmay's grief knew no bounds, and she continued without appetite or motivation for life.

Sak K'uk was almost embarrassed by her own strength and vitality. But not enough to wish Hohmay and her brother an heir.

"To what purpose is this private conversation?" Sak K'uk asked, not knowing how to enter the topic more gracefully.

Hohmay fixed an angry stare upon her husband's sister.

"There is much talk concerning your son Pakal." She almost spat the words. "That he has called the wind, and even that he commanded Lord Chaak to bring rain during the dry season. Of these things have I heard, not just in the palace or among the ahauob. The most humble of my attendants bring stories of Pakal's feats, lauded at the market and around the hearthstones of the villagers."

"Well, yes," replied Sak K'uk, trying to keep pride out of her voice. "He has indeed shown advanced abilities in his training."

"Why has he even been trained by the High Priest?" demanded Hohmay. "He is only now attained of eight tuns, and they say he began training at five tuns. This is unheard of!"

"He showed abilities so early, it was for his safety. He could have entered realms of danger or used these abilities unwisely."

"You are not telling the entire truth! You pushed his training forward out of your own ambitions. I know you believe Pakal will be the next ruler of Lakam Ha." Hohmay's bitterness blazed from sunken eyes.

"We must be prepared. The royal heir may not come from my brother." Sak K'uk could not summon compassion as her own anger swelled.

"I will conceive again!" Hohmay cried wildly. "We will produce an heir, unless your spells are preventing a successful pregnancy."

Sak K'uk narrowed her eyes and shot an energy bolt that caused Hohmay to recoil.

"I cast no spells. This is the product of a sickened mind, Hohmay. Seek counsel with the High Priest, bring yourself into mental balance."

"Pasah Chan is your ally! You both are plotting against me. . ." Her voice trailed off into stifled sobs.

"Hohmay, listen. I bear you no evil intentions. Surely such events, such recurring patterns are the will of the deities. We cannot always know their intentions, what they decree for our lives and our destinies. You must see that Aj Ne has little interest in ruling our polity. Perhaps your desire for a dynastic heir is not shared by your husband. His art is his first love, and could be his greatest contribution to our city."

Both women sat in silence for some time.

"I have failed in the most sacred duty of a royal wife," Hohmay whispered. "I have produced no sons, no heirs. Aj Ne must take another wife. My life is over."

Sak K'uk could indeed believe that the fragile, emaciated woman might die momentarily. A wave of pity swept over her and she tapped upon a ceramic bowl to summon attendants.

"Bring warm fermented maize drink," she ordered. After Hohmay sipped from a finely decorated clay cup, her color deepened slightly. Sak K'uk attempted to bring some comfort to the distraught woman.

"Aj Ne loves you deeply, and you can encourage his creativity," she suggested. "I have seen how you inspire his poetry. He expresses no interest in another wife, or dynastic succession. What ensues in the governance of Lakam Ha is the purview of the Triad Deities."

For a moment, it appeared that Hohmay slipped into acceptance. Then suddenly she threw her cup of maize on the floor and sprang to her feet. Eyes blazing fury and hatred, she pointed a scrawny finger at Sak K'uk and shouted: "You are deceiving me! You wish me to give up, to admit defeat, to resign myself that Pakal will become heir designate for the Bahlam dynasty! Never, never will I succumb to your spells! You and your shaman mother, you think you can control the future of rulers and cities. I curse you both, and your precious son Pakal the magnificent! Much suffering and misery I call down upon you, even such as I have known!"

Sak K'uk reeled at the powerful energy blasting from Hohmay, who appeared as a shimmering apparition with daggers for eyes in a cadaverous skull, teeth bared in a death grin. Staggering momentarily, the thin woman spun and rushed away in a cascade of ghastly howls.

It took Sak K'uk some time to recover her composure after the encounter with her sister-in-law. She was deeply disturbed by the prophetic nature of Hohmay's last utterances. An underlying sense of danger had been forming in her subconscious, now brought to the surface. Something was amiss, something beyond the continued dissention in the Council House and the tension between her family and her brother. Now she wished ardently that she had paid closer attention to her mother's teaching, had concentrated more on techniques for visioning and divination. Yohl Ik'nal would seek a vision in such circumstances to discern what forces were at play. But Sak K'uk did not possess similar abilities and had not enacted a visioning since the last time with her mother when they both foresaw her marriage to Kan Mo' Hix.

That was when Yohl Ik'nal foresaw the attack upon Lakam Ha, a vision that aided her city to prepare and defeat the attackers.

Was something similar brewing? Sak K'uk had not been attending Popol Nah sessions but heard about them from her father and husband. Even so, the network of informers used by Yohl Ik'nal, following the example of her father Kan Bahlam, had deteriorated under the poor leadership of Aj Ne Ohl Mat. Information about the plots and intrigues of neighboring cities was spotty at best. Usihwitz had extricated itself from Lakam Ha's dominion, and relations with other cities in B'aakal polity were growing more distant. Tribute had declined, and Aj Ne's chumtum—stone binding ceremony at the period end of 13 katuns (9.8.13.0.0) had been lack-luster, not as powerful and compelling as prior ceremonies by his predecessors.

She queried Hun Pakal in one of their long evenings together. Sipping warm cacao, father and daughter leaned close on adjoining mats and spoke in hushed tones.

"What information comes forth from Popo' and Yokib and B'aak? Hear you anything of Usihwitz?" she asked.

"Ah, it is not such as the times of your esteemed mother, Sacred Ancestor Yohl Ik'nal, wife of my heart," he lamented. "Our informers are few and not well connected. Hix Chapat of Popo' seems to forget his obligations, or even that his sister is married to our ruler. He basks in peace and abundance but is meager in tribute. Without firmness bordering upon threat, I doubt this will change. It is rumored that Yokib's ruler plays host to traders and ahauob from Kan, more so recently but we cannot obtain specifics. B'aak on the far western plains seems removed from such plotting and remains our most firm ally. As for Usihwitz, our sources have been silenced for some time. It is my assessment that they are courting alliance with Kan."

"And gloating in the absence of repercussions for flaunting their tribute obligations," Sak K'uk added glumly.

"Just so, and reveling in their defeat of Lakam Ha in the ballgame. We should have sent a foray against them right away to remedy their attack on us. This I still do not understand, except that Yohl Ik'nal was becoming more ill, and must have thought leaving the polity in peace was best." It pained Hun Pakal to offer any criticism of his wife's decisions.

"Hmmm. She had her reasons, I am certain."

Sak K'uk told her father about the encounter with Hohmay, and the woman's wild curses at the end.

"These things are much troubling me," she admitted. "Is there any way to find out if other cities have intentions against us?"

"I will try to send scouts for information, though it will not be easy in the current climate of the Popol Nah. Perhaps surreptitiously, if I can find reliable men."

Sak K'uk sighed.

"If only I had mother's vision," she murmured.

Thunder rumbled in the distance as dark rain clouds gathered in the east. Sak K'uk dabbed her sweaty face and signaled the fanner to more vigorous action. The rainy season was beginning when humidity became unbearable, keeping clothing constantly damp and skin covered with a fine wet film. Only the sudden gusts of wind blowing rain clouds toward the city provided momentary coolness. Soon the sky would unleash a deluge upon mountains and buildings alike, cascades of water pouring down pyramid steps and across plazas, waterfalls burbling down hillsides and rushing to swell the many rivers coursing through Lakam Ha.

She hoped Pakal would arrive before the rain. He was released temporarily from the Temple of the High Priest, given a short time to rest from training and to visit his family. It was difficult for her, knowing that her young son must endure so much discipline. But she also knew that sending him for training was the right decision. She missed him immensely, missed his sunny disposition and endearing presence. Would the rigorous shamanic training change him too much?

Just as the sky darkened overhead and fat raindrops began to splatter on the plaza, she heard his rapid footsteps in the portico. He burst into her chamber before the steward, who managed a breathy announcement from behind.

Sak K'uk opened her arms to embrace her son, noting with surprise that he seemed even taller. His presence made the entire chamber seem brighter. After a long hug, she held him at arm's length and examined his appearance. In these humid conditions he was wearing only a short loincloth, chest bare except for a jade pendant. Pakal's long and sinuous limbs promised that he would be unusually tall. Already he had good muscle development with large hands and feet.

Pakal smiled broadly into his mother's eyes, and she once again appreciated why calling him "K'inich" or sun-faced was perfect. His tilted almond eyes held a warm glow hinting of fire as his large, perfectly shaped teeth sparkled. Although his face was long and narrow with pronounced high cheeks offsetting a large arched nose, his countenance projected brightness and light. Just as K'in Ahau— Sun Lord brought heat and life to the Middleworld, this child Pakal the Shield of the Sun enlivened his surroundings.

"Beloved, I have missed you so!" Sak K'uk exclaimed. "Tell me everything. What you are learning, what you are doing, how it is going for you."

They sat on mats as rain pounded the roof and plaza, bringing a pleasant coolness. Attendants brought maize cakes and fruit drinks, while fanners continued their duties.

"It is most remarkable, Mother," Pakal began. "This world we live in every day, that seems ordinary, is actually full of magic. Hiding behind the surface are wonderful things! I am learning about them and how to see them—which you cannot do with ordinary eyes. Pasah Chan has taught me how to change the way I see, how to change my energy and consciousness so I can communicate with nature, animals, plants, birds, waters, even the rocks. Only a few days ago I was able to bring a small deer to eat from my hand. It was able to overcome its fear."

"How did you do that? The forest deer are very timid and fearful."

"It is done with a meditation technique," he explained. "I must become perfectly quiet in body, mind, and emotions. Every part of my being must be in harmony, and also I must attain harmony with the forest and plants. It is becoming one of them, so the deer sees me as another growing thing in nature. Then the fruit in my hand is like fruit hanging from a plant, and the deer feels safe to take it."

"That is so, that I can imagine," Sak K'uk murmured.

"But what is most important, Mother," Pakal added, "is to be in a state of complete peace. No shred of anger or aggression or tension can be present in your being. If there is any, the deer will sense it, and will be frightened and run away."

He nodded solemnly, almost to himself. Sak K'uk frowned slightly as she wondered if teaching Pakal to be so peaceful was good for a future ruler who would face opposition and potential attacks. But she sensed no weakness or reticence in his energy; on the contrary, he felt to her exceptionally confident and strong.

"What else have you done? Tell me again about calling the wind and rain," she entreated.

Pakal dutifully recounted these stories, emphasizing the necessary states of consciousness to interact with deities of the elements. Sak K'uk basked in shameless pride and genuine wonderment over her son's accomplishments. It mattered not that only servants were present to listen, for she knew it was the talk of the city. For her, it was enough simply to be with him, to share moments from his life, to revel in his presence.

When these stories were finished, she asked what came next in his training.

"In the coming time, Pasah Chan will prepare me for entering the Sacred Mountain Cave," Pakal said.

"The K'uk Lakam Witz?" Sak K'uk recalled childhood stories of her mother Yohl Ik'nal doing vision quests at the mouth of this cave, high on a southern peak bordering the city.

"Already have I done vigil at K'uk Lakam Witz," Pakal replied. "This is a different cave, one that is more difficult to find. It is a cave with a hidden opening that only those capable of attaining a certain state of consciousness can find. It is called the 'Cave of Immortal Wisdom' and leads into Xibalba. Only when all fears have been overcome, even fear of death, can you enter this cave."

"A cave into Xibalba?" Sak K'uk was alarmed. Surely her son was not old enough to begin encounters with the Underworld. This was dangerous territory; only skilled shamans attempted to work with Death Lords.

"Just so. One who has not overcome fear of death cannot be truly alive. This is an important step, Mother. Remember that the Hero Twins had to face and outwit the Death Lords in order to resurrect their father the Maize God, Hunahpu. If I want to have the most advanced skills, I too must face Death Lords and bring to life the creative force of resurrection within myself. To embody the Maize God for our people."

"But now? You are so young to take this advanced training. Might it not be best to wait until you undergo transformation rites into adulthood?"

"Pasah Chan will decide when the time is right for me." Pakal reached to place his hand upon his mother's arm, radiating compassion and soothing her with his touch. "You are worried, this I can understand. There is certain timing for entering the Cave of Immortal Wisdom. It only opens one time each year, and only for those who can find its entrance. An enormous amount of spiritual energy is needed to open this entrance. My next phase of training will be to build up my capacity for this enormous energy. Both body and mind must be prepared, because the energy moves like lightning through blood and nerves, and can cause serious burning if not channeled properly. Pasah Chan will not let this happen. He will not have me attempt this cave until he is convinced I am ready."

"So it might not be this year?" Sak K'uk felt shaky simply thinking about the risk Pakal would be taking.

"Possibly not. Possibly yes. I do not know the time of opening, but from the planned training it is many moons away. Ah, Mother, through this many things will become accessible to me. Through the Cave of Immortal Wisdom I gain access to many masters, many ancestors who have become deities of our people: Itzamna, Xaman Ek, Ah K'in, Ix Uc, K'ukulkan. From them, I will learn much wisdom."

"Yes, yes I see." Sak K'uk took a deep breath and tried to appear at ease. She had brought on all this training; she bore the responsibility if harm came to Pakal.

Pakal smiled playfully and stroked her arm reassuringly.

"Do not worry, Mother. It was shown to me by Unen K'awill, Baby Jaguar, that I am destined for these things. He told me in the Sak Nuk Nah where I visit with him whenever I have time. You remember our visits there, how he would play with me? He told me a secret; only those who are pure in heart can enter this cave. So if my heart is not correct, not purified, I will not be able to enter. And if it is pure, then I am ready to enter. All is in alignment in the domain of our Deities."

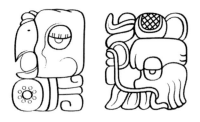

SAK K'UK/MUWAAN MAT—III

BAKTUN 9 KATUN 8 TUN 14 — BAKTUN 9 KATUN 9 TUN 0 (610 CE—613 CE)

1

UC AYIN HAD to admit that he was no longer a young man. Although the passage of years had been kind to his body, which still remained slender and straight, it took a toll upon his mind. Somehow, his life felt unfulfilled. It was not that he failed in attaining goals, for he had few of these. Nor that hopes had been dashed, for the only strong hope he could recall was the desire to stay alive. And while he was undeniably living, his seemed a pointless life. He regarded his status mercilessly. Here was an aging courtier in the city beloved of the Triad Deities, blessed with peace and prosperity, in the upper echelons of artists in the ruler Aj Ne Ohl Mat's intimate circle, who had done absolutely nothing significant in his life.

Except to survive the traitorous attack made by Ek Chuuah and warriors from Usihwitz. Nearly every other man involved in the insurrection had been killed. The insurrection leader Yaxun Zul had been spared, obviously part of a greater strategy to co-opt the rebels and keep the Bahlam family in power, since his son was quickly married to the ruler's daughter.

Uc Ayin had no delusions about his survival during the attack if he had been in Lakam Ha. He would not now be contemplating his lack of fulfillment; he would be cavorting with the Death Lords in Xibalba. Although he was not among the close circle of plotters, just having knowledge of their plans was enough implication to cost his life. Anticipating the worst, he decided to visit his sister in Sak Tz'i, a short distance southeast along the Chakamax River. There he remained for two moon cycles, giving time for Lakam Ha to re-settle after the attack.

His sister Manik now wanted him to come for another visit. Only two days earlier a messenger arrived bearing her request, a matter she considered urgent. Her health was declining and he felt obliged to leave immediately. Perhaps time away from the royal chambers and vacuous arts of Aj Ne Ohl Mat would clear his head and bring perspective on his discontent.

Travel during the rainy season was always a challenge, and quite risky when heavy rains cascaded down mountains to swell rivers into angry, boiling serpents hungry to devour trees and boats alike. The long canoe's paddler waited until the rains slackened and rivers fell from turbulent heights. They embarked early while mists hovered over the plains and draped Lakam Ha's mountaintops. The first day was spent on the Michol River that passed just below Lakam Ha, followed by a day over land through a well-cleared jungle trail to connect with the Chakamax River to the south. Another four days were necessary traveling with the current, past the small village of Nututun to reach Sak Tz'i.

Seated on a bench in the canoe with a deerskin canopy overhead, Uc Ayin was reasonably protected from the constant drizzle that persisted during their voyage. He wrapped a damp cotton shawl more tightly around his shoulders, shivering in the cool breeze. The hard wooden bench bruised his thin buttocks and his toes had congealed into numbness. Feeling perfectly miserable matched his dour mood. The river swirled in gray eddies and shimmered in slate expanses, the sky echoed grayness with its low cloud cover and intractable rain. Dripping water and the rhythmic slap of oars were the only sounds; not even a bird or monkey chattered to break the gloomy monotony.

Days of seamless repetition on the river gave small impetus to Uc Ayin's life review. He found himself always in the same loop of what he was beginning to identify as self-pity. It was not his fault he was born a two-spirit, *xib'il-x-ch'uup*, known among the Maya as a male-female. The two-spirits comprised a third gender group, different from men or women, that blended qualities of both sexes. Children were identified early as two-spirits because of their interest in dress and activities of the opposite sex. Most had an androgynous appearance and character and often took sexual partners from both sexes. Ultimately, sexual preference was based on their primary gender identity.

Maya society clearly recognized and accepted this third gender, based on a well-established place in mythology. Primordial and creator deities were often androgynous, the "changing ones" with special shamanic powers who brought many inventions and technologies for the benefit of humanity. The androgynous persona of the Maize God, who represented First Father and wore feminine symbols of the net skirt, earth associations, flowers and ix-woman face with the Ik' marking, created a powerful context for mixed-gender expressions. The Moon Goddess, while feminine, was often conflated with symbols of the Maize God. Twins often represent the combined male-female qualities, repeating the Maize— Sun God and Moon Goddess complementarities, seen in the *Popol Vuh* creator couple Xpiyakok and Xumkane, as well as in the Hero Twins, Hunahpu and Xbalanque, who became the Sun and Moon. Two-spirit humans often received their powers from one of these androgynous deities.

Uc Ayin regretted that even in this, his two-spirit nature, he had not attained anything of note. He was not called to spiritual leadership, possessed no shamanic abilities, was not a seer or prophet, not even a dream or vision interpreter. In the arts he had a modicum of talent, both with poetry and vase painting, but when these abilities were carefully scrutinized he had to admit his products were mediocre.

His life as a male-female two spirit was of the mundane type. With an inward grimace, he reflected again that the "shameless couple" dance often depicted on pottery or murals perfectly captured his character: An old man cavorts with what appears to be a young woman wearing an entirely feminine costume, but without breasts. The younger is a male two-spirit enacting a woman's role. The explicitly sexual postures and leering expression of the old man make it clear theirs is a profane act, having nothing to do with spiritual or transformational ceremonies.

Although this cross-gender role was accepted within Maya society, Uc Ayin felt a subtle discrimination. He had never married, finding he preferred male sexual partners exclusively. This set him apart, for he had no family and children as did most two-spirits. Because his life had produced nothing particularly useful for others, and he had not received much artistic recognition, he perceived a muted judgment among his peers.

Dissatisfaction crept more deeply into his bones with the evening chill.

Camping on the wet banks along the river further darkened his mood. The small campfire built by the paddler barely warmed his hands, and the cold maize cakes offered little satisfaction. His sister needed to produce a very good reason for requesting this visit.

The next day the canoe arrived at the modest town of Sak Tz'i as daylight began to wane. Paying the paddler, Uc Ayin hoisted his damp pack over his shoulder and trudged up the bank along muddy paths lined by wooden-walled thatched huts, until he reached the central plaza with surrounding stone buildings and a modest pyramid temple. Across the plaza, he recognized his sister's form hurrying toward him. After their initial embrace and greeting, he was surprised to see how she had aged. She clasped his arm and led him to her modest dwelling several lanes distant from the plaza.

"How many times has the sun made its passage since last we met?" Uc Ayin asked. Now that he was in dry clothing and finally the chill had left his limbs, his mood improved as he sat sipping hot maize laced with cacao at his sister's hearth.

"Ten, perhaps twelve sun passages," replied Manik. Her family house was small, having three interconnected rooms with the entrance facing a shared patio. It was a typical stone and plaster, one story structure that served the modest needs of minor ahauob families. Manik's husband had died several years earlier, but Uc Ayin did not attend the transition rites, for which he felt a twinge of shame. She now lived alone, her only daughter's husband having fulfilled his marriage obligation by working several years for his wife's family. Now the couple lived in Nututun in a house built adjoining the husband's family structure. Manik lived alone, a marginal widow given occasional assistance by cousins.

"Are you well?" Sliding his eyes toward his sister, Uc Ayin gauged her age was approaching 60 solar years, quite elder for most elite Mayas. Her hunched posture and loose skin bespoke advanced age, though her deeply sunken eyes still sparked with life.

"As you see," she said, spreading her hands. "I am old, but my health is good. You are looking well. Has life been good for you these years in Lakam Ha?"

"There is little of which I can complain," he demurred, surprising himself with the truth in this statement. A meaningless, disappointing life with little to complain about.

"Tell me things of your life, your city, your holy rulers the K'uhul B'aakal Ahauob."

Uc Ayin spun a few tales about court life, the ruler's art and music interests, and the precocity of the only Bahlam male descendant, Janaab Pakal. He off-handedly mentioned his solitary existence, understanding that his sister knew of his two-spirit nature. Having passed an appropriate time in such pleasantries, he asked about her summons.

"It appears all is well with you and your family, sister, so why have you requested this visit from me?"

She smiled secretively, making a puzzle hand gesture.

"That it is good to see you after such a long time, for my years here are surely few to come. Is this not enough reason? Truly I am happy to see you again, brother. But the request came not from me, I regret to admit. It is from one who knew you well in the past and now has important business with you. His name I do not now speak, for his business is secret. He will come here after darkness has established its cover; he desires not to be seen or spoken of. Rest from your long journey, and then we will eat. You will know soon enough."

After a hearty meal of turkey stewed with taro roots, tomatoes and herbs, Uc Ayin and Manik drowsed in silence around the glowing hearthstones. A wall torch flickered, casting dancing shadows across the stucco walls. Hot maize drink laced with cacao and chiles bubbled in a clay pot, awaiting the visitor. Steady raindrops beat softly upon the patio and small rivulets coursed down the sides of the entrance, pooling on the doorway before trickling outside. The sound of footsteps sloshing through puddles across the patio brought both to instant alertness.

Manik stood, holding the door-blanket aside for the visitor to enter. A muscular man of middle height removed his cloak, giving it to Manik to hang as he settled onto a floor mat next to Uc Ayin. The two men exchanged looks, finding both recognition and the alterations of age in each other's faces.

"Ek Chuuah?" Uc Ayin's voice sounded breathy with surprise.

"Speak softly," the man replied. "And do not say my name again. Good it is to see you, Uc Ayin, after so many years."

Uc Ayin shot a puzzled glance at his sister, who whispered, "He is the one who requested your visit, for very important purposes of which I know not, nor do I seek to know. Now I leave you to talk. Keep your voices low."

After pouring each man a cup of maize-cacao drink, she took a cup for herself and disappeared behind two sets of door-blankets into the farthest room. The heavy blankets reduced the men's voices to an indistinct murmur. Humming softly, Manik knelt on her floor mat and poured out the contents of a leather pouch. Wall torches glinted off shiny black obsidian blades and brought out the warm glow of amber. She caressed the golden chunks of amber, some light as honey and others mysteriously dark as dense cacao drink. She carefully stroked the sharp blades and admired their precise workmanship. Finally, her knobby fingers slid toward two lovely jade beads, green as the jungle in early spring when new leaves sprang forth.

Manik felt no remorse in accepting this small fortune from Ek Chuuah for summoning her brother. She thought of it not as a bribe, but as a gift from the Gods to sustain a poor widow. Happily, she contemplated the ceramic pots and pure white cotton cloth she would buy at the next market, already creating designs for the hem of her new huipil. Her sustenance needs were assured for a long time, maybe more time than she required. Why the visitor from Usihwitz wanted to meet her brother troubled her not at all. Men had their intrigues and manipulations; women wanted only a comfortable life.

Ek Chuuah sipped thoughtfully, remarking in a low voice: "You are looking well for your age. We are of similar age, if I recall rightly."

"Hmmm, yes that is so," replied Uc Ayin. Although he maintained a calm exterior, his mind was racing with memories of the controversial times when he and Ek Chuuah joined in the plotting of Yaxun Zul to overthrow the Bahlam dynasty. Since then, he heard nothing of Ek Chuuah's activities or even if he was still alive. Yet here he was, looking older but vigorous, and seeking something that made Uc Ayin's heart pound.

"Are you living in Usihwitz still? Politics have been of little interest to me, and I have not kept abreast of events between our cities."

"Yes. Now my son Yax Chapat is co-regent of Usihwitz, married to the ruler's daughter, his only heir. Of you, I do know some things, although my sources in your city are not as good as they once were. That your interests lie in arts, and not politics, a mirror of your ruler Aj Ne Ohl Mat, of these things, I am aware. But now I must draw you into politics because things of immense import are about to happen. There is a role for you in this, a role that will bring you great rewards."

"A role for me?" gasped Uc Ayin. His hands shook as he lifted the cup to sip, hoping the peppery drink would clear his mind.

"Let me cut to the central issue. Usihwitz is allied now with Kan, the most powerful polity our region has ever seen. Uneh Chan, K'uhul Ka'an Ahau, has ambitions to dominate this region south and west of the K'umaxha River. Already Usihwitz, Pa'chan, Pakab, and Yokib have formed alliances with Kan. The strength of Kan reaches far to the south with its ties to Uxwitza and their mutual defeat of Mutul. Kan plans to form an empire, and the next target is Lakam Ha. Once Lakam Ha falls, the other cities in the B'aakal polity will succumb to the power of Kan. Tribute and wealth will flow to Kan and its allies."

Uc Ayin stared, shocked and confused.

"How can I possibly have a role in such power struggles among cities?"

Ek Chuuah glanced around, signaling to keep voices low.

"You possess a piece of information that is key to the Kan attack on Lakam Ha," he murmured, leaning closer. "Information that I do not have, despite my years in your city. With this information, the plan to defeat Lakam Ha is certain to succeed."

"Surely you are mistaken. What could I possibly know that is helpful to warriors? Even if this is true, why should I give you information to defeat my city? You are thinking of that ill-fated conspiracy many years ago. I was never in favor of it, and did not stay to learn all your plotting. Those that knew are all dead now. There is no reason for me to be part of another plot against Lakam Ha." Uc Ayin's whisper was more of a hiss.

"There is a very good reason for you to join with us," retorted Ek Chuuah. "Why are you still alive, when all other plotters from Lakam Ha were killed? Because you fled to stay here with your sister. Are you surprised that I know this? I know many things. I know how to destroy your current life in Lakam Ha, or. . ."

Ek Chuuah let this threat hang heavily in the air between them. He slowly lifted his cup and drained the thick liquid in several swallows. Setting the cup down and wiping the back of a hand across his lips, he shifted into a relaxed, open posture.

"Let us not become antagonists. In truth, our interests are aligned. You are not satisfied with life in Lakam Ha, is this not so? Your ruler is weak and distracted and lacks inspiration, and even though you are in his close circles, you find this discouraging. It is time for major change—change for you and for Lakam Ha. Your help in accomplishing these changes will lead to a new, promising life for you in Usihwitz or another city in the Kan alliance. You can begin anew, without the set attitudes your colleagues now hold. Uneh Chan will owe you a huge favor, and he wields influence widely. Consider this well, Uc Ayin. . . what do you owe Aj Ne Ohl Mat and Lakam Ha? Would not a new life well-positioned with support from the most powerful men in the region outweigh any such obligation?"

Embers sparked as Ek Chuuah added wood to the hearth fire. Smoke wafted lazily around the two men, wrapping them together like floating rope. Uc Ayin stared into the nascent flames, watching them come to life, grow and dance. Mesmerized, he observed a flicker of hope kindle inside him, the image of his new persona emerging as a sudden flame. It was possible, it could happen; he could have a new life. A satisfying life.

"What must I do?" he whispered, nearly inaudible. But Ek Chuuah heard and smiled.

"Tell me one thing, a closely guarded secret among the upper elite in the ruler's confidence at Lakam Ha. I am certain that you know this, because you are close to Aj Ne Ohl Mat. Where is the entrance into the Sak Nuk Nah?"

"The White Skin House? Did you not know when you lived in Lakam Ha?"

"No. Remember my status there; my family was not among the higher echelon."

"How will this knowledge serve the Kan attack?"

"It is critical to our success. Simply an attack to destroy structures, take captives and loot the city's coffers is not Kan's goal. Our goal is to break the portal that connects Lakam Ha with the Triad Deities, to desecrate this sacred space, so they cannot provide gifts and sustenance to the Gods. Then the Gods will no longer support B'aakal, and the power of the Bahlam dynasty will be ended. Lakam Ha will be axed, chopped down, brought low never to resurge again. To accomplish this goal, we must know how to enter the Sak Nuk Nah quickly."

Ek Chuuah's voice trembled with passion. Uc Ayin stared blankly as if not comprehending, his eyes wide and unblinking. He also trembled, but from fear.

"Desecrate the Sak Nuk Nah? Destroy the portal to the Triad Deities? Surely I would be struck dead by the Gods for being part of such a horror!"

"No! Understand this well, Uc Ayin." Ek Chuuah spoke deliberately, each word falling as a prophetic stone from his lips. "There are deities more powerful than the Triad, I have encountered them, and they guide us in this attack. We have secured the assistance of the Death Lords through a devastating spell created by Kan's most accomplished shaman. You have no idea of the forces that will be called into play, forces that will overcome any other deities. Your life is in greater danger if you remain loyal to Lakam Ha, and not just from warriors. Their curse will fall upon you for not cooperating. You will die a thousand horrible deaths in Xibalba, and never escape."

Uc Ayin was terrified. He thought Ek Chuuah looked like a Death Lord himself, the fire etching every line in his face with dark shadows while red flames glowed on his cheekbones and lightning sparked from his eyes. Drawing his lips taut over his large teeth filed into points with jade insets, Ek Chuuah's mouth seemed huge as the Witz Monster maw that opened to caves leading into the Underworld. Hypnotically the monstrous mouth moved forming words that Uc Ayin felt as vibrations more than heard.

"Tell—me—the—location—of—the—entrance!"

Teeth chattering, Uc Ayin could hardly form the answer he was compelled to give. All volition had been sucked away by the Underworld forces emanating through Ek Chuuah. With clacking noises from chattering teeth punctuating his words like a stone-carver's mallet, Uc Ayin gasped the answer.

"It. . . it is in the Ix Chel Temple, in a storage structure. . . y-you enter from a chamber within the Temple. T-t-the door is concealed behind a. . . a panel with. . . uh, Ix Chel's serpent carved on it. The panel swings open leading to a stairway. . . goes down into a tunnel. . . t-t-to the sacred shrine underground."

Uc Ayin burst into a bout of coughing and sputtering, his body wracked with intense tremors. Ek Chuuah firmly placed a hand on each of the trembling man's shoulders, squeezing and willing him to be calm. Eyes locked, the men stared in silence. Ek Chuuah smiled and nodded, resuming again the guise of an aging human.

"This is well done, brother. When you are able, let us discuss more details. You are one of us now, in the great alliance of Ka'an polity. It is best that you remain in Sak Tz'i with your sister. Send word back with your paddler that your sister is ailing and needs your assistance indefinitely. The attack is planned for the dry season, only a few moon cycles from now. Stay here, remain silent, and you will be safe."

2

The dry season arrived near the time of spring equinox when the sun reached halfway in its journey along the horizon from the position farthest north to its southerly point. The jungle came to life as rains diminished and longer sunlight warmed treetops and soil. Rivers began to flow more gently and currents became less dangerous, encouraging travel and trade once again. Farmers burned dead corn stalks and plowed the carbonized nutrients back into the fields to mingle with rich muddy sediment deposited by overflowing rivers during the heavy rains. The people of the mountain cities brought their lives outdoors, glad to cook and clean and gather in plazas instead of staying inside their stone residences.

Sak K'uk strolled in the interior courtyard of her chambers at the palace, face lifted to the sun's warmth. Tender yellow-green leaves sprouted from ficus trees and buds swelled on hibiscus bushes, soon to unfold their opulent yellow and red blossoms. She smiled at various bird calls: the sibilant vocalizations with trills and twitters of the azure tanager, the metallic *plihk* or soft *hu-oi* of the yellow-white-black grosbeak, the high thin *tsiu* or *tseeip* of the lovely pink warbler.

Looking quickly at the treetop, she sighted the tiny warbler with its silvery-pink head and chest, dark red back and brown eyes. From an adjoining courtyard that served the royal kitchens came the bongo-like bass tones of male ocellated turkeys, calls which quickened and rose to a crescendo, followed by a high-pitched but melodious series of chops.

She was glad that the dry season had arrived after a long period of extremely heavy rainfall. It had been a difficult season for her, not simply because of the weather, but rife with family conflict. Her personal frustration over the lack of purpose in her life added an undercurrent of dissonance. Her strong will and leadership abilities could find no suitable outlet since she avoided the Council House and court, and had given over her son's training to the High Priest. Gathering with her women courtiers to weave and paint on gourds and ceramic pots failed to provide enough challenge to satisfy her. Surely her parents had trained her for greater things, and her ultimate destiny must be more than being a secondary member of the ruling family.

Now she felt happy, however, because early the coming morning she was to meet with the High Priest Pasah Chan for an update on her son's training. And what made her happiest was anticipating a visit with Pakal, the sun-faced—K'inich who always brought joy and the sun's warm glow with his presence.

The footsteps of her steward echoed before him as he approached through the long corridor between the entrance and her courtyard. She looked up quizzically, not expecting anyone for audience today. He bowed low and spoke softly: "My Lady, your esteemed husband Kan Mo' Hix approaches to speak with you."

Sak K'uk frowned slightly then signaled acceptance to her steward, but before he could turn around her visitor entered the courtyard. Giving a slight shrug and apologetic smile, the steward left. Kan Mo' Hix was not known for his politeness.

She offered her husband her hand and their fingers met momentarily as he nodded slightly then strode restlessly across the courtyard, returning to face her. Clearly he was agitated. She did not bother to invite him to sit on a mat.

"What troubles you?" she asked.

"Your brother, our illustrious ruler, has completely taken leave of his wits!"

She laughed softly. "Have you not said this before? What particular foolishness has he accomplished?"

"The dry season is upon us. Chakab as Nakom—War Chief wants to begin warrior training and conduct mock field battles. It is some time since our men have seen any serious battle preparations. They are becoming soft, slack from easy living. Our defenses are weakened and we live in uncertain times. Does this not sound reasonable to you? To conduct battle training?" Kan Mo' Hix spoke so forcefully that the veins on his neck stood out.

"Yes, you speak wisely. This sounds both reasonable and necessary. What is the problem? I assume Aj Ne is creating a problem."

"Aj Ne is both stupid and a complete fool! He does not support Chakab in his desire to train the warriors. He has other more important things in mind! Lakam Ha cannot spare the men for battle training because he needs them to organize a grand festival of arts for all the cities of B'aakal. The warriors must travel to other cities to bring his summons and organize groups for travel, and supervise building a new structure for these performances, and keep order in Lakam Ha during this arrogant folly! What is he using for a mind? He will put our city at risk, keep us vulnerable and less able to defend ourselves, to give himself a platform for self-aggrandizement." He stopped to catch a breath, shaking his head vigorously.

"The Council in the Popol Nah is giving support for Aj Ne's plans?"

Kan Mo' Hix sighed and spread his hands.

"They argue and discuss and take issue but there is no solid core of agreement. Never have I seen the Council so disjointed, so unable to deal with the real issues. Although Aj Ne frequently is absent, when he does appear he carries the weight of the K'uhul Ahau, and few are willing to stand in direct opposition of his wishes. He reasons that as May Ku, it is our responsibility to host cultural and ceremonial events. Your father and I argued along with Chakab about the importance of shoring up our defense capacity, but it has been too long since we faced attack. Many are lulled into belief that these are times of peace and we have no need to prepare. Our lack of information hampers our arguments; we cannot reliably report on what plots may be afoot in polity cities."

"Aj Ne has a point. Our responsibility as the May Ku city for this cycle—the central city for religious and social activities in B'aakal—mandates that Lakam Ha should organize such events."

"Do you defend this foolishness? Take his side against the wise reasoning of your father and the Nakom? I am disappointed in you," shot Kan Mo' Hix, eyes glaring.

"This I do," Sak K'uk retorted with heat. "What I do is take the side of truth and right. What I say about our May Ku duties is only what is true, and you know it."

"Hrumph! Aj Ne cannot conduct authentic ritual; you saw that at the last katun ceremonies. The only deities that act through him are the Alux tricksters! And we are the ones to suffer from their nasty pranks."

Sak K'uk was torn between acknowledging the truth of her husband's criticisms, and the desire to give support to her brother in his role as K'uhul Ahau.

"What good is this? Aj Ne is our K'uhul Ahau, our link with the Triad Deities. What would you have?"

"Better leadership, have I not said so many times? And now, this new foolishness that will only lead us into greater danger. Surely you see this, Sak K'uk."

"Truly am I sad over this," admitted Sak K'uk. She decided that arguing with her husband was pointless. "What you say is well advised. We should not quickly forget the attack from Usihwitz and Pakab. What information we do have points toward Kan becoming ever more aggressive, and this could be dangerous for us."

"Just so. Many times have your father and I argued this in Council, to no avail," said Kan Mo' Hix, now somewhat calmer.

"Is there something you want me to do?"

"Speak with your brother. Perhaps he will listen to you."

Sak K'uk laughed and shook her head.

"When I have offered him advice, he is either offended or disregards me," she said. "But I will try again, for surely using our warriors in this way will put us at a disadvantage. Perhaps other men can be found to fulfill the tasks Aj Ne needs to organize his art festival."

"This do I appreciate, though as you say, he may not take heed. It is one last attempt to sway him toward the city's good, instead of his own." Kan Mo' Hix's cheek muscles bulged as he set his jaw tightly. His eyes narrowed as he spoke his next words in a deadly whisper.

"If he does not heed us, the time may have come to depose him."

Sak K'uk met his eyes then looked down. She dreaded this possibility, although she had seen it brewing for some time. Civil strife in Lakam Ha, the struggle of unseating a K'uhul Ahau with its destruction, loss of life, and instability was not something she wanted her city, or her son, to face.

"This will only make us more vulnerable," she murmured. "Have you the forces to even attempt it?"

"Perhaps. It is yet uncertain, but may be inevitable," he whispered, glancing around to be sure they were not overheard.

"Give me some time. I will try to get my brother to act sensibly."

He nodded, inclined his head ever so slightly, and strode away without any gesture of affection.

Tears welled unwanted in Sak K'uk's eyes, and the golden sunlight created tiny sparkles in the droplets trickling down her cheeks. The birds still sang, but she no longer heard them. Her heart was heavy.

Pakal woke just before dawn, as was his habit. Quickly washing his face from a gourd bowl and wriggling into his loincloth, he stood in the east-facing doorway of his chamber to greet the rise of K'in Ahau. After chanting the sunrise greeting and using hand gestures to draw down the sun into his body, he opened his bark-paper codex and inscribed the date that would emblazon upon his mind and change his life forever:

Baktun 9, Katun 8, Tun 17, Uinal 15, Kin 14 in the Long Count (April 7, 611 AD)

4 Ix 7 Uo, in the Calendar Round that meshed the Tzolk'in and Haab calendars

Golden sunbeams streaked across the sky as Sak K'uk finished dressing and left the palace compound. She walked briskly through deserted plazas and raised walkways; glad to be unhampered by her slower-paced attendants. Crossing the stone footbridge over the Bisik River, she climbed wide stairs past the Hidden Complex with its immense raised plaza, and followed the road west toward the Temple of the High Priest. Another stone footbridge spanned the chasm of the Kisiin River, tumbling through its deep canyon carved into the rising mountainside. A series of switchback stairs led up the mountain to the lofty temple. Her breath came fast as she climbed; she found the exertion exhilarating and mind-clearing. Twice she paused to catch her breath and give her pounding heart a moment's rest.

Surmounting the final set of stairs, she stepped onto the temple plaza and turned to look upon the city below. This was her favorite view of Lakam Ha, from the highest and farthest west structure nestled partway up the mountainside. Looking east, she could see nearly all the city from the Hidden Complex to the Temple of Ix Chel, across the Bisik River to the palace and Temple of Kan Bahlam, past the spacious squares bordered by stately homes of ahauob, and to the clustered dwellings of commoners grouped between the next two rivers, the Tun Pitz and Ixha. Beyond that, the hills rose with fewer structures and she could barely make out the roofcomb of the Nohol—South Temple. Looking north, she watched the Bisik River cascades tumble over the edge of the plateau, disappearing into steep gorges before breaking into tributaries that flowed into the large Michol River, a major artery of transportation and commerce.

She turned at the sound of sandals slapping the plaster and smiled broadly as her son raced across the plaza, followed by Pasah Chan, the High Priest. Wrapping her arms around Pakal in a tight embrace, she nuzzled his hair and pressed her cheek against his. The boy's arms felt strong and muscular around her waist.

"Greetings of K'in Ahau, happy am I to see you, Mother," Pakal said.

"Greetings of Father Sun," she murmured, relishing the sense of warmth and joy his presence always brought her. Holding him at arm's length, she looked over his lithe, muscular body clad only in a loincloth and neck collar.

"You have grown, of this I am certain, although it is only two moons since I last saw you," she observed. His head now reached her ear; he was unusually tall for his eight solar years.

Pasah Chan joined them and exchanged greetings, inquiring into her wellbeing.

"Now that the dry season is here, I am more content," Sak K'uk replied. "Especially now that I am with my son. Slept you well, Pakal?"

A shadow crossed his sun-visage face and he knotted his brows.

"Not well this night. Strange dreams disturbed me, and I am still ill at ease. Sadly, I do not remember the details," he added, looking at Pasah Chan. Dreams were often important messengers, and part of his training was to recall details for examination.

"Perhaps some details will return," Sak K'uk remarked, thinking of her own unsettled feelings. She glanced again over the city, now bathed in early morning sunlight. A few cooking fires in residential plazas sent up thin columns of smoke. As the sun glinted on waters of the Michol River, she noticed several large canoes.

"See, there are traders on the river, several canoes are approaching," she pointed out.

"Ah, as soon as the rivers move less rapidly, the traders are about," said Pasah Chan. "Can you tell from which city they come?"

"No, they do not have their standards raised," replied Sak K'uk.

Pakal peered intently at the canoes, noting that five were moving along the river.

"These canoes appear to be in the K'umaxha style," he observed. "They carry large bundles and several men each."

Sak K'uk smiled with anticipation of the many new goods and jewelry this heralded.

"The market will be busy today," she said. "Shall we go down later, Pakal? You are growing so fast, you will need new sandals and clothing soon."

"Yes, Mother, I would like that."

The canoes moved out of view as they docked at the base of the mountain, hidden by the steep cliffs. The men would unload the canoes and carry their large bundles by tumplines spread across their foreheads. Balancing carefully, they would ascend the steep, winding steps that bordered the cascades, leading up into the city. Eventually, they would lay out their wares in the main market not far from the palace complex.

Pasah Chan and Sak K'uk settled onto mats spread near the edge of the plaza, as attendants brought fruit, maize cakes and warm maize drinks. While the High Priest discussed Pakal's training with his mother, the boy continued to perch on the plaza ledge and watch the river. He saw more large canoes with bundles, and more men than he thought was usual for traders. He was counting canoes, and when the number reached ten he became perplexed. Never had so many trading canoes arrived at the same time in Lakam Ha. His sense of being disturbed grew more ominous.

He was distracted by his mother calling to him to eat and drink. Taking his portion, he returned to the ledge but saw no more canoes. While he munched, his eyes traveled to the small plaza bordering the Temple of Ix Chel. There he saw several men, apparently the traders, arrive carrying burdens that they deposited in the plaza. Why would they bring their wares to the Ix Chel Temple plaza? He watched as they unwrapped the large white cloths and removed objects, quickly putting on vests and thigh guards. To his astonishment, they grasped long spears and knives and began moving toward the Temple entrance. He realized these men were not traders, but warriors.

"Mother! Holy Priest! Those men from the canoes, they are warriors! See, they are in the Ix Chel plaza and enter the temple!" he cried.

Pasah Chan and Sak K'uk leapt to their feet and joined Pakal. Puzzled, they watched for a moment as more men armed themselves and ran into the temple. When they saw one warrior lift the standard of the Ka'an polity and another lift the standard of Usihwitz, they exchanged horrified glances. Immediately both understood the situation: this was an attack aimed at the Sak Nuk Nah, the most sacred shrine in Lakam Ha.

"Pakal!" shouted Pasah Chan. "Run and summon the trumpeters! They must come at once and sound the attack warning. Hurry, go now!"

The boy dashed across the plaza and disappeared into the temple. Agonizing moments passed as Sak K'uk watched helplessly, heart pounding as more men streamed into the Ix Chel plaza. The forces entering Lakam Ha were huge; she had never seen such a large group of warriors. Looking toward the river, her heart dropped as she saw even more long canoes arriving. She knew that the warriors of Lakam Ha were dispersed in their homes, just awakening or now sipping hot maize at their hearth fires. Recalling her conversation yesterday with her husband, she realized their warriors were not battle-ready and might not even have weapons at hand. She was gripped by panic.

Four trumpeters rushed onto the plaza, dragging their long wooden trumpets awkwardly behind them, half dressed and looking dazed. Pasah Chan barked orders to sound attack alert. The men positioned the trumpets, longer than their bodies, along the plaza ledge and began a short series of low bass blasts: "Bom! Bom! Bom! Bom-bom!"

Repeated in rapid succession, the trumpet blasts carried over Lakam Ha easily, resounding from stone and plaster walls, echoing off plazas. A swelling murmur grew in the city below as people flowed out of doorways and swarmed into plazas. Men's shouts punctuated the rising buzz, but there seemed to be mass confusion.

"We must tell them the attack is on the Ix Chel Temple," Sak K'uk cried. "Send runners! Find Hun Pakal and Kan Mo' Hix and Chakab!"

Pasah Chan moved across the plaza, now filling with people and selected several men as runners. Giving quick instructions, he sent them away to find warrior leaders. Gathering a group of priests and acolytes, he began planning for defense of their temple.

Pakal returned to stand beside Sak K'uk, both mesmerized by the action in the Ix Chel Temple plaza. Some of the priestesses tried to stop warriors, who roughly tossed them aside. Other priestesses stumbled out, supported by their attendants, and were pushed aside into a huddled group surrounded by warriors. The High Priestess, Usih Ch'ob, ran out into the plaza, then turned and ran again inside the temple door, her hair streaming and gown flapping.

"Oh, Mother, what are they doing?" cried Pakal.

Uneh Chan, K'uhul Ka'an Ahau, and Yax Chapat stood inside the small storage chamber flanked by numerous warriors from Kan and Usihwitz. One man dragged the High Priestess into the chamber and threw her at the Kan ruler's feet. Lifting her roughly, Uneh Chan hissed into her face: "Show me the doorway into the hidden tunnel."

Large storage jars and wrapped cloth bundles cluttered the storage room and were piled up against the walls. Uneh Chan wanted to enter the tunnel quickly and avoid time spent clearing out the room.

Usih Ch'ob glared defiantly at him, shaking her head. With the back of his hand, he slapped her across the cheek, his large rings drawing a trickle of blood.

"Speak, woman, or die!"

When she remained silent, he slapped her again and grasped her neck in a crushing elbow hold. She gasped and struggled, then slumped against him. He released her onto the floor where she crumpled in an unconscious heap. A warrior brought him another priestess, the young woman shaking in fear.

"Show me!" His commanding voice bore no refusal.

This priestess caved under her terror, and slowly extended an arm toward one wall.

"Clear that wall!"

Quickly his men removed jars and bundles, opening a lane to the wall on which Ix Chel's snake coiled sinuously. Yax Chapat and Uneh Chan exchanged satisfied looks, and the Kan leader pressed the glyph below the serpent. With a deep groan, a large wall panel began to move. Warriors pushed it fully open and rushed down the stairs, carrying hand torches. The two leaders followed, Yax Chapat carefully cradling a small bundle against his chest. Footfalls echoed through the dark underground tunnel, flickering torches lighting the way.

The men entered an underground chamber with a center altar-throne, walls painted white with flower motifs. Effigies of the Triad Deities, ceramic figurines standing waist high, surrounded the altar. A removable slab with four corner holes was positioned in front of the altar, over a cyst that held offerings made over many tuns by rulers of Lakam Ha—the bundles of adornments, the gifts that maintained their relationships with the Gods in proper order.

Silently, surrounded by warriors holding torches, Yax Chapat placed his small bundle on the altar and carefully untied its white cloth. The human-sized crystal skull caught light from the torches and leapt to life, dancing inclusions rippling deep inside the cranium, eye sockets glowing, teeth grinning with reflected sparkles and starbursts. Its smoky quartz seemed to absorb light and transform it into swirling pockets of dark evil. It leered into the sacred place, ready to decimate the pure white harmony.

Uneh Chan stood in front and Yax Chapat stood behind the crystal skull. Their eyes met across its glistening crown.

"Speak the unlocking spell, Yax Chapat," whispered Uneh Chan. "This is your inheritance, your father's dream realized."

Yax Chapat's lips curled into a snarl. This was his father Ek Chuuah's day of vindication. The older man had stayed with the main corps of warriors, no longer swift and agile enough for the advance invasion of the Sak Nuk Nah.

The young man nodded, closed his eyes and recited the chant to unleash the skull's destructive potential.

"Mixekuchu kib' ronojel Xibalba	All the Xibalbans have gathered together
Are k'u retal wa chi qak'ux	Here is the sign in our hearts
Chojim ab'aj kamik qe b'ak.	Their instrument for death will be a skull."

Opening his eyes, Yax Chapat watched with amazement as the skull's colors began changing, the swirling dark pockets morphing from black to rose to red, and then two flashes of brilliant yellow light burst from its eye sockets. The dank air inside the chamber seemed to tremble and the warriors stood frozen in terror.

"Now! Begin the destruction now!" yelled Uneh Chan.

He moved first, striking an effigy with his obsidian sword and sending it crashing to the floor in pieces. Yax Chapat attacked a second effigy, and then the men jumped into action, using axes to deface the walls. Four men lifted the slab and began removing offering bundles, as others took the bundles and chopped them with axes and swords. Grinning maliciously, Uneh Chan destroyed the third effigy as Yax Chapat continued to strike blows at the other two.

Upon their ruler's signal, the warriors set aside their weapons and urinated on the broken Triad Deity figurines and the torn bundles with their crushed offerings. Those who could also defecated, especially around the throne and upon the effigies. The crystal skull's toothy grin seemed to widen as the desecration of holy objects proceeded. Now it appeared to be surrounded by an angry red aura, pulsating rapidly.

"Set the bundles on fire," ordered Uneh Chan. "Then we leave the skull to its work."

Those men with torches quickly lit the cloth bundles, which burst into flame, soon filling the chamber with acrid smoke. Some men retched while others covered their noses as smoke poured forth, reeking with excrement odors. They gladly followed the leaders into the tunnel and away from the smoldering and desecrated chamber.

Sak K'uk was shaking with fear and outrage. From her high view, she watched as Lakam Ha warriors gradually grouped and made their way to the Ix Chel temple plaza. To her dismay, another contingent of Kan warriors burst into the wide plazas surrounding the palace complex, diverting much of the Lakam Ha counter attack. Clearly her city's forces were badly outnumbered. Plumes of dark smoke billowed as the attackers set fire to wooden huts and lintels of stone structures.

Pakal stood beside her, transfixed with disbelief and shock. She turned to put her arms around him but stopped as his expression changed. His eyes became fixed upon something in the far distance, pupils wide and unblinking. Pure terror as she had never seen blanched his face, and his mouth opened wide in a soundless scream. He raised both hands as if fending off a monstrous attacker.

"Pakal! Pakal! What is it?" she shouted, grabbing his wrists and holding them tightly.

His mouth worked soundlessly, his tongue trying to form words. The ghastly stare continued, now showing the whites all around his irises. He gasped and forced out choking words.

"Noooo! Noooo! The Wakah Chan Te—Jeweled Sky Tree is falling down! It is falling into the maw of the Underworld Monster! It is being swallowed, oh nooo! Mother, Mother, can you stop it? Stop it from falling. Oh, this is terrible, oh Mother, see the portal is closing! We are lost! All is lost! We have lost our portal to the Triad!"

Tears streamed from Pakal's eyes as he crumpled onto the plaza floor. Sak K'uk knelt beside his sprawled figure, afraid that he had died of shock. She scooped him into her arms and shook him, placed her ear on his chest and breathed again as she heard his rapid heartbeat. His head lolled for a moment, then his entire body stiffened and he thrashed out of her grasp. Rolling over, he sprang to his feet and looked around wildly.

"I must try to help!" he cried. "I must stop it from disappearing!"

Pakal bounded across the plaza and descended the steep stairs in leaps, taking several steps at a time.

"Pakal, come back!" Sak K'uk cried. "Don't go to the plaza! There is nothing you can do—it is too dangerous. Come back!"

He turned a corner and disappeared from sight. Sak K'uk ran toward the stairs, glancing back as Pasah Chan called to her. "Don't leave, Sak K'uk! This is the safest place, stay here!"

"I must protect my son," she called over her shoulder as she descended the stairs. She ran panting toward the Ix Chel Temple plaza, bumping into terrified women and wailing children who scurried around aimlessly. The sound of stone blades clashing, axes thumping, and men groaning and cursing assaulted her from the plaza. Dodging struggling warriors and screaming priestesses, she swept the plaza searching for Pakal. At the temple entry, she saw her son in the grasp of a muscled warrior and threw herself upon the man, pounding his chest with her fists and kicking his shins.

The warrior grunted and used one arm to push Sak K'uk aside, and another warrior wrenched her arms behind her, bringing her down with his weight. Stunned by her fall onto the stones, her vision blurred and she could hardly breathe. The warrior's hot breath on her neck felt repulsive and she squirmed uselessly. It was some relief when he tied her arms behind her back with rope and moved away. She saw that Pakal was similarly bound, along with the High Priestess. Many other priestesses huddled just inside the temple, guarded by two warriors. As the battle slowly ended in the plaza, Sak K'uk was overwhelmed by the number of Lakam Ha warriors lying dead or dying in the bright noonday sun.

The march of prisoners from the Ix Chel plaza to the central plaza of the palace was painstakingly slow, for many were wounded. The hot spring sun beat down mercilessly. Cries and wails filled the air along with smoke and the sickeningly sweet smell of drying blood. Victorious forces from Kan and Usihwitz spread unimpeded through the city, smashing ceramic idols, setting fires, axing delicate panels and colonnades, taking food and drink from emptied households, scooping up booty. Some warrior groups were assigned to collect younger women and strong children to bring back to their home cities as slaves. These were bound by their wrists with a long rope creating a cadre, and guided to waiting canoes. Many women would become concubines of warriors, but Maya attitudes toward sex prohibited rape during an attack.

The main plaza of the palace complex was filled with Kan and Usihwitz warriors. Many bound captives crouched in the center. The captive group from the Ix Chel plaza was pushed along to join them. Sak K'uk and Pakal stood toward one edge, and noted that their ruler Aj Ne Ohl Mat, along with Hun Pakal, Kan Mo' Hix and most Lakam Ha leaders were already there, and some were wounded. Many warriors were missing, however, including the Nakom Chakab.

Numerous townspeople were herded to the plaza borders by Kan warriors. Many others had fled into surrounding forests to hide out until the invaders left. The victory protocol required an audience of subdued people. They stood silently, disheartened and filled with remorse, fear and sorrow.

Drums and conches sounded the victory march for the invaders. A group of finely dressed warriors entered the plaza, carrying the standards of Ka'an polity and the Kan dynasty high in front. The Usihwitz and Wa-Mut standards followed close behind. Cheers arose from the other warriors in the plaza. The procession crossed the plaza, stopping at the stairs leading to the Lakam Ha royal throne. Uneh Chan proudly ascended the stairs and seated himself on the throne, to another round of cheers. Ek Chuuah, Yax Chapat, Wamaw Took the Kan Nakom, and the Wa-Mut ruler and war chief followed and stationed themselves on either side of the throne. The standards, embroidered cloth with emblems of each city attached to two long poles, were brought atop the stairs for all to observe. Lakam Ha's standard had already been burned.

Uneh Chan rose to speak. He was adorned with the finest jewelry, feathered headdress and richly woven fabric. His handsome face glowed with satisfaction.

"Warriors of Kan, of Usihwitz and Wa-Mut, first do I speak with praise for your bravery and prowess. Today is a great victory for our cities, a further proof of the grand destiny of Ka'an and our alliances. None can withstand the force of this destiny. We will spread our rule through all the lands of the K'umaxha, and to the south and east. Let us celebrate and honor our Gods!"

Roars and cheers resounded across the plaza, contrasting starkly with the silence of captives and townspeople. Drums, whistles and conches tried to fill out the sound, but still it was thin in the wide Lakam Ha main plaza.

"Bring before me the ruler of Lakam Ha and his chief advisor," ordered Uneh Chan.

Warriors dragged Aj Ne Ohl Mat and Hun Pakal up the stairs, hands bound behind their backs and all clothing removed except a plain white loincloth. The hair of both men was cut short and rough ends bristled in an irregular chop. Both had bruises and blood trickled down Hun Pakal's leg. Never had Aj Ne looked so small and pitiable, his eyes deep pools of terror.

"Kneel," commanded Uneh Chan.

Aj Ne sank to his knees but Hun Pakal stood defiantly. A warrior shoved him onto his knees, and then pushed both men into a deep kneeling bow, foreheads to the floor.

"Aj Ne Ohl Mat, K'uhul B'aakal Ahau and Hun Pakal, you are to return with me to Kan. There you will be displayed in our victory march, the living symbol of a defeated city and tribute to Kan's power. You will stay as prisoners, so the people of Lakam Ha will never forget who is their new master and leader."

In the silence that followed, hot tears of fury stung Sak K'uk's eyes. She quickly blinked them away, not wanting her captors to see any sign of weakness. In her heart, she knew the fate that awaited her father and brother. They would be sacrificed for a katun-ending or other important ceremony at Kan. She stood tall seeking a glimpse of her father's face but was unable to see beyond the men nearby.

Uneh Chan waved for his warriors to remove Aj Ne and Hun Pakal. As they were taken down the stairs, Sak K'uk caught a side view of her father. He walked firmly with chin lifted and eyes ahead, showing no fear in contrast to the hunched and staggering Aj Ne. A mixture of pride and despair filled her, for she knew this was the last time she would see her father. Her heart was aching, and she silently projected her love toward him as she watched his form recede in the distance.

On the platform of the throne room, Ek Chuuah leaned toward Uneh Chan and whispered in his ear. The Kan ruler nodded and said, "Bring before me Sak K'uk and her son."

She snapped to intense alertness. Why was she being called? She could not imagine that Uneh Chan knew much about her or Pakal. She looked upward and scanned the men on the platform beside the Kan ruler. An older man with a dark countenance appeared to be smirking, while the younger man beside him assumed a posture of pride. They stood next to the standard of Usihwitz. Quickly searching her memory, she recalled her mother's concerns about a man from that city, the one behind the failed attack on Lakam Ha many years before. She could not remember his name.

Warriors yanked on her and Pakal's wrist ropes and guided them up the stairs. They stood in front of Uneh Chan and he commanded them to kneel. Defiance blazed from Sak K'uk's eyes, which she shot at both the Usihwitz men and the Kan ruler. Uneh Chan's handsome face softened into a tiny smile, for he appreciated spirited women. But Ek Chuuah frowned and gave the hand sign to force her to kneel.

The warrior pushed Sak K'uk on both shoulders and forced her to kneel. Suddenly Pakal fiercely attacked the warrior, kicking and head butting the much larger man in the groin. Caught by surprise, the warrior lost balance and fell with a loud thump, causing a few chuckles among observers. Sak K'uk swiveled and rose up, her eyes commending her son's bravery. Two more warriors closed in and shoved both mother and son roughly onto their knees. Sak K'uk remained still, but Pakal continued to struggle and kick and bite until more rope was wrapped around him and a rag bound his mouth.

"This royal whelp shows much courage," observed Uneh Chan.

Ek Chuuah looked surly but held his counsel. He did not want to derail the plan that the Kan ruler had agreed upon as his reward.

"Sak K'uk, granddaughter of Kan Bahlam and daughter of Yohl Ik'nal, here I bring reparations for a wrong done by your ancestors to my ally from Usihwitz, Ek Chuuah. He was wrongfully wounded in a Flower War long before your birth, and exiled from his home city of Lakam Ha. This was by the command of Kan Bahlam. Now the balance will be restored, for Ek Chuuah shall preside over your city in my stead. The throne that wronged him will now acknowledge his superiority, his regency."

Uneh Chan rose from the throne and stepped away, signaling for Ek Chuuah to take his place. Another fanfare of drums, conches and trumpets sounded. The older man took a deep breath and straightened to his fullest height, walking slowly and regally to take a seat upon the royal throne of Lakam Ha. From this perspective, he could look across the main plaza, see all its occupants and scan the buildings that bordered the other three sides. Forested green mountains rose beyond the city, reaching toward the cerulean sky. The sun hovered above the western range and cast lengthening shadows in rosy hues. The air never smelled sweeter, the day brighter or more potent with promise. Ek Chuuah felt the power of the double-headed jaguar throne beneath him. For a moment, his deepest longing was fulfilled.

"Sak K'uk, look upon he who sits on your throne," he ordered. "I am Ek Chuuah, perhaps your family spoke of me. Now am I vindicated for the wrongs done by the Bahlams."

Despite herself, Sak K'uk had to raise her head. It was not that he commanded it, but her own amazement that he went to such extreme ends to fulfill a longing of his youth. She took in his dark countenance, narrow eyes, irregular features now wrinkled with age, and hair showing streaks of white. Only years of deep-seated anger and resentment could carve such severe lines across his forehead and along the sides of his mouth. She wondered if he ever smiled, for his lips seemed to hold a permanent downward curve. Still burning in his black eyes was the heat of hatred that had propelled his drive for vengeance.

Her dark eyes bored into his, and she would not break the gaze. Conviction surged within that she would never succumb to his command. By whatever means he had placed himself upon Lakam Ha's throne, it would come to naught. Her very bones knew that Pakal would rule their city. Every cell in her body would work ceaselessly until this was accomplished. The only emotion she felt in that moment was stone-solid determination.

Pakal wriggled beside her and grunted through the gag in his mouth. Both Sak K'uk and Ek Chuuah broke gaze simultaneously to look at Pakal.

"Take them both to their palace quarters and guard them there," he commanded.

Once Sak K'uk and Pakal were taken away by warriors, Uneh Chan returned to the throne to continue orders for the sacking of Lakam Ha's treasures, food and wealth. He made plans for containment of the city's leading ahauob and remaining warriors. Most of Kan's forces would leave in the morning to return home. Usihwitz and Wa-Mut were closer to Lakam Ha, so a contingent of their warriors would remain for a time. Eventually, these occupying forces would return to their cities, for Maya rarely stayed to live permanently in cities they raided or attacked.

The Kan ruler believed he had accomplished his primary goal: to devastate Lakam Ha so thoroughly that the city would never regain its prominence and power. He fully expected that the crystal skull had destroyed the portal to the Triad Deities, although he did not possess the extrasensory ability to ascertain this himself. He would consult with the High Priest Tajoom upon his return to confirm this.

Walking down the palace stairs, a minor leg wound annoyed him. During the battle at the Ix Chel plaza, a warrior's knife had slashed his left leg and cut into the calf muscle. It was not deep and he barely noticed it until the battle had ceased. Now his wound ached and caused a slight limp. It was wrapped, and he felt certain it would heal quickly.

3

For three days Ek Chuuah sat upon the double-headed jaguar throne in the palace of Lakam Ha and held court. Warriors gathered a group of ahauob and herded them to the court, including members of the royal Bahlam family. The ahauob were forced to bring tribute each day and offer it to the "three-day mat person," as Ek Chuuah was later called in inscriptions. He relished the feeling of power that emanated from the jaguar throne with its sky bar linking the two heads, symbolizing command of the greatest forces in the natural and celestial worlds. The woven mat that covered the throne represented ruling status and presiding over the Popol Nah. This mat design was reflected in short skirts worn by rulers during ceremonies.

Tribute dwindled over the three days, for the homes of ahauob were raided by conquerors and stripped of most objects of value. Food was quickly becoming scarce; the palace storage chambers were almost empty and every temple was depleted of its reserves. Usihwitz warriors began grumbling and Wa-Mut forces left two days after the attack. Ek Chuuah became concerned that his reduced manpower might prove inadequate for maintaining control. Farmers among the Usihwitz forces were vociferous about their need to return and prepare the fields for spring corn planting. They had been conscripted to augment the number of fighters and were not happy about it.

By the third day Ek Chuuah tired of his game, finding little satisfaction in the dour faces and unspoken hostility of his artificial court. Even Sak K'uk and Pakal remained contained and distant, offering no response to his taunts. They knelt and bowed unresisting, offered their tribute as required, and kept their silence. Bitterness began to flavor the taste of success, for even as he reveled in assuming the throne he recognized that it was false. The ahauob and people of Lakam Ha would never acknowledge him as a true ruler, as K'uhul B'aakal Ahau.

The following day, Ek Chuuah ordered the Usihwitz forces to leave. By the time the shadows lengthened from the west, their canoes had all departed.

The people of Lakam Ha slowly returned from hiding in the jungles and mountains, shocked by the devastation of their city. In the days immediately following the attack, those who had remained undertook the heart-wrenching yet critical task of burying the dead. Leaving bodies in the hot sun led to rapid decomposition with risk of pestilence. Many buried their family members under the floor in their home, as was the Maya tradition. But time worked against them, and lack of manpower forced many quick burials in trenches dug at the forest edges. Abridged transition ceremonies were performed, but the spirits of many could not receive the expected offerings to facilitate their journey through the Underworld.

Food became a primary concern. The maize, bean, squash and tuber stores in nearly every home and storage chamber in the city were decimated. Household gardens offered a few straggling chaya leaves and peppers but were just emerging from their winter slumber. Women planted what seeds they still had and retrieved turkeys and dogs as they could. Men ventured into the jungles to find wild fruit, berries and tubers. Some formed hunting parties and sought deer, rabbits, birds and tapirs, sharing their catch with neighbors. Hunger settled onto the people as a way of life for several moons, until their plantings were ready for harvest.

In the palace chambers of Sak K'uk, the days of Usihwitz occupation dragged interminably. Pakal and Kan Mo' Hix were confined with her, and little conversation passed among them. The shock of this stupendous defeat had not worn off; it was too soon for analysis or examination or planning for recovery. At times when her eyes met those of her husband, both acknowledged the prophetic quality of their last normal conversation, but neither wanted to speak of it. Pakal seemed lost in another world, eyes distant and vacant. His expression remained neutral and he never cried, which concerned Sak K'uk. She could only imagine the emotional damage this was inflicting on her son. She felt some relief when Pakal settled against his father as Kan Mo' Hix wrapped an arm around his shoulders. His father's presence seemed a comfort. She was surprised that she also felt comforted. They were, at least, all alive.

When Ek Chuuah's forces departed, a new surge of energy enlivened Sak K'uk and she analyzed what actions to take first. A day spent walking around the residential compounds with Kan Mo' Hix and Pakal convinced her that first the people must plant, both household gardens and fields on the plain. When farmers cried that they had very few seeds, she sent runners by canoes to Nututun and Sak Tz'i to request more. She organized children to scour every storage chamber, even in outlying temples, for beans, corn and squash seeds that had been missed by invaders. The Temple of the High Priest had escaped being thoroughly pillaged because of its distance and height, and Pasah Chan distributed seeds generously among the townspeople.

Both Sak K'uk and Kan Mo' Hix met with farmers and gave encouraging speeches. They projected confidence that they really did not have because it was necessary to show strength in the royal family. When farmers worked in the fields, preparing the soil for maize, squash, tomatoes and beans, they were surprised by visits from the royals offering praise and blessing the fields. Always Sak K'uk kept Pakal at her side, for she could not bear being separated, and hoped their bravado would reassure him.

Fires smoldered for many days after the attack, and the haze of smoke hung overhead longer. During the dry season, there was little wind to clear it away. The smoke was a constant reminder of their tragedy. Once the planting process was underway, the royals agreed they must face the destruction and take stock of the damage wrought upon Lakam Ha. Two places in particular concerned Sak K'uk: the Temple of Kan Bahlam and the Sak Nuk Nah. She knew that her grandfather's burial pyramid would be a target since the core of Ek Chuuah's vengeance sprang from the Flower War affront. The Sak Nuk Nah was the primary focus of destruction, as she had observed during the attack.

From the palace, they crossed the stone bridge over the east tributary of the Bisik River and approached Kan Bahlam's temple first. Even from a distance they saw that the roofcomb had fallen, but upon reaching the lower platform they were appalled at the temple's condition. Fires had been lit in all chambers of the upper temple, using every burnable object and raising temperatures to the point that the wooden door lintels also burned. The lintels supported the upper doorways, so when they burned structural support for the corbelled arches was weakened, causing the arched roofs to collapse. These roofs held the roofcomb; now all upper structures lay in crumbled heaps inside the temple chambers.

With tears stinging her eyes, Sak K'uk climbed the long stairs to the upper temple level. Kan Mo' Hix and Pakal followed after her. They stood in stunned silence, for the once lovely carved outer piers and interior panels had been axed and chipped until their stucco figures and glyphs fell into fragments. Chips of vibrant colors caught the sunlight amid heaps of blackened ashes. No remnants of Kan Bahlam's portrait on the middle panel could be identified. She could barely imagine the destructive fury unleashed upon this temple, no doubt expressly commanded by Ek Chuuah.

Shaking her head, Sak K'uk took Pakal's hand and led him down the stairs. She could think of no comforting words, and her heart ached at the boy's severe, tearless face. The family walked slowly north toward the Sak Nuk Nah, past several noble residential complexes where they nodded or spoke briefly to ahauob whose confused, distraught expressions spoke more eloquently than their words. Blackened stucco on the walls of many houses marked the sites of multiple fires that racked the city. The three-tiered stone bridge over a wider section of the Bisik River remained intact, because it had allowed the invaders passage to the path descending along the cascades to the Michol River below.

Sak K'uk hesitated as the Ix Chel Temple came into sight. She was uncertain whether it was a good idea for Pakal to view the damage to the Sak Nuk Nah, where he had many joyful visits as a young child. His eyes met hers, pools of unfathomable darkness. He looked ahead and began walking with determination. Exchanging glances with Kan Mo' Hix, she followed close behind her son. The Ix Chel Temple's roofcomb stood intact, for its interior was not the target. A short distance from the temple, an area of open ground had collapsed into a huge hole.

There, she knew, the tunnel and underground chamber of the White Skin House had collapsed, opening to the sky.

Pakal stood on the edge of the ragged hole, clumps of soil and rocks tumbling into the shadowed chasm. His body was rigid for a moment, and then he dropped to his knees and peered down. Sak K'uk hurried to his side, but before she reached him, the boy clambered over precarious rocks down into the hole.

"Pakal! Do not go into the hole, it is dangerous!" she cried.

He paid no heed, disappearing into the partially collapsed chamber full of soil debris, charred wood, smashed ceramics and fallen rocks.

Kan Mo' Hix quickly descended into the hole, Sak K'uk following more carefully. Smells of burnt charcoal, earthy peat, and old excrement assaulted their noses. Most of the chamber roof had collapsed and also part of the tunnel leading to the Ix Chel Temple. As their eyes adjusted to the filtered light, they viewed the total destruction and desecration of their most sacred shrine. Nothing was recognizable, even the floor was disrupted; everything left in tiny fragments or burned heaps. A few fat flies buzzed lazily around dried excrement.

They called for Pakal, unable to see him as their eyes swept the open area. He emerged from the semi-darkness below a tipping section of chamber ceiling, cradling something in his arms. Now tears streamed down his cheeks, splattering into sooty drops on the small ceramic piece he held.

"They killed Unen K'awill, the Baby Jaguar," Pakal uttered between soft sobs. "Here is his head, but it has no life. . . he is gone, my friend is gone. . . Oh why, how could they do this?"

He cradled the decapitated head of the Unen K'awill figurine that once graced the sacred chamber. The chubby flattened jaguar face stared blankly, smeared with dirt and excrement and one stubby ear broken off. Sak K'uk took Pakal in her arms and cried with him. Kan Mo' Hix stood stiffly, fists clenched in fury and despair.

Moments passed in anguished silence. The remaining royal family of Lakam Ha felt as desecrated and damaged as their holy Sak Nuk Nah. As the morning sun moved more directly overhead, light fell upon the altar still standing in the chamber, and a flash of brilliance startled them. Thousands of glistening crystal shards covered the altar and spilled onto the floor below. The sunlight seemed to ignite the fragments and exploded a kaleidoscope of colors into the chamber.

Pakal leapt from his mother's arms, clutching the Baby Jaguar head to his chest. His surprised parents backed away from the brilliant light.

"It is what did this!" Pakal exclaimed. "Here it is; these are its crystal remnants. It has been shattered by doing its evil work."

"What are you saying, Pakal?" asked Kan Mo' Hix.

Sak K'uk approached, shielding her eyes to examine the fragments more closely.

"It has chopped down the Jeweled Tree, it has broken the channel, it has closed the portal to the Upperworld," Pakal intoned as if entranced. "The portal has fallen. It is closed. It is no more."

"Look," Sak K'uk whispered, pointing to a large crystal fragment that had fallen under the legs of the altar throne. "This was a crystal skull, see there is an eye."

Pakal and Kan Mo' Hix stooped to see, recognizing the arch of an upper orbit and the hollow space of a partial eye socket now displaced from its position in the skull. Sak K'uk understood from her shamanic training.

"They used a crystal skull, embedded it with a powerful curse that was released to destroy our sacred shrine. . . and our link to the Triad Deities and ancestors. That must be why the skull shattered when those forces were activated. This must be the work of a dark shaman-priest using the evil might of the Death Lords."

She shuddered as the mantle of ominous intentions wrapped closer around, making her acutely aware of evil presence. The dislodged eye socket seemed to fix its gaping stare at her, sending emanations that chilled her bones. Skin prickling and hairs of her arms standing on end, the sensations of danger were intense.

"Quickly, we must leave this place," she whispered. "Here is great evil intent. The forces of the Death Lords are still present."

Pakal was also trembling, but she saw it was from fury and not fear.

"They will not escape without suffering for what they did." His voice held deadly resolve. "It must be rectified. We must avenge this horrible affront and restore our portal. The Jeweled Sky Tree must be raised again."

His parents stared, feeling an intensity and strength beyond imagining emanating from their son. Even in her distraught state, Sak K'uk marveled that he so readily sensed the closed portal and envisioned the fallen Jeweled Sky Tree. She did not perceive these things, perhaps due to her shocked state but more likely because her intuitive and visionary abilities were not so well developed.

"It must be raised, as you have spoken, Pakal," she murmured. "But first, we must leave this profaned and evil place. Come, let us climb out quickly."

She reached to take his hand, but he stepped back, his sandals crunching on the shattered crystal fragments.

"Kan Mo' Hix!" she commanded. "Take your son out of this danger."

He moved quickly and grabbed Pakal before the boy could jump away. As he began to climb out, partly carrying and mostly pulling Pakal, she barked another command.

"Pakal, the Baby Jaguar must remain here. He has been contaminated. You cannot take his head with you. As you have said, he no longer inhabits this image."

Pakal started to protest, but as his eyes met his mother's, a bolt of understanding shot through him. He sensed the evil and menacing energies. Slowly, reluctantly, he bent with his father still firmly grasping one arm. With his free arm, Pakal cradled the broken head once more to his heart then placed it reverently beside the altar. He turned and began to climb upward out of the hole, in tow behind his father. Sak K'uk scrambled behind them, moving nimbly.

They gathered a safe distance from the edge of the hole. Pakal felt soothed by the bright midday sun, lifting his face to receive its warm rays. Sak K'uk brushed dirt off her knees and palms, finally sensing they were out of danger. She took several deep breaths and drew in calmness, becoming clear on what was necessary.

"This desecrated place is filled with evil. We must do ceremony to purify and cleanse it, to remove the destructive forces implanted here by our enemies. Let us prepare to ritually terminate this shrine, to bury all within through correct ceremony, to close this wound upon our souls."

Without looking back, they all walked to the palace to prepare the ritual termination of the Sak Nuk Nah.

The ahauob of Lakam Ha formed a circle around the gaping hole that contained the remnants of their sacred shrine. Most of the city's residents gathered behind the ahauob, and inside the circle standing close to the collapsed edge were the High Priest Pasah Chan, High Priestess Usin Ch'ob, and remaining members of the royal family except for Hohmay, wife of captured ruler Aj Ne Ohl Mat. Hohmay was too distraught to leave her chambers, and her already fragile emotional state was clearly deteriorating.

The High Priest and Priestess would conduct a ritual for cleansing and purification, using plant medicine and incantations to dispel the evil magic that had been performed. Sak K'uk, closest in bloodlines to the ruler, would undertake the ceremony to ritually terminate the shrine.

First, the High Priest and Priestess called upon the Lords of the Four Directions, the Bacabs and Pahautuns who held up the sky, and the Chaks of the Four Colors to be present in support. Usin Ch'ob signaled her fire priestesses to light 13 censers that surrounded the hole; 13 embodied the sacred number of spirit and holiness, and there were 13 levels of the Upperworld. As spirals of copal smoke rose from the tall censers, the High Priestess circled four times counter-clockwise and added crushed dried leaves of Kaba-yax-nik (Vervain), mingling the herb's fragrance with copal's earthy pungency. Copal, also called Pom, and Kaba-yax-nik were powerful plants for counteracting evil magic when used in ritual ceremonies. They warded off evil influences and repelled dark spirits.

Pasah Chan and several priests began the purification chant, circling clockwise around the hole nine times, once for each level of the Underworld. In each hand, they held bundles made up of four herbs and plants, each infused with specific powers. Pixoy (bay cedar) had long serrated leaves and gray-brown bark that released "bad winds" carrying off spells and bewitchments. Cacal Tun (basil) could cure spiritual ailments such as grief and evil magic with its highly aromatic, fresh green leaves. The multiple leaflets on branches of the Chink-in (Bird of Paradise flower) that had absorbed sunlight for half a day were capable of relieving sadness and grief. The square-shaped stems of Pay-che (skunk root) were peeled to release their strong skunk-like odor and used in two ways: Whole stems were burned to dispel evil magic, and shaman-priests drank a tea of boiled stems to strengthen their spiritual powers. All those participating in the ceremony, including Sak K'uk, had partaken of this tea in the morning.

Waving the bundles and shaking them toward the hole, the priests completed their nine circles as they chanted. They stood, facing the hole, as Pasah Chan and Usin Ch'ob alternated voices in a final prayer requesting that the evil magic be permanently dispelled, and the ground purified and cleansed. The priests then tossed their bundles into the hole, upon a mound of fragrant cedar branches piled at the bottom.

Sak K'uk stood at the edge of the hole, facing north, and lifted her arms to chant.

"Here was the most sacred shrine of Lakam Ha, the Sak Nuk Nah.

Here was born, of the earth, of the sky, the Jeweled Sky Tree—Wakah Chan Te.

The tree of many splendors, the portal tree to the Gods and ancestors.

Here our rulers for generations, back to the founder of our lineage K'uk Bahlam, made their offerings to the Gods, gave the gifts, made the bundles that clothed and adorned and honored the Triad Deities and the deities of the First Sky: the 9 Sky Yoch'ok'in, the 16 Ch'ok'in, and the 9 Tz'aak Ahau.

Here they performed all the duties required of the K'uhul B'aakal Ahau, nothing was left undone, all needs were satisfied.

Many are the blessings, many the boons given to the people of Lakam Ha as the rulers satisfied the Gods, and the Gods gave themselves, their powers, to the rulers.

This is the sacred covenant of K'uhul B'aakal Ahauob. This keeps the balance between the three levels; the Underworld, the Middleworld, and the Upperworld. This maintains harmony between the worlds of Halach Uinik—Real Humans and the celestial realm of spirits and ancestors, of stars and space.

But now this most sacred shrine has been desecrated, has been destroyed.

By the actions of Unen Chan, K'uhul Ka'an Ahau, through the evil magic of his ruthless priests,

By the treachery of Ek Chuuah of Usihwitz, by the cowardice of Wa-Mut.

They abandoned the traditions of our people, the Maya; they have forsaken our honorable agreements of the May cycles, they have subverted our ideals of ritual battle and distorted them into destructive warfare,

Against a city that gave them no affront, no insult, no challenge.

Their actions are immoral and insulting to the order of the worlds. They have violated the ways of the deities, the sacred agreements that keep the actions of humans in accord with the purposes of the Gods.

For this will they suffer. For this will their lives, their cities, their people be troubled. It will be so, for the Gods are not mocked nor ignored."

Sak K'uk paused, standing tall and slowly turning to meet the eyes of all in the circle. Solemn faces of the ahauob met her gaze. Commoners craned their necks to catch a view. The priests and priestesses held sacred space with their intense stillness. Sak K'uk signaled for Pakal to come next to her, and for attendants to bring torches. She took one torch and gave another to Pakal. Turning to face the hole, she continued.

"It is time to terminate this once sacred shrine. The Sak Nuk Nah has been cleansed, it has been purified, it has been prepared for proper closure according to the ordained rituals. The evil magic has been dispelled and removed, it has no more power, it exists here no more. Now shall the burning begin for the final termination."

She and Pakal raised their torches and threw them onto the pile of branches and herbs. Immediately the pile burst into flame, releasing waves of sweet-pungent smoke. As smoke billowed, tongues of fire lapped the edges of the hole and leapt upward in fierce abandon. The inner circle moved back to escape the heat while all eyes stared transfixed upon fantastic forms dancing in the flames. The participants remained until the fire had consumed everything and died back to glowing embers.

Sak K'uk moved farther away and signaled waiting men to begin filling in the hole. Using sturdy digging sticks they moved rocks and dirt from the edge into the cavity. More soil and rock was brought from other locations to completely fill in the hole and level the ground. This activity would take considerable time, so Sak K'uk led her people away from the now-terminated shrine back into the city.

The hot summer sun blazed mercilessly on the destitute city. People listlessly carried out daily routines, rationing food carefully to last until the next harvest. Already seeds were planted in gardens and fields, waiting for the late summer rains to initiate sprouting. Small efforts were made to clear debris from structures, but no restoration was undertaken. The people lacked the heart, and the leadership, to rebuild their city. It was widely understood that the elite ahauob could no longer access the main portal for communicating with deities, and uncertainty reigned as to whether they had any other methods. Lakam Ha had lost its ruler and the status of their captured K'uhul B'aakal Ahau was unknown. This created a vacuum in leadership, a void that could not be filled until the fate of Aj Ne Ohl Mat was ascertained.

Sak K'uk felt confused and despondent. After her show of determination in organizing the ritual termination ceremony, she descended into this unfamiliar state because she could get no sense of direction. She simply did not know what to do next. Lakam Ha's present situation was utterly different from any other time, either in her own experience or in the city's history. There was no functioning royal court, no tribute from polity cities, no visitors or traders, little food, and no resources to repair the damage done to numerous structures. Even the Popol Nah had not yet assembled, for who would call it into session?

If her father Hun Pakal were here, he would call the Council and lead it. But he also was a captive in Kan, possibly not still alive. This thought wrenched her heart and caused her stomach to clench. She felt lost without his calm wisdom. She considered whether her husband, Kan Mo' Hix, could assume leadership. He had certainly wanted this before, complaining frequently about Aj Ne's weakness and distraction with arts. But now, in this desperate situation, he was not stepping forth. When she encouraged him to take leadership and call the Council, his uneasiness was clear. Whoever moved into top leadership needed to communicate with the Triad Deities.

She pressured her husband to undertake a private vision ritual, to let blood and seek the Vision Serpent. Perhaps the great serpent would arise from its hidden chambers in the earth and ascend through the Middleworld into the Upperworld, even without the Wakah Chan Te to climb. Kan Mo' Hix retorted that she should be the one to try this since she had shamanic training from her mother. They had a nasty confrontation, fed by the frustration and underlying guilt both felt over the devastating Kan attack. Each realized they should have taken action during the years of Aj Ne's ineffectual leadership. Each bore responsibility for their city's incapacity to anticipate and defend against the attack. And now, each was equally confused about how to proceed.

After exchanging heated and harsh words, they discharged considerable emotions and calmed down enough to reach an accord. They would both let blood and seek the Vision Serpent, secretly and within their private chambers, with only the most trusted priests and priestesses in attendance. The High Priest and Priestess came with one assistant each, bringing prepared hallucinogenic brew, stingray spine bloodletters and bark paper and bowls. The royal couple had participated in the last Katun ceremony conducted by Aj Ne Ohl Mat nearly five tuns ago and performed the bloodletting ritual then. They would draw from that experience.

When the three days of fasting and purification were completed, in the evening by light of only a few torches, when all was in readiness and the hallucinogenic brew had taken effect, the royal couple drew their blood from tongue and penis in the prescribed manner. Dropping blood-soaked bark paper into waiting bowls filled with glowing coals, they concentrated on spirals of smoke twisting upward as the paper burned. The attendants, who served to anchor the spirits of the visionaries and provide support as needed, waited breathlessly. The semi-dark chamber hovered in anticipatory silence; only crackling sounds from burning paper were heard.

Through her altered consciousness, Sak K'uk strained to focus on the smoke from her bowl. She waited for the serpent form to resolve from the diaphanous billows. A few times the snake seemed to be taking shape, but it did not hold. Try as she might, she could not see the Vision Serpent. She held focus for a long time until all the bark paper had crumbled into ashes and only tiny wisps of smoke drifted up. Finally, crestfallen, she had to admit that for her, the Vision Serpent did not appear. One look at the face of Kan Mo' Hix told her this was also his experience. Both exchanged glances then met the eagerly waiting eyes of the priests and priestesses. Sadly, shaking their heads, they made the hand gesture for "nothing" to indicate the failure of their vision quests.

During the humid, steamy days of late summer, Pakal wandered through the damaged city. His feet followed familiar paths across wide plazas, along paved pathways linking different complexes, across narrow stone bridges spanning burbling streams, and up wide stairways leading to pyramids and temples. It was the latter that caused his heart to ache. Most pyramid-temple structures were defaced at minimum, or nearly destroyed at the worst. He could not visit the pyramid-temple of his great-grandfather Kan Bahlam often, but he was compelled to climb the long stairway mounting its terraces from time to time. The utter destruction of this once lofty and noble monument sat like an immense boulder upon his chest, taking his breath away and crushing his heart to the point he felt faint. He would sit upon the top stairway, back turned to the ruined temple, forcing in deep breaths. When the pressure lessened and he could breathe normally, he gazed over the city spread below and toward the tree-covered hills in the distance. From this high perspective, the residential complexes with multiple plazas appeared almost as before. He could, for a moment, forget that his city lay in chaos and disarray.

His wanderings occasionally took him past the area where the Sak Nuk Nah had been terminated and buried. Now it was covered with new grass and small shrubs, finding nourishing soil between rocks and drinking moisture from dew. The area felt cleansed to him; he could not detect malign or evil energies. But his sorrow was uncontained, and visits here always brought tears. He felt that his soul had been rendered, that a deep gash was sliced into his essence. The wondrous Jeweled Sky Tree, the magnificent Wakah Chan Te that arose from the depths of earth, its roots boring into the farthest regions of the Underworld as its limbs soared to the heights of the Upperworld, was no more. The great trunk that once rose straight and regal through the Middleworld, that gave access to all three realms, the tree that was used by shamans and the Vision Serpent for travel across dimensions, had fallen.

In profound sorrow, Pakal wondered if he would ever be with Unen K'awill—Baby Jaguar again. Was the portal forever, irrevocably destroyed? Could it ever be recreated? He had no idea how this might be accomplished, were it possible. Despair flooded his young body like a torrent of frigid rain, causing spasms of tremors that threw him to the ground. Curled in a tight ball, he shivered and twitched, rolling from side to side and wailing. His fingers dug into the pebbles and moist soil, his face pressed on the fresh grasses and became streaked with dirt. The very earth seemed to embrace him, the sun poured its warmth on his back, the birds chirped and whistled and clacked until his shaking ended.

Pakal sat up and lifted his face to K'in Ahau, Sun Lord. Even with eyes closed, the sun's brilliance nearly blinded him, but he would not look away. Far in the distance, as though from another realm, came the long throaty roars of howler monkeys.

K'in Ahau, help me. Pakal did not speak but projected his plea to the sun.

The sun's warmth flooded him with compassion, heated his chilled bones and shot vibrant energy through his blood vessels. Wave upon wave of empowerment washed through him, pushing away sorrow and despair and filling him with potential. He breathed sunlight, he bathed in golden rays, and he absorbed sun energy through his pores. As long as Father Sun, K'in Ahau, returned every day to light the sky and bring life anew to the earth and its creatures and people, Pakal would find courage and draw power. He was, as they called him, "K'inich" the Sun-Faced One. The Sun Lord would guide him, support him, sustain him through these troubled times.

Pakal rose to his feet and spread his arms wide, lifting them to the sun.

"Father Sun, with your help may my resolve be carried to fulfillment. With your power may this human, this child of yours who is called K'inich Janaab Pakal, restore this sacred city Lakam Ha, raise again the Jeweled Sky Tree, revive the home of the Bahlam dynasty. Father Sun, more than restore the city and our portal to the Gods . . . It will be so, this is the resolve made this day before your shining face, that Lakam Ha shall be greater than it ever was, shall be lifted to the heights of beauty and perfection and strength to prevail as never before in the land of B'aakal."

Forming both hands into the gesture for manifestation, used for bringing intentions into reality, Pakal pointed directly overhead with extended index fingers, thumbs uplifted and the other three fingers curled toward his palm. Slowly he moved his hands in an arc from overhead until they pointed down to the ground. He held this posture and hand sign until he felt jolts of electric energy moving through him from the top of his head, down his arms, and shooting out through his pointed index fingers into the earth.

The breeze first whispered, then the trees sighed and rustled, and the birds and monkeys added voices into a chorus that sang: "So it will be. So it will be. So it will be."

The rains came in late summer, soaking fields and gardens. Seeds opened and sent tiny shoots into rich soil, drawing nourishment for rapid growth in the hot climate. Beans, tomatoes, peppers, summer squashes, and large green chaya leaves were soon ready to satisfy the eager appetites of Lakam Ha's residents. Trees flowered and set fruit, eaten a little less ripe than usual this season. Corn stalks grew tall and green, setting ears and dangling tassels. The fall harvest would be abundant and hunger reduced. The people felt reassured that at least some ahauob were communicating with the deities, in some way, and satisfying those Gods in charge of foods and harvests.

Indeed, the priesthood made offerings according to established agricultural schedules and performed rituals following the sun, moon, and star calendars. The royal family and top elite nobles gathered for seasonal rituals in the temples of the High Priest and High Priestess. These were mundane levels of ceremony that followed planting and harvesting cycles. They honored moon cycles, sun positions, and movements of the traveling stars (planets).

But these were not the arcane, hidden high rituals required of the ruler to satisfy the Lords of Time and keep covenant with the Triad Deities and First Sky Gods. Only those ahauob of the purest bloodlines in the Bahlam dynasty could perform these rituals. To do these, the Jeweled Sky Tree rising in the sacred portal was necessary, and it had been destroyed.

Sak K'uk felt immensely troubled about this situation, although most nobles preferred to avoid facing it, waiting for the outcome of Aj Ne Ohl Mat's fate. Some nobles found the chaos and social upheaval advantageous to their personal ambitions. They cultivated circles of supporters who enjoyed complaining and scheming without having to take responsibility. They hoarded food, especially maize after the harvest, and were able to stockpile larger supplies since they were not held to tribute for the ruler and court. Others collected pottery and cloth as it was made, storing these away to augment personal assets. After the cacao harvest, more wealth in the form of these highly prized pods was sequestered in the storage rooms of ahauob.

Kan Mo' Hix was frustrated that the nobles acted selfishly, but was powerless to command tribute. Without the palace reserves of maize and dried beans, many commoners would go hungry during the winter. Their hard work in the fields would benefit the nobles for whom they labored. Although the harvest was good, there was not enough to feed everyone through winter's season and still have seeds for spring planting. With nobles hoarding, the situation was even more difficult. Despite concerns for the people, he found himself following the noble's suit and putting away the bounty of the ruling family's fields and orchards. He would use this store for winter rations although these would be slim for commoners due to holding seed for spring.

Sak K'uk reminded him to also provide supplies for Hohmay. She seemed incapable of taking charge of her household and workers, and it required much effort by Kan Mo' Hix to keep things in reasonable functioning order. It was difficult to prevent workers and minor functionaries from skimming the royal fields, as the city's warriors were severely decimated in the attack.

The winter rains and cold further dampened their spirits. Kan Mo' Hix called the Popol Nah into session a few times, but attendance was sporadic and most of the time was spent arguing about who could take charge of the Council. Sak K'uk attended now but sensed resistance to her assuming leadership. When she tried to garner support for rebuilding pyramid-temples, the ahauob complained they could not spare any workers or offer any tribute because of the difficult times.

When the next dry season came, traders began to arrive again at Lakam Ha. Markets formed and ahauob used their accumulated assets to trade for salt, foreign foodstuff, flint, obsidian, and a few luxury goods. With the traders came information about other cities in the region. Traders from up-river cities of Yokib, Pa'chan, and Usihwitz brought dire news just one moon cycle short of the anniversary of Lakam Ha's defeat. In a ceremony performed to commemorate accession dates of Kan rulers, Hun Pakal had been sacrificed by their High Priest on the main pyramid-temple altar.

Ironically, the leader of the attack, Kan ruler Uneh Chan, died only three moon cycles earlier from infection of the leg wound incurred during battle. Controversy racked Kan's leadership in Dzibanche over who would be his successor, with two noble contenders of royal lineage. Most observers believed that Yuknoom Ti' Chan, son of the deceased ruler, would win out. This hiatus in leadership weakened Kan's influence; a new dynasty at Saal had emerged and schemed to sever Kan's patronage. Belligerence was escalating between the Kan dynasty and the nearby Bat rulers at Uxte'tun with frequent skirmishes. Rumor had it that Kan was plotting an attack augmented by Usihwitz forces to eject Bat rulers and take over residence in their city, the ancestral Kan home.

News of Ka'an polity's political upheavals brought little comfort to Sak K'uk, who mourned her father's death. She feared that her brother would also become a human sacrifice, a practice done on occasion by the Maya since times of great antiquity. The ritual offering of a human life usually took place at times of extraordinary need or significance such as Baktun ceremonies at the end of 400 tuns (396 years), or during droughts and other natural disasters. For most other occasions, letting blood was considered the suitable sacrifice. To offer life itself was the supreme religious expression of the blood sacrifice, the ultimately potent ritual to directly communicate with and petition the life-sustaining divine forces.

Human sacrifice was thus reserved for extraordinary circumstances in Maya traditions. However, Sak K'uk was aware that these practices were changing. Certain of the most powerful cities, including Mutul, Uxwitza, and Kan had escalated their use of human sacrifice recently. The usual method was either heart excision or decapitation, quickly and skillfully performed on the drugged victim by trained priests. She felt this had less to do with religious zeal than as a means of ostentation by political and religious authorities. Although these sacrifices followed the rules and sequence of predetermined steps that ensured a purified and sanctioned offering, she could not believe that the deities who created humans and sustained them in a co-creative process would desire this level of sacrifice very often.

Even though she was not surprised, having anticipated this outcome when her father was captured, his loss struck her heavily. She arranged transition rituals using his clothes and eating implements, but had few jewels and fine ceramics to offer as grave goods. No funerary monument could be built, so she followed the time-honored tradition of locating his symbolic grave inside his chambers in their household. The only good news was that Kan was preoccupied with internal affairs and distant conflicts, making another attack on Lakam Ha very unlikely.

In the season of late summer rains, traders again brought news of loss to Lakam Ha. The struggle for Kan rulership was decided in favor of Yuknoom Ti' Chan, and as part of his accession ceremonies, Aj Ne Ohl Mat was sacrificed. This symbol of Kan's prowess and victories lent prestige to the new ruler. The Lakam Ha royal family organized a large transition ceremony, using resources they truly could not spare for grave goods, ceremonial dress, burial in the palace, and feeding the people in the main plaza. Sak K'uk commissioned a small plaque to commemorate her brother's death, carved with his likeness and the date on which he was taken by the paddlers in the celestial canoe to the Underworld.

Baktun 9, Katun 8, Tun 19, Uinal 4, Kin 6, on the date 2 Kimi 14 Mol (August 11, 612 CE).

Within three days of this ceremony, the deceased ruler's wife Hohmay committed suicide. Her despondency had deepened as time passed, to the point she never left her chamber and often refused food and drink. Her husband's death was the final blow to her fragile mind, and she obtained poisonous herbs that she took in a maize drink. Her choice was not questioned, nor the assistance that her attendants provided. Suicide under such circumstances was both accepted and acknowledged among the Maya.

Lakam Ha was officially without a ruler. Since the ruling couple had no surviving children, a vacuum in succession arose. Turmoil over succession spread, adding to the pall of loss and destruction hanging over the city. Kan Mo' Hix and Sak K'uk knew they could be contenders, but both were restrained by acute awareness of their inability to communicate with the deities. In her heart, Sak K'uk believed that Pakal was destined to become ruler, but now he was too young. She could not imagine a plan for achieving recognition of Pakal as royal heir, given the chaotic and contentious atmosphere among the ahauob. The legacy of failure hung over her family, for clearly they had not kept the deities satisfied. If they had, the disastrous attack from Kan would not have occurred. She blamed her brother most but felt her own deficiencies too painfully. Her training was not deep enough; she did not make proper effort or master shamanic techniques for attaining the realms of Gods and ancestors, for making prescribed communications.

What concerned Sak K'uk as much as succession was the approaching katun end, a time when the Long Count calendar reached a point of completion, moving from Katun 8 to Katun 9. It was obligatory to perform K'altun ceremonies, the binding of the tun, to honor and recognize the deities and Lords of Time. Otherwise, the Order of Time and the well being of B'aakal people would be jeopardized for the coming 20-tun time period. The katun end would arrive in nine more moon cycles as the three lower stations set to zero.

Baktun 9, Katun 9, Tun 0, Uinal 0, Kin 0, (May 12, 613 CE).

Who in Lakam Ha would be capable of conducting this important ritual? Sak K'uk could bring no one to mind.

The moon, Lady Uc, progressed gracefully through her cycles. From a tiny sliver of arched light she grew steadily, night by night, her concave belly becoming fuller until it began to swell like a pregnant woman. She swelled into the full roundness of completion, shining her lovely silver light in the star-studded sky, ducking behind drifting cloud tendrils that wrapped veil-like around the resident rabbit. Usually, Sak K'uk loved Lady Uc, rejoiced in her waxing to fullness and waning into darkness where she hid for only a few nights, allowing the stars their moments of unimpeded glory. But now Lady Uc brought worry, for every cycle she completed moved Lakam Ha closer to a point of immense danger. What would happen if the K'altun ceremony was not performed correctly, or even at all? Such a thing had never before occurred.

Sak K'uk felt increasingly desperate. Everyone she discussed this problem with offered no solutions, including her husband and father-in-law, and even the High Priest and Priestess. If only her mother Yohl Ik'nal were alive, she would know what to do. Even her father, now also in his journey through Xibalba, could have given wise advice. Never had she felt so alone and without moorings.

When her internal tension was at the bursting point, Sak K'uk realized she must take some action. She instructed attendants to prepare the Pib Nah, the sweathouse, for a ritual purification. She would undergo maximum preparation to make herself a pure and potent receptacle for communication with deities or ancestors, in the hope that one might find a way to reach across dimensions and bring her guidance. She fasted and meditated for three days, and then entered the steaming darkness of the Pib Nah. Already faint from lack of nourishment, she wilted rapidly in the stinging steam billowing from water poured over hot glowing rocks. Collapsing onto the stone bench lining the Pib Nah walls, she felt awareness drifting off as her naked skin singed on the heated stone.

In the semi-darkness of her mind, she drifted in space aware of the stately movements of stars far in the distance. An image began to form and she heard her mother's voice telling a story about the cave high up K'uk Lakam Witz, the Sacred Mountain of her city. It was a story re-told many times, one of her favorites that she begged for frequently. It recounted her mother's first vision quest upon coming of age, during which the future of the dynasty was revealed – the coming of the glorious ruler, son of Sak K'uk. The image was coalescing, taking form as the tones of her mother's voice soothed her heart. Now she saw it clearly: it was the mouth of the Witz cave where her mother's vision occurred. The cave had a large opening, tall enough to walk through and wide enough to allow four people abreast to enter. A shimmering Witz Monster mouth was superimposed over the cave opening, its squared eyes above and jowls wrapping around the sides as fangs protruded upward at the base.

The Witz cave was a portal into liminal space, that evanescent zone separating dimensions. It had not been desecrated during the Kan axing attack because it was so remote and infrequently used. The monster's eyes stared directly at Sak K'uk, beckoning her, even commanding her presence. A light glimmered deep inside its throat, glinting off sharp fangs, pulsating with hints of hidden possibility.

Sak K'uk knew what she must do. She would go alone to the Witz cave, enter the maw of the monster and seek the portal that might allow communication with the denizens of other dimensions.

She did not confide her real purpose to others but said only that she felt called to keep solitary vigil overnight at the Witz cave. Kan Mo' Hix was alarmed about the dangers of night in the jungle, though she reassured him that she would be inside the cave by nightfall, and would have torchlight. Pakal worried about what she might encounter in the cave. Her women courtiers could not imagine doing such a thing alone and begged her to take assistants. When her resolve did not waver, they capitulated to her strong will, urging that she take a long obsidian dagger and flint stones for starting fire. When thus equipped, and carrying a sack with her water gourd, maize cakes, shawl and mat, she set out in the early afternoon to climb the mountain that rose steeply to the south of the palace complex.

In all her years living in Lakam Ha, Sak K'uk had never ascended K'uk Lakam Witz. It was a fabled mountain of mystery and danger, with a few trails leading to a succession of tall peaks and deep gorges channeling seasonal streams and small lakes, according to the few who had explored these regions. Walking briskly, she followed the course of the Bisik River uphill until it disappeared into the mountainside. A faint trail continued upward and she found her breathing labored from the steep climb. In places, draping lianas blocked the path and she carefully stepped around or over them, mindful of snakes and biting insects. Once she caught a glimpse of the thick brown body of a yellow jaw snake just off the path, looking exactly like a fallen branch. The noise of her steps alerted the snake and it moved slowly away; only this movement warned her. It was the most poisonous snake in the region and its bite meant certain death. Heart beating wildly, she forced herself to walk evenly up the path as the snake disappeared into the underbrush.

The hunters she had questioned about the mountain told her the climb to Witz cave would take half an afternoon or morning. The condition of the trail was uncertain, they advised, so it was hard to know the exact time required. Her progress was slow, for she frequently had to push limbs or bushes away and pick her way through fallen forest debris. On a few occasions, she regretted not taking a strong man along to wield a brush knife. But the sense she had that this must be a solo endeavor was very strong.

The simple white huipil that she wore, completely without adornment, was soaked with sweat and suffered several small rips from thorny shrubs. Her legs ached and her hands throbbed from scratches, her chest burned from deep breathing. Her sandals and feet were coated with dirt and many bites smarted around her ankles. Keeping eyes focused on the trail and scanning nearby brush for dangers, she paid no attention to the sky until a loud clap of thunder stopped her in her tracks. Lifting eyes upward as the thunder rumbled into the distance, she saw immense black-bellied storm clouds gathering. A late afternoon rainstorm was fomenting, and in very little time cool winds whipped through jungle foliage carrying the earthy smell of freshly wet humus.

Sak K'uk quickened her pace but was soon pelted by fat raindrops, harbingers of the deluge that followed. Shivering from sudden coolness and quickly drenched, she struggled upward as the path turned into slippery mud. The rain was so heavy that she lost her bearings and wandered off the trail, losing time in backtracking. Already the light was fading under the high canopy of thickly interwoven branches. The edges of panic jabbed at her mind and she fought to remain calm. Using lianas and branches to steady her ascent, she kept placing one foot carefully ahead of the next, slipping to her knees or staggering against prickly shrubs.

It is penance, she thought. *Contrition for my negligence, for the imperfections of our offerings, for our weakness when we knew all was not in proper order. This suffering and difficulty is my offering. This do I bear without complaint.*

Keeping intense focus, she repeated these words as a chant in rhythm with her steps. She forbade fear to enter; she defied panic. It was nothing, being lost in this storm as night gathered. There was only one thing, and that was the mouth of the Witz cave. Step by slogging step, she climbed and slipped and slithered until suddenly the narrow trail topped a rise and tangled branches yielded to a circular opening. Several large boulders huddled in semi-darkness and across the opening appeared the faint outline of a large, dark hole in the mountainside.

The Witz cave. As the last shreds of light faded, Sak K'uk approached the gaping entry into the Sacred Mountain. Water streaming down her hair, huipil soaked and tattered, feet and legs muddy, she stood uncertainly and peered into total darkness. She tried to remember details of her mother's story. Was there not an old priest, keeper of the cave? But that was many years ago; surely he had passed into the spirit realm. She had no knowledge of whether other caretakers had assumed his duties. From the darkness of the interior, she doubted it.

Closing her eyes, she sensed into the energies present and immediately the image of the Witz Monster mask surrounding the cave entrance returned. Again its square eyes beckoned, so she moved forward and stepped high over the imagined fangs at the base of the entrance. Once inside, the musty odor of bat droppings mingled with the dankness of deep earth. A gust of wind startled her and the air churned around her head with a hoard of flapping wings and high screeches. Instinctively she ducked as numerous small brown bats streamed out of the cave.

Feeling inside her sack, she removed the mat and sat down. The cave floor was cushioned by a layer of dust. She felt for the torch that was wrapped in skins; it was dry enough, so she rummaged for the flint stones inside a small hide bag treated with oil to repel water. With chilled fingers she struck the flints together, sending tiny sparks of redness into the darkness. After a few tries, the torch caught and slowly its fire grew, casting flickering light against wide cave walls. She found stones to prop the torch, drew her wet shawl around her even wetter dress, and assayed her surroundings.

The nearest cave walls rose steeply to a ceiling that disappeared into gloom. Several stalactites hung their tips into view, but the torchlight did not penetrate far into the cave's throat. The remnants of a fire were nearby, the charred wood so old it had no odor. A fine film of dust covered the small rocks surrounding it. Glancing around, Sak K'uk saw that some branches and twigs had blown against the walls, and used these to build a small fire that she lit with her torch. The fire gradually warmed her shivering body. She removed her muddy sandals and scraped mud off legs and feet with her knife. Taking a drink of water from the gourd, she settled cross-legged on the mat and relaxed into the fire's warmth.

Her mind stilled as she watched dancing flames and heard reassuring crackles of burning wood. Her aching muscles and painful scratches slowly eased and she drifted into semi-torpor. Heaviness descended upon her. The weight of her body pressed downward as if melting into the cave floor. Her eyelids became heavy; too heavy to hold open and she allowed them to close. She struggled to stay conscious, remembering her mission. Barely formed thoughts swam in her mind until a suddenly clear stream of words emerged powerfully, and she whispered them into the darkness.

"Guardians of K'uk Lakam Witz, Lords of the Witz cave, I have nothing to offer, neither tribute nor gifts that are sufficient and proper. Deities of B'aakal, I have no techniques to propel me into the vision state, no method to attain the Wakah Chan Te. I have only myself —this is my offering— all that I am and could be. Humbly and respectfully do I offer this Halach Uinik, this woman, this ahau of royal lineage called Sak K'uk. Not with bloodletting offerings, but with all the blood coursing within this body, the sacred itz that flows within this vessel. Use me as you will, but guide me to help my people."

Having expressed these thoughts, she sank again into drowsiness, the liminal state between sleep and awakening. Time passed but she was unaware, as the fire burned down to glowing embers. A subtle sound reached into her trance, the scurrying and scratching of tiny, clawed feet. As if detached, her mind registered the sound but her body took no action. More scurrying sounds occurred, now closer. The embers seemed to shine through her eyelids, tiny points of bright red. Only two red points and they were moving. Lazily, her mind asked how she could see with her eyes closed, but it really did not want an answer.

Were her eyes closed or open? What did it matter? The tiny red points moved again accompanied by scurrying sounds. They waved up and down repeatedly as if calling for her attention. Now she could see the outline of their host, now its form filled in and she beheld a small green lizard staring at her with unblinking, bright red eyes. Once she had noticed it, the lizard waved its head toward the deepening darkness of the cave interior. It was a clear signal to follow and enter the depth of the cave. The lizard slowly ambled into the cave tunnel, and Sak K'uk followed, her body drifting off the mat effortlessly. . . or did her body move at all? A quiver of fear shot through her but the compulsion to follow the lizard was intense.

The lizard led Sak K'uk through a large tunnel that descended steadily. Soft, dim light emanated from its walls, lighting the way. They took a tunnel that branched to the left and descended more steeply. They encountered water slowly moving along the tunnel base that soon deepened, and they were swimming in an underground stream. The cool, clear water felt refreshing and cleansed mud from Sak K'uk's clothes and body. The tunnel opened into a large vaulted cavern filled with a shining pool of turquoise water. On the far side was an island, and on it sat nine shamans drumming. Each shaman had a small fire in front and incense burners emitting copal smoke.

Sak K'uk and the lizard swam closer and watched the shamans from the water. Looking at each shaman in turn, Sak K'uk realized they were the nine Death Lords of Xibalba. With leering grimaces, protruding eyeballs in open sockets, bony arms and legs, bloated bellies, and revolting odors, they filled her with terror. Their teeth clacked and bones rattled as they drummed and chanted, occasionally emitting foul-smelling belches or vile farts. Even the pungent copal incense could not overcome the hideous odors. Sak K'uk tried to swim away but the lizard blocked her and commanded her to stay with its eyes. She turned back toward the island and gasped.

A cold blue fire had started in the center of the Death Lords. It leapt upward, twisting and turning, darting fingers of yellow flames twining with blue tentacles and slowly morphing into a huge snake. The serpent undulated and danced in the flames, merging and separating, turning partially into a woman who waved her arms sinuously and danced on flaming legs. The woman-snake also had red eyes, much larger than the lizard's eyes, with brilliant gold slits for pupils. As the apparition resolved back into serpent form, it protruded a split tongue between huge fangs, and its back became covered with shimmering blue-green feathers while the underbelly retained opalescent scales.

The snake beckoned Sak K'uk to come, holding her in a relentless, hypnotic stare. Unable to resist despite her terror, Sak K'uk swam to the island and climbed out of the water, her dripping huipil clinging to her body. Passing between two Death Lords—she believed they were the leaders, One and Seven Death—their hoarse whispers sent shivers up her spine.

"Let us take her, she is a fine catch."

"We will feast well and dance with this luscious morsel."

"I will take her heart."

"Ah, but her belly is more delicious."

One Death reached a bony hand toward her but was stopped by the snake hissing and flashing its fangs near his hand.

"Iiit—iiis—nooot—heeer—tiiimeee," hissed the snake.

Quickly Sak K'uk went to stand next to the snake, as the cold blue-yellow flames wrapped around them. Keeping eye contact, she and the snake danced together, matching each other's movements. The snake hissed words and communicated directly into the woman's mind: "Feeed—meee."

Sak K'uk's eyes widened with dread. Had the snake saved her from the Death Lords to make her own meal? But the snake did not bite; it waved its huge head from side to side, flicking its tongue repeatedly. Looking around, Sak K'uk saw that each Death Lord was holding up a small bundle. She recognized that these were for the snake, and took from each their bundle, feeding these one by one into the jaws of the snake. In this act, she understood that the snake needed the Death Lords to feed her so she could feed the world and give sustenance to life. The snake fed the soil that fed the roots of trees and plants that fed animals and people. The essence of the snake fed the serpent of life within the spine of all creatures, so this life force could reach all their cells.

Once fed, the snake seemed to want something else. She glanced at the water and rubbed her head against Sak K'uk's clothing. It was a request to be bathed. Sak K'uk took a gourd from one of the Death Lords, filled it with water from the pool and tore the hem off her huipil. With this soft cloth, she washed the snake's scales and feathers carefully; making certain each was wiped thoroughly. Then she took a reed growing by the island, shredded one tip and used this to clean the snake's fangs and jaws.

The snake seemed satisfied, closed her eyes, coiled up and dozed. The Death Lords began to fade away, their forms becoming less substantial until they dissolved into nothingness. Sak K'uk stood beside the snake in puzzlement about what to do next. Her mind formed a request and she whispered: "How can we fulfill the requirements for the next K'altun?"

The snake did not respond, and Sak K'uk sat beside her, discouraged. The red-eyed lizard had climbed out of the water and settled next to Sak K'uk. They waited.

Sak K'uk tried again: "This have I done: I have offered myself completely, I have traveled to the Underworld, I have fed and bathed you. Now I request this, help me know how my people can fulfill the requirements for the next K'altun."

The snake stirred, yawned to display an enormous maw with long fangs, and rubbed her head against Sak K'uk's legs. Her long feathered body slipped under Sak K'uk's legs until the woman straddled the snake. As the snake undulated into the water, Sak K'uk wrapped her arms around the snake's neck and held on during a rapid journey through another water-filled tunnel and into another cavern. An island in the center of this cavern supported the immense root system of a huge tree whose trunk rose through the roof of the cave. The snake deposited Sak K'uk on the root-filled island and swam away.

Sak K'uk's heart beat riotously as she recognized the Underworld roots of the Wakah Chan Te. She threw herself onto the roots, laughing and crying as she embraced their radiant tendrils. No sooner had she touched the roots than she felt herself dissolving into sap and quickly ascending the massive trunk, flowing through sap vessels upward into large limbs, then smaller branches until she reached the tiny tips of twigs at the top of the tree. The treetop soared into the Upperworld, surrounded by clouds and twinkling stars. A sea of indigo rippled away into the incalculable distance.

Perched on an uppermost twig, Sak K'uk yearned to fly into the sky. As her yearning became intense, a large white quetzal approached, its long tail feathers waving in the breeze, and she leapt onto its back. The white quetzal was her uay, her power creature for whom she was named. Her being merged into the white quetzal; soaring upward in spirals through rippling cloud waves, looking down at the round globe of earth below with its green lands and blue waters.

What did she seek? What must she do now that she was in the Upperworld?

Faintly, as if from far away, came the whispers of her mother's voice, the last thing she said before transition to the spirit world: "When in difficult times, turn to Muwaan Mat."

Muwaan Mat, the primordial mother, the progenitor of the B'aakal Triad.

As Sak K'uk formed these memories into a request, she perceived a huge dark bird flying toward her. Its long body was sleek, its wings wide and curved, its neck elongated, its head with rounded eyes and a pointed beak—the cormorant or "duck hawk" called Muwaan Mat in her language.

The white quetzal and the cormorant flew together, side-by-side, diving and gliding, sweeping and soaring in circles and spirals. Pure joy flooded Sak K'uk as she reveled in the ecstasy of freedom and union, the reconciliation of all differences. As the two celestial birds cavorted, the white quetzal understood the immense power of the cormorant, and her guidance became clear. Muwaan Mat would take on the responsibility of the K'altun offerings for the people of B'aakal, her own creations. She would give the proper bundles to the deities in the Upperworld, and this would appease them. Sak K'uk would become her representative in the Middleworld, and would perform abbreviated rituals in Lakam Ha that were primarily symbolic. The people must understand that humans would be unable to perform the full rituals until the Wakah Chan Te was restored, and that would take some time. Muwaan Mat would continue her Upperworld ceremonies as a substitute until Lakam Ha re-established its portal to the Gods and ancestors.

Muwaan Mat would assume the actual rulership of Lakam Ha, with Sak K'uk as her earthly ambassador. As soon as Pakal came of age, he would become ruler—and his destiny was to rebuild the portal.

4

"Let me understand this correctly," said Kan Mo' Hix, sounding more annoyed than usual. "You journeyed to the Upperworld and met Muwaan Mat, and she told you that she will do the K'altun ceremony there while you undertake a limited ritual here. That will appease the deities until Pakal becomes ruler and is able to reconstruct our portal."

"In essence, that is what I have spoken," replied Sak K'uk, holding back irritation at her husband. She needed his support in the Council meeting.

"Did you not also say that The Primordial Mother instructed you to assume rulership in her stead until Pakal reaches 12 tuns?" inquired Yaxun Xul.

Sak K'uk nodded to her father-in-law, who despite his advanced age remained mentally sharp.

"To be accurate, the ruler will be Muwaan Mat, but I will act in her behalf in the Middleworld," she said.

Kan Mo' Hix looked over her head with an exasperated expression.

"How can a Goddess in the Upperworld become our ruler? There is no precedent for this."

"Historically, there is precedent," interjected a young man among the group. "U Kix Kan, predecessor of our founder K'uk Bahlam, was a divine being but also had human form. He was not born in a human way, but came into being by the instigation of Muwaan Mat, and thus he is of the B'aakal Triad lineage. He lived a very long time, many human lifetimes before K'uk Bahlam was born fully human. In a sense, U Kix Kan was a representative of the Primordial Mother, who passed rulership into the B'aakal lineage through him."

Sak K'uk smiled and looked around at the small group gathered in her reception chamber. These were the ones she believed would support her plan. In addition to her husband and father-in-law, the group included Pasah Chan the High Priest; Usin Ch'ob the High Priestess; Chakab, elder Nakom-war chief; Oaxac Ok and Ch'amak, her distant cousins; and Yax Chan, the young man who just spoke. He demonstrated remarkable talent as an architect at an early age, and she intended to put that skill to good use in rebuilding Kan Bahlam's pyramid-temple.

"Words of wisdom spoken by the youngest among us," she remarked wryly, but quickly caught her mistake. "Except my son Pakal, even younger but equally wise."

By Sak K'uk's insistence, Pakal attended the gathering. He was to play an integral role in her plan and needed to know every nuance. Much would be expected from him, and his preparation could not omit any aspect, however small. She smiled at him, noting his serious and determined expression. He acknowledged her only with his eyes.

"In extraordinary circumstances, unusual measures must be taken," observed Pasah Chan. "There is great truth in this, for only one residing in the Realm of the Gods could perform the rituals without an existing portal."

"Muwaan Mat is the perfect choice to assuage the Triad Deities, for what sons could deny their mother? And the Lords of the First Sky are her companions in the starry vastness. This plan is brilliant," added Usin Ch'ob.

Oaxac Ok, a seasoned courtier, spoke to other concerns.

"There may be difficulty convincing the Council to accept Pakal as heir, the first prince—ba-ch'ok, designated as the ruler to follow Muwaan Mat. They are disgruntled with the Bahlam family, and other contenders have ambitions for rulership, although few will risk revealing their goals in our current turmoil."

"Can they not see that something must be done, and quickly?" retorted Sak K'uk. "The katun-ending is closing upon us; we have little time to establish the procedure for the K'altun ceremony."

"Perhaps they can be convinced of Muwaan Mat's intercession, but will balk at designating Pakal," said Ch'amak.

"This must be overcome. Here you have the totality of the Primordial Mother's instructions, and these include both her intercessory rulership and Pakal's designation. His hoof-binding must closely follow the K'altun ceremony to keep the ahauob from becoming contentious and fractured again." Sak K'uk spoke forcefully, her eyes blazing.

"Pakal must be at least 12 tuns of age for accession to rulership," added Pasah Chan.

"And none would expect him to fully assume rulership responsibilities for several tuns following," observed Yaxun Xul. "That means, in actuality, that his parents will be acting regents for some time." He looked meaningfully at Kan Mo' Hix.

"Just so, as you say," sighed Sak K'uk. "Much is yet to be accomplished, even after Pakal becomes ruler. This will not be easy. It is of utmost importance that I have all your support when I bring it before the Popol Nah."

She looked intently at each person, her eyes hardening as they met those of Kan Mo' Hix. He still perplexed her, shifting positions unpredictably, but almost without fail offering criticism. She feared that his ambitions to be ruler would undermine his support for Pakal. However, he had already admitted that he was unable to establish the necessary communications with the deities. Perhaps he was chafing over her assuming stand-in rulership for Muwaan Mat. Dropping her gaze and softening her demeanor, she attempted to lure his cooperation.

"It will be made clear that I am not actually acceding to rulership of Lakam Ha," she said with subdued voice. "I am well aware of my opponents, that many care not for my manner and believe I am not closest in line of succession. With royal lineages from both Kan Bahlam and Yaxun Xul, in whose families course the most pure bloodlines from K'uk Bahlam, Pakal is clearly the leading choice for ba-ch'ok. This must be our emphasis."

Many were nodding agreement, but Kan Mo' Hix appeared preoccupied, his expression stony. The well-respected High Priestess and skilled Ix Chel healer, Usin Ch'ob, spoke to their higher duties.

"It has come, this time of extreme hardship that was foretold by our beloved visionary ancestor and ruler, Yohl Ik'nal. In times such as this, we are called to surmount our personal goals for the survival of our city, the well-being of our people. The covenant that binds the royal ahauob of B'aakal is to serve our deities, to give what is required and proper, that they may also provide for us. This mutual exchange of sacred itz, in its many forms, is what sustains the world, this Fourth Creation of the Gods that brought forth the real people—Halach Uinik. Look deeply into your hearts and find your inner knowledge that all this is so, that it is the way of our people the Maya. When we break this covenant with the Gods, we are putting in motion forces that will lead to our destruction."

Silence descended upon the small group as all reflected upon the priestess' words. Kan Mo' Hix kept his eyes lowered, but Sak K'uk could tell by his body language that he was deeply affected.

"Let it not be said by our descendants that we were the ones to initiate the forces of destruction." The tenor voice of High Priest Pasah Chan rang clear notes of celestial command inside the stone chamber.

"Be it so," rejoined Yaxun Xul and Chakab in unison.

"Be it so," Oaxac Ok and Ch'amak repeated. Sak K'uk bowed her head and crossed both arms over her chest, the ultimate gesture of respect. Pakal's eyes were bright with unshed tears as he mimicked his mother's gesture.

In the charged silence following, all eyes turned toward Kan Mo' Hix. He looked at his son, their eyes locking for long moments. The profound trust and belief in the boy's expression struck deep into the father's heart.

"Be it so," he repeated softly. Taking a deep breath and releasing it in a long sigh, Kan Mo' Hix subsumed his ambitions to the collective good. "Usin Ch'ob and Pasah Chan, you have spoken well to remind us of our sacred covenant. To all present, I give my respect. And to my wife, I give acknowledgement for her courage to seek this guidance and her strength to carry out the Goddess' instructions. I am in full support. Let us proceed."

The stone benches along the sides of the Popol Nah were crowded with ahauob of Lakam Ha, mostly men but a few women. The call to Council had come from Sak K'uk and Kan Mo' Hix, declaring an announcement of great portent to the city's future that addressed the need for leadership. Rumors ran rampant through the city, inciting heated discussions and fueling the fire of opponents to the Bahlam family. Leading the opposing group were two young ahauob, Kitam and Pax Koh, whose family bloodlines traced through several branches to K'uk Bahlam, making them contenders for rulership.

The raised platform upon which the ruler would sit was draped with jaguar skins but was vacant. The High Priest stood beside the platform holding his staff, tipped with shining crystals and red macaw feathers. Several spaces on the benches near the ruler's platform were kept open for the royal family. Whispers circulated among ahauob, seated on stone benches lining the walls, that one of the royals might have the audacity to sit upon the ruler's platform, a clear declaration of assuming rulership. The hum of voices hushed as a conch was blown four times outside the Council chamber, announcing the beginning of a Popol Nah session.

In the ensuing lull, Sak K'uk and Kan Mo' Hix entered the chamber. All eyes riveted upon them, watching as they slowly walked from the entrance toward the central ruler's platform. When they sat in the open spaces on benches near the platform instead of on the throne, there was an audible release of breath. For the moment, crisis was avoided.

The High Priest intoned prayers for opening the Popol Nah session as attendant priests passed along the benches waving burners of copal incense, a ritual for purification that all present might enter into deliberation cleansed of negative energies. The sweet-pungent Pom smoke filled the room. Raising his staff, Pasah Chan rapped it four times on the stone floor—the number four for the directions of the quadripartite world—and declared the session begun.

Kan Mo' Hix stood and addressed the Council first. It was a strategy aimed at defusing resistance to Sak K'uk's message. As a man from a well-respected family, he hoped to build a foundation of support among ahauob.

"Honored Council of Lakam Ha, this session is called to address serious problems within our city and our polity. It has been well past one tun since our city suffered the wicked and immoral attack from Kan and two uinals since their foul and despicable murder of our ruler Aj Ne Ohl Mat. We have also lost the wise leadership of Hun Pakal, another victim of the ruthless Kan. Our city still lies in ruin, many sacred temples defaced and pyramids damaged, our larders depleted, our fields laid waste, our idols of Gods and ancestors destroyed, and most of our jewelry and adornments stolen. Not a single family has been spared personal loss and suffering; many of you lost kinfolk, brave warriors during the battle, or your women and children taken as slaves. Never before has Lakam Ha suffered such a defeat. In the memory of our ancestors, all the way back to our noble founder K'uk Bahlam, nothing of this magnitude has befallen our people, beloved of the Triad Deities.

"We know that treachery and betrayal by some of our own people underlay this defeat. We suffered the infamy, the insults of the three-day mat person, that vile and despicable Ek Chuuah. He profaned the throne of Lakam Ha by sitting upon it. May his soul be damned before the Gods and ancestors so he is lost forever in Xibalba, never to escape the grasp of the Death Lords. Even in this Middleworld, his evil conspirator Uneh Chan of Kan met an untimely death, delivered upon him by our avenging Gods. Our deities have not deserted us, but their ability to provide for and protect us has been seriously diminished.

"The collapse of our portal in the Sak Nuk Nah has taken away our ability to access the Gods and ancestors. Without this portal, we are unable to perform the ceremonies required, to give to them their bundles in the traditional and time-honored way. We cannot adorn the Triad and the First Sky Gods. We cannot keep our covenant with them. We all know this but in our confusion and dismay, we have avoided facing what is soon before us: the ending of Katun 8, which will be upon us in less than one tun. It is our sacred obligation to perform the K'altun ceremony, to bind the last tun, to set the auguries for the coming katun. The stone-binding ceremony is necessary to invoke patronage of the Lords of Time, to assure their favor for a prosperous new katun. We know the auguries of Katun 9, the attributes of the number 9. Katun 9 can carry the burden of limitation, but with proper rituals these limits can turn toward our enemies, can stop adversity and thus ensure times of expansion for Lakam Ha.

"We must have a plan. We must take action soon. Through the grace of the B'aakal deities, such a plan of action has been revealed to my wife, Ixik Sak K'uk. This is a powerful demonstration that our Gods have not abandoned us. But extraordinary means are needed to maintain our relationships; unusual measures are required in these times of great calamity. Now we shall hear from Sak K'uk of her message from the deities."

Kan Mo' Hix clasped his shoulder and bowed to his wife, resuming his seat on the bench as she rose. Sak K'uk wore a simple white huipil bordered in yellow, an amber neck collar and earspools, with hair braided and twisted into a modest headdress of white cloth with intertwined bronze discs that clinked softly as she moved. She walked along the benches filled with ahauob, drawing herself to full height and straightness. Lifting her chin, her eyes swept the assembly then focused in the distance.

"My mother, Honored Ancestor Yohl Ik'nal, came to me in a dream. She re-told a story from my childhood about her vigil at the Witz cave on K'uk Lakam Witz. The quadripartite monster mask surrounded the Witz cave and called me to come there for my own vigil. This I did, unaccompanied as instructed and without any offering but myself. Within the maw of the cave, I was taken down into the Underworld where there exists a portal, one that was not damaged in the Kan attack. There in the cave depths were the roots of the Wakah Chan Te, through which I was able to ascend into the Upperworld."

Sak K'uk continued, giving details of her encounters both inside the cave and in the celestial realm. She entered a semi-trance in telling the story, and ended with the instructions of Muwaan Mat.

"Muwaan Mat, the Primordial Mother Goddess, will give the K'altun offerings. She will give the proper bundles to the Triad Deities and Lords of the First Sky in the Upperworld. She charged me to become her representative in the Middleworld, and perform symbolic rituals so the people can see that these requirements of the Gods are being carried out. But the people must understand that we cannot perform the full rituals until the Wakah Chan Te is restored, until Lakam Ha has re-established our portal to the Gods and ancestors.

"Muwaan Mat is to accede as our next ruler. I am to act as her earthly ambassador. When my son Janaab Pakal reaches 12 tuns, he is to accede as ruler. The Goddess has ordained that it is his destiny to rebuild the portal.

"Thus has our Great Mother spoken to me, and charged me to bring her communication to you, the Council of the people of Lakam Ha."

Still dazed with her sight blurred from revisiting the encounter with Muwaan Mat, Sak K'uk stood in the center of the Popol Nah, trembling slightly.

All around her arose murmurs as the ahauob exclaimed to each other, a few phrases penetrating her awareness: "The Primordial Mother has spoken . . ." "Can this be so?" ". . . Who observed this?" ". . . Self-serving story. . ." "Our deities still care for us."

As voices became more strident, Pasah Chan stepped forth and pounded his staff several times on the floor.

"Let the Council come to order! Hold your speech!"

When there was quiet, he continued. "In the absence of a ruler, let us select our Nakom to preside over the Council."

"Yes, yes, the Nakom!"

"Come forth, Chakab!"

From the bench, Kitam and Pax Koh exchanged dark glances, knowing well the long alliance of Chakab with the Bahlam family. Neither dared challenge the choice of the honored elder warrior to preside, however. Kan Mo' Hix suppressed a smile, for this was part of their plan. He went to Sak K'uk and assisted her to sit on the bench, as Chakab stood in front of the raised platform holding the throne. Kitam signaled a request to speak and was recognized by Chakab.

"It is with great respect that now I pose some questions to esteemed Ixik Sak K'uk. Surely what she has told us is an amazing event. She deserves our acknowledgement for braving the dangers of the Underworld to seek assistance. Such a dangerous endeavor should have received some protection by assistants. Were there not any with you at the Witz cave?"

Kan Mo' Hix murmured in Sak K'uk's ear as Kitam spoke, bringing her back into the present. Although she felt shaky, she stood near her husband to reply.

"There were no assistants. The calling I received required that I do vigil alone."

"This she told us before embarking up the mountain," Kan Mo' Hix confirmed.

"Then no one was present to hold sacred space, to anchor your soul, or to observe what transpired?" continued Kitam.

"No one."

"With no disrespect, Sak K'uk, perhaps this was your imagination and not actually a journey to the Upperworld. There is no one to verify what you tell us."

Oaxac Ok leapt to his feet and exploded before Chakab could restrain him. "What is Sak K'uk if not honest? Her honesty has often been criticized by those who oppose her leadership. How dare you imply she is fabricating her experience?"

He sat quickly upon Chakab's glare.

"It fits too perfectly into her ambitions," retorted Kitam. "We are not ignorant of her desire that her son Pakal sit upon Lakam Ha's throne. How convenient that Muwaan Mat would give her just such instructions."

A round of murmuring and nodding showed that Kitam had made a strong point. Satisfied, he returned to his seat. Ch'amak signaled next to speak.

"It does strike me as unusual that Sak K'uk, alone in a dangerous place, was able to attain such a journey when by her own admittance, she has not journeyed very often and has not been able to raise the Vision Serpent. Perhaps her desire to be helpful to our city has clouded her perceptions and brought these images into her mind. We can all identify with her desperation to bring Lakam Ha out of its chaos. Do not we all feel disheartened and confused?"

Cries of "That is so!" and "Well spoken!" erupted, and Ch'amak continued his speech.

"Sak K'uk is correct in her desire to revive leadership in Lakam Ha, so we can begin moving toward recovery. This is good, this is correct. She is right, we must take action soon for the katun-end is upon us. It is my contention that other leadership will serve us better. Let us choose a new ruler, but from another family of royal lineage. The time of the Bahlam dynasty has waned, and fresh leadership is needed. Let us consider my kinsman Kitam, of correct bloodlines, a youthful and vigorous statesman, and a brave warrior who distinguished himself battling Kan. Kitam has the vision to lead Lakam Ha forward!"

Shouts of agreement mixed with lower growls of disapproval.

Yaxun Xul spoke next, predictably in support of Sak K'uk's proposal. The fervor grew as one then another ahau rose to speak, showing an even division among those present. Sak K'uk had resumed her seat, now fully present and sinking into desperation. Clearly her explanation had fallen short; she had not convinced the Council. They even doubted the truth of what she told them, a blow that pained her heart. Maybe they were right and she was incapable of providing leadership, even as a proxy. Maybe her earlier visions had been false and Pakal did not have the destiny she foresaw.

Sak K'uk was overcome with a wave of despair. Her mind cried out in anguish: *Great Mother! How could you give me these commands and not the authority to carry them out?*

Suddenly her ears were bombarded by a roaring sound, so loud it caused pain. Her vision darkened and she could not see the chamber or people around her. A blaze of brilliant light flashed into her forehead, like a lightning bolt splitting her skull and flooding her brain with vibrant energy. The periphery of her awareness recognized this as the axe of K'awill penetrating her forehead, the symbol of divine dynastic lineage. Her mind and her body were no longer her own, for she was possessed by K'awill and his mother, Muwaan Mat.

"STOP—THIS—DISSENSION!" she yelled, springing to her feet.

Everyone in the Popol Nah froze and stared dumbfounded in her direction. Kan Mo' Hix, Pasah Chan, and Chakab, who stood closest to her, shrunk backward lifting their hands to shield their faces.

The pounding force of giant wings beat the air within the chamber, sending vortexes of dust swirling and flapping the loincloths and feathers worn by ahauob. Blinding light emanated from around the form of Sak K'uk, sending forth flashes of lightning that crackled the air. Hair rose on forearms and necks and some dropped to their knees, while others covered their eyes. Those who looked saw a huge dark cormorant settle its shape around Sak K'uk's body, then morph into a blazing-eyed hawk-goddess with sharp beak and long talons, frightening and awesome.

"DARE—YOU—QUESTION—MY—COMMANDS?"

It was not Sak K'uk's voice, although her mouth-beak spoke through the shimmering form of the Goddess.

"All that my daughter Sak K'uk has spoken is true. She came to me from the depths of Xibalba, risking her life, overcoming her terror, in order to help you. What ungrateful wretches you are! Were it not for her love for you, and my love of her, I would leave you all to destruction. Now listen closely and do not doubt me again. Every word Sak K'uk has spoken must be followed exactly. You are to provide her every support that is needed. My intercession in the Upperworld will save you for a time, but then the reparations must be done by yourselves. Pakal has an enormous challenge as ruler to re-establish your portal, and you must support him in that.

"DO—YOU—UNDERSTAND—ME?" she roared.

The cowering and shaking ahauob whimpered pitifully under the merciless glare of the Goddess. Many blubbered a tremulous "yes" while others nodded their heads.

With another round of pounding wings and crackling lightning that threw more ahauob onto the floor, Muwaan Mat ascended through the corbelled arch ceiling of the Popol Nah and disappeared.

Sak K'uk slumped to the floor unconscious. Usin Ch'ob the High Priestess, who had been sitting at the farthest corner of the chamber, rushed to her side. Cradling Sak K'uk in her arms, the Priestess pressed an herb paste below her nostrils and signaled for a cup of water. Kan Mo' Hix knelt next to his wife, awe-struck and flooded with new respect. Pasah Chan and Chakab circulated among the ahauob, helping them up from the floor. Some remained in shock while others appeared exuberant. This encounter with the Primordial Mother

Goddess would be the high point of their lives, repeated for generations in story and fable. They felt incredibly privileged—or soundly rebuked.

When Sak K'uk was revived, the Priestess and Kan Mo' Hix supported her to stand. Her confused look prompted her husband to whisper in her ear: "You are validated. Muwaan Mat took over your form and commanded them to follow your plan."

His arm firmly around her shoulders, he addressed the Council.

"We shall prepare for the accession of Muwaan Mat as K'uhul B'aakal Ahau."

The main plaza of Lakam Ha teemed with its residents, both ahauob and commoners, gathering for the accession rites of the newly designated ruler. Tall censers with deity faces lined the stairs of the Royal Palace at the west side of the plaza. Fire priestesses tended the censers, dropping copal crystals over glowing coals to produce undulating columns of pungent smoke. Many of the censers were newly crafted to replace those destroyed in the Kan attack. Musicians played flutes and beat drums of wood and turtle shells, accompanied by clacking gourd rattles. From the highest pyramids nearby, resounding blasts of conch shells saluted the four directions. Several bass rounds from long wooden trumpets announced the appearance of the royal procession.

The crowd became silent as the procession entered the plaza, led by the High Priest and Priestess and their entourage. Several rows of elite nobles followed, all dressed in the finest regalia they could assemble in the short span of two uinals (40 days) since the decision of the Popol Nah. The miraculous happenings in the Council House had spread like wildfire through the city, and all were eager to see how the new ruler would appear. A cadre of musicians blowing short trumpets and beating hide drums preceded dancers who enacted the rejoicing of animals, birds, and humans over the appearance of their K'uhul Ahau to continue royal succession and keep covenant with the Gods. The newly woven standards of Lakam Ha, carried by warriors on tall poles, flapped in the soft breeze and reminded the people of their city's past glories.

Four powerfully built men bore upon their shoulders decorated poles supporting the ruler's palanquin. Its square wooden platform was ornately decorated with red and yellow tassels, bordered by white cloth embroidered with blue and green trim resembling waves. Cavorting among the waves were fish, frogs, and turtles. Green rushes attached to corner poles swayed with the movements of the carriers. The aquatic theme of the palanquin was evident to all.

Seated upon the palanquin was an impressive being, clothed in a white sheath with a cape of pure Maya blue and large neck collar of turquoise and creamy jade. More jade and shells adorned wrists and ankles, secured from coffers that ahauob had sequestered. None dared refuse to give adornments to Muwaan Mat's earthly representative. The headdress and mask of the ruler brought murmurs of admiration from the observers. Towering above, fully half the height of the small form sitting on the palanquin was an immense headdress on a backstrap frame. The chest and long neck of the cormorant, called duck hawk, rose from her elongated skull and arched above her forehead. A band of glittering bronze feathers flared and curled on the bird's forehead. Its long beak ended with a sharp curve and dangled a fish between its jaws. Rounded eyes sported red stone pupils staring fiercely out of white shell corneas.

The backstrap frame supported a soaring display of shimmering quetzal tail feathers, their blue-green iridescence repeating the watery motif. Along the back of the frame were carved masks of Bahlam royal ancestors surrounded by dangling silver medallions and clinking seashells. The facemask worn by the ruler repeated elements of the cormorant with shorter beak and enlarged round eyes, while reedy embellishments and prominent catfish whiskers invoked affinity with the Hero Twins myth.

To complete the royal accession imagery, the ruler held a K'awiil scepter fashioned from rare white jade. This exquisite piece had remained hidden deep within the Temple of the High Priest, buried under a storage chamber floor. Legend told that it traced back to the founder K'uk Bahlam, though none really knew its origins. Generations of High Priests had guarded this treasure. The scepter was as long as two men's feet, carved in high relief and fully fashioned on every surface. The lightning-forehead snake-foot deity of royal lineage had a snaky face, a flaming torch spouting and curling from the forehead, wore an Ik—wind pendant and had one elongated leg that ended in an open serpent mouth issuing fiery breath scrolls. K'awiil was the divine patron of noble lineages, the essence of fertility, and integral to the potency of the Maize God.

The power radiating from this imagery overwhelmed the people, who dropped to their knees and clasped both arms across their chests. None doubted that the Primordial Mother Goddess Muwaan Mat had descended into the form on the palanquin. This impressive figure far exceeded and completely eclipsed any presence of the personage known as Sak K'uk.

Behind the palanquin walked members of Sak K'uk's family and her closest courtiers. It was Pakal's first royal procession, and he stood tall with head proudly upraised. His mother's transformation made a strong impression upon him, furthering his understanding of the embodiment of deities that was required of rulers.

The procession moved into the main square and along each quadrant, giving all assembled a clear view of the ruler's palanquin, finally crossing through the center to the palace stairs. Lesser priesthood and ahauob lined the stairs near the smoking censers. To the single beat of a huge turtle carapace, the carriers set down the palanquin and assisted the ruler to rise, for the weight of her apparatus was considerable. Once balanced on her feet, she slowly and carefully ascended the stairs, feathers waving and adornments jangling. Reaching the top platform, she turned to face the plaza and raised the K'awiil scepter in one hand, making the scattering gesture with the other. The crowd broke into cascading roars, crying the Goddess' name over and over.

"Muwaan Mat! Muwaan Mat! K'uhul B'aakal Ahau Muwaan Mat!"

Coming to stand beside the ruler, the High Priest and Priestess chanted incantations for a prosperous, peaceful and creative reign. They also did ritual to dispel adversities and bring healing to the people and land.

Although much time elapsed in the ceremony, and the bright sun shone warmly on this clear autumn day, the ruler stood still and straight, showing no signs of fatigue. Kan Mo' Hix, standing near the top steps, worried that her strength might fail under the heavy costume and her preparatory cleansings. Pakal, standing near his father, sensed that his mother was completely immersed in divine energy and marveled at her ability to subsume her consciousness so totally to the Goddess.

When the chants and rituals were complete, the conches blew four times and the long trumpets gave four blasts. In the hush that followed, the ruler moved slowly toward the throne room in the central chamber facing the square. Only her clinking adornments and distant birdcalls broke the silence. On the double-headed jaguar throne, covered with dappled black and gold jaguar pelts, the newly acceded ruler K'uhul B'aakal Ahau Muwaan Mat sat regally, accepted the white headband from the High Priest and tied it around the cormorant headdress, to rapid drumbeats and the wild cheers her people.

The date of Muwaan Mat's accession was later carved and inscribed.

Baktun 9, Katun 8, Tun 19, Uinal 7, Kin 18, on the date 9 Etznab 6 Keh (October 22, 612 CE).

The hoof-binding ceremony to designate Pakal as heir, as ba-ch'ok, took place 5 moon cycles later at the time of spring equinox. This pre-accession ritual was called *K'al May*. The symbolism of renewed life as K'in Ahau-Sun Lord reached his halfway point, the time when light and darkness are perfectly in balance, created the proper framework for initiating the process that would prepare the next ruler. The ceremony was simple and pure. Sak K'uk in modified Muwaan Mat costume tied two deer hoofs around her son's waist with woven cords of red, yellow, and black. To bind the deer hoofs meant that his path was established, and set the direction where his footsteps would lead.

The deer was an important symbol to the Maya. As a major food source, it was a prognosticator of rain and renewal, but when portrayed as dead it augured drought and death. In winter the deer carried the sun quickly across the sky, denoting shorter days, while the peccary carried it slowly during the long days of summer. In a particular rendition, the deer was associated with Mars, depicted as the Mars Beast with a fret-nosed snout, starry eye, and cleft hoofs. When suspended from the sky band, it referred to periods when Mars was moving in retrograde while crossing the Milky Way. During this period typical weather conditions that occurred led to rainfall. Mars crossing the Milky Way often brought rain, and its recurring cycles were used for weather predictions. Rain was the essential source of itz needed to bring new plant life and stimulate maize seeds to grow.

The hoof-binding ceremony signaled that Pakal had embarked on the path of rulership, and he assumed the accoutrements that activated deer qualities to bring life-giving rain to the land. The ritual began in the forest where deer lived, and involved a procession from the low forests to the plains, where Pakal enacted rites of sprinkling water upon cornfields. A select contingent of priesthood and ahauob witnessed this event, accompanied by musicians rapping wooden sticks on hollow tubes for the clacking of hoofs, and shaking long hollow bamboo rain-tubes full of seeds to simulate raindrops.

This also initiated a period of intense training for Pakal. His instruction included further shamanic training by the High Priest, lessons in statesmanship from his father, grandfather, and leading courtiers, and review of the history, calendars and cosmology of B'aakal with experienced scribes. Sak K'uk made certain there was time for study of construction and architectural arts. The Nakom taught about strategies of competition and battle, and young warriors trained Pakal in basic fighting techniques. The boy's natural inclinations were toward the creative and mystical aspects of Maya sciences, rather than disposing him to become a mighty warrior. But he was required to become competent in battle skills and develop strength.

Two moon cycles later arrived the much-anticipated ending of Katun 8. Sak K'uk and Pasah Chan conferred frequently about how and where to enact the K'altun ceremony. They decided to conduct it at the High Priest's temple, the least damaged pyramid remaining in Lakam Ha, in its large plaza overlooking the plains below. Period-ending rituals were concerned with time and cycles, part of the Maya's esoteric knowledge and special relationships with the Lords of Time. These were not public rituals and had always been conducted inside the hidden Sak Nuk Nah in the past. The elite ahauob, those with closest ties to the rulers, usually attended the rituals to bear witness to the ruler's completion of the prescribed and proper offerings.

Now the location was no longer hidden and all were acutely aware of Lakam Ha's unusual predicament. Interest in attending this ceremony was intense, and Sak K'uk chose to include all ahauob, although this meant the temple plaza would be packed. The ceremony took place around dawn and had two parts; the ending of Katun 8 as darkness began to yield to light; and the beginning of Katun 9 when the sun rose above the horizon. Just as Muwaan Mat performed her offerings and gave bundles to the deities in the Upperworld, Sak K'uk enacted her truncated ritual in the Middleworld.

Pakal as ba-ch'ok was given a place of honor close to the altar where the ritual would be conducted. He eagerly watched the eastern sky for the first signs of dawn.

In the pale pre-dawn light the ceremonial entourage entered the crowded plaza accompanied by a single slow drumbeat. The High Priest and Priestess preceded Sak K'uk and several attendant priests followed carrying ritual items. Sak K'uk was dressed in a pure white huipil bound at the waist by thick cords that also encircled her hands, tied behind her back in captive position. She wore no headdress or adornments and her hair was tied into a single topknot, the long black tail hanging down her back. This was the characteristic appearance of noble captives taken in battle. A barely audible gasp rippled through the gathered ahauob at the implication of captive sacrifice.

Solemnly the entourage crossed the plaza and ascended the stairs to the temple atop the highest pyramid of the complex. Censers carried by attendants were placed at both sides of the top platform, their smoke curling into the stillness. Sak K'uk knelt between Pasah Chan and Usin Ch'ob as an attendant placed a large bowl filled with bark paper next to her. The High Priest addressed the assembly.

"Ixik Sak K'uk, royal lady of B'aakal, brings Katun 8 to a close by her sacrifice, by her surrender into servitude to the Primordial Mother Muwaan Mat. The Lord of Katun 8, Oaxac Tiku, has extracted severe payment from Lakam Ha. May his desires now be satisfied and set aside. With the rise of K'in Ahau this day, we finish Katun 8, it is done, it is completed. As the penance of Muwaan Mat brought forth the birth of her sons, the Triad Deities, so now the penance of Sak K'uk will birth the next Katun. People of Lakam Ha, witness the travail of Sak K'uk and the penance of she who is the form and essence of Muwaan Mat among us."

Usin Ch'ob grasped and lifted the long tail of Sak K'uk's hair while the attendant lit the paper in the bowl with a small torch. Pasah Chan drew a long obsidian knife from his waistband and raised it high for all to see. Torchlight glinted off the knife's sharp edges. Pakal's eyes widened with terror as he stared upward from his vantage point at the foot of the stairs. With a sudden swipe, Pasah Chan slashed off Sak K'uk's hair, leaving the long strands dangling in Usin Ch'ob's hands. The High Priestess dropped the hair onto the burning paper, releasing an acrid smell that burned the nostrils as flames sputtered and crackled. Sak K'uk remained perfectly still, head bent over her knees and hands tied behind. Pakal held his breath, his body stiff with tension.

The first rays of sunlight crept over the eastern mountains and tinted the temple roofcomb with rosy hues. From the four corners of the temple platform, conches sounded their blasting tones to the four directions. Lilting clay flute melodies mingled with twittering birdcalls as the surrounding jungle awakened. Several drums took up a commanding rhythm as nine strong men entered the plaza, each carrying a large stone on his back using tumplines across foreheads. The men climbed the temple stairs and deposited the nine stones in a pyramid shaped heap near the platform's east corner.

Quickly the sunlight swept across the face of the temple and illuminated the top platform, shining golden tones on the heap of stones and the figures standing nearby. When the drums ceased, the High Priest released Sak K'uk's hands from the cords and unwound her waist. The High Priestess lifted the magnificent cormorant headdress Sak K'uk had worn for the accession ritual of Muwaan Mat, and with help of attendants placed it upon Sak K'uk's head, attaching the feathered wooden back frame that stabilized it. They helped the ruler to rise and Pasah Chan placed the cords in her hands.

"Muwaan Mat now welcomes the arrival of Bolon Tiku, Lord of Katun 9. With the light of Sun Lord—K'in Ahau, we welcome the new Score of Tuns. The burden of the nine stones was born to our temple by strong men; the binding of the nine stones is done by the vessel of the Goddess. We witness the stone binding, so that Katun 9 may arrive properly acknowledged, rightly recognized and honored."

Sak K'uk—Muwaan Mat walked slowly to the heap of stones and wound the long cords around the nine stones several times. She tied the cords into a large knot, then stood tall, lifted her arms to the sun and chanted the K'altun ritual.

"Five Ahau settles into Three Ahau,
Lords of the final days of each Katun
One releases his burden to the next.
This is its word and its burden,
Face of the Lord Sun is the seat of the Three Ahau Katun.
There its mat will be present,
There its throne will be present,
There it will reveal its word,
There it will reveal its might.
Yaxal Chak, Green Rain, is the semblance of the katun ruling the sky.
In the face of its rule is the balance of three,
Is the limit of nine, the master of endings.
Lords of the Katun, Bolon Tiku, Ox Ahau,
They who bring the ending of Lakam Ha's suffering
And restore the balance of humans and Gods."

Sak K'uk turned to the crowd below, spread her hands and held them, palms outward, in the sign of universal blessing. The High Priest and Priestess stood beside her and led the assembly in the chant to welcome the dawning of a new day. Then the three turned and entered the temple chambers to enact a symbolic offering to the deities. A small select group of ahauob, including Sak K'uk's family, climbed the stairs to join this ceremony. It was understood that no bundles could be given, that the Triad Deities and Lords of the First Sky could not be adorned with the usual hats and jewelry because the portal did not exist. The customary bloodletting by the ruler and high ahauob would not take place because the Vision Serpent could not be invoked without the portal through which it rose into the Upperworld.

Instead of these usual bundles of gifts, the group sat and gave thanks to Muwaan Mat who was making these offerings to her sons in the celestial realm. Many years later, Pakal's son would have the commemoration of this occasion carved on the hieroglyphic panels in his father's funerary monument called Temple of the Inscriptions.

"Less than a year after Ix Muwaan Mat K'uhul B'aakal Ahau
Became seated as ahau, it was the K'altun of 3 Ahau 3 Zotz.
It was the ninth Katun (9.9.0.0.0—May 12, 613 CE).
Muwaan Mat K'uhul B'aakal Ahau gives the bundle of her Gods
for the 9 Baktun 9 Katun.
On the back of the ninth Katun, god was lost; ahau was lost.
She could not adorn the ahauob of the First Sky;
She could not give offerings to the 9 Sky Yoch'ok'in,
The 16 Ch'ok'in, or the 9 Tz'aak Ahau.
On the back of the 3 Ahau Katun, Ix Muwaan Mat could not give their
    offerings.
Ix Muwaan Mat gives the bundle of her god."

SAK K'UK/MUWAAN MAT—IV

Baktun 9 Katun 9 Tun 1— Baktun 9 Katun 9 Tun 2 (613—615 CE)

1

I N THE SEASONS following the K'altun ceremony to bind the stones of the new katun, Pakal thought deeply about time. He was keenly interested in the Lords of Time, having studied their dominion over the calendars that ordered many cycles, immense to small that gave structure to Mayan life. He saw how time permeated all aspects of life, a dynamic force that imbued temporal existence with spiritual significance. Earthly life was enmeshed with natural and celestial rhythms. Time ordered the sequence of daily events and gave a framework to remember the past and anticipate the future. With the Long Count, sacred Tzolk'in, and Haab annual calendars, his people could prepare for repeating patterns that brought either good or bad fortune.

Stones became the bones of history. By imprinting ephemeral moments onto the solid medium of stone, the Maya turned time into an enduring presence. Defining specific moments in the lives of rulers, commemorating endings and beginnings of katuns and baktuns, and documenting significant events in the history of cities constituted a work of spiritual magnitude. The life of the ruler was memorialized through the carving of dates into stone, inscribing the ruler into the history of the cosmos.

Recalling his lessons with the old calendar priest Ah K'uch, Pakal reviewed how certain deities ruled over time. Each unit of time and each number had a named lord. The Lords of the Tun and Katun took the name of the day and number on which their cycle ended. Tuns always ended on an Ahau day. Katuns ended after 20 tuns, thus likewise always ended on an Ahau day. The numeric count of the K'altun, the Wheel of the Katun, followed a regressing count separated by 2 digits: 13-11-9-7-5-3-1-12-10-8-6-4-2. Every 13 cycles the count began anew; every 260 tuns a new Katun Wheel turned. The mathematics of this calendar led to the great cycle of the Tzek'eb or Pleiadian Calendar of 26,000 tuns: 260 + 260 = 520, 520 + 520 = 1040, and 1040 x 25 = 26,000.

Indeed, Pakal concluded, time brought to the Maya many opportunities to encounter Gods and ancestors. Reverently, the newly designated heir recited the names of the Lords of Time who carried the burden of the passing and beginning katuns.

"Lord of Katun 8—Oaxac Tiku (8 Deity).

Lord of Katun 9—Bolon Tiku (9 Deity)."

The Lord of the ending day was Ahau for both katuns, and each Ahau had accompanying numeric lords, numbers 5 and 3. Pakal continued his recitation.

"Numeric Lord 5—Ho Ahau Katun for Katun 8.

Numeric Lord 3—Ox Ahau Katun for Katun 9."

Pasah Chan judged that the time was right for Pakal to make the dangerous journey into the Underworld and encounter the Lords of Death. Training for this intense challenge had been interrupted by the city's devastation following Kan's attack, and the long chaotic phase that followed. Now that a measure of stability was established and succession was secure, he wanted no delays in completing the ba-ch'ok training. At the dark of the moon, when Ix Uc was hidden in the night sky, he knew the inter-dimensional Sacred Mountain Cave would open its mouth for those who could find it. Called Cave of Immortal Wisdom, only adepts who could overcome all fears, even fear of death, were able to enter. If their hearts were not pure, they would either be prevented from entering or would be unable to leave the Underworld, trapped forever in Xibalba, the domain of the Death Lords.

The High Priest knew that Sak K'uk was worried about the dangers for Pakal, but the heir to the throne could not assume proper rulership powers without facing them. The evening before the moon's disappearance, when she hung as a mere sliver over the darkening horizon, he led a small group into the steep, rugged terrain of mountains to the south of the city. They toiled upward on barely visible paths, picking their way gingerly over lianas and rocks, avoiding spiny bushes and fanning roots of towering trees, until they faced a cliff so perpendicular that climbing was impossible.

At the base of the cliff, Pasah Chan set up camp for the night. His two attendant priests started a small fire and set mats around it. He and Pakal prepared for a night spent in meditation. He instructed Pakal that the cave mouth would open in the few moments between the dim light heralding dawn and the rising of the sun. During the night Pakal must use divinatory training to pinpoint the cave opening, and prepare his consciousness so that he could gain entry. Giving any intimation of where the cave mouth was located would invalidate the challenge. In truth, the High Priest could not remember which of the many small hollows pocketing the cliff held the cave mouth. His final instructions were about returning from the cave. At dusk, moments before sunset, the cave mouth would re-open and allow Pakal to exit. If he missed this small window of time, he would be trapped in the Underworld.

The three priests kept vigil with the ba-ch'ok through the night. Two attendant priests maintained the fire and watched for jungle dangers, such as jaguars and snakes. The High Priest attuned his consciousness to Pakal and entered the trance state with the boy. Pakal maintained intense concentration and practiced breath meditation, not allowing drowsiness to creep up. Immobile as a stone statue, he floated for hours completely absorbed in the fresh air moving in and out of his nostrils, following its channels flowing within his body through his lungs into every organ, muscle, blood vessel, nerve, and deep into the bones.

From time to time, he scanned the cliff mentally to detect the cave mouth. Although he sensed nothing, he firmly controlled any thoughts of worry or inadequacy. It was just such thoughts that derailed intuitive processes. He breathed in confidence and trust that the Gods would show him the entrance in good time. Years of training had prepared him to hold meditation postures for long hours, and ascetic disciplines allowed him to ignore pangs of hunger and thirst. The occasional night sounds, the insect chirps, bat shrieks, rustling leaves, and frog croaks wafted through his awareness like thin smoke, passing and exiting without leaving any traces.

Although his eyes were closed, Pakal could detect a slight decrease in the darkness that surrounded him. Dawn was not far away, and still he had not found the cave mouth. He concentrated harder, shooting a stream of consciousness toward the cliff face, probing into every hollow and depression. Nothing was apparent. Behind scraggly brush that clung to boulders, he detected no hint of secrets or energies that would give clues. Small ripples of uncertainty began spreading in his lake of mental calmness. His heartbeat quickened and his breathing became irregular. He noticed his aching limbs and felt nearly irresistible urges to move them.

Relax, relax and breathe, open your heart and trust. Pakal repeated this mantra silently until he felt complete calm returning. Un-summoned, an image of Baby Jaguar—Unen K'awiil floated before his inner vision and his heart smiled. His special friend was here to help. The plump little jaguar cavorted in front of the cliff, waved a paw at Pakal and disappeared into a hollow near the east edge where jungle took over.

A bolt of certainty shot through Pakal's awareness. *This is it!* Heartfelt gratitude flooded toward Baby Jaguar, now hidden within the cave.

The light grew brighter and Pakal stirred. He opened his eyes and glanced east. Although dense trees blocked his view of the horizon, he knew earliest sunlight would quickly dance through the top of the forest canopy. Judging from the light and twitters of awakening birds, this would occur momentarily.

It was time. The few moments between dawn light and sunrise were upon them.

Pakal leapt to his feet, ignoring protests of stiff muscles and bounded toward the hollow entered by Baby Jaguar. Pasah Chan was fully aware of Pakal's actions and opened his lids a slit to watch. The other priests were drowsing on their mats.

The lithe boy covered the space to the hollow almost instantly. He paused for a moment, looking through brush, and saw a jagged opening into the cliff. It appeared to be a hungry mouth waiting to swallow him, full of pointed rocky teeth. Fear flashed but he immediately extinguished it with a blast of love, totally trusting Baby Jaguar. The cave mouth seemed to vibrate and then started closing. Pakal made a headfirst dive into the opening, landing inside on sand and pebbles as the rocky teeth snapped closed.

The darkness was total. Silence reigned inside the cave. Pakal waited for his vision to adjust and his heartbeat to slow down, and gradually he could see faint light emanating from deep within the tunnel that went steeply downward. The cave was high enough for him to stand, so he proceeded carefully down the tunnel. Down and down he went, following curves and stepping over puddles. After what seemed an interminable descent, the tunnel opened onto an immense cavern, so huge that he could not see the far sides. Canyon after canyon, ridge after ridge swept away to an unfathomable distance.

Xibalba. It was the domain of the Death Lords.

Pakal listened and sniffed the dank air. Sounds of rushing rivers, hoots and squawks came from the distance. Foul odors wafted out of canyons, sickening smells that turned his stomach. Baby Jaguar was nowhere in sight, but he detected a narrow path wending through slippery rocks toward the canyons. There seemed nowhere else to go but along the path, so he followed it slowly, grasping damp boulders at times to steady his steps. This brought him to the brink of the first deep canyon, and he gasped to see that instead of water, a thick stream of pus flowed through its precipitous walls. The smell gagged him.

Suddenly a hideous creature jumped from behind a boulder, its face a grinning skull, its limbs skeletal, and its belly bloated. From numerous sores on its body, pus was running. Shreds of skin hung off its back and arms, putrefying and dripping more pus. Its headdress contained dangling eyeballs, flapping tongues, severed fingers, and slimy entrails. Bloodshot eyes popping out of sockets, it pointed a clawed finger at Pakal and shrieked: "Why come you here? What are you, that you invade my domain uncalled?"

Pakal quickly got grip of his emotions, clasped his left shoulder and bowed.

"Greetings, Lord Demon of Pus. I am K'inich Janaab Pakal, ba-ch'ok of Lakam Ha. Here came I to learn from the Lords of Death. It is part of my training to become K'uhul Ahau of B'aakal. Humbly and respectfully I request your instructions."

"Ah-hah!" Pussy dribble sprayed from the decayed teeth of Demon of Pus. "Another ambitious Halach Uinik who thinks to master the realms of Xibalba. Foolish boy! You must pass two tests before you earn the right to learn from the Death Lords. Few manage to pass our tests; soon you will become food for our denizens. Ha-ha-ha-ha!"

His laughter tapered into throaty gurgles as he coughed and spat more pus.

"Give me the first test," said Pakal calmly.

Demon of Pus regarded the boy disdainfully.

"As you wish. First you must enter the Dark House. I will give you a burning torch and a cigar. You must return them both to me when I come, but they must be intact. Nothing must be consumed of either the torch or cigar. But you must keep them burning the entire time."

"Let us proceed," Pakal replied.

The pus dripping Lord led Pakal to a stone house with two narrow windows, placed him inside with a burning torch and a lit cigar, rolled a heavy slab to cover the entrance, and called from a distance: "Remember, nothing must be consumed but both must be kept lit. Here shall I stay, watching that the burning light glows through the window."

Pakal thought furiously about how to accomplish this task. Somehow, it seemed familiar, a story he vaguely recalled from early studies. Then he remembered that the Maya creation story of the Hero Twins included this test, and the Twins overcame it by getting help from fireflies and a macaw. Concentrating, he envisioned a swarm of fireflies and mentally called to them, and then did the same for a scarlet macaw. In a short time, the twinkling bodies of several fireflies appeared through the window on the side away from where the Death Lord waited. Pakal snuffed out the cigar and the fireflies clustered on its tip, keeping it glowing. The scarlet macaw appeared next, and Pakal smothered the torch under his sandal. The macaw clutched the torch shaft and waved its brilliant red tail feathers over the tip, looking exactly like wavering flames. Pakal held his insect and bird friends in deepest gratitude as they kept the glow shining through the window near the Death Lord.

Demon of Pus knocked at the door and began removing the slab. Pakal quickly released his assistants and they flew away. The torch and cigar were intact.

"Show me the torch and cigar!"

Pakal stepped through the door and held them up for inspection. The Death Lord gasped and howled angrily.

"How did you do this? The glow and flames were always present, these I saw!"

"This is the work of some magic that I know," Pakal replied.

Demon of Pus had to accept defeat.

"So be it. You have passed the first test, and now shall I conduct you across the River of Pus that you may encounter your next test."

He summoned a large owl that carried Pakal on its back to the other side of the river. There Pakal saw that the path continued, and he followed it to the next deep canyon where he saw flowing inside a river of blood. He waited, knowing another Death Lord would appear.

Before long a figure ambled slowly along the path toward Pakal. It had the usual Death Lord appearance of bony limbs, bare skull, and bloated belly. Its thin arms ended not in hands with fingers, but in long claws from which dripped steady streams of blood. Its headdress of red feathers and shredded organs sent bloody droplets flying when its head moved.

"Greetings, Lord Bloody Claws," said Pakal, bowing with left shoulder clasped.

"Arrgh! Know of you, do I. News travels fast in this realm. Upstart human, think you to defeat all the Lords of Death? Now comes your undoing. You will never pass my test." Bloody Claws grimaced at Pakal and flexed his dripping claws close to the boy's face. Pakal did not flinch but stared defiantly into bulging eyes with perpetual bloody tears dripping over bony cheeks.

"My test is the Jaguar House. It is packed with hungry jaguars, and they like nothing better than to crunch human bones and munch tasty flesh. Soon you will be turned into a bloody skeleton exactly as I am. Hah! Follow me to your death."

As they walked to the Jaguar House, Pakal formulated his plan. Only Baby Jaguar could stop his feline tribe from the slaughter. The boy knew Baby Jaguar was inside the cave, and focused upon the intuitive center between his eyebrows to mentally call his friend.

Please come! Come quickly, for I desperately need your help.

Bloody Claws approached the door into a large wooden structure, its tall poles ending in pointed tips. Growls and grunts increased as the jaguar herd rose and clustered near the door. Quickly opening the door, he pushed Pakal inside and slammed it closed. His eerie laughter trailed off into the distance.

Pakal faced about fifteen jaguars; all were thin and looking exceedingly hungry. The nearest jaguars crouched and prepared to spring at their prey. Pakal called again to Baby Jaguar and furiously hoped he would soon show up. Meanwhile, he must do something to ward off attack. Drawing his body to full height, Pakal slowly raised his arms and formed the hand sign for blessing, palms cupped and fingers together facing outward. Closing his eyes, he dropped quickly into his heart and invoked loving kindness. He emanated waves of compassion and gentleness, feeling deeply his oneness with these animals.

The jaguars sat back on haunches and blinked golden eyes at this strange creature. The lack of fear perplexed them. Some waved their heads side to side, as if to get better views. Some sniffed, seeking the sharp smell of terror but only finding the scent of a mammalian body. One large female found this flesh smell too delicious. Her hunger took over; she would eat this creature even if it were peaceful. She began warily stalking closer to Pakal and he sensed her intentions.

Baby Jaguar? he pleaded mentally.

Suddenly the little jaguar bounced over the posts carrying a large bundle. He dropped the cloth and from inside rolled out chunks of meat and juicy bones, enough to satisfy all the hungry jaguars. They pounced upon the feast, while Pakal joyfully embraced and thanked his friend. The sound of bones being crunched and flesh being chewed soon brought Bloody Claws back. As he opened the door, Baby Jaguar vanished.

"What is this? How can this be so? Arrgh! Arrgh!" exclaimed the Death Lord upon seeing Pakal standing unharmed by the door.

"This is the work of some magic that I know," Pakal said again.

"Who are you? No mere mortal can defeat Death Lords repeatedly."

"You know me. You know my destiny. This is not my time. I have much to accomplish in the Middleworld. Now I request what it is that I am to learn from Xibalba."

"Arrgh! You have learned it already. You have mastered fear of death. You have visited our realms and will return to your world. It is sufficient."

"No, there is something yet for me to experience here," Pakal said thoughtfully. He did not know where this idea came from, but felt its truth strongly.

"Well, then you may continue deeper into Xibalba to find what you seek."

Bloody Claws summoned the owl again, and it carried Pakal across the River of Blood, depositing him near the path that wandered into the distance. The boy continued walking and the terrain became swampy with tall reeds and lily pads. Frogs croaked and bats cried "eek-eek" as they flitted over the surface, seeking insects. An occasional evil-countenanced crocodile eyed Pakal hungrily, and the boy kept carefully to the raised path that now had water on both sides.

He did not know what he was seeking, but knew something waited. Feeling tired, he sat on a stump beside the path to rest. The water close by began rippling and churning, pushing lilies away to reveal the long scaly body of a serpent. Loops rose and fell, as large as a man's chest. With loud splashing and a fountain of spray, the snake lifted its huge fanged head from the swamp. It hovered close to Pakal, opening its jaws to display rows of sharp teeth and a flickering forked tongue.

Pakal recoiled instinctively but quickly managed his fear once again. He watched the snake with growing curiosity, for it appeared to be gagging and trying to extrude something from its throat. With a loud cough, the snake brought forth a human head between its jaws. The face appeared to be that of a middle-aged woman wearing regal jewelry and headdress. On her cheek was the Ik' sign for wind.

It was a Vision Serpent. Pakal knelt reverently and looked into the ancestor's eyes.

"Honored Elder, with great veneration do I bow before you," he said. "My name is K'inich Janaab Pakal, descended from the sacred Bahlam lineage of Lakam

Ha. Ixik Sak K'uk is my mother, now serving as ruler of our city by the auspices of our Progenitor Goddess Muwaan Mat."

"Of this know I well," the ancestor replied. "Do you not recognize me, Pakal? Ah, you were but a babe when my feet set upon the Underworld path. Look again; see the mother of Sak K'uk, your own grandmother."

"Holy Lady Yohl Ik'nal? Much blessed am I to be in your hallowed presence!"

"Much honored am I to be in your blessed presence, Sun-Faced One. You are the hope and future of our people. The Gods are much pleased with your accomplishments, and many more are anticipated. What you have achieved here in Xibalba exceed all expectations. My congratulations."

"Have you words to instruct or inform me? There remains much that I must learn."

"This will I tell you: remember the highest needs of all your people, humblest to greatest. Your world is changing, Pakal. The ways of rulers before you must also be changed. The shaping of society is in your hands. Include the common people in the spiritual practices that satisfy the Gods. Assist them to develop their own spiritual natures. Bring together talents from all ranks of society so each may contribute their best to re-creating Lakam Ha as the most advanced and glorious of Maya cities. Your powers are extensive, but you will need assistance from the meekest and least proud to accomplish your greatest challenge – rebuilding the portal to the Gods and ancestors."

Pakal listened intently and committed his grandmother's words to memory. He needed to review them and deeply ponder their import once back at home. Nodding in acknowledgement, he gave thanks.

"Accept my deepest gratitude for these words of guidance that I will take into my heart and carry out to my utmost ability."

"Of this I am certain," Yohl Ik'nal replied. "There is one other thing that I request of you. A woman who is my friend from times long ago, whom I met as a girl on a time-travel journey, a golden-haired stranger from a far-away place, has become trapped in Xibalba. She is not of our culture; she does not know our ways. Without powerful help, she will never escape the clutches of the Death Lords. I have tried to release her, but without success. My domain now is in the sky with the stars, but you have greater access to the Underworld. Will you help her?"

"With utmost pleasure, to serve you, will I seek to help release this woman. What is she called? How shall I find her?"

"The name by which I knew her is 'Elie.' She is somewhere here, in this swamp, wandering aimlessly. Her courage is nearly gone. You cannot imagine the importance of her release; it is both personal and for our family's future. Her soul must return to the Middleworld and find another expression in life."

The image of Yohl Ik'nal began to shimmer and grow transparent. The snake's slit eyes glowed and its tongue lashed back and forth. Pakal knew the vision was ending.

"Honored Grandmother, I vow to accomplish this task. Your appearance here is dear to my heart, something I shall always treasure. For you and for my family shall I release the woman Elie from Xibalba."

He bowed, crossing both arms over his chest in the gesture of highest respect as his ancestor's image disappeared into the snake's throat. Slowly the huge serpent sank into the murky waters.

Pakal resumed walking the raised path, looking across the vast swamps that stretched into the misty distance. He listened for a woman's voice but heard only insects buzzing, water dripping, and a few frogs. Lizards skittered across the path and an annoyed scorpion lifted claws and tail to threaten him. Though he kept alert for more Death Lords, the fearsome Underworld rulers made no further appearances. He began to worry about time, although it seemed insignificant in this timeless domain. Remembering Pasah Chan's instructions, he attuned his intuition to the sun's trajectory across the sky and realized it was hovering not far above the western horizon. There was little time left before the cave mouth re-opened to allow his exit.

Far away, the glint of something shiny and golden caught his eye. Quickening his pace, he reached the nearest point on the path and saw corn-silk colored hair fanning out on the water's surface. Was this the woman, and was she dead? The irony of that thought caused Pakal to chuckle; of course she was dead here in the Underworld realm. He marveled at the mystery of life after death, and the continuance of consciousness and form in Xibalba. Hearing a sound, the woman turned to face him, standing neck deep in the swamps. She looked terrified and dazed, staring with wide eyes sunken deep into her thin, pale face.

He raised a hand in greeting and spoke in soft, reassuring tones: "Be not fearful, I have come to help you."

She only appeared more confused and backed away. He realized she did not know his language, so tried communicating only with thoughts. This was more effective and after a few trials, they understood each other.

Are you called Elie?

She nodded.

Allow me to help you. I am Pakal, grandson of Yohl Ik'nal. Do you remember her?

More nodding and a spark of recognition in her eyes were encouraging.

Can you leave the water? I will come and bring you out. Then I will help you leave this dreadful place.

He felt her flood of gratitude and realized she was caught in an underwater bog. Entering the water, he pushed through lily roots and rushes, carefully placing his feet on places where the bottom felt firm. When his feet felt squishy mud beneath, he was close enough to reach out an arm for her to grasp. Hesitantly she stretched out her arm until their fingers met. He smiled encouragingly and gently grasped her hand. Pulling while slowly backing up, he freed her from the bog and brought her to the path.

She sat trembling, drenched and naked. Her body was almost emaciated and ghastly white, the skin wrinkled and loose. Pakal unwound his waistband and draped it around her, leaving only his short loincloth. He wanted to comfort her and warm her in his arms, but realized this might frighten her more. Tears streamed down her face and she managed a wan smile of thanks.

How came you here? he asked mentally.

Images formed in her mind of strange lands and people, immense seas and huge boats that seemed to have trees standing upon their decks. She and several men appeared in unusual clothing, climbing through dense jungles to arrive at tall stone structures half-covered with vegetation, their stairs and roofs in crumbling disarray. With shock that stabbed his heart, Pakal realized this ruined city was his home, Lakam Ha. Quickly he contained his emotions, for little time remained and he could not explore the meanings now. Re-focusing on her imagery, he saw her arguing with one man, being shoved and thrown to the floor, slapped around viciously. Then there was another trek through jungles, this time with a different man who was dark-skinned and had Mayan features. Next, she was being fed and comforted in a plaster-walled hut, very similar to those the village people used in his city. Elie and the Maya man embraced, Pakal realized they were together as a pair. Rapid flashes of village life followed: cooking, tending children and gardens, evening walks along a forested path to maize fields and orchards.

What happened? he queried.

She tried to form words but failed, sending images to him again. The villagers never completely accepted the strange pale women, although she worked hard and tried to learn their customs. The angry man and his companions departed and returned to their land far away. The village shaman distrusted her and became an enemy, refusing to teach her Mayan spiritual practices. When her Maya husband died, his family helped with the children and provided sustenance. But when she became ill, the shaman would not attend and forbade village healers to assist her. Soon she died, unaware of how to make transitions into the spirit realm. She knew this was necessary for Mayas, but had no training. Finding herself in the terrifying Xibalba realm, she had passed miserable times and suffered much from the vile Death Lords.

Be comforted, he communicated. *Here I am to help you. But time is short and I must leave soon. I will teach you this incantation to our Father Sun, K'in Ahau. By his shining power and radiant strength, you will be freed from the Underworld. You must chant it without ceasing, over and over. Never let it leave your mind. When I am back in the Middleworld, I will do this incantation for you at sunrise and sunset, until I know you are free.*

She nodded, a tiny spark of hope lighting her sky blue eyes as Pakal continued.

You must memorize the Mayan words and chant them. The Sun Lord does not speak your language, so you must use the sounds he understands. Listen and repeat with me until you commit this incantation to memory:

"Ahau K'in, ubah ten okotba	Lord Sun, hear my call
Yubte ten thanoklal tah ten okotba	Give me help when I call
Chaab ten a-eex saasil	Bring unto me your light
Tul ten yetel a-eex uchucil	Fill me with your might
Uchebal ten tulpach ti yokolcab.	In order that I may return to life on earth."

They chanted in unison, voices blending softly in the watery vastness of Underworld swamps and caverns. Pakal felt a quiver around his heart and realized the sun was setting. The moments for escape were upon him and he could delay no more. Quickly he summoned the owl that was his transport and heard large wings flapping nearby.

Elie, I must leave now. You will be safe; you will be able to return to life in the Middleworld. Keep on chanting without end, believe and trust Ahau K'in. Farewell.

Pakal leapt onto the owl's back and urged it to speed toward the cave opening. Faintly he heard the voice of Pasah Chan calling him to return, not with his ears but with intuition. *Hurry, hurry!* The priest kept repeating. Wings flapping madly, the owl soared over the canyons, the River of Blood and the River of Pus. It swooped into the tunnel and ascended steeply. Golden sunlight sent shafts through the cave opening, tingeing the walls with rosy hues that dimmed rapidly.

Pakal jumped off the owl, gave quick thanks and ran through the cave mouth just before its rocky teeth crunched down.

2

The sun reached perfect measure with the moon, day and night of equal length at the fall equinox. Slowly the sun's path traveled southward as the days shortened and the season of rain intensified. Whether the sun rose and set in clear skies, or hid behind tumbling clouds or pounding rain, Pakal stood outside with arms uplifted, chanting the incantation he taught the strange woman Elie. Twice daily he chanted, holding an aura of protection around her, and envisioning her being released from Xibalba.

One morning as the time of greatest darkness approached, he began the chant but spontaneously stopped. Alert to every nuance emanating from K'in Ahau, he sensed that something was different. Opening his eyes into slits, he squinted at the first brilliant rays of sunlight streaming through layered clouds to the east. Before the question could form in his mind, the answer was there. Elie was freed from the Underworld. Bowing with both arms folded across his chest, Pakal gave profound thanks to the Sun Lord, bringer of life anew upon the earth.

Although Pakal attempted to discover where the woman's soul might have re-appeared, he could get no clear image. The only sense of location he could get was that her feet again touched the earth not far from where he stood. She returned to the lands of the Maya. That triggered the image he had seen while in Xibalba, the heart-rending vision of his city in ruins. It evoked strong emotions, too strong for him to effectively seek intuitive answers.

Perhaps his mother could help him reach some understanding. She must have heard stories from his grandmother about this strange woman.

When next visiting Sak K'uk, Pakal pursued information about Elie after their usual greetings and embraces.

"When you were a girl, did your mother, Honored Ancestor Yohl Ik'nal, tell you about her visions and journeys?"

"That she did, on many occasions," Sak K'uk replied. "Most seemed so odd to me that I could not understand. She went to exotic places and interacted with many deities."

"Did she ever mention a woman, maybe it was a young girl, named Elie?"

"Hmmm, not that I can recall. So many years and events have passed; I rarely visit these childhood memories. That is an unusual name."

"She comes from foreign people, I believe," said Pakal. "From somewhere far away."

"Why are you asking this? How did you learn of her and what is the connection with my mother?" Sak K'uk was now thoroughly perplexed.

"You will recall my journey into the Underworld required by Pasah Chan, some moons ago."

"Indeed, for I was much worried, and thankful for your safe return."

"While inside the caverns and swamps of Xibalba, after the tests and meeting with Yohl Ik'nal through the Vision Serpent, which I described to you, I had another experience that I was not yet ready to discuss. It involved fulfilling a request my grandmother made of me, and I could not mention it until it was completed. Recently I did complete it."

"And this request involved the woman Elie?" Sak K'uk had a quick mind.

"Just so. My grandmother said Elie was her friend, a golden-haired woman from a distant place who became trapped in Xibalba. Grandmother asked me to help Elie escape the clutches of the Death Lords, saying it was of great importance to our family. And something else appeared during the time I was helping Elie . . . I saw our city nearly covered by jungle, in ruins and being explored by Elie's companions, who were angry and violent men seeking treasures."

Sak K'uk frowned, concentrating. She dredged up faint recollections of stories her mother told, flitting impressions that she could not decipher.

"I remember once my mother tried to explain a visionary experience that showed the future of our people, and how the immense cycles of the calendar worked. She talked about rising and falling of cultures, but it was too complicated for my young mind."

Sak K'uk sighed, giving the hand signal of regret.

"Much do I wish that I had listened more carefully, learned more from my mother about visioning."

"But you do not recall any mention of the golden-haired girl?"

"No, my dearest. To my dismay, for I see it holds significance, I cannot recall anything."

Time was once again much on Pakal's mind. Since the Katun 9 ceremonies, K'in Ahau had completed two journeys from north to south, two full seasonal cycles. The passage of two tuns brought changes in both his body and mind. With the approach of his twelfth tun, Pakal had grown noticeably taller, his body well muscled from physical training, and his face assuming mature proportions with a prominent straight-bridged nose that swept in a clean line from tip to elongated forehead. His long oval face had high cheekbones, arched brows over tilted almond eyes, and sculpted lips offering a sensitive expression. Immersion in esoteric sciences expanded his inquisitive mind and created a thoughtful quality in his manner. Constant awareness of his ba-ch'ok status and the heavy responsibilities that accompanied it, as well as the expectations placed upon him to repair the city and renew links with the deities, gave him a solemn character.

The attainment of 12 tuns not only signaled his accession to rulership, but also his transformation from childhood into early adulthood. Another 6 tuns were needed for full adulthood; although many young people assumed adult responsibilities, married, and began families before then. The signs of a maturing body, of developing manhood, were evident and Pakal was instructed in management of sexual energy. Pasah Chan taught him the spiritual meanings and techniques for directing this powerful force.

"Sexuality is a very important tool of spiritual development. Sexual acts have procreative and recreational ends, but the greatest purpose is sacred union—more valuable than jade, more exquisite than cacao, and sweeter than ripe figs. All creatures of earth, air and water, the fruit and flowers, exchange masculine and feminine energies. The subtlest exchange, however, is between humans and the divine, and this requires spiritual contemplation and practices.

"First, you must learn to sublimate your sexual impulses and use their power to boil the vapors within your body that propel spiritual expansion. This mix of desire, sexuality, and breath creates the water and fire of these vapors. Take the principles you have mastered for movement of Ik'—wind breath to control your mind, physical posture, and respiration. Apply these now to the surges of sexuality moving through your being; bring this intense energy deep into your core and channel it upward along the spine to the center of spiritual awareness between your brows. Then will you experience the ecstatic explosion into sacred union.

"The woman is earth, is sweet, is cold, and is night. The man is sky, is fire, is heat, and is day. The two together create a vaporous force that awakens the Plumed Serpent to climb the central column of the body and open its energetic centers to the fullest, until both attain the cosmic realm and know the infinite. Thus can you fully participate in the game of life and the miracle of creation.

"The lower centers along the spine have masculine nature, are filled with heat and fire, have to do with control, force, and sexual drive. The upper centers are feminine and have to do with love, compassion, self-transcendence, and spirituality. Dark shamans work with the lower centers and evoke their powers for harm or manipulation. Mystics work with the upper centers, but may be unable to accomplish practical worldly things. A real human, Halach Uinik, must master both lower and upper forces. True mystical guidance must be grounded in the earth, or it takes flight into mere imagination. Your accomplishments as a child in applying subtle energies have been impressive. Now your real work begins. You must become master of your body and mind, to serve your higher divine nature."

Pakal listened to his mentor with avid interest. He recently began experiencing sexual urges, a mixture of intense surges of pleasure and disturbing agitation. The new things his body seemed capable of doing, particularly his genitals, made him bemused and eager. Pasah Chan was still a young man, and had married shortly before the Kan attack. Pakal was curious.

"Yum Ah K'in," he said, using the honorific title Yum—Master, "have these things been your experience since you married?"

Pasah Chan tilted his head and eyed Pakal warily. The boy was nothing if not clever in probing for the information he sought.

"To some degree, yes," the priest replied. "Mastery of sexual energy is a lengthy process. The innate skill and depth of insight possessed by the woman is the key. Of this will I speak next."

"Women must also learn control of sexual forces?"

"Indeed. In particular those women who will unite with rulers and ahauob leaders. These are ancient arts but sadly overlooked among many families."

"With all respect, Master, was your esteemed wife so trained?"

Pasah Chan hoped the slight flush he felt spreading across his face did not show.

"Not well-trained," he admitted, quickly shifting focus back on Pakal.

"The woman chosen in the future as your wife must have outstanding training," he said. "Your destiny calls for a consort whose ability to apply esoteric sexual techniques can match those you will develop. Where to find such a woman I do not yet know. Such training in Lakam Ha has lost favor among noble families. We shall search when the time comes."

"When will be that time?" Pakal asked with more eagerness than pleased his teacher.

"Not for many tuns," the priest replied sternly. "Great care must be taken, and you need time to perfect your abilities and assume your rulership responsibilities. Let such questions fall from your mind, Pakal. You have much to accomplish."

Pakal lowered his eyelids and accepted the reprimand.

Pasah Chan continued on a cautionary note.

"Many women will look at you with eyes of desire, and you can choose to have them because of who you are. But you should choose not to have them, because of who you are. Your mission in life is ultimate service to your people. Your life is not your own, it belongs to the B'aakal lineage. It belongs to the deities from whom you are descended. Those in the most powerful positions have the greatest obligations, the grandest opportunities, and the most profound risk. Your people's destiny rests upon your shoulders; you may take it to new heights or plunge it into abysmal depths. For you—for rulers—the dangers to overcome arise from selfishness, greed, pride, and sensuality. Each danger has its snares that will entrap your spirit and cloud your mind.

"To avoid the snares of the sexual drive, you must master its forces and move them according to your intention. For this, you will need knowledge and experience. The first I can provide, the second a special Lunar Priestess will give at the appropriate time. She will teach you to manage your sexual energy using the force most powerful upon the earth—the feminine essence. Woman is a gift of Hun Ahb Ku to men, and is considerably stronger on the spiritual and energetic level than men. When male and female sexual energies combine in sacred ways, immense creative forces are produced. The Lunar Priestess will give you techniques for shaping sexual intentions and focusing sexual forces. But not until you are united with the woman chosen as your royal consort, who is also well-trained and carries the correct bloodlines for your dynasty, will the fullness of this potential be realized.

"Until then, practice as I am teaching you with breath, meditation, physical postures, and mental focus. Do not allow your mind or body to run away with you. Discipline is essential every moment. Apply the enormous will that you possess, and you shall successfully become master of yourself, as well as of vast knowledge, wisdom, and power."

Another aspect of time engulfed Pakal while studying the dynastic history of B'aakal. He memorized the lengthy recitation of origins tracing back to Muwaan Mat in the celestial realm, and the names and ruling dates of all his human predecessors from K'uk Bahlam. This story would be told during his accession ceremony, as it had been told by all designated as carrier of the royal bloodline. He reflected upon the character and qualities of each ruler, their accomplishments and building programs. He imagined how Lakam Ha appeared during the different time periods, and how the Lords of the Katuns influenced the city's fortunes.

During one meditation about the Bahlam dynasty, he slipped into a spontaneous vision. On a cloud-enshrouded mountain, several gentle hills surrounded a valley that cupped a small lake. Tall reeds grew along the shore, their narrow spires waving in soft breezes. Among the reeds, long-legged herons speared the shallow waters with pointed beaks. Clusters of green-backed ducks swam while numerous dark cormorants swooped and dove into the water. The forests beyond the lake were full of colorful red and blue macaws, magnificent iridescent quetzals, doves, owls, and sparrows. Howler monkeys cavorted in treetops. On the forest floor walked deer, peccary, coati, and jaguars. Across the grassy hills near the lake, several snakes, turtles, and lizards slithered.

The creatures began to form a procession, led by a jaguar with a quetzal perched on its back. Other strange combinations included a ghost-like figure, a howler monkey grasping the long tail of a white coati, an open-mouth turtle with a macaw on its carapace, a snake twining around the neck of a peccary, a jaguar with a snake coiled on its back, a wind blowing from the north, a cormorant wearing a heart pendant, and a hawk-cormorant paired with a white quetzal.

The creature combinations morphed into the forms of Maya men and women in royal regalia. They bore the countenances of the succession of B'aakal rulers, and Pakal recognized them from portraits in codices and from their animal symbols. He recounted their names.

K'uk Bahlam I—Quetzal Jaguar
Caspar—Ghost
Butzaj Sak Chiik—Howler Monkey White Coati
Ahkal Mo Nab I—Open Mouth Turtle Macaw
Kan Joy Chitam—Snake Binds Peccary
Ahkal Mo Nab II—Open Mouth Turtle Macaw
Kan Bahlam I—Snake Jaguar
Yohl Ik'nal—Heart of North Wind
Aj Ne Ohl Mat—Heart Cormorant
Muwaan Mat—Duck Hawk-Cormorant
Sak K'uk—White Quetzal

When the White Quetzal—Sak K'uk had passed, a brilliant sun face appeared on a shield. Pakal recognized himself in the progression of rulers: K'inich Janaab Pakal—Sun-Faced Lord Shield. After this, there followed what appeared mostly a reverse order of creature combinations, but with less distinct appearance to later rulers. Most of these rulers had an added "sun faced" to their names.

K'inich Kan Bahlam II—Sun-Faced Snake Jaguar
K'inich Kan Joy Chitam II—Sun-Faced Snake Binds Peccary
K'inich Ahkal Mo Nab III—Sun-Faced Open Mouth Turtle Macaw
U Pakal K'inich—His Shield Sun-Faced
K'inich Kan Bahlam III—Sun-Faced Snake Jaguar
K'inich K'uk Bahlam II—Sun-Faced Quetzal Jaguar
Wak Kimi Janaab Pakal II—Six Death Lord Shield

When K'inich K'uk Bahlam II—Sun-Faced Quetzal Jaguar passed, darkness began falling over the hills and lake. Mists from the high mountains thickened and swirled around, dissolving the creatures. One final apparition lingered among the mists, the face of Six Death Lord upon a shield. Then the scene faded into total darkness, complete emptiness, and chiasmic nothingness.

Tears streamed down Pakal's face as he returned to waking consciousness. His heart felt wrenched by a sorrow so profound he thought it might cease beating. Confused and distraught, he searched for meaning in this dynastic parade through past and future time. Nothing made sense to him; he needed someone with deeper insight to interpret this vision. At once he thought of his mother, Sak K'uk.

She had slowly changed since becoming the earthly vessel of the Primordial Mother Goddess. Now she seemed distant, less involved in his activities, and preoccupied with her duties as K'uhul Ahau. Although he reasoned this was to be expected, emotionally he felt the loss of her closeness. His own training took him away for uinals at a time, and they had not visited for over two moons. Knowing her many obligations, he sent ahead by messenger to request an audience.

He arrived at her small reception chamber in the palace with both anticipation and trepidation. The dynastic procession vision haunted his mind, and he reached the conclusion that he was the "central sun" of his dynasty. This imagery emerged from the brilliant sun faces linked with the rulers following him.

When they met, Sak K'uk embraced Pakal warmly but her eyes remained remote. Settling down on mats, they exchanged small updates before she inquired about the purpose of her son's visit. He described the vision in complete detail, every nuance of and color and image, every shadow of light and sense of setting. Her eyes became bright with focus as she listened, her mind no longer partly distracted with other thoughts. She nodded a few times as he spoke, making hand signs for understanding.

Pakal finished with his sense of being the "central sun" and of the dynasty that faded away into non-existence at the end. Once again he choked with emotion but kept it under control with breath and determination.

"What you have seen is indeed prophetic," said Sak K'uk. "The Gods have chosen to reveal difficult things to one so young. This vision takes place in Toktan, the place where our dynasty began in the confluence of the Upperworld and Middleworld. As with everything in life, our dynasty has its cycle of beginning and ending. You have been shown what is to follow, the sequence taking our people toward the cycle closing. It is destined that those so named will be our rulers in the reverse order of our ascension."

"Is such destiny then unalterable? Did not the Gods give us, as Halach Uinik, the rights of making choices that can shape our future?"

"We can affect how the future unfolds through choices we make now, and choices that have been made in the past," his mother replied. "But we cannot alter the broad strokes of destiny, or the patterns set into the stones of the katuns. These things will play out, for they are woven into the fabric of the cosmos as it is reflected in our realm, the Middleworld. How we anticipate, how we deal with and adapt to these patterns is within the domain of our choices. Lord Time, *Ahau Kinh,* is the primary reality, divine and limitless. *Ahau Kinh* embraces all cycles, all solar and cosmic ages. There is no beginning and ending, only cycles upon cycles that continue and repeat and circle into the immemorial past and the infinite future, until it curves back into itself and we understand that all time is one. Nothing is lost and nothing is new, only the surface of appearances changes."

Pakal shook his head, confused.

"Honored Mother, this is too abstract for me. I am seeing the end of my entire world, the dissipation of everything I hold valuable, the erasing of my life purpose. If all is to end, why should we continue to make efforts? It all seems useless to me."

"Your life here is but a small sliver of your eternal existence," said Sak K'uk, gently laying her hand upon Pakal's arm. "Here we live in the world of space, but it is only another aspect of time. Time and space are the same primordial reality, time is the spatial measure of our everyday life, it shows how the sun is maker of the day, how stars are directors of celestial cycles, how the Witz Monster opens inner earth, the squaring and measuring of earth, the Quadripartite Gods who support the pillars of the sky. Every city reflects the cosmos above and the cycles of stellar movements. Our lives fulfill our destiny given by endless time, played out in earthly space, to be consummated in the immortal universe."

"And then we return to the stars," Pakal reflected. "We become ancestors and shine in the night sky, to give wisdom and guidance to those still walking in earth space."

"You have said it truly. This is the grand cycle of life. The spatial world exists, changes, dies, and is reborn in each Sun—Age. This is the consequence of the actions of the Gods whose countenances are time. Space is not static. It changes like colors change with the daily passage of K'in Ahau. Space and our lives on earth exist as the handiwork of the Gods, and have in themselves divine meanings. We ourselves are embodied time and are always changing throughout our lives. Without time cycles there is no life, nothing happens, even death. The primeval darkness would return, devoid of all meaning. So we must live our lives in this time-space reality and understand that everything is both fleeting and significant."

"Even if our dynasty were no more," Pakal began, "our people no more, our cities abandoned and lost into ruin, you say we would still exist in the great time-space cycles? We would still make our ancestral wisdom and guidance available to others?" This idea made Pakal a bit more hopeful.

"This do I believe, Pakal. Nothing is ever truly lost. The essence of being never dies. What is required for this earth-walk is to fulfill our life path with courage and creativity. To accomplish the destiny the Gods have given us, and to do it as completely and artistically as we can."

Pakal's face was brighter, and this brought gladness to Sak K'uk's heart. Her deep love for her son had not diminished, although responsibilities kept her away more than she wished. She was saddened by the burden he already bore but knew it could not be averted or lessened.

"You remember our talk about visions of your grandmother Yohl Ik'nal that I had trouble recalling? Much have I thought on these, and now memories have awakened. She also had a vision about the future of the Maya people that frightened and dismayed her. She foresaw immense changes for our people and cities, with dispersion of populations and changes of customs. Our great civilization appeared lost, the people fallen into ignominious conditions, the cities lying in ruin among jungle vines and trees. But, yet to come is another cycle in which our greatness will be rediscovered. Foreign people of many lands will come to study and learn; to marvel and appreciate what the Mayas accomplished. Much is written upon the face of time and space that we now cannot read, but that comes to fruition as the cycles unfold."

"Then what lies before me to do, my destiny as ruler of our people, does matter," Pakal reflected.

"Yes, it matters greatly," Sak K'uk reassured him. "It will shape Lakam Ha, the B'aakal polity, and the lives of our people now. It will leave a legacy for future people, both Mayas and foreigners that will affect their worlds. You are here in the space-time reality of earth and you cannot avoid taking actions. Even not making decisions or choices is taking an action. All actions have consequences, and your actions have larger influences than most. So you must act, my son, even when your heart aches under the burden of your knowledge."

Pakal nodded, for he immediately grasped the truth of his mother's words. His destiny would have its way; he could not avoid actions, so he must make those choices that brought the noblest outcome.

4

The day of Pakal's accession was at hand. He had passed twelve tuns, stood half a head taller than his mother, and matched his father's height. He had undergone the transformation rites moving him from childhood into adolescence a short time before. Time signatures of calendars and cycles of wandering stars figured prominently in determining the date of accession.

Chak Ek (Mars) was already linked with Pakal during his hoof-binding ceremony. This harbinger of rain and bringer of watery itz formed an important symbol of the ruler's capacity to bring fertility to the land and sustenance to crops. Pakal's accession was timed to the planet's first stationary point in its 780-day cycle. The interval between its conjunction with the sun and first stationary point was 352 days, close to the 360-day Haab calendar cycle. After that point, it moved retrograde for 75 days, and then reached its second stationary point from which it traveled another 352 days until sun conjunction.

The combined symbols of rain bringing, crop nourishing, and two Haab agricultural cycles firmly established Pakal in the role of Yum K'ax, the young maize god. All Maya rulers had deep associations with sprouting corn stalks, and the God's youthful face framed by foliated and tasseled imagery attested to the powers of renewal, both of plant growth and human life.

Another important wandering star entered the timing of Pakal's accession. Yaax Ek (Jupiter) was in conjunction with the sun. This large stellar body was associated with the deity of royal lineage, K'awiil, who also embodied rulership, lightning, and thunder. He was frequently depicted with a snake foot and mirror on his forehead, or emerging from the jaws of a double-headed serpent sky bar that Maya rulers used as a royal insignia. Yaax Ek was linked to katun endings, and his head was the insignia of Katun Lords who were usually depicted seated on sky-band thrones. Presenting the head of Yaax Ek to the new ruler in katun ceremonies or during accession rites signified the passing on of the royal lineage. When Yaax Ek was conjoined with K'in Ahau—Sun Lord, the two most powerful symbols of rulership merged. Selecting this day for Pakal's accession was a potent declaration of his right to rulership.

The ceremony followed the model used for Muwaan Mat, except that Pakal wore minimal regalia when he was borne by the palanquin around the palace main plaza. The palanquin was decorated with symbolism of Chak Ek and Yaax Ek, along with foliated maize stalks. Pakal was adorned with a simple headdress that held a forelock of hair over his forehead and a ponytail behind, with water lily and flower motifs. Around his neck and over his bare chest hung a large jade pectoral with an Ik' symbol carved in the center, and in his earlobes were heavy jade ear pendants. Wrist cuffs of grooved bronze had jangling disks and beads. His loincloth was white trimmed by a red border and waistband, and his feet were bare.

The simplicity of Pakal's regalia emphasized his youthful freshness and the newness of rebirth. The bright midsummer's day was graced by wispy clouds overhead and a soft, cooling breeze. The birds seemed to sing more sweetly as he lithely ascended the palace stairs to the throne chamber, accompanied by a slow single drumbeat. Following enunciations by the High Priest and Priestess stating his lineage and rightful position in accession, he entered the chamber and sat upon the double-headed jaguar throne.

Sak K'uk was seated on a mat next to the throne where she awaited his entry. In the side chambers stood his father Kan Mo' Hix and his grandfather Yaxun Xul, along with many elite ahauob and warriors. Only his mother was in the throne room, not clad in Muwaan Mat's regalia but wearing the classic costume of royal women: a cape and skirt in the woven mat pattern over a white huipil, with embroidered fringes and waistband, wrist cuffs matching Pakal's. Her feet were bare feet, and she wore a small headdress of ancestor faces with white cloth flaps hanging behind. She ceremoniously lifted a large "drum-major" headdress, its tall dome decorated with four rows of round silver discs with obsidian dots in the center. The headdress was lined top and bottom by a row of thin, square white stones, and the Sun God's face was set in front above the stones. Several long quetzal tail feathers soared above two rows of green leaves.

This headdress was associated with sacred battle on several levels. It signified the struggle each person was fated to have with his or her own baser nature in order to ascend to higher levels of consciousness, and expand that animal nature into the divine essence of all true humans. In addition, the headdress implied battle with forces of disruption and decay that inevitably confronted human society. Political and economic systems needed to be surmounted and subdued to serve the people's well-being. Lastly, sacred battle on the physical level often was necessary to defend one's city against oppression and exploitation by bellicose neighbors.

Pakal first removed his simple headdress and tied on his forehead the white headband of rulership. This symbolic act had been passed down from ruler to ruler since the dynasty began. In primordial times, Muwaan Mat was the first in the lineage to tie on the white headband, and it had become the ultimate symbol of assuming rulership in B'aakal. With this gesture, Pakal was tied into the rulership, *hok'ah ti ahaulel*. He then took the "drum-major" headdress from Sak K'uk and placed it securely on his elongated skull.

Two and a half katuns later, Pakal would have this scene immortalized in a lovely sculpted panel that adorned the back wall of his new Sak Nuk Nah. This panel was called "The Oval Palace Tablet" by scientists who later visited the ruins of Lakam Ha. The date of Pakal's accession was commemorated in stone glyphs at several locations in the city.

Baktun 9, Katun 9, Tun 2, Uinal 4, Kin 8, on the date 5 Lamat 1 Mol (July 29, 615 CE).

The High Priest approached and handed Pakal the white jade K'awiil scepter. Taking the scepter in his right hand, Pakal lifted it that all below might see. He twisted his body to face the plaza and made scattering gestures with his left hand.

Throaty cheers arose from the crowd gathered in the plaza, followed by several rounds of chanting their new ruler's name and title.

"K'inich Janaab Pakal, K'uhul B'aakal Ahau!"

Pakal stood and moved regally to the edge of the palace platform. Standing between tall censers, carved with faces of K'in Ahau and Yum K'ax, he recited his dynasty's long history and retold the story of their people's creation, as his grandmother Yohl Ik'nal had done in the same place nearly a katun and a half ago. Lazy, fragrant smoke curled upward from censers, perfuming the hot, still air in the plaza. The people of Lakam Ha stood silently, rapt in the tale so beloved by all, the lilting cadences of Pakal's strong young voice carrying them into the intoxication of trance.

Later most people indulged in more worldly inebriation during the feasting that lasted well into the night. Balche flowed freely and washed down savory stews of deer and peccary, simmered with squash and tomatoes, fragrant with spices of coriander, oregano, annatto and chile. Music and dance, conversation and story-telling filled their celebratory evening as the people of Lakam Ha rejoiced, for their royal dynasty continued in the inspiring form of this exceptional young ahau, who brought promise of a bright future.

SAK K'UK—V

BAKTUN 9 KATUN 9 TUN 5— BAKTUN 9 KATUN 9 TUN 8 (618—621 CE)

1

THE YOUNG ARCHITECT stepped back from his model for a critical look. Slowly circling the table, he examined it from every angle making certain he had considered horizontal and vertical gravity loading in the design. He checked the model against drawings sketched on bark paper demonstrating the actual dimensions and heights of the structure. Once again he re-calculated the mathematics of gravity resistance by the axial forces generated by the compression and tension members of the structural design. All seemed in order. The structure should stand solidly and resist natural stresses from wind and seismic effects.

Yax Chan recalled his conversations with K'inich Janaab Pakal, K'uhul B'aakal Ahau, leading to this exploration of new construction design. Pakal had dreams of building extensive new structures in Lakam Ha, as well as repairing and improving the older temples damaged in the Kan attack. The young ruler's overall intention was to have taller temples and buildings with loftier roofs, higher arches, and wider chambers. This posed an architectural challenge and spurred Yax Chan into a flurry of creative thinking. What techniques of building would permit higher arches capable of supporting chambers with wider roofs?

Maya buildings were constructed of cut masonry stone blocks using native limestone that had great compressive strength. Ancient technicians had invented the process of making hydraulic cement using a firing kiln far in the past, over two baktuns ago (around 300 BCE). The kiln was an assembly of self-consuming timber fuel in a geometric shape that induced very high temperatures by drawing oxygen rich air from below the wood into a central shaft. Small limestone blocks sat on top of the woodpile, and the extreme heat changed their chemical composition. These were allowed to cool and be exposed to dew and rain, which expanded the stones into a dome of fluffy white powder several times the original bulk. This substance, hydraulic cement, was collected and ground into a fine powder. The powder was later mixed with water, loosely ground limestone, and aggregate pebbles to create cast-in-place concrete. This concrete was used as mortar for stonework and pavements, and to make stucco for plastering both exterior and interior walls of buildings.

Residential buildings had rectangular chambers with straight walls and often had multiple stories. Palaces were larger with more rooms and interspersed patios; some chambers were residential and others for administration and reception purposes. Pyramids usually were constructed in stages, growing in size and height over time. Most did not contain functional interior spaces but were a mass of stone and fill material, such as compacted clay, rubble, and broken pottery. The exterior façade was made of composite stone and concrete encapsulating the interior mass, stepped upward in three to nine levels, and terminating in a temple platform accessed by staircases leading from the ground to the top. When an existing pyramid was enlarged by later construction, a series of retaining walls were used to confine the new fill material, built just inside the perimeter of the new exterior. A new exterior skin was then applied, decorated, and painted.

The key structural element that concerned Yax Chan was the arch that supported the chamber roofs, whether in pyramids, palaces, or residences. This was the limiting factor in both the height and width of rooms. The huge gravitational pressures of building with stone required construction design that guaranteed adequate support. The Maya used a design called the corbelled arch. It was formed by stair-stepping successive blocks of masonry stone from the spring line, the point where the arch began, and moving upward. Adding one block that protruded outward a little further than the one below formed an upside-down stair, and gradually brought the wall of the chamber inward and upward, until the two sides met in the center of the ceiling where a capstone was placed.

The vault created by this corbelled arch assumed an upward pointing wedge. It was not a true rounded arch and used different force dynamics to support the load of the ceiling. It required thick walls and an abutment to counteract the horizontal stresses generated by this gravity load. The chamber could neither be very wide nor tall. To meet Pakal's requirements for new buildings, a different arch structure was needed.

An innovative arch structure was the subject of Yax Chan's model. He had pondered the mechanical and gravitational forces involved, had made calculations and consulted other architects, and had arrived at an ingenious idea. By adding a high strength timber thrust beam, he could both raise the ceiling and thin the walls. This created a trapezoidal linear truss of great stability and strength. Due to its trapezoidal structure, this arch resisted large gravity loads through pure compression and tension members. Placing the timber thrust beam at the spring line of the arch, a tall ceiling wall could be angled inward to meet the opposite ceiling wall at the capstone.

The model chamber began at the foundation, its walls lined with stone masonry and filled with cast-in-place concrete. When the height for beginning the arch was reached and the concrete had hardened, the timber thrust beam was placed to span the two walls and inserted deep into the walls. The exterior wall continued straight upward, while the interior began its inward angle using pinion shaped stones carved to form a smooth slope where their faces met. Concrete was put inside after the placement of several pinion stones, and allowed to harden. This process continued until the interior walls were close enough to place the capstone. The interior walls thus formed a smooth ceiling that later was covered with plaster. If an especially tall arch was desired, a second timber thrust beam could be inserted some distance above the first.

Timber with long-term resistance to insects and degradation, with dense fibers of high strength, was readily available in such trees as the zapote and mahogany. The tensile strength was similar to low-grade steel and many beams continued to hold ceilings in place long after the Maya no longer occupied their great cities. Although Yax Chan could not imagine this distant future, his goal was to engineer a structural spanning system for permanency, as well as one with inherent strength capable of resisting large levels of vertical and lateral gravity loading. This he believed he had accomplished.

With both anticipation and concern, Yax Chan revealed to Pakal his model chamber with its innovative trapezoidal linear timber truss. Even in its small size, Pakal could see that the proportions created a sense of harmony. The slender walls and smoothly angled interior ceiling were elegant, and the greater width brought spaciousness to the chamber. Yax Chan explained the principles used in creating the trapezoid.

"This is excellent, Yax Chan," Pakal said as he circled the model. "It is clever to use a thrust beam to give more strength and stability. How did you think of this?"

"After much time visualizing corbelled arches, I kept seeing the shape of a triangle," Yax Chan replied. "I imagined the triangle getting larger and larger, but soon the ceiling would collapse. After watching many ceilings fall in my mind, it occurred to me that adding something to support the walls might help hold them up. This idea led to the thrust beam."

"Remarkable. We already use hard wood timber for door lintels, and these timbers are known to last for baktuns."

"Just so. The strength of the hard wood is not much less than stone."

"Your use of pinion stones is also fascinating. Why this did not occur to our builders before is strange, for they have long used pinions in wall and bridge structures," Pakal observed.

"Yes, to achieve a resistant yet smooth façade. Then plaster can be applied and painted, or carved panels can be attached. I wondered too why no builders have used pinion stones to create interior chamber ceilings," said Yax Chan.

"Possibly because only the corbelled arch was used for chamber ceilings," Pakal offered. "The stepped stones make it impossible to apply plaster for a smooth surface. With your new approach, we can now have murals and paintings on ceilings. This appeals greatly to me."

Pakal traced his finger along the exterior roofline. The four sides of the roof sloped gently upward to meet the border framing the rooftop.

"Why is the roof slanted?" he asked. "All the temple roofs I have seen are square and flat."

"The interior arch construction functions better with a sloped roof," Yax Chan explained. "The roof runs parallel to the interior slope of the vault inside. This reduces the gravity weight of roof masonry stone, thus making the structure more resistant to collapse. It allows the walls to be thinner, rooms wider, and entryways larger. It also adds an esthetic quality, giving the structure an upward thrust and creating an illusion of lightness."

Pakal re-examined the model, both exterior and interior. He stood back and viewed the roofline from several angles.

"That is so, it does create an impression of lightness and elevation," he agreed. "Making the roofline sloped is brilliant. It is truly pleasing to the eye."

The two young men gazed in silence at the model, each lost in his thoughts. Pakal spoke first.

"You are quite certain that the force dynamics will hold up in a full-scale building?"

Yax Chan spread his palms and gestured to signal his personal view.

"Many times have I re-checked my drawings. I can find no errors; certainly by mathematical and geometric calculations this trapezoidal linear truss should support many forms of buildings. We will know beyond doubt when one is built."

"Then let us proceed with building. It is time for Lakam Ha to begin its restoration. Your design must be presented to my parents, who may want to review a construction program with the Council. Some still resist putting our resources into building when we have not yet restored our orchards and fields to full production."

Yax Chan bowed his head, but not before Pakal caught an expression of disdain. The young ruler smiled and placed a hand on the architect's shoulder.

"Many lack your imagination and do not share my vision for a grander city," he said. "They are caught in the energy of limitation and scarcity. It is difficult for them to see how expansion through creating beautiful new structures will change the attitudes of our people and others in the polity; will draw resources and manpower to us that will launch the city into a new era."

Yax Chan met Pakal's eyes and shared his smile. There was another idea he had yet to mention, but hesitated because it was not fully developed. Pakal sensed this.

"Have you other ideas about building?" he asked.

"This is now just a thought, an image in my mind," said Yax Chan. "I have not yet made drawings or models, but I think it is something you would appreciate, especially in terms of creating beautiful structures."

"Then you must tell me, I am interested."

"It is a new way to construct roofcombs. With longer and wider chambers on top of pyramids, there will be longer and stronger rooflines to support tall superstructures. What if we could build lighter and more open roofcombs that would be elegant and graceful? It would be possible using hollow spaces between the opposing faces and making many openings in the faces themselves. This open matrix would allow light and wind to penetrate through the roofcomb. It would also minimize lateral and vertical loading and make roofcombs less susceptible to wind and seismic forces. We could have larger roofcombs that are lighter and more attractive."

Pakal reflected on these ideas and immediately saw the advantages.

"Yes, this would be very good. It will give additional height to pyramid-temples so they truly soar to the skies, and allow artistically crafted carvings to dance among sunrays. Mirrors could be used to amplify light effects. With wind freely blowing through the open matrix, we could attach wind chimes to project lovely melodies across the plazas. It is as you suggest, Yax Chan, a way to enhance the magnificence of our structures. Bring me drawings as soon as you can."

Yax Chan crossed both arms on his chest and bowed deeply. He was going to enjoy working as chief architect for the new ruler.

2

Sak K'uk was glad for the outing with her son. Although they were together more often since his accession, their interaction was mostly formal as they conducted the activities of the royal court and the Popol Nah. Sak K'uk and Kan Mo' Hix acted as co-regents with Pakal, advising him and making joint decisions as he honed his skills and gained experience administering the city of Lakam Ha. In the ten tuns that passed since Lakam Ha's axing by Kan, the political structure had been largely restored as the city's ahauob coalesced behind Pakal's rulership. Nobles brought regular tribute to support the activities of the royal court, courtiers attended the ruler and his family in daily gatherings in the throne room, and the Popol Nah met regularly to address issues that affected their city's operations.

Most of the agricultural lands and orchards had regained their former productivity. Surplus food increased and this spurred trading with other polity cities. Frequent visits by traders plying their long dugout canoes through the river network brought many valued items from distant mountains and coastal regions. Several B'aakal cities that had fallen away from bringing tribute mended their ways, observing the progressive recovery of their May Ku city. Usihwitz and Yokib, however, remained recalcitrant and did not send emissaries with tribute. Traders reported that these cities were ever more tightly drawn into the net of Kan.

Such concerns were far from Sak K'uk's mind as she met Pakal at the main plaza to begin their outing. He had requested her company for a trip across three rivers and multiple hills toward the eastern escarpment, where a meadow spanned one of the largest flat plateaus in their mountainous homeland. Few structures existed in this outlying area, but she remembered the small building sitting in the middle of the meadow near the Otolum River, used occasionally by hunters and warriors. Pakal had expressed interest in seeing this building, though she could not imagine how he remembered it from the many stories she told of her childhood. On the way there, they planned to stop at the burial pyramid of her mother, Yohl Ik'nal, where they would make offerings of copal, maize and flowers.

Sak K'uk had a small retinue of attendants carrying baskets with noonday food and drink, and a canopy on four poles in case of rain. During this time of year, afternoon showers were frequent although the days began clear and sunny. Pakal brought only one attendant to carry his mat, writing materials, and cloak. After embracing, Sak K'uk and Pakal linked arms and led the procession along the sakbe that traveled east to the edge of the built area of Lakam Ha, terminating at the Lakin Temple of the East. After that, they would follow footpaths.

In the time since she conducted the truncated K'altun rituals at the turning of the 9th Baktun, Sak K'uk felt a diminished presence of the Primordial Mother Goddess Muwaan Mat. For this she was grateful; the Goddess was an all-consuming energy that took over body, mind, and spirit. She had not felt herself during the three tuns during which Muwaan Mat had ruled using her human form as Middleworld agent. Gradually that powerful presence had diminished after Pakal was seated as ruler and tied on the white headband. Sak K'uk felt lighter and more interested in her immediate life, especially her family.

She listened avidly while Pakal described his work with Yax Chan, chief architect to the ruler. Smiling to herself, she felt a surge of pride that she had identified the young architect as one having special talents, and included him in their close circle of ahauob. Although she did not fully comprehend the engineering details of how this new trapezoidal arch functioned, she clearly grasped its conceptual advantages. Her heart was thrilled at the image of soaring pyramid-temples with light, airy roofcombs that made magic with sound and light.

"These ideas are marvelous!" she exclaimed. "What a creative genius is that Yax Chan. Such structures will be the envy of the entire polity."

"This is but the truth," Pakal agreed. "If only we could begin a concerted building effort soon. It seems to me that Lakam Ha is reaching an even state, and ahauob are increasing their reserves and wealth."

"Yes, these things are happening, but the sense of uncertainty persists. It takes time to recover from such a devastating blow. And it takes many tuns to replace the manpower of our men lost in battle or taken as captives. We have not yet reestablished a large enough warrior contingent."

"Hmmm. It is unfortunate that cities must devote human resources to battle preparedness," Pakal reflected.

"Unfortunate, but the way of our emerging world," observed Sak K'uk dryly. "I doubt the Maya lands will ever again see the widespread peace and cooperation that existed during the height of the May Ku system."

"A divinely given way for humans to live in harmony, in synchrony with the cycles of nature and the cosmos, now dishonored by such cities as Kan and Usihwitz."

Pakal appeared deep in thought as they walked along the raised white roadbed, covered with plaster making it smooth underfoot. Such sakbeob, white roads, stretched long distances between some Maya cities located in the flat lowlands to the north. In the mountainous terrain of their region, intersected by numerous rivers, it was impractical to build inter-city sakbeob. River travel was more efficient.

"It will be necessary for me to take action against those who defiled our sacred shrine and plundered our city." Pakal's voice sounded solemn. "Not in the spirit of revenge, but to restore balance and bring justice. Those perpetrating such atrocities must be made to understand that they cannot escape the consequences. As you well know, Mother, I am not a hot-blooded warrior who lusts for combat. Violence does not please my nature, for I would have all people live in cooperation and harmony. But the actions of Kan and its allies cannot remain unanswered, and raids upon their cities must be undertaken. The time is not right, I know. This will be something for future times when our warrior power is well developed."

Sak K'uk watched her son with a mixture of admiration and compassion. She was not aware that such thoughts were playing through his mind. Of his gentle nature she was fully appreciative, and she knew that military action was not something he desired. However, he understood the ways of humans far more than such a young man might. He would do what was required as Lakam Ha's ruler, setting his own preferences aside.

"These things can wait, my dear," she said gently. "Now we can focus on kinder activities, such as rebuilding our city. Perhaps you and Yax Chan could start with the Temple of Kan Bahlam. Every time I see its crumbled stones, my heart is deeply sad. Your great-grandfather's burial temple is a symbol, reconstructing it would send a message to Kan and Usihwitz. What think you of this? Might we convince the Council that we have adequate resources?"

"It is possible, but I am eager to proceed even without their full accord," Pakal replied. "Have we the family wealth to achieve this rebuilding effort, including the materials and manpower?"

"Of this I am uncertain. When we return from today's outing, I will consult with your father and the scribes to assay our holdings."

Pakal nodded, and both turned their attention to the surrounding landscape, enjoying the tree-covered hills replete with wildlife. Birds chirped and twittered, monkeys chattered, and leaves rustled in the soft breeze. They crossed the second river, spanned by a short stone bridge and passed in front of the tall Nohol Temple of the South. It was an older structure and dark mold covered the walls of stepped tiers and staircase. Pakal noted the solid carved roofcomb, imagining how much lighter and more attractive Yax Chan's open matrix design would appear.

The sun was directly overhead as the group reached the Lakin Temple of the East, where the sakbe ended. From there a path curved up the steep hillside, causing the attendants to breathe heavily under their burdens. Pakal offered his mother a hand for the climb and she clasped it tightly, grateful for the assistance. Once they reached the summit, a view of the large meadow spread below, transected by the Otolum River. Across the river and somewhat south was the crest of Yohl Ik'nal's temple, situated atop a low hill that nestled among others of greater height. Breezes swept up the hillside and ruffled their clothing while cooling their sweaty skin.

Sak K'uk recalled the time she stood on this hill with her parents. Closing her eyes, the image she saw then returned, the ephemeral shape of a glorious city spread across the meadow. Turning to Pakal and blinking to clear her vision, she noticed a distant view in his eyes.

"When I was young I came to this hill with my family," she murmured. "Only that small stone building, as you see in the distance, was in the meadow. But an image appeared to me of a great city situated there. Somehow I knew that I would live in that city."

Pakal nodded and replied softly, "That image also comes to me. This meadow is calling for our people to build here. That is one reason why I wanted to visit."

Mother and son entwined fingers as they stood side by side, sharing a common vision for their city's future. Sak K'uk felt close to Pakal, closer than she had since he was yet a boy under her care. Her heart swelled with overwhelming tenderness as tears glistened in her eyes. She vowed to hold onto this closeness, no matter what happened.

The shuffling feet of attendants brought them back to the present, and the group descended the hillside to the small valley beside the river that bordered Yohl Ik'nal's temple. Here mats were spread and the canopy set up for shade, as the sun was hot. Sak K'uk and Pakal waded across the shallow river to make their offerings before having the noonday meal. The pyramid was of modest height and the temple simple, having a single doorway to the interior chamber and one nicely carved panel featuring the buried ruler. Pakal noted the square shape of the temple roof and solid roofcomb constructed in the old manner. Inside he joined his mother in chanting ancestor prayers, placing the incense, maize, and flowers on the small stone altar under the panel.

Over lunch Pakal asked Sak K'uk to repeat some stories about his grandmother, Yohl Ik'nal. Munching maize cakes, dried deer meat, and tart dried plums; she talked of the Flower War when Yohl Ik'nal was betrothed to Hun Pakal. She described the injury of Ek Chuuah that set in motion the chain of revenge. From her own childhood, she described grand court scenes when tribute was received from many cities, festivals of vast abundance, and her mother's most renowned visions, including the prophecy that neutralized the first Usihwitz raid. Pakal never tired of hearing about his remarkable grandmother, the first woman to rule in her own right.

Leaving the attendants with their accoutrements in the small valley, Sak K'uk and Pakal followed the river's course down a gentle slope until the large meadow spread before them. Tall grasses waved in the wind, now brisker as afternoon clouds with dark bottoms billowed overhead. Sak K'uk wondered if she would regret leaving the attendants and canopy behind, but they could not keep up Pakal's rapid pace. She was getting a bit winded herself. He waved at her to rest as he forged ahead, seeming drawn to a certain region near the old building.

The structure sat next to the river on the north bank. Pakal peered across toward the south bank, interested in something. The river was wide but Pakal plunged in, the water reaching his thighs before he made the opposite bank. He wandered around the area, then re-crossed the river and disappeared into the structure. Sak K'uk felt a twinge of worry because the walls had partially fallen and the roof had caved into a pile of rubble. She stood tall and craned to get a better view, and then proceeded towards the building. When she arrived at its standing wall, she heard Pakal's voice chanting inside and hesitated. Listening carefully, she recognized a prayer to the Triad Deities and decided to remain outside.

The wind swirled and moaned through the ruins, making eerie noises as though the Gods were replying to Pakal. He kept chanting, seeming in response to the wind sounds. The dialogue became louder and stronger, rising to gusty shrieks and dropping to muttering groans. The hairs rose on Sak K'uk's neck and arms as a chill ran up her spine. She recognized the presence of otherworldly entities and felt a strong vortex of energy swirling around the structure, enveloping her and Pakal. Thunder sounded in the distance, its booming voice rumbling over the mountains.

Quickly the clouds darkened and bumped together, sending flashes of lightning over the meadow. Loud crashes of thunder followed, deafening her ears. She could not stand it anymore and had to make certain that Pakal was safe. Passing around the wall and stepping over fallen stones, she wove her way to the interior just as the storm clouds opened their bellies and poured out heavy rain.

Pakal was seated cross-legged among the rubble; his cheeks wet but not from rain, for an overhang of ceiling protected him. His face was lifted upward with eyes pressed closed and a rapturous expression. Sak K'uk stood, transfixed by the sight. Rain streamed over her head as wind whipped wet strands of loose hair across her face, but she would not move or speak. She lost track of how long she stood there, guarding her son in his trance, holding the space of sacred energy.

The rain had diminished to a drizzle and the clouds were scurrying toward the western horizon before Pakal opened his eyes. He appeared disoriented and gave his mother a confused look. She smiled and extended her arms toward him, moving forward to help him rise. Grasping his hands, she drew him up into her arms and held him closely. He returned her strong embrace, his chin resting on her crown. He was trembling and she held him until his body was still.

They carefully picked their way out of the crumbled building and walked back along the river. Sak K'uk's wet clothes dripped but the air was warm and muggy. She pushed loose tendrils of hair behind her ears. Neither spoke until they reached the bend and saw the attendants in the valley. Pakal turned back to face the meadow and pointed toward the old building.

"The vortex around that building is very powerful," he said slowly. "It has the potential to become a portal. I could feel the presence of the Triad Deities more strongly than I have since our old portal was destroyed. I could hear them calling me through the voice of the wind. That place will be the location of our new Sak Nuk Nah. There I will construct a new portal to reach the Upperworld, to communicate with the Gods and ancestors, to restore our ability to give their proper bundles. Thus will it be; the portal to birth the Jeweled Sky Tree, the *ikatz*-charge of the earth and sky, so we may adorn our patron Gods and the Gods of the First Sky."

3

The large patio of the royal residential area was full of people talking, feasting, and drinking. Every ahauob of Lakam Ha who could stand and walk crammed into the patio and terraces of the surrounding chambers. They were present to partake in the festival celebrating the adulthood transformation ceremonies of their K'uhul B'aakal Ahau, K'inich Janaab Pakal. The popular young ruler had reached eighteen tuns and all wanted to show their respect, their love, their support. Many ahauob contributed food, fermented drinks, and servants for the feast. Dressed in fine clothing with jeweled wrists and ankles, large earspools, neck collars and pendants, the nobles competed for elegance and richness. Their attire was not heavy and unwieldy as were ceremonial costumes, but were made for lightness and comfort as well as show.

Steaming bowls of deer and peccary stewed with sweet potatoes, peppers, and mixed spices were scooped up with flat maize breads. Beans and tomatoes seasoned with chile and greens, boiled iguana eggs, fresh and dried fruits steeped in honey were passed around on curved ceramic platters. Savory pit roasted peccary and turkey, rubbed with herbs and covered with maize dough then wrapped in palm leaves, were taken from the pib, a pit oven in the ground, where they had cooked for most of the day. Chunks were served in ceramic bowls and eaten with fingers or flat breads. Guests were plied with cups of alcoholic balche, fruit drinks, and spicy cacao mixed with chile.

Musicians played softly in the background, lilting wooden flute melodies hovering over gentle rhythms of hide drum and gourd rattles. Groups of ahauob sat together on mats eating, drinking, and talking, while some wandered around the area mixing with other groups. The royal family's mats were on the largest terrace, where they sat surrounded by their closest courtiers and relatives. Sak K'uk and Kan Mo' Hix were enjoying the savory food, giving compliments to ahauob who had provided certain outstanding dishes. Yaxun Xul sat behind them, propped by pillows against the chamber wall. He was very elderly and absent several teeth, but would not miss the celebration and feasting. Attendants selected the softest food and kept him regularly supplied with balche.

Pasah Chan and his very pregnant wife Kab' sat nearby as Sak K'uk inquired solicitously about how she was feeling. The two women discussed childbearing while the men engaged in topics mostly related to hunting and the condition of crops. Pakal remained beside his family until he finished eating, then excused himself and went to join a group of young men standing close to the terrace.

They greeted him with effusive compliments and deep bows, which he gracefully acknowledged. Standing almost a head above most men, Pakal was among the tallest Maya that the region had ever seen. It made him easy to identify in a crowd, even without an official headdress.

The architect Yax Chan eagerly drew Pakal into the conversation.

"It is good you have joined us, we were hearing of some remarkable structures being developed at Pa'chan. Here is our visitor, Ho' Tok from the city of Nab'nahotot. He travels with his father's traders. They recently returned from a long voyage up the K'umaxha River and stayed at Pa'chan."

Pakal and the young noble from Nab'nahotot bowed to each other.

"Welcome to Lakam Ha," said Pakal. "You have traveled an impressive distance. Is not your city located on the coast of the Great Sea of the West?"

"That is correct, Yum Ahau," replied Ho' Tok, using the formalized phrase meaning Master Lord. "We have traveled for nearly one tun, and I am most eager to complete the trip and return home. From here, it requires less than one uinal."

"Has your trading been successful?" inquired Pakal.

"Most certainly. My father will be pleased with the fine inland fabrics, obsidian, and wood we obtained, as well as magnificent feathers from highland birds. Although not much remains of our coastal products, we have traded well here in Lakam Ha for our salt, seashells, and ritual stingray spines. Your pottery and weaving are exquisite; we are bringing a good supply home."

"Not the least due to the brilliant designs of our scribe, K'anal, transferred onto ceramic bowls and cups by our potters," added Ikim, whose family specialized in fine ceramics.

K'anal bowed to Ikim and added, "Where would a scribe's designs be without gifted potters to provide the vessels for their display?"

"On bark codices? On carved glyphs?"

"On jewelry? On painted panels?"

The young men laughed as K'anal shrugged and raised both hands in the gesture for "of course."

"But more about the Pa'chan structural designs," Yax Chan insisted. "Although Lakam Ha does not have congenial relations with this city, we hear about its impressive location rising up the steep slopes that ascend from the K'umaxha River."

"It is located in a sharp u-shaped bend of the river, making it almost an island. With its height, the river below, and tall mountains filling the space behind the city, it is readily defendable and cannot easily be assailed," remarked Ch'amak, a distant cousin of Pakal and emerging warrior leader.

"That is so, and its alliance with Kan makes it even more impregnable," said Pakal.

"Pa'chan does have one serious problem in the wellbeing of the people, however," said the visitor Ho' Tok. "The terrain upon which the city is built cannot be farmed because it is too steep and rocky. The river cuts the city off from flatter lands on the other bank that serve as their fields. The K'umaxha is a very wide river. During the summer season when the river flows gently, crossing in canoes is no problem. In the winter during the rains, however, the water rises more than two men's height. The river becomes a raging torrent, carrying uprooted trees and brush in its wake. Canoes cannot readily cross because of the treacherous currents and debris. If the rainy season is long, the farmers have difficulty getting across to begin spring planting. If fall rains start early, they cannot harvest their crops efficiently. Many men and canoes have been lost to the river's fury."

"So they need a bridge," observed Pakal.

"Exactly!" said Yax Chan excitedly. "That is the remarkable structure their engineers are now developing, as Ho' Tok explained to me. It must be a long span bridge because the river is so wide. This demands new technology, new ideas of bridge building."

"Here is what I learned about their plans for this long span bridge," expounded Ho' Tok, having captured the full attention of all. "You are familiar with medium span bridges that use heavy stone and concrete pillars on each bank, with high strength timbers spanning the pillars and cross-decking covered with a plaster coat. I saw one such bridge in your city and several short span bridges of simpler support. A long span bridge requires structures of lightweight tension members. They must use geometry principles based on pure tension, not massive strength in pillars to bear the weight. Higher strength materials and lighter gravity loads are necessary. How does this get accomplished? By using a cable suspension structure."

Several young men nodded, but Pakal frowned quizzically.

"We are familiar with rope and wood suspension bridges across canyons. Several are built along mountain trails," he said. "But these bridges cannot carry much weight and certainly would not span a river so wide. How is their design different?"

Yax Chan appeared delighted at Pakal's question and jumped in before Ho' Tok could respond.

"This is what makes the design brilliant! They have conceived of building tall concrete and stone support towers, placing two in the river not far from each bank. These towers will be tall enough to hold the bridge well above water level at flood stage. The roadway will be held up by high-tension sisal rope, connecting to grooved stones embedded high in the towers. Lines of rope attach in an upturned crescent moon (parabola) configuration to the crossbeams made of high strength timbers. Wooden planks will span between the crossbeams and be covered with a thin plaster coat. On each river bank, elevated causeways will be constructed at the height of the roadway, the west causeway leading into the main city plaza that borders the river, and the east causeway linking to a sakbe that connects to paths into the fields."

"The architects of Pa'chan are already familiar with building on steep hillsides," added Ho' Tok. "Their main city plaza is considerably higher than the river bank, to avoid flooding. Constructing tall towers to hold suspension cables that support the bridge is not a great challenge."

"What about placing the tower foundations within the river? How will that be accomplished?" asked Pakal.

"Of course, they must construct the foundations when the river is at its lowest," explained Ho' Tok. "They will use large, heavy masonry stones carved exactly, so their fit is tight. Then cast in place concrete and rubble will be put inside, it will dry and set up in time. From there the tower column is built upward in the usual manner. Engineers are now calculating the exact placement of the towers, determining how long a section can be supported between them given the maximum number of people assumed to walk across the bridge at one time, plus the dead load of the roadway deck. The bridge deck will be wide as a man's height, and the hemp cable system made of ropes half the span of a hand."

"It can work, I have done some calculations and it appears all the tension and gravity forces are adequate," said Yax Chan.

"This is truly remarkable," Pakal acceded. "If they accomplish it, this will be the longest suspension bridge in the Maya region."

"A thing of awesome beauty," Yax Chan effused, making hand gestures of admiration.

Laughter rippled among the young men, and Ch'amak patted his shoulder.

"Spoken like an architect," he said.

"Ah, but here come other things of great beauty," observed K'anal.

All heads turned to watch as three young women crossed the patio, weaving among the seated feasters, stopping to bow, touch fingers, and chat.

"Who are those girls?" asked Pakal.

"Hmmm, let me see. . . Yonil, daughter of my kinsman and yours, Oaxac Ok; Tulix and Muyal who are sisters in the family of Chakab the Nakom," said Ch'amak.

"Lovely young women grace your city," Ho' Tok observed.

"Without doubt; and there are more," Ikim assured him.

"How goes your courtship with Muyal?" teased K'anal.

Ikim smiled and spread his fingers suggestively, murmuring "Not so badly."

"And you, Pakal? Now you are a man, is it not time to seek a woman?" said Yax Chan. "Rather, a young woman as your royal consort, not just the Lunar Priestess."

Smiles passed among the young men, for all had received sexual training from Lunar Priestesses, as was the custom for nobles. These priestesses acted in professional and sacred capacity, and could never marry. Once the training was complete, they never interacted with their students again. They kept to themselves, secluded in the Temple of the Moon. Their position and responsibility were highly respected; for the price was exclusion from the main course of life and relinquishing their opportunity for a family.

Pakal shrugged and made a dismissive gesture, but his eyes lingered on the lithe forms of the young women.

The feasting was nearing completion and attendants began removing bowls, cups, and platters. A large contingent of musicians gathered on one side of the patio while guests folded their mats and moved to the edges, leaving the center clear for dancing. Some of the elders made evening-end acknowledgements to the royal family and left; some mothers departed to attend their children. Pasah Chan's wife also returned home as her pregnancy made her tired, but he remained next to Sak K'uk and Kan Mo' Hix, whose aged father had sought his bed earlier.

Sak K'uk looked around for Pakal, but the group of young men with whom he was talking had dispersed. She could not locate him among the milling group waiting to begin dancing.

"Ah, well," she murmured, "he has precious little time to enjoy simply being a young man, let him be with his companions."

As if he read her thoughts, Kan Mo' Hix remarked,

"Our Pakal seems to be enjoying his manhood celebration."

"So it appears," she replied. "It is good to see him relaxed and talking with the young men. Usually, he is solemn and focused upon his duties."

"That is so. Perhaps his responsibilities can be sweetened with someone to lift his spirits in his chambers. He is well grown into manhood. It is time we seek a suitable noble woman for his wife."

Sak K'uk was startled by her intense response to this suggestion. Her gut wrenched and a flash of anger surged, making her reply testily to her husband.

"He has only now reached adulthood; surely it is soon to make such a significant move. Give him time to become comfortable assuming more leadership duties. There is much additional training to undertake, is that not so, Pasah Chan?"

The High Priest carefully considered his reply, not wishing to offend either by taking sides.

"Plumbing the depths of our people's wisdom and history, perfecting spiritual practices and shamanic techniques, these are the work of a lifetime," he equivocated.

"Exactly!" responded Kan Mo' Hix. "Pakal will keep studying for katuns. Finding a suitable wife and starting a family need not be delayed. It will take time to identify a woman of proper bloodlines, with whose family it is advantageous to form strategic alliances. The process should begin."

Sak K'uk made a dismissive gesture. The thought of another woman becoming close to her son, sharing the intimacy of his bedchamber, pained her heart. She had only just revived their closeness and treasured it beyond measure. Every fiber of her being resisted the idea of his marrying any time soon.

"You are pushing this too rapidly, Kan Mo'," she said firmly, holding on to her temper. "Let us discuss it another day."

"You are not being reasonable," he retorted. "This is but a common sense step following transition to adulthood ceremonies. Why you desire to delay escapes me."

Rising with abrupt movements that bristled with annoyance, Kan Mo' Hix strode away and merged into the crowd.

Pasah Chan raised his cup toward a servant, who filled it with more balche. He was well aware that Sak K'uk and Kan Mo' Hix often argued, but he did not relish the tension it created. It put him in an awkward position.

Sak K'uk sat pensively, fingering her wrist bracelets. She shifted position to face the priest, her back toward the dancers filling the patio.

"Pakal is yet so young," she murmured. "He must contend with so many forces, often at cross-purposes. Need we add another complication to his life?"

"It may be that he would find it a diversion, not a complication," the priest offered.

"You are a married man. You know full well that having a spouse complicates your life. It certainly adds stresses to mine."

Pasah Chan smiled ruefully, signaling accord.

"This idea must pass from Kan Mo's mind for now. It is not necessary to seek a wife for Pakal. He has shown no interest yet in women," she said with finality.

Pasah Chan wondered where to go with this conversation. The idea of seeking a wife for Pakal was much on his mind, although he had not discussed it with the parents. He glanced over Sak K'uk's shoulder at the patio, and saw Pakal dancing close by with Yonil.

"That may be changing," said Pasah Chan. "Look how he dances."

Sak K'uk swiveled quickly toward the patio. The music pulsated in sensuous rhythms as singers joined voices in extolling the joys of spring, of life bursting forth in youthful vigor, of potency and fertility. Sweet harmonies rose and fell with measured drumbeats and lilting flutes as couples danced, facing closely and mirroring each other's movements. Pakal danced with a slender young woman, her black hair swaying with each step as her arms snaked in parallel with his. Torchlight glistened on her warm brown skin and lit sparkles in her jewelry. Their eyes were locked, Pakal gazing down into her upturned, rapturous face. Her lips were slightly parted, wide and full and voluptuous. Her small firm breasts rose and fell with her breathing and she arched into him, their midriffs almost touching. As they turned into the next step, a slow twirl, her hand brushed against his exposed thigh and he smiled, allowing his arm to slide along hers although the dance did not call for touching.

"Who is that girl?" snapped Sak K'uk.

"Her name is Yonil, daughter of Oaxac Ok," answered Pasah Chan.

"She is dancing too close to him. That is not proper."

"He does not seem to mind."

"It is I who mind! What she does is very suggestive. How can noble girls behave so?" Sak K'uk huffed.

"They are young, their bodies are full of passions, and they are lost in the music."

"This music is unfitting," she complained, then fell silent and watched her son. She had never seen him this way, and it unnerved her. His bare shoulders and chest muscles rippled and gleamed in the torchlight; his feet stepped confidently in the complex dance patterns. White teeth glinted as he smiled at his partner, displaying the carved "Ik" pattern in his two front incisors. He moved closer still until their bodies brushed and both laughed, unaware or unconcerned with disapproving elders.

"Water and fire mix within his veins to ignite the boiling vapor of sexual desire," observed Pasah Chan softly.

"Let him spend more time with the Lunar Priestess!" hissed Sak K'uk. "Is that not her work? He need not expend his sexual urges on these young women."

"Ah, Ixik Sak K'uk, it is not the same. The Lunar Priestess is a professional trainer, she is older and experienced and dispassionate. Yes, he knows sexual pleasure with her as well as perfecting techniques of sex magic, but there is little emotion. The heart is not enflamed and he does not sip the intoxication of young love. Look at him. You can feel the rising passions, the thumping heart, and the swelling groin."

She took a deep breath and turned her head again to observe Pakal. The dance ended and he bowed, touching fingers with Yonil and whispering in her ear. She giggled and fluttered her eyelids, looking down then back up into his eyes. They were standing so close together that Sak K'uk knew they felt the heat radiating from each other's bodies.

"Pakal is a handsome young man," said Pasah Chan. "He is striking in his presence and power. These are irresistible combinations for young noble women. Even if he were not ruler, he would attract women. Being ruler makes him the ultimately potent sexual symbol. Any young woman in Lakam Ha would give everything for him."

Sak K'uk swallowed and looked back at the High Priest.

"What you say is true. It is clear to see, tonight has revealed it to me beyond doubt."

"These women will pursue him, for they cannot help themselves. He is remarkably clear-minded and strong-willed, but when the fire of sexual passion burns in his veins, he may not be able to contain it despite all his training. Is it not better to select a suitable wife and provide him the proper channel for this drive? Then can he harness this immense sexual energy for the creative projects needed to fully restore Lakam Ha."

Sak K'uk equivocated once again. Angry demons of jealousy tore at her heart. She was shocked by the scene she had witnessed, for it clearly revealed Pakal's enthusiastic response to the young woman's sexual charms.

"It will be necessary to find the proper consort, but it will take time, considerable time," she said. "We must make the absolutely correct choice and there are many qualifications the woman must have. Kan Mo' and I shall meet and discuss these, begin considering noble daughters in our city and others. Yes, it will take time."

Somewhat reassured by the thought of a lengthy search, she gazed again at the plaza where dancers were turning and stepping. Soft laughter mingled with clinking disks and rhythmic music, but all felt flat to Sak K'uk. She would not yet give up her son to another woman. She would delay this process as long as possible. She would find reasons to seek a wife for Pakal from outside of Lakam Ha, someone who would not usurp her in his heart.

"We must avoid his involvement with young women here," Pasah Chan advised. "Pakal must not be touched by any hint of impropriety, nor dissipate his energies in sensual indulgences. I will speak of this to him, and soon."

"With that I am in full agreement. No further contact with this nubile Yonil will be allowed. She is completely unsuitable for royal wife."

Pasah Chan raised his eyebrows, surprised by the charge with which Sak K'uk spoke about the girl. He perceived spiteful emotions and wondered from what source these welled. Yonil came from a minor noble family without solid bloodlines, but that did not totally disqualify her as the ruler's wife. Deciding to avoid this charged topic, he still pressured the ruler's mother to proceed with searching for a consort.

"Speak quickly with Kan Mo' Hix and set up the search delegation. Finding a wife for Pakal should not be delayed."

"Yes, yes," Sak K'uk said, looking annoyed. "It is so, it must be done. We will begin the search for a royal consort for Pakal. Tomorrow will I speak to Kan Mo' Hix and give my consent."

FIELD JOURNAL

ARCHEOLOGICAL CAMP

Francesca Nokom Gutierrez   Palenque, Chiapas, Mexico

July 30, 1994

Big news at the archeological camp today! We just heard a rumor that the Mexican archeological institute INAH is sending Arturo Romano Pacheco to Palenque to examine the skeleton in the Temple XIII sarcophagus. Romano is Mexico's leading physical anthropologist, chosen to examine Pakal's skeleton when it was found forty-two years ago. Our entire team is very excited. Our discovery two months ago of the Temple XIII substructure with its pristine sarcophagus, containing bones of a person given a rich burial, is getting the attention it deserves. It's not official yet that Romano is coming, but word got out through the reporter who covered the opening of the sarcophagus lid on June 1st. Adriana Malvido has written several articles for her newspaper *La Journada* detailing our discoveries and bringing them to the public. We owe her a big *gracias* for these insightful articles.

Curious to find out the skeleton's sex, Adriana interviewed some specialists in Mexican archeology and physical anthropology, including Arturo Romano Pacheco. He noted that the absence of inscriptions was unusual for Palenque, a city with panels and walls full of glyphs. Fanny Lopez Jimenez, our team member who uncovered the substructure in Temple XIII, thinks the lack of inscriptions points toward a woman's interment. We know that several carved reliefs at Palenque emphasize the important function of royal women. Several are shown handing objects of power to their sons, including Sak K'uk giving the "drum major hat" to Pakal. This extraordinary role of women was depicted most often in Palenque, but is portrayed at other sites such as Yaxchilan. The sides of Pakal's sarcophagus in the Temple of the Inscriptions are carved with his female and male ancestors, honoring the role of royal women and acknowledging the rulership of Yohl Ik'nal and Sak K'uk.

If the person interred in Temple XIII is a woman, she is obviously very important to be buried in this structure joined to Pakal's pyramid. Everyone believes this would lead to politically important repercussions. One concerns the controversy over Pakal's age at death and the split between Mexican and North American archeological schools of thought. Las Mesas Redondas de Palenque (Round Tables) organized by Merle Greene Robertson in 1973 brought together the first interdisciplinary teams—archeologists, anthropologists, epigraphers, linguists, art historians—to work on deciphering the glyphs at Palenque. This group interpreted the names and dates of Palenque's ruling dynasty and produced a "king list." They proved that Mayan writing was a true work of literature and told the histories of rulers and cities.

Unfortunately, very few Mexican archeologists participated in the Round Tables. The politics of the time led to animosities and growing disagreement between the schools of thought. Mexicans believed the North Americans were not giving enough weight to their discoveries, especially Alberto Ruz' and Arturo Romano's work with the tomb of Pakal. The North Americans held that Pakal was 80 years old at death based on epigraphy; Ruz and Romano stated he was around 40 based on physical anthropology.

Now with a new skeleton to analyze in Temple XIII, this question will be revisited. Advances in scientific methods of bone analysis, including regional mineral content and DNA, will give us firmer conclusions. This work could lead to "a great un-sticking" of Mexican archeology, as Adriana Malvido so astutely writes.

At the Palenque camp, we feel it could be explosive—especially if the bones turn out to be a woman's.

Arturo Romano explained in an interview how these advances in technology would give answers. A comparison between the bones of Pakal and the person interred in Temple XIII would reveal whether they are related. Better restoration techniques now available will preserve bones for future analysis, though it's a costly and time-consuming process. Romano looked at photos of the new discovery, noting that the sarcophagus is much deeper than Pakal's, that the position of the skeleton's feet showed that it was shrouded upon burial, and that the skull had the typical royal cranial deformation. Since there was no bone deterioration from insects, it proved that the tomb was perfectly sealed.

He concluded, "This is a great discovery. It is another link in the chain of knowledge about the Mayas. Congratulations to the archeologists at Palenque and we wait for results of their studies."

Soon Romano will come to Palenque to visit the tomb. He wants to see the skeleton *in situ* for his initial analysis. Like forensic pathology, physical anthropology knows that seeing the evidence in its natural setting provides important clues. As soon as he finishes his examination, we will prepare the bones for transportation to the INAH laboratories in Mexico City.

What we are all eagerly anticipating is his conclusion about the sex of the mysterious inhabitant of Temple XIII.

My roommate at the archeological camp, Sonia Cardenas, and I like to chat about Maya archeology and review timelines of the discoveries at Palenque. Since both of us specialize in restoration, our discussions often focus on how data were obtained and preserved in the steamy tropical jungles of the Maya world. In his upcoming visit, Romano will examine the tomb and skeleton, and take many photographs. We reviewed how field photography has changed over time and contributed to research.

Photography initiated a new era in documentation of Maya ruins. Before the camera, on-site drawings or white paper cast molds were the best techniques available. Drawings depended on the skill and perseverance of the artist, and molds were subject to melting in the extremely wet and humid tropical climate. In 1839 Daguerre invented the first camera using a complicated "wet" chemical process. The enterprising French explorer Desiré de Charnay used this camera on his expedition to Palenque in 1860. He spent nine days there, using the cumbersome process to take the first photos of the ruins.

One important image shows the central tablet from the Temple of the Cross. Charnay found it where John L. Stephens and Frederick Catherwood saw it earlier, described in their popular book *Incidents of Travel in Central America, Chiapas and Yucatan* (1841). It was abjectly lying by a stream and covered with muddy debris. Charnay cleaned it and lifted it sideways for better light, taking the first photo of this famous piece. The missing right tablet had found its way to the Smithsonian Institution in Washington, D.C. Partly due to Charnay's work, all three tablets have now been united in Mexico's Museo Nacional de Antropología.

A folio of Charnay's photographs of Palenque and other Maya sites was issued in 1863. This prompted Australian Teobert Maler to launch his field career in photographic documentation of Maya sites. In the summer of 1877, he went to Palenque and took a series of excellent photos of the Palace and Cross Group, using the cumbersome wet process with a large format camera. His photos are the clearest early images of tablets, stelae, and lintels from Palenque and a wide range of undiscovered sites. What lay behind these discoveries was chicle, the basic ingredient of chewing gum, increasingly popular with North Americans. Chicle trees grew abundantly in Central American tropical forests, and opportunistic chicleros cut hundreds of trails through the Peten that uncovered dozens of unknown Maya cities.

Maler received funding from Harvard's Peabody Museum to explore and survey these newly found sites, and from 1901 to 1911 he took numerous excellent photographic plates of sites now called Yaxchilan, Piedras Negras, Seibal, and Tikal. The accuracy of his work provided a foundation for later decipherment of Maya glyphs.

English explorer Alfred P. Maudslay took invaluable photos at Palenque in 1891, producing exceptionally clear images of sculptures and glyphs. Technical progress in cameras made his work possible. Factory-made, ready-to-use photographic dry plates became available three years before his expedition. Images taken by new cameras on dry plates were far superior to the old wet plate process. Maudslay also made paper molds of stone and stucco reliefs, facing the same issues as Charnay. In one disastrous rainstorm, three weeks of molds were transformed into a sodden blob, so the tedious procedure had to be done over.

The trip that Maudslay made to Palenque interests me since it reveals much about the region and its people, my people. From Progreso at the northern tip of the Yucatan Peninsula, he took a boat bound for Frontera at the mouth of the Grijalva River. A bad storm forced them into port at Laguna de Terminos (now Ciudad del Carmen), the lagoon outlet of the other navigable river leading to the Usumacinta, the major artery of river travel. After two weeks clearing customs despite ample official permissions from the Mexican government, he secured a small steamer to take his equipment up-river to the village of Montecristo (now Emiliano Zapata). Finding pack-mules and carriers was difficult and he faced the same problems that plagued most expeditions of his time.

Maudslay commented: "As the Indians had all been hopelessly drunk the night before, we did not get off very early, although our efforts to start commenced before dawn, and what with bad mules, sulky muleteers, and half-drunken Indians we had a hard day of it."

The ruins of Palenque were 40 miles from Montecristo, so they went first to Santo Domingo de Palenque (my village). Maudslay described it as a sleepy little village of twenty houses with one grassy street leading to a thatched church. A few white stucco houses lined the grassy square, with Indian huts (palapas) scattered around. When Chiapas was part of Guatemala, the town was on the main trade route but this commerce had been diverted. The village was struck by cholera that wiped out half the population. Many of the homes were abandoned and falling into ruin. Palenque village was "so far out of the world" that he was surprised to find the two most important inhabitants were sons of a Frenchman and a Swiss doctor.

Trouble with workers seemed endemic. Maudslay asked for 30 laborers, and the jefe políticos (leaders) of local towns promised them, but only 15 showed up and that quickly dwindled to three. Finally, he got 20 men from the nearby Chol Maya village of Tumbala (my grandmother's family is from there). His team included an engineer, a young Frenchman planning to write books about his travels, and some cooks. At the Palenque ruins, they set up beds and camp furniture in the Palace corridor by the eastern court, supposedly the driest area. "Driest" was a relative term, however.

Maudslay wrote: "The great forest around us hung heavy with wet, the roof above us was dripping water like a slow and heavy rainfall, and the walls were glistening and running with moisture . . ."

Despite unpredictable laborers, Maudslay's team managed to cut down many trees around the structures, clear out the Palace eastern court, and remove all but one of the trees growing from the Palace Tower. The top story of the Tower was half destroyed and the whole in danger of falling over in heavy winds. To prepare Palace piers for photography, they had to remove limestone incrustations that formed small stalactites on the pier faces. The limestone coating varied from a thin film to 5 or 6 inches thick, and it took six weeks to remove it carefully with hammer taps and scraping. Underneath they found colors of the stucco paintings still fresh and bright in some places.

Next was photography, requiring platforms supported by scaffolding. The piers sat on narrow terraces above stairways, and Maudslay needed to get enough distance to frame good pictures. His engineer made plane-table surveys of the site center, producing detailed floor plans of the Palace and other structures that are still among the most accurate ever done.

Maudslay suffered from malaria contracted in Nicaragua, but his health was good during the four months at Palenque. Despite many difficulties and "hot and mosquito-plagued nights" he recalled pleasures such as finding a cool breezy spot, where they escaped mosquito attacks and enjoyed "the beauty of the moonlit nights when we sat smoking and chatting on the western terrace looking onto the illumined face of the ruin (Temple of the Inscriptions) and the dark forest behind it . . ."

August 17, 1994

Last weekend was the celebration of Ascención de la Virgen on August 15, the day the Holy Mother María was assumed into Heaven. I brought Sonia with me to visit my family and attend mass in Palenque town. It's the custom in my town, after our holy day obligations have been met, to finish our celebration with a fiesta.

Mexicans love fiestas and we have one at the least excuse. Thank goodness there are so many Catholic saints; they give frequent opportunities to take off work and have fun. Our many revolutions also contribute their share to our celebrations. On fiesta days, the town sets up bandstands in the central plaza, and we have music and dancing late into the night. Street vendors sell food and trinkets while the entire town walks the streets, old and young alike, eating and drinking and talking.

Sonia and I had lunch with the family first and then took to the streets and plazas to mingle. She was very curious about my part-Mayan family. I think my father Luis's knowledge of the ruins surprised her, for they spent much time discussing technical points that few non-professionals can appreciate. My mother María and grandmother Juanita watched Sonia with an appraising eye, partly impressed by her urbane manner, but there was subtle disapproval of her forwardness. I know they're worried that I'm becoming like her, unfit for village life.

She quizzed my little grandmother, Abuelita as we fondly call her, about life in her village Tumbala, even farther into the forests than the Palenque ruins. Abuelita Juanita seemed flattered as she described the wood-and-mud walled palapas with thatched roofs, the muddy village streets and the one stone church. About 150 people lived there when she was young, but that has dwindled because many villagers migrate to cities seeking work and a modern life. The village routine was familiar. Men left in the mornings for work, either in the milpas or at larger towns doing labor; women tended backyard turkeys and pigs, washed, cooked, sewed, and cleaned. The children walked through forest paths to the regional school about an hour away. The single road into the village is still unpaved and turns into deeply rutted mud during the rainy season. My grandmother doesn't visit there anymore since she has trouble walking.

Later Sonia and I sat on cement benches in the central plaza, the band blaring Mexican disco in our ears, and discussed my family. My grandmother used to come into Palenque to get work sewing and cleaning house, I told her. There she met my grandfather, a mestizo shopkeeper with more Spanish than Maya blood, and he wooed and married her. I've seen pictures of Abuelita Juanita when she was young, and she was striking. The photos are not in color, but her pale eyes fairly jump out of her dark face framed by lustrous black hair. My father and his brothers and sisters were all born in Palenque. Of the six children, only three remain here. Visiting with my uncle in Mexico City first exposed me to a metropolis and I was hooked on the excitement and culture. I spent untold hours at the archeological museum that fueled my desire for researching Maya civilization.

Probably my mother regrets those visits, though my father always wanted me to be educated. My sister and brother, who were at our lunch with their families, never had the aptitude for academic study. They seem happy in Palenque town, which now has 37,000 people and a thriving economy in tourism, artisan crafts, restaurants, and fiestas. Whether Abuelita Juanita misses her little village I don't know; she keeps her secrets well. It's intriguing how she insisted that my parents give her family name, Nokom, to me. I'm the middle grandchild but the only one with blue eyes.

Invariably, our conversations wander back to archeology; a passion Sonia and I share. We sought refuge from the afternoon heat by having a beer inside one of the soothingly dark bars that dot the main streets of Palenque town. Strains of popular tunes drifted through open windows, played loudly and somewhat badly by a local band heavy on brass. Sipping the foamy bitterness that cooled our palates, we reviewed our progress preparing artifacts for shipment to Mexico City. Our restoration skills were required to clean and stabilize many ceramic shards and a few nearly intact bowls. Just as we dropped into some technical details, a familiar form entered the bar and approached our table.

How my father knew he would find us in this obscure bar escapes me. Maybe he's psychic or just plain lucky. After hugs and greetings, he sat contentedly and ordered another round of beer. His black eyes twinkled and animated his narrow face with aquiline nose; his dark hair was sprinkled with silver. I knew he relished this opportunity to delve deeply into archeology, one of his favorite topics, with a couple of experts. Probably he tracked us down just for this. And the best thing was that no other family members were around to complain about being bored or make us change the topic.

"Don Luis, tell me more about your recent visit to San Cristóbal," Sonia entreated with her seductive smile. It works every time. I've watched it turn a number of men in our team into panting puppies eager to please. My father is a bit more self-contained, but he was happy to elaborate. San Cristóbal de la Cases is a captivating city set high atop a 2200-meter mountain south of Palenque. It has a distinct European ambiance, or so people who've been to Europe tell me, with its many espresso cafés, bookshops, art galleries, and fine international restaurants.

"Ah, the lovely San Cristóbal," he responded with the hand wave we use to signal a distant place. "Yes, I took a group of tourists there to visit the Frans Blom museum and enjoy the mountain coolness. A good place to go during the summer in Chiapas, no?"

We clinked beer bottles in acknowledgement.

"I must go there before returning to Mexico City when our project ends," Sonia said with enthusiasm.

"Yes, yes, and be sure to visit the museum. Do you know much about it?" When we both shook our heads, he continued with relish.

"It was originally a monastery in ruins when Blom and his wife Gertrude bought it in 1950. They rebuilt it around the existing interior patio, preserving the style with colonnaded walkways and large rooms. It's brightly painted in deep yellow and red, with beautiful walled gardens full of native plants and trees that are still donated for reforestation. They created a cultural center where Frans' Mayan artifacts and Trudi's documentary photos were featured. Frans had an exceptional collection of books on Mayan culture, and he opened this library to the public. To raise funds, they took in guests who dined at the long table in the dining room. Many were tourists and locals, but they also housed archeologists working in the area.

"They named it Casa Na Bolom, a pun on Blom's name and the Mayan word for jaguar, Bolom or Bahlam. Did you know that the locals called Frans 'Pancho Bolom'? It was a great compliment to associate him with the sacred jaguar. They both had a special relationship with the nearby Lacandon Maya, always keeping a free room open for them when they came to San Cristóbal. The Lacandon Mayas lived deep in the jungles and were the only indigenous group never conquered by the Spanish. Now the complex is operated by a nonprofit group of volunteers, who keep it open as a museum, hotel, and restaurant. They donate funds to community projects and the jungle Mayas."

My father paused to sip his beer, looking pensive. Then he launched into tour guide mode, regaling us with Blom's contributions to Mayan research.

"Frans Blom loved the Mayas and Palenque in particular. Some say that modern scientific investigation of Palenque began with him. He was Danish, an explorer and archeologist who came to Mexico in 1919 and worked in Tabasco oil fields.

He became fascinated by Maya ruins in the area, especially Tortuguero. While in Mexico City recovering from malaria—seems that most European Mayanists got this nasty disease—he worked for Mexican archeologist Manuel Gamio who was impressed by his sketches and notes. Gamio sent Blom to Palenque in 1922 to survey the site and report on ideas for conserving the ruin, which was by then quite famous. Those drawings were so good they inspired archeologists Sylvanus Morley and Alfred Tozzer to help Blom get a scholarship to Harvard University, where he earned a Masters Degree in Archeology in 1925."

My father went on to describe more of Blom's life, over another round of beers. I'll try to summarize what he said.

In the 1923 report on Palenque, Blom mapped structures beyond the central area and assigned roman numerals to unnamed buildings. We still use Blom's numbering system. He improvised to make some repairs, noted buildings that were damaged, drew floor plans, and copied hieroglyphic texts. He emphasized that a road from Montecristo to Palenque was essential to reduce expense and delay transporting material from the river to the site. He cut logs for later construction of buildings to house guardians, a museum, and laboratory.

Before doing his work, Blom had to cut down forest growth. He arrived by the old trail that led to a "fairy tale palace beyond description." He was so struck that he could not begin cutting for days as he walked past ancient temples immersed in the "world's most beautiful forest. Lianas and orchids and other tropical verdure" covered all the structures and his job was to tear that floral beauty down. The roofs of every temple and palace were covered in "a solid carpet of wild pink begonias" and with "each machete slash my heart was bleeding."

When Blom returned to Palenque in 1925, he found that objects from the museum had been taken. The caretaker had saved fragments with glyphs and figures from the Cross Group. Two stucco reliefs from the Temple of the Cross were now flanking the front doors of the town church, the same reliefs that Stephens had seen in a private house in the 1830s. Due to such pilfering, Blom stressed the importance of protecting and conserving Palenque's precious art.

Blom had some precocious ideas about Maya hieroglyphs. He believed that a linguistic approach was necessary because the glyphs express sound and the writing system was at least partly phonetic. He spoke four languages and could read earlier studies in those languages. This exposed him to ideas about phoneticism and historical content that ran counter to the established view. His mentor Morley believed Maya glyphs did not express sounds but were ideograms expressing ideas. Morley thought the inscriptions were calendrical and astronomical observations, not historic information. Much later, however, the sciences of linguistics and epigraphy vindicated Blom's ideas

My father was getting a bit worked up, and spoke adamantly.

"Blom thought scholars needed to learn the Mayan language before they'd unravel the secrets of the glyphs. And more important, they should study Maya thought processes to get a true picture of Maya culture. All those Europeans, they think they know the Mayas, but until they enter the Mayan mind they won't really understand."

We three sat quietly, pondering European hubris. I wondered if Sonia was offended, she is of pure Castilian descent as are most Mexican archeologists; not mestizos like my family. But more of us are entering the scientific world; we mixed breeds of Spanish and Mayan blood.

"So what happened to Blom's work?" I asked mainly to get the tale finished.

"Ah, that's a sad story," my father replied. "He had problems with alcohol and his first wife divorced him in the 1930s. He was never so productive again. Blom loved the Maya world and finished his life in San Cristóbal. He met his second wife Gertrude in the surrounding jungles, where she was photographing the legendary Lacandon Mayas in the mid-1940s. With her inheritance, they bought the monastery and turned it into a Maya cultural and scientific center. It is their tribute to the Mayas."

Dusk was gathering, the streets swelling again with revelers and the bands blaring interminably on. Glancing at his watch, my father sighed.

"I must return home, María will not be happy if I stay out any longer."

"We've got to get back to camp," I said patting his arm fondly.

"Don Luis, thank you so much for telling us about Frans Blom." Sonia's smile was now softer and appreciative.

We paid our bill and said our goodbyes, my father trudging homeward and the two of us finding a combi to take us back to the archeological site.

Ensconced in my cot with journal in lap, I'm finishing a few remarks of the day.

Here is my favorite Blom quote, probably because I'm part Maya.

"The scientist trained with a foundation of European knowledge has absorbed the arrogant idea that his learning is a world pattern and that it is impossible for other peoples to develop individual lines of thought that amount to anything. Not until he shapes himself to the psychology of the people will he succeed in understanding *them* and their characters."

In 1939, President Lazaro Cardenas created INAH, Instituto Nacional de Antropología y Historia. It's the government agency responsible for exploration of archeological sites, conservation and restoration of monuments and artifacts, and publication of research. Cardenas visited Palenque many times and valued the ancient Maya cities as part of Mexico's cultural heritage. INAH has done much to stop the removal of artifacts from the sites.

German scientist Heinrich Berlin joined the Palenque team in 1940. He directed the renovation and conservation of the Palace Tower, which was especially vulnerable because of its height. It had sustained damage by trees growing out of cracks in the masonry. Berlin supervised excavations at Templo Olvidado, the best-preserved structure found in the forests west of the central area, and first reported by Frans Blom. The temple's well-preserved date glyphs fascinated Berlin, and his long career studying epigraphy had its beginning there.

Berlin's great epigraphic discovery some years later was that each Maya polity had an Emblem Glyph that combined a pair of phonetic signs, one standing for "ahau" or lord and the other representing the city itself.

For Palenque, these glyphs would read: K'uhul B'aakal Ahau.

August 22, 1994

Standing at the base of the pyramid, head tilted back, my eyes travel up its steep front, level by level. This is Pakal's burial monument, and it is magnificent. Constructed in a short time between 675—683 CE, the Pyramid of the Inscriptions is the dominant pyramid of the central plaza. It stands just west of the Palace and has a string of smaller pyramids jutting from its northwest side. Soaring 23 meters above plaza level on an almost square base, the pyramid's nine stacked levels decrease in size as they rise. The base is 60 meters wide by 42.5 meters deep, making it a massive structure. A narrow stairway ascends the front, flanked by two decorative slabs. A few short, wider stairs complete the descent to the ground.

On the top level a platform supports the pyramid's Temple. The shape of this harmonious building reflects the central canons of ancient Maya architecture: rectangular structure with mirror-image symmetry, sloping roofline, overhanging eaves, corbelled arches supported by trapezoidal linear trusses, and a delicate roofcomb. Inside, a wall divides the structure into two long parallel rooms and supports the capstone, where the faces of both interior vaults converge to form the corbelled arch. Five doors flanked by panels open into the long front gallery, with three interior doors giving access to rear chambers. The central rear chamber is largest and holds the amazing hieroglyphic tablets that give the Temple its name. These are attached to the back wall and figuratively look out over Palenque's main plaza. Exquisitely carved in the flowing glyphic style unique to Palenque, the panels are covered with a single continuous inscription of 617 glyphs, the second longest in any Maya site.

Although the text carved on the tablets is not fully deciphered, we know the themes interweave Palenque's dynastic history with specific rituals performed by rulers to honor their three patron Gods, the Palenque Triad. Rituals celebrating Katun endings from 514 CE (9.4.0.0.0) to 672 CE (9.12.0.0.0) are included. These calendar rituals devoted to the Gods are juxtaposed with realities of politics and warfare, including the 611 CE attack by Kalakmul. The inscriptions conclude with records of the death of Pakal's wife, Tz'aakb'u Ahau in 672 and of Pakal in 683. The final passage notes the accession of his oldest son, Kan Bahlam II. We believe that Pakal's son completed construction of the Temple of the Inscriptions shortly after his father's death.

The late afternoon sun sends shafts of golden light through the Temple roofcomb, and the beauty moves me. Behind the pyramid a steep hill rises;

the builders used its bedrock face to support the back terraces. Ancient Maya architects often used already existing hills to amplify the terraces of buildings, effectively merging pyramids into sacred mountains. The dense foliage covering the hill is deepening green and I realize only a couple of hours of daylight remain. If I'm to visit the burial chamber of Pakal, I must hurry.

Skirting the left side of the pyramid, I scramble up the stony path that climbs the hillside toward the upper platform. This is the way we access the Temple since the front stairs are roped off for cleaning and stabilization. From this high vantage, I can see the last few tourists straggling down well-worn paths toward the exit. I waited until the archeological site was near closing to avoid contending with tourists inside the cramped interior space of the pyramid. As I step on the top platform, the guard casts a scowl at me until he recognizes that I'm with the archeological team. He smiles and we exchange a few niceties; I sympathize with his boredom and eagerness to get home for dinner. Explaining that I need to check a few details for our research, I'm relieved as he gestures for me to enter the Temple.

I cannot walk into the Temple of the Inscriptions without a sense of awe descending upon me. Stucco decorations still survive on four of the six front piers, though the outer two are badly eroded. These four piers depict rulers standing atop monster masks; each holding an infant who we believe is Pakal. One foot of the infant turns into a long snake with a Vision Serpent mouth, a well-known symbol for the youngest Triad God, Unen K'awill, who was patron of royal dynasties. The adult figures appear to be ancestors, and it is likely that the two on the central piers are Pakal's parents, Sak K'uk and Kan Mo' Hix. In this powerful symbolism on Pakal's mortuary monument, the people of Palenque would understand that their beloved ruler was being born into the otherworld as their own dynastic god.

Entering the Temple through the central door, I pass into the rear chamber containing the tablets of inscriptions. Standing before this incredible artistic masterpiece, I bow my head in homage as if entering a cathedral. Once again my eyes feast upon the intricate carvings, glyph after glyph of stylized beings, fanciful creatures, perplexing symbols, and the dots and bars of Maya numbers. For me, it's a near-mystical experience. I yearn to spend more time studying epigraphy so I can read these glyphs myself.

To my right is the stairway that descends to Pakal's tomb. Only the upper few steps are visible in the dim lighting, and the stairs plummet quickly into semi-darkness. Although I've gone down these stairs many times, I never overcome a feeling of uncertainty, as if treading any further might put me in danger. Maybe it's my sense of intruding into an extremely sacred space, still watched over by disapproving spirit guardians. Pakal's people went to great lengths to prevent his tomb from discovery and to discourage entry by totally obstructing the passage with rubble. I murmur a few prayers to placate the spirits and respectfully request permission to enter.

Taking a deep breath, I step down and carefully descend. The stairway is very narrow, the steps slippery, and the walls feel oppressively close. When I touch them to stabilize myself, my hands feel moisture on the irregular surfaces. Above me the corbelled arch ceiling gives an eerie impression of pressing downward. The stairs ahead come into faint view as I move from one suspended overhead light to the next. Is it purposeful that INAH keeps the lights dim, maybe to prevent deterioration? The deeper I go inside the pyramid, the more humid and dank the air becomes. It was quite warm outside, but the heat within is intense and stifling. Soon I'm covered in sweat.

Reaching the landing about halfway down, I know the stairs take a sharp 180-degree turn before completing the descent. Here I rest momentarily and wipe sweat from my eyes. I note the small, square stone tube that lines the entire stairway and leads into the burial chamber. This is the psychoduct that served as a conduit for the ruler's spirit to communicate with the world above. With renewed determination, I continue slowly, step by slippery step, until I arrive at the bottom landing that is slightly below ground level, 22 meters under the Temple platform above. The huge triangular slab closing the entrance to the burial vault stands to one side, where it had been moved by Alberto Ruz' team when Pakal's tomb was entered in 1952. INAH had a barrier gate placed to prevent tourists from entering the chamber, but that allows a view inside. Resting my forearms on the gate, I peer into Pakal's tomb.

The chamber is almost completely filled from wall to wall with the huge stone sarcophagus in which Pakal was interred. It is rectangular, 9 by 4 meters, made from a single slab. The lid is a quarter of a meter thick and weighs five tons. Amazing arrays of carvings adorn the sarcophagus lid, considered perhaps the finest work done by any ancient Mayas. Pakal is shown in a slightly curled position, hovering over the maw of an earth monster. From his torso rises the Wakah Chan Te, the Maya World Tree. Flourishes of emerging corn sprout from its arms and a celestial bird soars above. Other figures and glyphs are carved on the lid and the border. The sides of the sarcophagus base are carved with the figures of Pakal's dynasty, including his grandmother Yohl Ik'nal and mother Sak K'uk. On the walls of the chamber is a curious parade of life-size figures.

The sarcophagus holds a fish-shaped box that originally contained Pakal's skeleton. Pakal's burial treasure is legendary, his jade death mask world-famous, his body covered with jade, pearls, obsidian, and shells. The funerary goods to accompany him on the Underworld journey were profuse. In addition, the bones of five sacrificial companions were found. Now most of these burial goods, including Pakal's skeleton, have been moved to INAH laboratories and museums in Mexico City for preservation and display.

As always, I am nearly overcome with emotion as I contemplate the burial chamber of Palenque's greatest ruler. Leaning forward to glimpse the carvings on the side of the sarcophagus, I strain to focus on their features. It's hard to see in the dim light, and I want to climb over the barrier and squeeze into the chamber, but my professional training restrains me. I yearn to know everything I can about these people in Pakal's world, how he related to his ancestors and relatives, who the figures are that line the chamber walls. We still don't fully understand the symbolism carved on the sarcophagus lid. There is so much more to learn from the Mayan glyphs.

Paying homage to the great ruler Janaab Pakal, to his lineage and his people, I bow my head and whisper my thanks for this visit. A sudden sensation of tingling spreads through my arms and chest and my ears are filled with buzzing sounds. My whole insides seem to be humming and I fear that I'm going to faint. Plopping to the floor, I take several deep breaths and shake my head to clear it. After a few moments, the sensations dissipate. Rising slowly and testing my balance, I feel reasonably stable. Maybe my brain oxygen level dropped in the stuffy air. I turn and begin the long ascent, taking the stairs as rapidly as I can although it makes me breathless and even sweatier. I know the guard is getting impatient for I've been down in the vault longer than I should.

This experience is so vivid that I've written in present tense. I am ever there.

K'inich Janaab Pakal is considered the greatest of all Mayan kings. He acceded when only 12 years old, in 615 CE. I'm sure his mother Sak K'uk co-ruled for several years. Ruz and Romano say he died at 40, but the American school contends he lived to the ripe old age of 80, dying in 683 CE. The city was in chaos during his early childhood, devastated by the attack from Kalakmul and Bonampak in 611 CE. It must have left deep impressions on his young mind. By middle age he had instituted a tremendous building program; he and his sons and grandson built most of the structures we now see. It's hard to even imagine what Palenque looked like before.

K'inich Janaab Pakal exploded dramatically on the archeological scene with the work of Alberto Ruz Lhuillier. Ruz was born in Paris to a Cuban father and French mother, went to college in Havana, Cuba, and specialized in pre-Columbian Mesoamerican archeology. He moved to Mexico in 1936 and became a citizen. In 1945 he took charge of INAH's investigations at Palenque with the goal of establishing a complete archeological chronology based on hieroglyphic texts, architectural and ceramic sequences. In 1949 he guided excavations in the Palace, finding the Palace Tablet relief and recording 150 unique images in House E that continue to challenge scholars. We believe House E was a very special sacred shrine during those times.

The Temple of the Inscriptions caught Ruz' attention because its size suggested possible substructures from earlier times. Probes into the supporting platforms did not find earlier structures, however, confirming that the pyramid was built in a very short time in the late 7th century, just as the glyphs stated. While workers were cleaning the floor of the Temple, Ruz saw it was made of huge flat stones instead of the usual stucco. One of the stones had holes drilled near the edges, into which carved plugs were inserted. Checking out this unusual stone, Ruz found a shallow cavity underneath, cleared it of debris, and saw a gigantic stone crossbeam. Under the crossbeam, he saw two stone steps leading downward. The stairs were filled with stones and rubble.

Ruz knew the stairs must lead to something. Soon the crew started clearing the stairs, laboring in a narrow space in sweltering heat and choking dust. They chipped away at the wall of rubble filling the passage from floor to ceiling, removing stones by buckets up the ever-descending stairway. At one point the workers reached a landing and thought the stairs had ended, but instead there was a sharp turn and the passage continued to descend into the heart of the pyramid. It required three years to remove all the rubble.

In June, 1952, the excavators reached bottom. They found a narrow vaulted chamber leading to a huge triangular stone, set vertically and slightly recessed. After they pried the stone open slightly with lever poles, Ruz squeezed through into a large vaulted chamber. Shining his flashlight into the dark chamber, Ruz beheld glistening walls and sparkling stalactites of limestone, like a subterranean crystalline cathedral. Inside, almost filling the chamber, he saw an immense rectangular box with elaborately carved top and sides, covered with figures and glyphs. Glistening limestone deposits on the walls of the chamber almost obscured the life-size, ornately attired figures in low-relief stucco carved on them.

At that time, Ruz and other archeologists had no idea who these figures might be. No one could read Maya glyphs in 1952, except for dates.

The archeologists thought the box was solid and functioned as an altar. Juan Chablé, the master stonemason, requested permission to drill a small hole into the side to confirm that it was solid. A few months later Ruz agreed, and Chablé drilled into the huge stone box, finding that it was hollow. They realized the cover was a lid. The team arranged to lift the lid, a five-ton slab, with automobile jacks. This revealed an inner fish-shaped box, set flush with the precisely carved insides of the huge stone box. Then they realized they were dealing with a sarcophagus. The lid of the fish-shaped box was raised using holes put there by the Maya. What Ruz and team saw inside is considered the greatest discovery of Mesoamerican archeology.

There lay the skeleton of a tall man, 1.65 meters, wearing an exquisite jade mask, necklaces, earspools, bracelets, and surrounded by treasures as never before seen. The richness of Pakal's burial has been compared to that of King Tutankhamen of Egypt.

It was clear to Ruz that the tomb was constructed before the pyramid and summit Temple, because the 15-ton sarcophagus and its five-ton lid could not have been carried down the narrow stairs. The foundation for the pyramid was dug out slightly below plaza level, floored with flagstones, and the sarcophagus was dragged into position. After that the crypt walls and vaults were built, along with the stairs and bulk of the pyramid. The structure was built from ground up, slowly rising to be crowned by the Temple as the final touch.

The discovery of Pakal's tomb revolutionized Maya archeology and caught the imagination of the public. It proved that stepped pyramids did not serve solely as platforms to support their summit buildings. The sarcophagus with portraits and texts set in the burial context of a ruler gave strong clues that glyphs expressed names and histories of real people. Other findings stimulated new research interests, such as the psychoduct that was an expression of spiritual beliefs. The sacrificial bodies suggested that in royal burial practices, companions were chosen to accompany their ruler in the afterlife. Veneration of ancestors was shown by evidence that the stairs were worn by repeated trips down to the tomb.

But Alberto Ruz was not the one to discover who was interred in the splendid sarcophagus. That fell to a group of foreigners who gathered in the first Mesa Redonda at Palenque in 1973. Ruz called the interred ruler "8 Ahau" from what he thought was a birth date. Later when Pakal's name was deciphered, archeologists realized this date referred to the beginning of the current Sun or Great Cycle.

Ruz was invited to attend the first Mesa Redonda, but declined. The same year INAH published his report on the Temple of the Inscriptions, which Ruz thought would be the definitive study on this rich burial. The next year, however, two papers came out from the Mesa Redonda proceedings that directly contradicted his conclusions about name and age of the ruler. Ruz continued to disagree with the North American group.

Ruz requested that when he died, his remains be interred at Palenque. The foremost figure of Mexican archeology died suddenly in 1979. Now a small shrine with his plaque facing the Temple of the Inscriptions fulfills this wish.

We know so much about Pakal, and yet so little. What was his life like between 615 CE when he became ruler and 647 CE when he dedicated the renovated Templo Olvidado? There is very little epigraphic data about this time period. We know he married a woman "of Toktan" and had three or four sons. What was their relationship? His mother Sak K'uk appears on several monuments, it seems they had a special bond. How did that play out over their lives? If only I could time travel and become part of their world in ancient Lakam Ha.

August 29, 1994

Romano is arriving in just over a week to examine the skeleton in Temple XIII. Only a couple of weeks later, our archeological season ends and everyone will be leaving the camp at Palenque. This saddens me, for I've become attached to our enthusiastic young group, to Arnoldo our leader, Fanny who is still ecstatic over her discovery, and my dear roommate Sonia. But most of all I'm attached to this incredible ancient city on a mountainside in the jungle. I'm in love with Palenque.

The irony of this does not escape me. I'm in love, but not with a nice young man who would make a good husband and give me a home and family. That is the dream of my mother and grandmother. No, I'm in love with a place, but more than simply a location. Palenque is another world, a state of mind that transports me into the ancient Mayan culture and connects me deeply with its people and traditions. I yearn to know them better and feel their presence and share their desires. I want to get inside the skin of an ancient Mayan woman and have all her experiences. Especially I want to know the queens of Lakam Ha and their lives.

When I looked recently at the ancestors carved on the side of Pakal's sarcophagus, and those remarkable figures on the chamber walls, it triggered reflections about lineage. It seems that emphasizing a pure lineage back to the founding rulers and even to the Creator Deities was ultimately important to Pakal. His artists' portrayals of these ancestors and nobles, male and female are stunning in their realism. The portrait style at Palenque stands apart from all other cities. Depicted in natural poses with minimal costumes, these graceful figures contrast with the rigid, stylized, and ornately costumed people carved on most Maya stelae and panels. Palenque portraits capture the unique faces of individual rulers. The other cities' carvings have standard faces and set expressions where every ruler looks the same. The difference is huge and striking.

While I'm scraping encrustations off jewelry, applying solvent to ceramics to dissolve clay deposits, polishing obsidian knives, coating figurines with protective pigment to stabilize them, I daydream about the Palenque queens and their people. Though my reverie creates its fantasy, my scientific brain demands data. It's a strange mind to inhabit, half imaginative and half materialistic. No wonder I find it hard relating to villagers, including most of my family members.

My mind jumped to my last interaction with Abuelita Juanita. Because I'm returning soon to Mexico City to continue university studies, I felt obligated to visit my family often. I spent last Sunday afternoon with my family in Palenque town. My parents left after lunch for a social engagement, and Abuelita and I settled into wicker chairs on the patio to enjoy the sunshine and plants. Since the afternoon was quite warm, we sought shade under the table umbrella.

Abuelita Juanita had that faraway look in her eyes, making me wonder where her thoughts had taken her. More and more she seems lost in distant memories. I suppose that is usual for aged people, whose early realities are more vivid than the present. Birds twittered, bees buzzed, and I waited.

She fixed her sky-blue eyes upon me with an unfathomable expression. I marveled yet again at how much her features matched those ancient Maya faces that mutely gazed back at me when I visited the tomb. Juanita's almond shaped eyes are set above high cheekbones in a narrow face. Her nose is large and straight leading to a high forehead. But her nose takes a dip at the bridge, and that distinguishes her from her ancient ancestors. Their nose bridges were completely flat and created a straight line from nose tip to elongated crown, the cranial oblique deformity favored by royals and nobles.

Of course, no Mayas have used headboards to compress and shape the skulls of infants for centuries. Even so, Juanita's cranium is higher and more pointed than most people. Interesting, it makes me wonder about a genetic factor in these elongated Mayan skulls.

Her lips are still full and well modeled, with that sensuous curvature repeated so often in ancient Mayan art. No doubt her false teeth help her lips keep their shape. Marvels of modern dentistry! With the addition of feather headdress, jade jewelry, and regal costume, my grandmother could have stepped off the sides of Pakal's tomb.

"You must always remember the importance of family."

Juanita's soft voice startled me back into the sunny patio at my parent's house.

"Family is your anchor, your foundation in this world. It defines what you are and can be. It is more than your roots, it is your destiny. Do you understand?"

I wasn't sure that I did, so I shook my head. Her eyes became fierce.

"Francesca, you are the continuation. Your brother and sister do not carry enough of the ancient blood. For some reason known only to the Gods, you are the chosen one in the family. Maybe that is why you are an archeologist."

"I'm sorry, Abuelita," I said. "I don't understand what you are saying."

"Look at you. You are different than all the rest. Always adventuresome, always curious. You followed your own ambitions to get a university education, the first in our family. You became an archeologist devoted to studying the ancient Mayas, your ancestors. What called you to do all this? You listened to the lightning in your blood, the blood of your people, your lineage."

I knew what she meant by "lightning in the blood," a particular electrifying vibration that revealed truths to visionaries. I couldn't recall ever experiencing anything like that.

"Abuelita, you give me too much credit. I am no Mayan visionary. I just followed my interests in a professional career. And technically I'm a specialist in restoration, not an archeologist."

She regarded me with disdain. Using a dismissing hand wave, she flicked away doubts.

"I know who you are, Francesca. Do not quibble about small details. You study the ancient cities and customs of our people, you do archeology. You have the ancient blood and it will speak to you."

Unclear what to reply, I just nodded. Juanita alarmed me, speaking with the certainty of prophecy. What did she know but would not say directly? I wondered if it was connected to the tale she always held out to tantalize me, the story of how I got my blue eyes. But she refused to tell me until I get married, and there is no sign of that on my horizon.

My grandmother sat back and closed her eyes. She appeared to be dozing, and indeed the moments of quiet began to lull me into somnolence. She shifted position and coughed, bringing me into strangely heightened awareness.

"When are you returning to Mexico City?" she asked.

"The middle of next month. Our project is ending, and there is no more funding to continue this research. So I don't expect to be back for the season next year."

"You must come more often, even if you don't have an archeological project nearby."

"Yes." There was no point saying how busy I would be finishing my degree. An inspiration popped up to use my departure as an excuse to pull information out of her.

"Since I am leaving soon, and it may be some time before I return, why not tell me the story about my blue eyes? If you keep waiting, it may be . . . uh . . . too late." I was a little abashed at myself for using this tactic, but she was getting very old.

Her sharp glance conveyed more than words.

"You have much to learn, querida." She softened her disapproval with a term of endearment. "That is why I cannot tell you the story now, you are not ready. I thought taking the responsibility of marriage and family would cause your heart to embrace the importance of continuing the lineage. When you understand this with your mind and take it deeply into your heart, then you will be ready to know everything about your heritage. There are things that the unprepared soul cannot handle. There are things for which you must be initiated. In these times, with much loss of our traditions, initiations take unexpected paths. I cannot prescribe it. I can only recognize it once it happens."

She had never talked to me in this way before. She was sounding like a village shaman, not a simple old grandmother. Now I was really alert and disconcerted.

"What are you saying, Abuelita? I am totally lost about this initiation."

"That is why I cannot speak more of it presently," she sighed. "And why I cannot tell you the story. But this you must remember: Watch for the lightning in the blood."

We had little more conversation after that. She seemed sad when I left, her face creased with the handiwork of the Lords of Time. Walking toward the main plaza to find a combi, I stopped dead in my tracks with a sudden revelation.

I *had* experienced the lightning in the blood. It happened just last week when I was standing at the entrance into Pakal's tomb saying my goodbyes to him. The memory of those sensations clicked with what I'd read about this shamanic phenomenon. Badly shaken, I stood trembling in the hot afternoon sun.

Across the street was the small Catholic Church that my family always attended. I'm no devout Catholic, mostly it's a social activity for me, but I felt drawn to enter the church. Dodging cars that refused to slow down; I maneuvered the street and entered the dim vestibule, breathing faint whiffs of incense and candles. Dipping fingers into the holy water and making the Sign of the Cross, I sat in a rear pew. I did not pray. I did not know what, if anything, to pray for. My mind went blank and I sat in silence, somehow comforted just by being in a sanctuary.

A door creaked to one side and I glanced around as the parish priest came in. I knew him well from years of church events while growing up. Father Julio Mendez was a kind man and more tolerant than most priests. I waved at him to join me in the pew.

"Hello, Francesca, it's good to see you. You don't visit here much since you moved away, just an occasional mass with your family."

"That's true, but it's nice to be here now."

He sat beside me and we embraced lightly.

"What brings you to church at this unusual hour?"

"Father Julio, I am disturbed by things my grandmother said to me today." I've no idea why I was so candid and to the point with him. Maybe years of making confession or the crack into my awareness that was happening.

"Ah, Juanita Nokom, she is quite a person. What did she say that upset you?"

I recounted our conversation, even sharing about my strange sensations inside the pyramid. He listened with wise and compassionate eyes.

"Sometimes I think your grandmother still follows the ancient religion, even though she does everything expected of a Catholic," he offered. "There are things about her that I have never understood. An undercurrent of wildness, perhaps. A nobility in bearing that is subtle but compelling. I do believe she keeps secrets, even as she implies to you."

"Do you have any idea what these secrets are?"

"Not precisely. I have heard rumors over the years from the village priests that served Tumbala. They said there was some scandal about her family, something very big and very significant. None had any details about it. Apparently the village still gossips and holds her family suspect. They keep some distance; that may be one reason why Juanita married outside the village."

"Would someone in the village know?"

"Maybe the shaman, for I am certain they still have one. Not that I recommend pursuing that route. Let us hope that your grandmother will come around to telling you. But for now, how can I be helpful to you?"

"You have been helpful simply by listening. I've got a lot to reflect on and pray about. Guidance will come, I'm sure."

I sounded more confident than I really felt. The part about praying was mostly for the priest's benefit, though later I thought it wasn't such a bad idea. I didn't need to say in which religion and to what Gods I would be praying.

September 5, 1994

It is three months after the discovery, and today Arturo Romano Pacheco visited the tomb in Temple XIII. It was an emotional experience for him, reviving the intense feelings evoked when he first viewed the bones of Pakal forty-two years earlier. Although he is an older man, he is still agile and athletic and climbed the stairs of the temple easily. Entering the chamber he felt the same astonishment as when he entered Pakal's tomb, gazing across centuries into the sarcophagus of a royal ancient Maya.

Arnoldo Gonzales Cruz, director of our project, stood close by Romano. I was fortunate enough to accompany the small group from our team who entered the chamber this day. Eager to document every detail, Arnoldo clicked on his recorder to catch each word uttered by the famous professor. I hoped I could hear clearly over the pounding of my heart.

Romano stood in silence, eyes traveling up and down the skeleton. His gaze came to rest on the pelvic bones, where he studied the pelvic outlet and shape of the iliac bones.

"Hmmm, it is a small pelvis with a very ample sub-pubic angle; at least ninety degrees . . . the bones are delicate, fine, graceful . . . hmmm . . ."

Sweat dripped from my nose and I tried discretely to wipe it away. The temperature inside the chamber was extreme and the humidity nearly intolerable. Romano looked cool and unperturbed, though everyone else present was coated with sweat. We remained still as statues, our breath bated, hanging in suspense.

With certainty born of profound expertise and his uncanny ability to dialogue with bones, Romano stated his conclusion without touching anything.

"It is a woman."

I took a quick inbreath and wished Fanny could be here. She was at the site museum preparing the bones of the companions found beside the sarcophagus for later examination by Romano. Everyone stayed hushed and motionless, awaiting his further words.

"Although it is difficult to determine precisely without touching the bones, the general configuration of the skeleton is feminine. Look at the skull, the ascending wings of the mandible, the superior border of the orbits, the vertebral bodies and lumbar vertebra, the sacrum that has come apart over time. The forearms are fine, as is true of all the bones . . . this person was undoubtedly of the feminine sex."

He further observed that the skeleton had remained untouched since it was placed in the sarcophagus, and it appeared to be a primary interment rather than a secondary burial. The bones were impregnated with cinnabar and were completely red in color, including the skull and teeth. The ankles were close together, showing that the body was shrouded before being deposited, evidence that great care was taken in preparing it for burial. Although the cranium had fallen into pieces, probably from the weight of the jade mask and diadem, he commented that the cranial deformation was the tabular oblique type, characteristic of high ranked persons in the Classic Period.

Next he examined offerings inside the sarcophagus, noting that diadems were not exclusive to women but were worn by all high ranked nobles. Looking around, he made further observations about the lack of glyphs.

"This person might have died much earlier than expected, and her tomb quickly prepared. To avoid decomposition, they moved rapidly to the interment and possibly did not have time to carve inscriptions . . . Without carved dates the exact time of burial is a mystery. We cannot know if this woman preceded or came after Pakal. We will have to wait for results of DNA testing, ceramic analysis, and carbon dating of organic remnants within the crypt."

Romano made one surprising observation while examining the lower extremities. In the lower third of the left tibia was the cocoon of a wasp, with a larva that never developed into an adult.

To his experienced eyes, the skeleton was that of a woman about 1.58 meters in height, who had attained between 38 and 40 years of age before she died.

A few hours later, Romano went to the Site Museum and informed Fanny that the sarcophagus held the bones of a woman. Fanny told me later that her skin crawled and her heart leapt. She always believed it was a woman and now the most respected physical anthropologist in Mexico had confirmed it. He examined the bones of the companions, concluding that they were sacrificed to accompany her, and neither was bundled in a shroud. The skeleton on the west side was a boy between 8 and 11 years calculated by his teeth, with tabular erect cranial deformation. He was placed with body extended in face-up position. The skeleton on the east was a woman between 25 and 35 years, of 1.55 meters height, her body placed extended with face down. She had a tabular oblique cranial deformation and insertions of jade and stones in her teeth.

Romano returned to Mexico City the following day to report his conclusions to INAH and the world. Arnoldo coined the nickname for the woman in the sarcophagus that we all immediately took to using: *"The Red Queen."*

The question now reverberating in everyone's mind is: "Who is this woman?"

Speculation runs rampant around camp. Because of the age determined by Romano, many think it must be Pakal's wife, Tz'aakb'u Ahau. But we cannot rule out his mother Sak K'uk or grandmother Yohl Ik'nal, although they probably had longer lives. As the two documented woman rulers of Palenque, there are glyphs stating their dates of accession and death, but not their birth dates. The final possibility, to me a distant fourth, is Pakal's daughter-in-law K'inuuw Mat.

Ringing across the plazas of Palenque, soaring over the mountains, coursing down the rivers, spreading onto the wide plains of Tabasco, and eventually wrapping around the world is the question we are all asking.

"Who is this woman?"

Who lies in the second richest burial ever found in the Maya world? Which woman was so honored that she was interred in a temple adjoining the mortuary pyramid of Pakal? Our archeological team keeps tossing possibilities around.

"She's his wife." "She's his mother." "She's his grandmother."

Or maybe she's someone else, an unknown royal woman we have yet to discover in the glyphic texts. On one thing we all agree, however.

In the sarcophagus in the unknown substructure of Temple XIII, a woman was interred with highest respect—a woman who was a Queen of Palenque.

The lack of inscriptions on the queen's sarcophagus is the main obstacle to learning her identity. If only we had some name glyphs! Then we would know now, and not have to wait for DNA testing. This put me to thinking about the long saga of deciphering the Maya glyphs. Since the earliest explorers, Mayanists have speculated about what these enigmatic carvings say. The history of Mayan language decipherment is fraught with dissention, quite a story in itself. Much to our shame it took over one hundred years, compared with only two years for Champollion to crack Egyptian hieroglyphic writing, and two decades for an international team to decipher Hieroglyphic Hittite, the Bronze Age script of Anatolia (modern Turkey). Of course, Champollion had the Rosetta Stone, but we had our own key in Diego de Landa's *Relación de las Cosas de Yucatán*, discovered in dusty recesses of a Madrid library by Brasseur de Bourbourg in 1862. Its importance was not recognized for about a century, however.

The Mexican Revolution of 1910-1917 and World War I created decades of turbulence, but scientific exploration at Palenque moved ahead. Justo Sierra Mendez, Mexican minister of public instruction and fine arts, visited Palenque in 1909. He was familiar with the Maya, since his father (statesman-poet Justo Sierra O'Reilly) had produced a Spanish edition of Stephens' travels. Two months after his visit to the ruins, he established the first school of archeology and anthropology in Mexico City.

Eduard Seler of Germany was the first director. Seler's specialty was Mesoamerican iconography, and he immediately attempted to interpret the complex inscriptions at Palenque. He brought together a huge amount of iconographic evidence, mostly from the central highlands, and did detailed comparisons with Palenque. In 1920 this school closed and its functions passed to UNAM (Universidad Nacional Autonoma de Mexico). Mexican archeology came of age by 1920, with an enlarging cadre of scholars and new outlets for rapid publications.

Important research in Europe set the stage for initial decipherment of Maya glyphs. Ernst Forstemann, Head of the Dresden Royal Saxon Library, found among its collections a curious fan-folded document filled with figures and groups of dots and bars. An earlier librarian had purchased it in a Vienna flea market in 1739. Forstemann photographed the document, compared it to photographs and drawings of Palenque and Yaxchilan by Maudslay and Maler, and to publications by Harvard University showing monuments of Copan. By 1900, he figured out the bars (fives) and dots (ones) in the Dresden Codex were a numbering system for the ancient Maya calendar. His analyses confirmed what others had already suggested: that Maya glyphs should be read in order from left to right and down, two columns at a time.

In 1905, American journalist Joseph T. Goodman was able to correlate the ancient Maya Long Count Calendar with modern calendars. This was no small accomplishment since the Mayas stopped using the Long Count in the late 10th century. In Guatemala and Yucatan, Mayan descendants continued using the Tzolk'in—Haab "Short Count" of 52-year cycles. Goodman studied the work of Diego de Landa, who first made connections in the 1560s between katun-end records of local villagers and current Julian dates. From these he worked out possible calendar correlations. With a few modifications added by later archeologists Juan Martinez and J. Eric Thompson, this GMT (Goodman-Martinez-Thompson) correlation is still used.

The foundations were laid for scientific archeology and epigraphic research. For the first time since Palenque was abandoned, we could read the dates carved by residents of the mysterious city. But for many more years, the other glyphs carved on monuments and written on ceramics or codices went undeciphered.

September 15, 1994

This is my last day in the archeological camp at Palenque. The INAH Special Project is ending and future discoveries must be made by some other team. The last few weeks here have been bittersweet. We are justly proud of the momentous work done by our team, for the Red Queen's tomb is opening an entirely new chapter in Maya studies. Though we've learned a lot, so much more remains unanswered. As Arnoldo said when the tomb was first opened, we need one hundred years of research to fully comprehend the messages contained in the burial chamber.

After Arturo Romano's visit, Fanny was charged with preparing the bones for transport to Mexico City. Sonia and I were assigned to assist since we are restoration specialists. We undertook removal of the Red Queen's bones as a sacred responsibility. A special swing was built so we could hang over the sarcophagus without stepping into the interior. Wearing protective gloves, we leaned over while suspended and picked up the fragile bones, one by one. Our hands were soft as velvet when we lifted first the skull bones, then arms, vertebra, ribs, hands and fingers, pelvis, legs, and feet. These bones were placed carefully in labeled bags and put inside airtight containers for their trip to the main INAH laboratories.

Fanny often spoke to the Queen, as though the red bones could hear and understand.

"It's in your best interests, to preserve you, so you can exist for a much longer time. This discovery is a way of assuring that you always continue living and that people will always talk about you. If you wanted to be present for a very long time, you have attained this goal."

Sometimes I found myself whispering to the Queen, too. She has entered into our imaginations and taken her place there on her throne. Never will our lives be the same again. We all feel compelled to find out exactly who she is, to learn all we can about her, to understand women rulers in Palenque and the ancient Maya world.

After the Queen's bones left Palenque, we all felt a vacuum. Many times I revisited the sarcophagus inside Temple XIII, where I could still feel her presence. At dinner we talked about returning to Palenque on another project. None of us want to release our ties here, for we have lost our hearts to this magnificent city in the Chiapas jungles.

Lingering over packing, my hands rested on my reference book that chronicles the decipherment of Maya hieroglyphs. I sat and flipped through the pages, even though I should continue getting ready to leave. It's an ever fascinating subject to me.

In 1952, even as Ruz was getting ready to excavate the stairway leading to the chamber beneath the Temple of the Inscriptions, important developments occurred across the Atlantic Ocean. Yuri Knorosov, a young Russian epigrapher, published his work interpreting the Mayan hieroglyphic system. Knorosov was an Egyptologist with keen interest in writing systems of ancient China and India and was versed in Japanese and Arabic literature. In one of the great coincidences of life, he was a Soviet soldier in World War II whose unit entered Berlin in May 1945, where he found the National Library on fire. He managed to snatch one book from the thousands being consumed by flames. It was a combined edition that reproduced the three Mayan codices that survived Diego de Landa's infamous book burning. Just consider that improbability!

With this trophy in hand, Knorosov returned to university studies and pondered the ancient writing. His professor challenged him to crack the code. The brilliant scholar learned Spanish and translated de Landa's *Relación* as his doctoral dissertation. Using this key, the earliest attempt to translate Mayan language, Knorosov set the foundation for decipherment. He said the glyphs were a mixed system consisting of ideograms or logograms that have both conceptual and phonetic value, purely phonetic signs, and classificatory signs with only conceptual value. Maya scribes wrote using principles shared by other hieroglyphic systems, and those rules gave multiple functions to various glyphic components. In Mayan writing, word sequence generally went verb—object—subject. It was a complex system, and Knorosov didn't get everything right, but his basic conclusion that Mayan writing was essentially phonetic proved to be correct.

This did not go over well with the established epigraphic expert of the time, J. Eric Thompson. The British "grand old man" of Maya archeology, Thompson was knighted by Queen Elizabeth for his work. By sheer force of intellect and personality, he dominated modern Maya studies until his death in 1975. Thompson believed Mayan society was led by priests and calendar keepers, and the impressive stone cities in the jungles were primarily places for ceremony and astronomy. His books were full of literary and mythological references, and he felt deep affinity for the wise Maya priests and astronomers. The main lasting contributions he made were to calendar studies and the influence of ancient Gods over Maya life.

As to interpreting the Maya glyphs, Thompson was completely wrong. He said the glyphs were "anagogical" and expressed spiritual and mystical concepts.

They were not to be taken literally or read as mundane daily language. Here's a quote from Sir Eric.

"That such mystical meanings are imbedded in the glyphs is beyond doubt . . . our duty is to seek more of those mythological allusions."

Thompson began attacking Knorosov in 1953 and continued the rest of his life. His arguments swayed an entire generation of Mayanists, including Alberto Ruz and most Mexicans. A new school of thought was emerging in North America, however, one that dissented with Thompson and pursued its own interpretations – mostly the epigraphers and linguists.

Another Russian, Tatania Proskouriakoff, working with the Carnegie Foundation, published a landmark paper in 1960 about her study of a pattern of dates at Piedras Negras, Guatemala. She showed that the texts on these stelae recorded history, naming the rulers of towns, both men and women, with birth and accession dates. Even though she could not translate their names, it was clear that the monuments showed real people and events in their lives.

In 1958, Heinrich Berlin published a paper that identified the Emblem Glyphs of several cities. He detected a particular pattern in which the third glyph varied according to the city to which it was linked. This had far-reaching effects, later enabling analysis of Maya political geography. Berlin studied Palenque texts and identified glyphs for the Palenque Triad Gods that are so important to the mythological history and spiritual practices of the city. With Emblem Glyphs identified, Proskouriakoff was able to work out dynastic history for an Usumacinta River city (Yaxchilan). She noted that the Emblem Glyph generally followed the names of rulers. The earliest pair of rulers she called "Shield Jaguar" and "Bird Jaguar" based on what the glyphs looked like.

Things began happening fast in the 1960s and 1970s. A corpus of Maya hieroglyphic inscriptions was being created, building on the photographs of Maudslay and Maler, augmented by discovery of more panels covered with glyphs in the Palenque Palace and Cross Group. The Peabody Museum at Harvard University sent Ian Graham to record all the glyphs carved on stone wherever they may be, using photographs and same-scale drawings. Done with uniform drafting standards, this guaranteed an impeccable source for epigraphic and iconographic analysis.

All this set the stage for the Mesas Redondas of Palenque.

On a hot August afternoon in 1973, a small group of North American "Palencophiles" gathered on the back porch of a thatched roof house in Palenque town. The home of Merle Greene Robertson and her husband Bob had become a

Mecca for foreign archeologists and Mayanists, and a few were always stopping by during the season. Merle was an artist who was enamored of Palenque. She gained permission from INAH to make impressions of the site's sculptures and reliefs before these deteriorated more. Over 10 years, she made photographs, drawings, and rubbings that surpassed Maudslay's in detail and accuracy.

Chatting about Palenque in the shady pavilion were Gillett Griffin, Curator of Pre-Columbian Art at Princeton, Linda Schele and her husband David, and David Joralemon from Yale in addition to Merle and Bob Robertson. Griffin suggested a "round table" on Palenque bringing together interdisciplinary experts to examine the art, iconography, and hieroglyphic inscriptions. All were in agreement, and soon invitations were sent out to the Primera (First) Mesa Redonda in December 1973.

The meetings were held at the motel and restaurant of Moises Morales, a northern Mexican fluent in four languages and connected with the Lacandon Mayas. Present were 23 North American and five Mexican scholars, plus eight students. For a week, this group focused on Palenque, moving back and forth between the motel and the ruins. When questions arose about details of sculptures or inscriptions, or to test ideas that came up in discussion, they could immediately visit the ruins and check things out. In addition, they had the art of Merle and a notebook recording all the published Palenque texts and their dates brought by Peter Mathews, a student of David Kelley. Kelley was invited but could not attend.

Linda Schele was an artist from Tennessee with a brusque style and thick accent. She fell in love with Palenque on her first visit and became friends with Merle. Although she didn't complete degrees in archeology until later in life, Linda became a leader in translating Maya glyphs. Her enthusiasm was infectious. Floyd Lounsbury was a linguist who mastered Amerindian languages, including impossibly complex Oneida. Also trained in mathematics and anthropology, he took up Maya glyphs as a hobby after reading the work of Knorosov. He was convinced the glyphs reproduced speech. He learned Yucatec and Chortí Mayan as well as ancient Cholan, the language used by Classic Maya scribes. Agreeing with Knorosov, he emphasized that Mayan script fit perfectly with other early scripts in the rest of the world.

George Stuart came as a neophyte; he became a major researcher of Palenque as his archeological career unfolded. He brought his family, including his eight-year-old son David Stuart who found Palenque "the place" for exciting archeology. David also focused his archeological research on Palenque and made important contributions to later Mesas Redondas. George was acquainted with Alberto Ruz and regretted his absence at that first meeting, but knew Ruz resented this group of foreign enthusiasts descending on the place to which he devoted his career.

The crowning achievement of the Primera Mesa Redonda was the decipherment of Palenque's "king list." Linda Schele wanted to work on identifying rulers at Palenque, and Peter Mathews and Floyd Lounsbury joined her in the library at Merle's house. The three of them sparked an intellectual chemistry. Working on the kitchen table with Peter's notebook and mathematical formulas Floyd had created to obtain Long Count dates from the Calendar Round used at Palenque, they examined copies of the inscriptions from Pakal's sarcophagus. First they identified a royal prefix that they read "makina" or Great Sun (now translated as K'inich). This pointed them toward the ruler's name glyph that followed. The next glyphs would be titles and include the Emblem Glyph. From Floyd's knowledge of linguistics, they knew a verb would come next and after that, the subject of the sentence.

The three constructed a provisional list of rulers with dates. But what to call them? Looking at the logograph, they assigned names depending on how the glyph appeared. The first ruler they called "Shield," the next "Snake Jaguar" and so on. It took three and a half hours to reconstruct the second half of the Palenque ruling dynasty.

That evening the three mesmerized other participants with their presentation, nothing less than the ruling history of Palenque from the Late Classic period in the early 7th Century through the end of the lineage. The lives of six successive kings were laid out, from birth to accession to death. It was the most complete king list for any Maya site to date.

The king called "Shield" was the mighty ruler whose burial chamber lay deep inside the Temple of the Inscriptions. Ruz called him "8 Ahau." Shortly after the Mesa Redonda ended, David Kelley and Michael Coe both came upon phonetic versions of his name glyph, which, following Knorosov's system was pronounced pa-ca-l(a). The "a" is silent, so it was pronounced Pakal. From his birth and death dates, they determined that he lived for 80 years.

In spring 1974, a group met at Dumbarton Oaks in Washington, D.C. and persisted in completing the Palenque king list. Linda Schele, Peter Mathews, Floyd Lounsbury, Merle Robertson, and David Kelley were almost "in a state of trance" as they deciphered some key glyphs related to lineage. Within three-and-a-half hours they identified the names and reconstructed the lives of the first half of the dynasty.

"Franci! What are you doing?"

Startled, I looked up and saw Sonia standing in the door, hands on hips.

"You don't have time for reading; we have to get out of here by two o'clock."

"What time is it?" I asked lamely, shutting my book.

"One-thirty so get going. Here, I'll help with your things."

We scurried around shoving clothes and toiletries into bags and boxing up the last books. Hoisting as much as we could carry, we hurried to the parking area where vans were waiting to take us to our busses in town. A couple of trips completed the task. With hugs all around and teary eyes, the team mingled and bid each other farewell, or as we like to say *hasta luego*—until later.

It's a long bus ride from Palenque town to Villahermosa, where we catch flights that will disperse us all around Mexico. Sonia and I are on the same flight to Mexico City, returning to the same university, now as good friends. But the others I may never see again, though we all vowed to come back to Palenque.

Deciphering the glyphs. They say that we've cracked the Maya code and can read 80% of the symbols. I'm not so sure that we fully understand their meanings. The ancient Mayas led a multi-dimensional existence and viewed their world in a very different way than we do with our western minds. Maybe I need to plummet into the depths of Maya thinking. Wasn't that something my father talked about? And might not my grandmother be saying the same thing, in her odd way?

The glyphs are the key to understanding the ancient Mayas. Through the glyphs, they speak to us. The inscriptions on Pakal's sarcophagus and the hieroglyphic panels in his Temple unfolded the history of Palenque's ruling dynasty. These inscriptions include names of the queens in Pakal's lineage.

But what about our new discovery, the tomb of the Red Queen?

There are no glyphs on the sarcophagus or chamber walls of the Red Queen's tomb. She keeps her identity hidden, as if teasing us. How will we know for sure which queen is buried in the Temple next to Pakal? If only I had the abilities of a shaman, I could journey to other dimensions, to that ancient Mayan world, and see for myself.

A Sneak Peek into Book 3 of the Mists of Palenque Series

THE MAYAN RED QUEEN: TZ'AAKB'U AHAU OF PALENQUE

THE ANCIENT MAYA city of Lakam Ha has a new, young ruler, K'inich Janaab Pakal. His mother and prior ruler, Sak K'uk, has selected his wife, later known as The Red Queen. Lalak is a shy and homely young woman from a nearby city who relates better to animals than people. She is chosen as Pakal's wife because of her pristine lineage to B'aakal dynasty founders—but also because she is no beauty. She is overwhelmed by the sophisticated and complex society at the polity's dominant city, and the expectations of the royal court. Her mother-in-law Sak K'uk chose Lalak for selfish motives, determined to find a wife who would not displace her in Pakal's affections. She viewed Lalak as a breeder of future rulers and selected her royal name to reflect this: Tz'aakb'u Ahau, the Accumulator of Lords who sets the royal succession.

Lalak struggles to learn her new role and prove her worth, puzzled by her mother-in-law's hostility and her husband's aloofness. She learns he is enamored of a beautiful woman banished from Lakam Ha by his mother. Pakal's esthetic tastes obscure his view of his homely wife. Lalak, however, is fated to play a pivotal role in Pakal's mission to restore the spiritual portal to the Triad Gods that was destroyed in a devastating attack by archenemy Kan. Through learning sexual alchemy, Lalak brings the immense creative force of sacred union to rebuild the portal. But first Pakal must come to view his wife in a new light.

The naive, homely girl flowers into a woman of poise and power, establishes her place in court, and after several miscarriages that bring her marriage to crisis, she has four sons with Pakal to assure dynastic succession. Her dedication supports him in a renaissance of construction, art, and science that transforms Lakam Ha into the most widely sought creative center in the Classic Maya world.

TZ'AAKB'U AHAU—I

BAKTUN 9 KATUN 9 TUN 9— BAKTUN 9 KATUN 9 TUN 12 622 CE—625 CE

1

THE MESSENGER BOWED deeply, clasping his shoulder and dropping to his knees. Head bowed, he waited below the raised platform in the reception chamber of the royal couple. All eyes were fixed on him and his sense of importance swelled. The mission entrusted to him was of utmost importance. It concerned nothing less than the future of the Lakam Ha dynasty. Now he brought his report to his patrons and the atmosphere of the palace chamber quivered with anticipation.

"Welcome, Worthy Messenger Budz Ek." Kan Mo' Hix spoke first. "Come forward and sit before us. We are pleased you have returned safely."

"Indeed, your journey has been swift," said Sak K'uk. "You are rightly named, for you travel as quickly as your namesake, Smoking Star—Comet."

Budz Ek smiled at the compliment and edged forward on his knees to take a position on the woven mat set in front of the platform. He was apprehensive, however, because he feared the royal couple would not be pleased with his messages. It was a risk faced by all messengers. Their powerful patrons often unleashed a barrage of fury upon the hapless bringers of bad news, though mostly this was an onslaught of words and not the thrust of a knife. He knew the ruling family of Lakam Ha would not resort to violence, but to be in disfavor would affect his status.

"Speak now of your visit to B'aak. We are ready to hear what you have seen and learned." Sak K'uk waved the hand sign ordering attendants to bring refreshments.

Before speaking, Budz Ek sat up straight and glanced around the reception chamber, his astute eyes taking in every subtlety. In addition to the royal couple, parents of K'inich Janaab Pakal, the youthful ruler of Lakam Ha and the B'aakal Polity, was a small audience including the steward Muk Kab, K'akmo the Nakom—warrior chief, the royal scribe K'anal, and two trusted courtiers who were distant cousins of Sak K'uk, the ruler's mother. The only other woman in the group was Zazil, her primary noble attendant. It was a select group, the messenger observed, so his information was meant for only certain ears.

It struck him as odd that the ruler, the Holy B'aakal Lord—K'uhul B'aakal Ahau was not there. Surely the report pertained most of all to him. But this was not the messenger's business.

He took note that his report was not being received in high level court protocol. Although the royal couple was dressed in typical Mayan finery, it was modest compared to courtly dress. Sak K'uk wore a white huipil with blue and gold embroidery at the neckline and hem, several strings of alabaster beads, dangling alabaster ear spools, and a small headdress of blue and yellow feathers set in bands of silver disks. Kan Mo' Hix was bare-chested with a short, skirted loincloth of colorful stripes. His small pectoral pendant symbolized the Sun Lord; jade ear spools hung from both ears and worked copper cuffs surrounded his wrists. On his elongated skull perched a tall white cylindrical cap topped with a ceramic macaw-mo, his namesake.

The messenger wore the usual runner attire, a white loincloth with red waistband and short cape loosely tied over his shoulders. A red headband kept his long black hair away from his face. He had arrived at the palace in the early morning, stopping the evening before to rest a short distance from the city. This allowed him to appear refreshed and in clean attire. His years of experience had taught him the wisdom of preparing well for reports to royal patrons. Arriving breathless and sweaty in the heat of midday did not create an advantageous scenario.

Bowing again to the royal couple, he began his report.

"It takes two days of travel, as you know, to journey from Lakam Ha to B'aak. Travel on the Michol River went easily, thanks to our skillful canoe paddlers.

More difficulties arose once we left the river and climbed through jungle-covered hills toward our destination. The path is not as well maintained as would be expected since the river is their main source for trade goods. It is said among traders I encountered along the path that B'aak has declined in prosperity. The ahauob of B'aak buy fewer luxury items such as red spondylus shells, carved jade, quetzal feathers, and fine obsidian for blades. In the city, while mingling among ahauob-nobles and craftsmen in the market, I heard mention of difficult years when crops were less productive. Rumors circulated that B'aak leadership was faltering during this time.

"The B'aak ruler, Ik' Muuy Muwaan, was apparently contending with internal dissension and a plot to overthrow his dynasty. His ambitious younger brother had recruited a cadre of ahauob and warriors, leading to several years of intermittent clashes, often taking place in cornfields and trampling crops. Between skirmishes, the insurgents hid in the jungles, re-grouping for more raids. Only two years ago was the rightful ruler able to suppress this group, when his younger brother was killed in battle. Since then, the ruler has re-established leadership, banished the traitors and is slowly bringing fields back to fertility. This history I confirmed with the calendar priests of the city.

"The day after my arrival, I was received at the ruler's court. There I presented your gifts of cacao, fine woven cloth, and copal incense. These were received with much enthusiasm, and most polite inquiries were made into the health of your royal family and our young K'uhul B'aakal Ahau."

"For the concern of Ik' Muuy Muwaan, we are grateful," interjected Sak K'uk. She was impatient for the messenger to arrive at the purpose of his visit. "What said he to your inquiries about his daughter?"

"Of this, he was most pleased. To have his daughter considered as royal consort for your son was beyond his imagining. He was eager to bring the girl for my viewing, and her mother to extol her virtues. The visit was arranged for that very afternoon."

"Not surprising that Ik' Muuy Muwaan leapt at the chance to wed his daughter to the ruler of Lakam Ha," muttered Kan Mo' Hix under his breath. Only Sak K'uk could hear him. "He is already counting the marriage gifts we will give him."

Budz Ek looked quizzically at the royal couple, observing the murmurings.

"Honored Messenger, do continue," Sak K'uk said, frowning at her husband. "We wish to hear your observations of the girl."

225

The messenger felt heat rising along his neck and face and hoped he would not sweat profusely. It was not due to rising morning temperature, for inside the chamber the air was cool and fresh. He knew the flush was caused by worry over what he was about to say. Sucking air in through nearly closed lips, he tried to cool himself and maintain composure as he continued his report.

"Her mother and attendant brought her to the reception chamber. First there came lengthy descriptions of her character and abilities. Lady Lalak is, by their words, a young woman of pleasant and quiet character, who treats all kindly and is well loved by her city's people. She is skilled in weaving and makes delicate cloth that has no match. She paints lovely patterns on ceramic bowls with a true artistic flair. Her voice is sweet and clear when she sings, her form graceful and sure-footed when she dances. Children flock to her and she entertains them with clever stories. In conversation, she speaks with a courtly flourish and can address many topics. In particular, she is knowledgeable about the animals and plants of the area. It seems she creates special relationships with animals and has several wild ones as pets."

"Excellent attributes, if these are all to be believed." Sak K'uk doubted everything was true; such praise was only expected when proffering a daughter as a royal bride. Her real interest was revealed by her next question.

"And of her appearance? Tell me not the words of her parents, but your own observations. Is she beautiful?"

Budz Ek hesitated, for this was the exact question he wished to avoid. The intense stare Sak K'uk gave him made it clear that avoidance was impossible.

"Holy Lady, this I must answer honestly although it pains me. The daughter of Ik' Muuy Muwaan has a sweet and gentle presence and spoke well when questioned. But she is not a beauty according to standards of our art. She is large-boned and, well, rather rounded of body. Her skin is a deep brown color, her hair thick and lustrous. She has the elongated skull that signifies nobility of the true blood, and her nose line is straight as a blade."

He glanced at the ruler's mother entreatingly, as if beseeching her to forgive him in advance. Only a stern glare was returned to the now copiously sweating messenger.

"Of the face of Lady Lalak, it must be said . . . much do I regret to say it, her face is . . . homely."

"She is unattractive?" Kan Mo' Hix sounded more curious than displeased.

"You must give more details," Sak K'uk insisted. "Describe her face carefully. You have great powers of observation, you have shown these before."

"As you command, Holy Lady. I wish not to disparage the worthy daughter of our neighbor city and their ruling family. I bring only what my eyes have seen, and it is your prerogative to make your assessment. Now come the details. Her face is wide and square, with a firm chin line. While large noses are common among our people, hers is uncommonly great. The tip is almost bulbous and the nostrils flare out widely. This feature dominates her face. By comparison, her eyes are small and recessed under heavy brows. They do have a nice almond shape and shine with intelligent light. Her lips are thick and down curving, except when she smiles. Her smile is captivating and her teeth straight and white. The ears are also prominent, standing out from her head with long lobes; good for wearing heavy ear spools."

He paused again, pondering whether to impart the next bit of telling information about the girl's appearance. Quickly he gauged it was folly to omit it, for the royal family would see this defect the moment they set eyes on her.

"There is yet one additional observation I made of her features," he continued slowly. "As a young child, she contracted an illness that caused a widespread rash over her face and body. Infection set in and she almost died. The healing skills of B'aak priestesses saved her life, but scars were left upon her face from infected bumps. These are most visible upon her cheeks, appearing as dark spots.

"This completes my description." He paused and glanced up expectantly. Did he see a smile curling the chiseled lips of the ruler's mother?

"An excellent description!" she exclaimed. "It is possible to picture the girl clearly. You have done well, Budz Ek, and will be richly rewarded for your work."

Kan Mo' Hix looked appraisingly at his wife. He knew more about her motives than would please her, but his concern was not the girl's appearance. Her bloodlines back to the dynastic founders, the stability of the ruling family and the political situation of the city, were his main interests.

"It is so, Worthy Messenger," he said. "Your report conveys much information about the daughter of Ik' Muuy Muwaan, and we are appreciative. Tell me more about the difficult times and leadership deficits that recently beset B'aak."

Budz Ek launched with considerable relief into details of crop failures and poor decision-making by the ruler and his administrators. This was safer ground, and the men in the chamber listened with avid attention.

B'aak was a small city to the northwest on hilly country not far from Lakam Ha. It did not possess the lofty vista across wide, fertile plains that his home city enjoyed. Lakam Ha, Place of Big Water, sat upon a narrow ridge one-third of the way up a high mountain range, K'uk Lakam Witz. Numerous small rivers coursed through the ridge, tumbling down the steep escarpment in cascades to join the Michol River. The plains below stretched north to the Nab'nah, the Great Northern Sea, transected by the K'umaxha River that served as the major transportation artery for the region. Named for the Sacred Monkeys that lived along its banks, when the K'umaxha River overflowed it deposited rich silt in the fields in which corn, beans, peppers, and squash were grown.

Lakam Ha was indeed blessed by its patron deities, the Triad Gods. This favored city abounded in water, flowering and fruiting trees, lush jungle foliage with numerous kinds of animals and birds, and cooling breezes from the soaring mountains to the south. It enjoyed a nonpareil view from its high ridge, and the steep cliffs plunging down to the plains below provided natural defense. The Michol River at the cliff's base offered easy transportation, and the plains rolling gently into the hazy distance supported abundant crops to feed the population.

B'aak had long been in the B'aakal Polity and was an ally of Lakam Ha. The ruling dynasty of Lakam Ha provided oversight for the cities within its polity, acting as *May Ku* or chief ceremonial center and dispensing privileges to rulers and nobles of these cities. This system of cooperation, in which leadership rotated among cities through choices made by a Council of ahauob and priests, followed regular cycles of 20 tuns and 260 tuns. The *May* system was ordained by the Gods and kept humans living in peace and harmony. However, recent developments were disrupting this hallowed system, most notably the aggressive actions by Kan rulers in the distant Ka'an Polity. Lakam Ha was still struggling to recover from Kan's devastating attack only twelve years before.

It was important for Lakam Ha to cultivate alliances with its polity cities. Already two cities had switched allegiance to Kan, and had joined in the attack. This was one motive the royal family had for considering marriage ties with B'aak. As Kan Mo' Hix listened to the messenger describing B'aak's troubles, he became even more convinced that the ruling family's daughter was the right choice. This union would guarantee the loyalty of B'aak.

There were other important considerations in selecting a wife for Pakal. However, these were not part of the messenger's report.

"Budz Ek, greatly do we give thanks for your thorough work," Kan Mo' Hix said. "Your report is insightful and provides much information. These things are important and we must consider them carefully."

"Receive also my appreciation for your work," Sak K'uk added. "Our Royal Steward, Muk Kab, will provide your reward to express our deep gratitude. One thing I must stress to you: Do not speak to anyone about this mission. As you see, we consider here things having utmost significance for our city. With this confidence, I charge you."

For moments the eyes of Sak K'uk, recent ruler of Lakam Ha, mother of Pakal the K'uhul B'aakal Ahau, locked with those of the messenger. What he saw in these pools of fathomless blackness made him quiver. She could be ruthless in the service of her son and her dynasty. Any misstep of his, any leaking of secrets, would be fatal.

"It is as you command, Holy Lady," he said, dropping his gaze and bowing.

With hand signs, she dismissed him and ordered the steward to give his recompense. After these two men left, further discussion ensued.

"Pasah Chan, made you study of the bloodlines of the B'aak ruling family?" Kan Mo' Hix addressed the High Priest of Lakam Ha, whose extensive library of codices contained histories of many B'aakal cities and dynasties. A man in his prime, the High Priest was slender with sinewy limbs, a hawk-like face and penetrating half-lidded eyes. From a minor noble family, he had risen to a position of prominence through both brilliant scholarship and shrewd competition.

"So have I done. Our records of the B'aak dynasty are complete." Pasah Chan always enjoyed being in the spotlight. He relished this authority among the highest echelons of Lakam Ha society, especially given his rather humble origins. For a personal reason, he felt sympathy for the "homely" girl under consideration as the ruler's wife. He also had a defect; his skull was not shaped in the fashion of the elite. His parents had failed to apply headboards properly during infancy, a technique used by aspiring nobles to mimic the hereditary elongated skulls of ruling families. Although he now wore headbands to push his hair up from the forehead to resemble this peaking crown, these efforts could not conceal the defect.

"The ruling family of B'aak can justly claim that they are 'of Toktan,' for their ancestors trace back in an unbroken lineage to K'uk Bahlam, founder of the primordial city of Toktan," said Pasah Chan. "These ancestors lived in Lakam Ha for four generations, then left to build their own city a short distance away. They have consistently inhabited B'aak for six generations. According to their traditions, the rulers can rightly call themselves 'K'uhul B'aakal Ahau' because their bloodlines are as pure as your Bahlam family. And, as you well know, their Emblem Glyph bears close resemblance to ours with its use of b'ak—bone and k'uhul—holy symbols."

"Much am I annoyed by this appropriation of our Emblem Glyph," Sak K'uk said, frowning. "Using our Holy B'aakal Lord title is preposterous. Their status in the polity is far less than that of Lakam Ha."

"But their lineage is pristine," observed Kan Mo' Hix. This satisfied his highest priority in selecting his son's wife.

"So have I verified," confirmed Pasah Chan.

"Here is another advantage of this match," Sak K'uk added. "The girl is not of our city."

Pasah Chan shot a quizzical glance toward the ruler's mother, and then recalled their conversation at the celebration of Pakal's Transformation to Adulthood ritual a year earlier. The scene played vividly in his memory. He re-witnessed Sak K'uk's shock upon watching her son dancing sensuously with Yonil, a lissome young woman of minor noble lineage. The strong words of the ruler's mother about preventing this relationship from progressing were as clear as on that night; she vowed to find a more suitable match from a neighboring city. Lalak filled those criteria and another one that would remain unspoken. The High Priest surmised that Sak K'uk did not want a beautiful woman as her son's wife.

Kan Mo' Hix had arrived at the same conclusion much earlier. He was fully aware of the special relationship between mother and son, one that Sak K'uk treasured and would strive to preserve. She did not want a beautiful woman replacing her in Pakal's heart.

More discussion ensued about the benefits this alliance would bring. The Warrior Chief K'akmo commented about strengthening defenses to the west, and the royal cousins speculated about sending expert farmers to help B'aak improve its crops so there could be more tribute and trade opportunities. The group seemed in concordance about this choice for Pakal's wife.

As the session ended and the others departed, Pasah Chan hung back. Sak K'uk alone remained in the chamber; even her husband had left to plan lavish marriage gifts and discuss timing with calendar priests. An event as extraordinary as the marriage of the K'uhul B'aakal Ahau must take place on a very auspicious day, one that promised longevity and fecundity to the royal pair, and abundance and prosperity to the people. Each day of the Mayan calendar held unique qualities based upon positions of stars, sun, and moon, and sacred numerology. It took years of study to develop expertise in interpreting calendar auguries, and well-trained calendar priests were required.

Noticing Pasah Chan's continued presence, Sak K'uk walked over so they could speak in low voices. She sensed he desired a private conversation.

"Have you more to say of this matter?"

"A small concern, Holy Lady."

"Then speak, I am listening."

"Your son Pakal is of age, he has undergone adulthood rituals, and he has a strong character as befits a ruler. Think you not that he should be included in selecting his wife?" Pasah Chan was among the few nobles in Lakam Ha who could question the ruling family directly. His status as High Priest put him among the upper elite.

Sak K'uk looked haughtily at the priest.

"Ruler he may be, but he is still my son. Tradition dictates that parents should select their children's spouses. Pakal is well steeped in the protocols of ahauob and ruling dynasties. You, Pasah Chan, also are well aware of this."

"That is so. But has not Pakal shown interest in the young woman of our city, Yonil? Perhaps he desires at least consideration of this possible match."

"Yonil!" Sak K'uk's eyebrows compressed and her eyes glowered. "That young woman is not a proper candidate. You know her family bloodlines. They are marginal at best; she is deficient in lineage. No, it is impossible to even discuss this with him."

"With her deficient lineage I have no argument," the High Priest replied. "It is only to be sensitive to Pakal's feelings that I suggest such a discussion."

Sak K'uk shook her head. Her jaw was set strongly.

"Men cannot make good decisions about their lifelong mate when driven by the passions of youth. If Pakal is continuing to see this woman, I will immediately put this to an end." Sak K'uk paused as a plan formulated in her mind. "Let us quickly arrange a marriage for Yonil to a noble of a distant city, perhaps Nab'nahotot on the shore of Nab'nah, the Great North Sea. Yes, this we must do, to remove any future temptation. Pasah Chan, see to it."

The High Priest clasped his shoulder and bowed. He felt an unexpected twinge of sadness for the lovely young woman Yonil and for Pakal, who clearly was attracted to her. However, those who served their people as intermediaries to the Gods, who invoked blessings through rituals to guarantee their city's wellbeing, who fulfilled the divine covenant to speak the God's names and keep their days properly, could not make purely personal choices. Pakal's destiny would shape his life.

2

Pakal sat cross-legged on the ruler's double-headed jaguar throne, his expression alert and his long body relaxed. Intelligence shone in his tilted almond eyes set above high cheekbones in a slender face. A prominent straight-bridged nose swept in a clean line to an elongated skull, on which perched a headdress of bright feathers and woven bands. Sculpted lips curved sensuously above a strong chin line, framed by large jade earspools. On his well-muscled chest hung a Sun Lord-K'in Ahau pectoral, and his wrists sported copper cuffs with dangling discs. He wore the mat-design skirt that signified he was a person of the mat, one who sat upon woven mats to govern and deliberate. Strong and well-shaped legs were left bare and he wore no sandals while sitting.

The overall impression created by his appearance was one of self-assurance without arrogance, incisiveness tempered by kindness. The Sun-Faced Lord of the Shield, as his name K'inich Janaab Pakal meant, was well liked by both nobles and commoners. His mettle as a ruler had not yet been tested, for times were returning to stability at Lakam Ha after the destruction of the Kan attack. The simmering issue remained, however, over the loss of the sacred Sak Nuk Nah—White Skin House that served as a portal to the Upperworld. This portal formed by the Wakah Chan Te—Jeweled Sky Tree provided the pathway for communication with the Triad Deities, and had been used for generations by B'aakal rulers. In the Kan attack, the shrine had been spiritually defiled and physically demolished; Pakal's mother Sak K'uk performed a ritual termination ceremony to close the structure permanently and remove lingering evil forces.

During the three years of her rulership, Sak K'uk drew upon the Upperworld powers of the Primordial Mother Goddess Muwaan Mat, mother of the Triad Deities, to perform the required rituals. Once Pakal acceded at age twelve, his mother continued to provide leadership until he reached adulthood. During this time, no major calendar periods came to completion, so the truncated rituals she was able to carry out were sufficient. When the next Katun ending arrived, however, the ruler would be expected to perform extensive ceremonies that reaffirmed his connection with the Deities and satisfied their requirements for tribute and acknowledgement. Upon this rested the sacred contract between the Triad Deities and people of B'aakal.

Without the portal in the Sak Nuk Nah, it was impossible to imagine how these ceremonies could be properly done. It was an issue that weighed heavily upon Pakal's mind and heart. He had pledged himself to restore the portal to the Gods but was uncertain how to accomplish it. Thankfully, he had several years to figure this out. The Katun ending was eleven tuns in the future. Pakal was considering a smaller ritual when the tuns reached 13 in the 20-tun count, a sacred number of spirit and wholeness. This was over three solar years away; it would be his first significant calendar ritual as ruler.

Pakal's duties today were more mundane. He was adjudicating a quarrel in a noble family over inheritance of a small housing complex in the city. T'zul was a middle-aged woman now living in the main house, the recent widow of the family head with only one living child, a married daughter. By Maya custom, the son-in-law lived for one year with his wife's family, offering his services to the household. After that, he returned with his wife to his own family compound, where they continued to live. In T'zul's situation, the son-in-law had remained in her household, as the family head was ailing and there were no sons to help out. T'zul wanted this arrangement to continue; her in-laws had many other sons and could surely spare one.

The challenge to this arrangement came from Ah Nik, brother of the family head. He argued that the housing complex by right should revert to him, as the second oldest male in the family that built the structures. He was living in a nearby house but considered it too small for his growing family of three sons, all married with children and more on the way. Ah Nik was arguing his position.

"It is only reasonable that my family should move into the complex. It is quite larger than our present house and has two other buildings that my sons and their families could occupy. T'zul has fewer members in her family and no grandchildren yet, though greatly do I wish her that joyous happening. Do you not confirm the rightness of this, Holy Lord?"

"It was the wish of my esteemed husband, your older brother, that I remain in the house." T'zul broke in, not waiting for Pakal to respond. Her cheeks were flushed and she stared venomously at her brother-in-law. "We have spent many years in this house. It holds our dearest family memories, and under the floor rests the bones of my poor husband, dead before his time. It is heartless to force us to leave. Ever have you been selfish, Ah Nik!"

"I am thinking only of what is best for my family!" he retorted testily. "You are the selfish one, clutching onto the complex that is too large for your needs. Think of your nephews and their children. Open your heart to their needs."

"Every day I pay homage to my husband's spirit at the shrine in my house. Why would you tear me away from what little solace this gives? It is only right that I remain close to my ancestor's bones, to receive their guidance and comfort."

"Forget you that my ancestors too are buried in that house? My own father and mother, and their predecessors also? Be reasonable, T'zul. We can exchange houses; you move your family into my current place, and I move mine into yours. It is all so very reasonable!" Ah Nik was becoming frustrated.

Tears were streaming down T'zul's face as she turned to Pakal and pleaded her case.

"Oh wise and kind Holy Lord, see a widow's grief! Have mercy upon a suffering one and let me have my small comfort. Do not separate me from my husband's bones!"

Pakal raised a hand, commanding silence. Everyone present hung on the moment, wondering how the young ruler could decide this emotional mess equitably. Several courtiers sat on mats lining the walls of the throne room, the royal steward Muk Kab stood attentively nearby, and a handful of other petitioners hovered along the stairs rising to the chamber.

"My heart is pained by the conflict in your family," Pakal said softly. "Yours has long been a kind and loving family, generous to your workers, and responsible in tribute. My parents spoke of the assistance you gave as our city began to recover after the villainous attack by Kan. Now remember what has come before. You dishonor your ancestors by such dissension. Take a moment, each of you, and look within your heart and conscience. Ask yourself, T'zul, what would your husband want? And Ah Nik, ask yourself what your brother would say of this argument."

The two petitioners hung their heads, feeling abashed. Until recently, their relations had been congenial and both did regret their current strife. Neither was yet willing to relinquish the position they had taken, and waited in silence.

"T'zul, it seems the most important consideration for you is your husband's shrine, is this so?"

Wiping tears from her eyes, T'zul nodded.

"Ah Nik, for you the need of a larger complex for your family is uppermost. You are willing to exchange houses. Would you also be willing to provide labor and materials should T'zul need to enlarge that house in the future?"

"That I would gladly provide," Ah Nik replied, brightening.

"Let me emphasize how important I consider the sacred shrines to our ancestors. These are the very foundations of our culture, for we seek ancestral guidance in every aspect of our lives. This is why we bury their bones in the central chamber of our homes. It is not common, but there are times when ancestral bones must be moved to other locations. This is undertaken with utmost care and all proper ceremonies must be performed."

The young ruler focused his gaze on T'zul and compelled her to look directly into his eyes. Her eyes widened as she was drawn into mesmerizing pools of darkness, from which flowed a force of overwhelming compassion. She felt a pinging sensation in her chest followed by a wave of relief. A sense of deep comfort descended upon her, and the anger she held for her brother-in-law dissipated.

"T'zul, if you will agree to the housing exchange, I will personally conduct the ceremonies to move your husband's bones. You may rest assured these will be done with complete correctness, and his spirit will be satisfied that it is truly honored. He will be happy with his new home, and continue to bless you with his presence."

The widow could not respond for several moments, overcome with gratitude. She had never imagined this solution, and it resonated deeply in her soul. Finally, she spoke.

"Blessed are you, K'uhul B'aakal Ahau, that in your wisdom you could see this path to mending the troubles of our family. With much happiness do I accept your suggestions, and with deep appreciation your personal effort on our behalf. No greater honor could be bestowed upon my husband, than the ceremonies for moving his shrine be performed by our Holy Lord."

Fluffy white clouds moved slowly across the blue sky, making a stately procession overhead. Gentle breezes stirred leaves of Ramón and Pixoy trees and rippled the summer grasses covering the hillsides. A flock of green parrots darted from one cluster of trees to another, squawking exuberantly. From the distance came the throaty roar of howler monkeys, echoing over forest canopy and resounding from steep mountainsides. Life was everywhere in the tropical jungle, bursting with song and sound. Even the insects added their incessant humming and clacking to the chorus.

A raised and plastered walkway called a *sakbe*, or white road, left the eastern edge of Lakam Ha and wended between hills, curving as it followed low ground between the temples rising toward the sky. At the summit of the closest hill stood the Temple of Nohol, dedicated to the warming yellow light from the south that brought growth and ripening. A nearby hill served as base for the Temple of Lakin, facing the eastern sunrise and expressing the awakening powers of red light that brought new beginnings. Swinging around this hill, the sakbe ended and a footpath ascended a steep hillside before dipping toward the Otolum River burbling merrily toward a wide grassy meadow stretching eastward. Across the river was the crest of Yohl Ik'nal's mortuary monument, a temple situated atop a low hill that nestled among others of greater height.

Pakal stood on the hill across from his grandmother's pyramid temple. From this vantage, he could see the far edge of the meadow, where the terrain changed suddenly and plunged over a cliff. The Otolum River crashed into tiers of cascades as it plummeted down the precipitous mountainside, joined by its parallel sister, the Sutzha River, in smaller cascades. Breezes ruffled Pakal's hair and cooled his sweaty skin. He wore only a white loincloth with green and yellow waistband, his hair tied into a topknot, for the day was hot. His eyes sought the small stone building situated next to the river, in the center of the meadow. The walls were partially collapsed and the roof had fallen into a pile of rubble. It once was used by hunters but was long abandoned.

Memories of his previous visits there floated into awareness, and even from this distance he could faintly sense the vortex of energy around the ruined building. His powerful experience of this vortex had convinced him that here was the site to construct a new portal, to build a new Sak Nuk Nah, to re-establish communication with the Triad Deities and divine ancestors.

Standing alone on the hill, Pakal relished his solitude. Rarely did he have an opportunity to be alone, surrounded as he usually was by courtiers, advisors, attendants, administrators, petitioners, and countless others who either wanted his assistance or simply wanted to view their ruler. It was no small accomplishment to carve out this time alone. He had used a visit to his grandmother's tomb as the excuse, explaining that he wished to commune with her spirit and bring offerings, and needed privacy to establish these sensitive and subtle connections. His personal attendant Tohom tried to insist that someone was needed to carry water and mats, and his courtiers offered to wait outside, but he had graciously declined.

It had not been easy, but he prevailed. Actually, there was truth in his excuse, for he greatly admired his grandmother Yohl Ik'nal, who had ruled in her own right for twenty-two years and steered the city through several crises. He did want to pay homage at her tomb and renew their spirit connections. His actual motive, however, was a secret meeting with the young woman Yonil.

She would be arriving soon, and he must complete his ritual first. He hurried down the path, splashed across the river and climbed the narrow stairs to the temple on top the pyramid. Sitting before the altar, he recited invocations and placed a round piece of amber over Yohl Ik'nal's name glyph. He had no means of lighting copal incense and had brought no food offerings. In his heart, he knew simply offering his love was enough. As he concentrated and sensed his grandmother's presence, the amber glowed as if lit from within. He asked for nothing, no guidance or information. He only wanted to experience the deep connectedness between them. Time passed; Pakal kept focus until he heard splashing in the river below. Thanking his grandmother, he bowed and rose to meet the young woman eagerly racing up the pyramid stairs.

The sight of her took his breath away. Her slender form perched on the edge of the temple platform, framed by verdant hills that brought her white huipil to startling clarity. Breezes fluttered the soft fabric so it outlined her thighs and clung to her breasts, where a multicolored band anchored it firmly, leaving her shoulders and arms bare. The shift ended at mid-calf, showing her supple ankles and small feet that slipped into embroidered sandals. Her shining black hair was tied in a topknot, as was his, but hers dangled a long ponytail that swayed sinuously.

She clasped her shoulder and bowed deeply, throwing her ponytail to the floor and exposing the graceful curve of her neck and back. A delicate necklace of copper and white shells clinked softly.

"Greetings, Holy Lord of B'aakal," she murmured without lifting her head.

"Please rise, Yonil," Pakal replied. "And please call me by my name."

He enjoyed watching her form uncurl, movements full of grace and ease. She stood a head shorter, her crown at the level of his shoulders. As their eyes met, he felt an unfamiliar jolt shooting through his body that left his insides humming.

"Did I interrupt you? For this am I sorry," she said, glancing into the temple toward the altar.

"No, no. I had just finished paying homage to my grandmother." Pakal glanced beyond her toward the footpath, relieved to see that no one was in sight. "Let us depart from here; people come often to honor our Holy Ancestor and it is best they do not see us. There is a secluded place I know, and want to show you."

She nodded and followed him down the stairs. At the base, he led her to a faintly visible deer path running alongside the river. The grasses became taller as they entered the large meadow, with an occasional tree casting shadows. Pakal helped Yonil step over some fallen branches and then re-cross the river where it was shallow, hopping on stones when possible but ending up knee deep in clear, cold water. They laughed while splashing onto the bank and Yonil took a moment to wring out the hem of her huipil. Pakal led the way to the partially collapsed building, heading to the far wall that stood highest and blocked them from view.

They found some smooth stones and sat, breathless from their efforts, laughing again at nothing in particular.

"Was it difficult for you to get away?" Pakal asked.

"Not so difficult. I am not constantly surrounded by attendants, as must surely be your lot. It is not unusual for me to leave home and visit my girlfriends. My father was away and my mother occupied with weaving, so I just slipped out unnoticed."

"Ah, yes. Much easier for you. I had to make excuses and almost plead to be allowed a visit to my grandmother's tomb alone. This is a rare moment for me."

Yonil lowered her eyes, blushing faintly.

"Truly am I greatly appreciative for this moment that we can share," she said softly.

"Tell me about your life. What do you do all day?" Pakal felt sadly ignorant about details of non-royal lives.

Yonil began an animated description of her daily life, but Pakal found he was not paying attention to her words. Instead, he was fascinated by her movements; the way her arms made delightful arcs, her supple finger signs, how she tilted her head to emphasize a point. The lilt of her voice was intoxicating, and he could almost catch the scent of honey on her breath. His body pulsed with the rhythm of her words.

Pakal felt both elated and disconcerted. Since the moment when his interest in Yonil was ignited by their dancing at his adulthood ceremonies, he had found very few opportunities to speak with her. These few occasions were always in the company of others, and he was aware that his mother disapproved. She gave him a lecture about the importance of not demonstrating interest in the young women of Lakam Ha, not encouraging their aspirations, because the process of selecting his wife was soon to begin. The High Priest, his mentor and spiritual trainer, also took him aside and reminded him about conserving his sexual energies, so vitally important to his ability to carry out demanding and esoteric rituals. Pasah Chan's admonitions were fresh in his mind about the character-sapping dangers faced by rulers—selfishness, greed, pride, sensuality—that would snare their energies and entrap their spirits.

In years of intense training, Pakal had learned how to master the forces of his sexual drive and move them according to intention. He learned these through experience with Lunar Priestesses, specially trained women dedicated to initiating young ahauob into the physical and psychic aspects of using sexual energies, the most powerful creative force in the Middleworld, *cab* the earth. He knew that combining male and female sexual energies in sacred ways would release immense creative forces. He fully realized how he was expected to channel and to sublimate his sexuality.

However, he had not anticipated his body's reaction to Yonil. Even sitting beside her, his body was vibrating with excitement and desire. He could begin now using breath techniques and meditation to control these sensations, but he did not want to. Instead, when she paused in her recital, he reached an arm toward her and cupped her chin, lifting her face.

"So beautiful!" he whispered, his eyes devouring her features.

Yonil was an exceptionally lovely woman. Her face was oval, with a narrow nose and long straight brow line leading to an elongated skull, the hallmarks of Maya nobility. Tilted almond eyes showed flecks of gold, wide and doe-like, soft as downy feathers. High cheekbones set off smooth cheeks, and her lips were wide and full and voluptuous. Her well-formed chin dipped to a long, graceful neck and softly rounded shoulders. Her skin was the color of light cacao and glowed with health and vitality. In her small ears were tiny amber earspools that reflected the gold in her eyes.

Eyes now wide and mesmerized by Pakal's gaze, Yonil parted her lips as if to catch her breath, her small firm breasts rising and falling rapidly. Pakal's hand dropped to her warm, bare shoulder then moved down, brushing against a breast and wrapping around her waist. She leaned into him, or did he draw her to him? Sparks ignited as their torsos touched; he brought his lips softly against hers then followed her chin to her throat, nuzzling the soft hollow at the base. Her arms wrapped around his neck and she gasped in ecstasy as his arms encircled her waist.

Pakal savored the sensation of her breasts heaving against his chest, aware that he was fully aroused. She was nibbling his ear gently, causing bolts of electricity to shoot through his groin. He could take her now, she would not resist. Her sexuality was exploding through every pore, eager and receptive.

He had to stop it. He could not let this happen. Somewhere, from some depth of determination, he summoned up the willpower to end their embrace. Lifting hands from her waist, he removed her arms from around his neck and gently pushed her body away from his. Still quivering with passion, he turned and walked a short distance away. Now he used the cooling breath technique with vigor, sucking air between nearly closed teeth in deep, steady in-breaths. Simultaneously he chanted a calming incantation until he felt his pulse slowing and the fire in his body retreating.

When he turned back to Yonil, he saw tears glistening in her eyes.

"Yonil, we cannot become lovers," he said with a voice not quite steady.

"Why not? It is what we both want. This passion that *I* feel, I also feel in you. Why must we deny it?"

"You know why. It is because of who I am. Yonil, as much as I desire you, I am bound by duty to my dynasty and the people of Lakam Ha. I must follow the traditions expected of me, and marry the woman selected by my parents. We both know that will not be you."

"Your mother hates me!" Yonil was crying now, tears streaming down her cheeks. Between sobs, she gasped a few words. "She . . . always disliked me . . . from that first time . . . we danced together."

Her tears tore at his heart, and he grasped her hands in his, pressing strongly.

"It is not you, she does not even know who you really are," he said, trying to sound reassuring. "It is that . . . that your family lineage is . . . not suitable for a royal wife. Please do not take offense. You are lovely, so beautiful you cannot imagine. Any man would be fortunate to have you for his wife."

His earnest praise seemed to comfort Yonil, and she stopped crying. Wiping her eyes, she glazed wistfully at Pakal.

"Any man but you," she murmured.

"Not so! I also would be fortunate, but . . . it cannot be."

"Then take me as your concubine." Her gold-flecked eyes locked onto his with the force of a female jaguar. "You are the ruler. You can have any woman, or all the women, that you desire. Your word is law. Your command is as binding as death. To be with you is all I want . . . to love you."

"Ah, Yonil . . . my heart is aching. There is so much you do not understand, cannot possibly know about me, my destiny. About what I must do and how I must do it. Truly am I sorry . . ."

His voice trailed off as her fierce eyes continued to bore into his.

"You can do what you want. You are K'uhul B'aakal Ahau." Her eyes softened into pools of honeyed delight. "All you have to do is command and I will become yours."

A tiny fount of possibility surged upward from the desolate place within Pakal. What she said was not impossible. He knew of other rulers, not in Lakam Ha but in Pa'chan and Uxwitza, who had married secondary wives, and who kept concubines. He was ruler here, and might he not begin a new practice in his dynasty?

He smiled and she relaxed, breathing out a deep sigh.

"Come," he murmured. "Let us part on a sweet note. As you wisely observe, many things may be possible, even for a ruler."

She melted into his arms, snuggling against his chest, reveling in his masculine scent and hard pectoral muscles. He lightly wrapped one arm around her and stroked her hair with the other, fingers combing through silky tresses, murmuring under his breath, "So beautiful, so exquisite."

Neither wanted their embrace to ever end. Long moments passed while the breeze sighed and the river warbled. White puffy clouds bunched over the southern peaks, forming tall thunderheads with gray bellies beginning to fill with rain. The sun was dropping closer to the horizon, sending lengthening shadows across the meadow.

Pakal's lips brushed her crown as he slowly disengaged from their embrace. She did not protest, lifting eyes bright with promise to meet his once again.

"Climb quickly over the hill, there is a deer path through the meadow," he said, pointing the direction. "I will return to my grandmother's temple, so we will seem to come from different places."

She nodded and turned to leave. Suddenly she whirled around, grasped his shoulders and pulled herself up to brush her lips against his.

"Remember that I am waiting, ever waiting, for your command."

Dynasty of Lakam Ha (Palenque)

CODES: B. BORN A. ACCEDED D. DIED R. RULED ALL DATES ARE CE

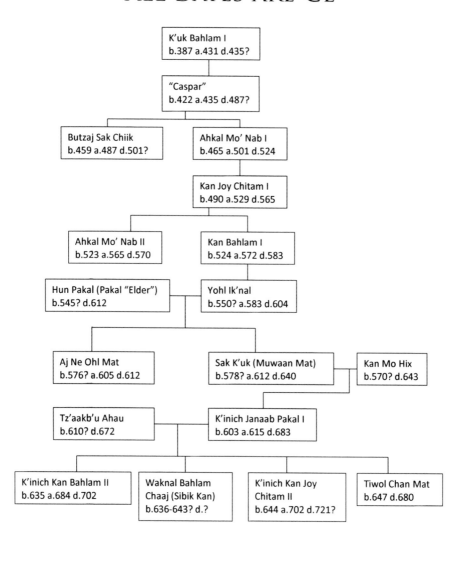

K'uk Bahlam I
b.387 a.431 d.435?

"Caspar"
b.422 a.435 d.487?

Butzaj Sak Chiik
b.459 a.487 d.501?

Ahkal Mo' Nab I
b.465 a.501 d.524

Kan Joy Chitam I
b.490 a.529 d.565

Ahkal Mo' Nab II
b.523 a.565 d.570

Kan Bahlam I
b.524 a.572 d.583

Hun Pakal (Pakal "Elder")
b.545? d.612

Yohl Ik'nal
b.550? a.583 d.604

Aj Ne Ohl Mat
b.576? a.605 d.612

Sak K'uk (Muwaan Mat)
b.578? a.612 d.640

Kan Mo Hix
b.570? d.643

Tz'aakb'u Ahau
b.610? d.672

K'inich Janaab Pakal I
b.603 a.615 d.683

K'inich Kan Bahlam II
b.635 a.684 d.702

Waknal Bahlam
Chaaj (Sibik Kan)
b.636-643? d.?

K'inich Kan Joy
Chitam II
b.644 a.702 d.721?

Tiwol Chan Mat
b.647 d.680

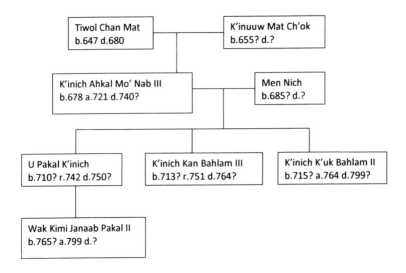

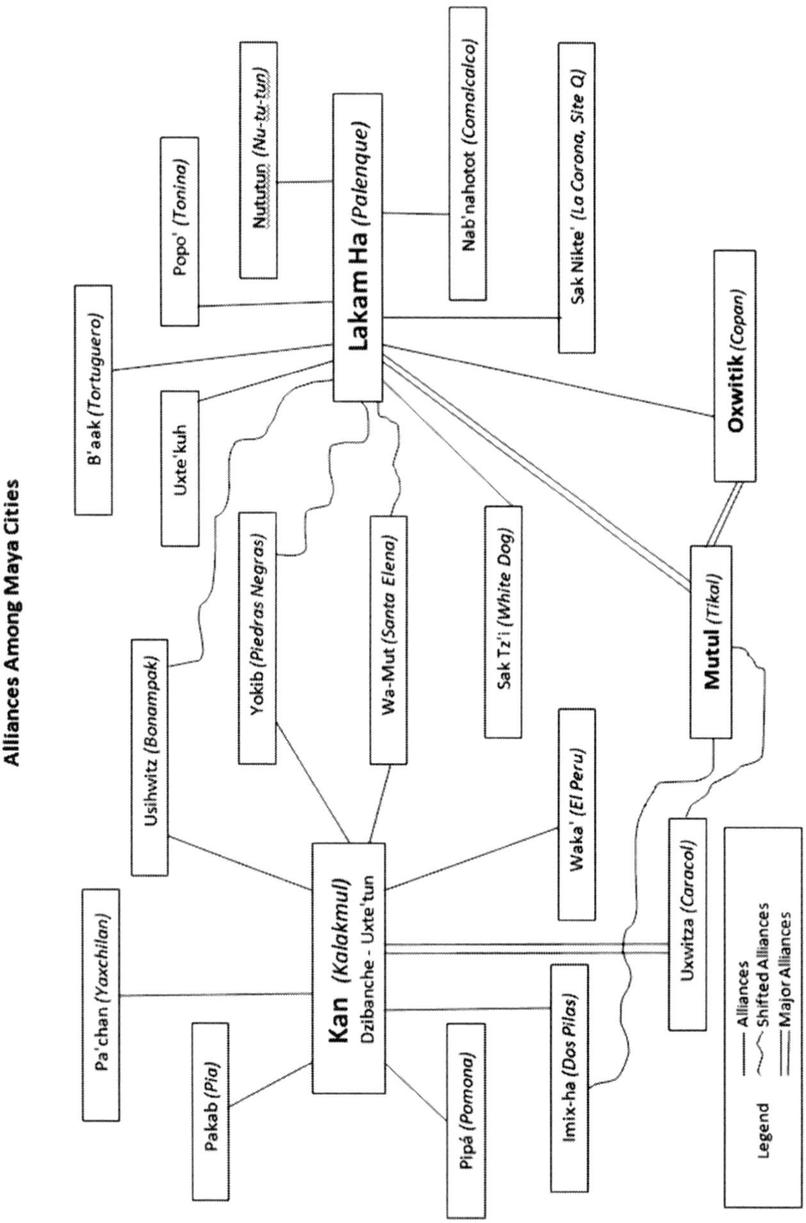

Alliances Among Maya Cities
B'aak (Tortuguero)
Popo' (Tonina)
Nututun (Nu-tu-tun)
Lakam Ha (Palenque)
Nab'nahotot (Comalcalco)
Sak Nikte' (La Corona, Site Q)
Uxte'kuh
Oxwitik (Copan)
Usihwitz (Bonampak)
Yokib (Piedras Negras)
Wa-Mut (Santa Elena)
Sak Tz'i (White Dog)
Mutul (Tikal)
Waka' (El Peru)
Pa'chan (Yaxchilan)
Kan (Kalakmul)
Dzibanche - Uxte'tun
Uxwitza (Caracol)
Pakab (Pia)
Pipá (Pomona)
Imix-ha (Dos Pilas)
Legend
Alliances
Shifted Alliances
Major Alliances

Long Count Maya Calendar

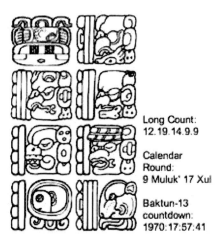

Long Count:
12.19.14.9.9

Calendar
Round:
9 Muluk' 17 Xul

Baktun-13
countdown:
1970:17:57:41

ALTHOUGH CONSIDERED A vigesimal (20 base) system, the Maya used modifications in 2 places for calendric and numerological reasons. In Classic times the counts went from 0 to 19 in all but the 2nd position, in which they went from 0 to 17. Postclassic adaptations changed the counts to begin with 1, making them 1 to 20 and 1 to 18.

Name	Count	Days/Kins per Time Period	Solar Years	Tuns
Baktun	0-19	144,000 Kin = 20 Katun = 1 Baktun	394.25	400
Katun	0-19	7,200 Kin = 20 Tun = 1 Katun	19.71	20
Tun	0-19	300 Kin = 18 Uinal = 1 Tun	0.985	1
Uinal	0-17	20 Kin = 1 Uinal	--	--
Kin	0-19	1 Kin = 1 Kin	--	--

After 19 Kin occur, the Uinal count goes up by 1 on the next day; after 17 Uinal the Tun count goes up by 1 on the next day, after 19 Tun the Katun count goes up by 1 the next day, and after 19 Katun the Baktun count goes up by 1 the next day.

Thus, we see this progression in the Long Count: 11.19.19.17.19 + 1 kin (day) = 12.0.0.0.0

Increasingly larger units of time beyond the Baktun are: Piktun, Kalabtun, Kinchiltun, and Alautun. These were usually noted by placing 13 in the counts larger than Baktun, indicating 13 to a multiple of the 20th power: 13.13.13.13.13.0.0.0.0

When a 13 Baktun is reached, this signifies the end of a Great Cycle of 1,872,000 kins (days) or 5200 tuns (5125.2567 solar years). But this does not signify the end of the Maya calendar. Larger baktun units occur on stela with numbers above 13, indicating that this count went up to 19 before converting into the next higher unit in the 6th position. When the 5th position (Baktun) reaches 19, on the following day the 6th position (Pictun) becomes 1 and the 5th position becomes 0. This results in a Long Count such as that projected by glyphs at Palenque to a Gregorian date of 4772 AD (GMT correlation), written as 1.0.0.0.0.0.

The Tzolk'in and Haab Calendars

The Tzolk'in (Sacred Calendar)

T HE TZOLK'IN IS a ceremonial calendar that orders the times for performing rituals honoring the Maya Deities. It is the oldest known Mesoamerican calendar cycle, dating back to around 600 BCE. The Tzolk'in has a 260-day count, believed to be based on the nine months of human gestation which averages 260 days. The mathematics of the Tzolk'in combines 13 numbers with 20 day names: 13 x 20 = 260. Mayan culture assigns the value 13 to the circle, a sacred number representing spirit and movement. This number also represents the 13 great articulations of the human skeleton, the 13 yearly cycles of the moon, the 13 planets known to the ancient Mayas, and the 13 constellations of the Maya zodiac. Additionally, they subdivided the day into 13 segments each divisible by 13, similar to modern hours, minutes and seconds.

The Maya "month" has 20 days, each with a name. To create the Tzolk'in, each day is combined with a number between 1—13. Since 20 is not evenly divisible by 13, the two sequences do not pair exactly. When the 13th number is reached, the count starts again at 1 while the day names continue from day 14 through day 20. This forms unique combinations until the numbers and names run through a complete 260-day cycle. Then, the Tzolk'in count starts again at day 1 and number 1.

The Haab (Solar Calendar)

The Haab is considered a secular or agricultural calendar, was in use by at least 100 BCE, and has deeply significant numerology. It is composed of 18 "months" of 20 days, creating a mathematical system that resonates through vast cycles and synchronizes with many other calendars through its multiples: 18 x 20 = 360. Each month has a name, combined with a number between 1—20 which is assigned to each day. In ancient Maya counting, the month begins with a "seating" that is recorded as zero, and then the patron deity of the month assumes the throne on day 1 and reigns for the next 19 days. The Haab is used to track solstices, equinoxes and eclipses of moon and sun. Since the Haab count is 360 days, it does not match the solar year of 365.25 days, and the Mayas add a short 5-day "month" to coordinate with the sun's annual cycle. They account for the fractional day by adding one day to the count every four years.

In ancient hieroglyphic texts, the Haab date is recorded next to a Tzolk'in date. This appears as a month name-number combination next to a day name-number combination: 4 Kan 12 Pax, for example. In operation together, the Tzolk'in and Haab create a larger, 52-year cycle called the Tunben K'ak or New Fire Cycle. It is known as the Calendar Round, and is used widely throughout Mesoamerica. The Haab also synchronizes with the Tzek'eb or Great Calendar of the Suns, which tracks cycles of the Pleiades over 26,000 years.

Most Mayan texts that track time combine a Long Count date with a Tzolk'in-Haab date. Using these two separate systems for counting time, the Mayas present amazingly accurate dates.

About the Author

LEONIDE (LENNIE) MARTIN: Retired California State University professor, former Family Nurse Practitioner. Author and Maya researcher, Research Member Maya Exploration Center.

My books bring ancient Maya culture and civilization to life in stories about both real historical Mayans and fictional characters. I've studied Maya archeology, anthropology, and history from the scientific and indigenous viewpoints. While living for five years in Mérida, Yucatán, Mexico, I apprenticed with Maya Elder Hunbatz Men, becoming a Solar Initiate and Maya Fire Woman in the Itzá Maya tradition. I've studied with other indigenous teachers in Guatemala, including Maya Priestess-Daykeeper Aum Rak Sapper. The ancient Mayas created the most highly advanced civilization in the Western hemisphere, and my work is dedicated to their wisdom, spirituality, scientific, and cultural accomplishments through compelling historical novels.

My interest in ancient Mayan women led to writing the Mayan Queens' series called "Mists of Palenque." Three books of the 4-book series are published, telling the stories of powerful women who shaped the destinies of their people as rulers themselves, or wives of rulers. These remarkable Maya women are unknown to most people. Using extensive research and field study, I aspire to depict ancient Palenque authentically and make these amazing Mayan queens accessible to a wide readership.

My writing has won awards from Writer's Digest for short fiction, and *The Visionary Mayan Queen: Yohl Ik'nal of Palenque* received a Writer's Digest 2nd Annual Self-Published eBook award in 2015. *The Mayan Red Queen: Tz'aakb'u Ahau of Palenque* received a Silver Medal in Dan Poynter's Global eBook Awards for 2016.

For more information about my writing and the Mayas, visit:
Website: www.mistsofpalenque.com
Blog: http://leonidemartinblog.wordpress.com/
Facebook: https://www.facebook.com/leonide.martin

Author Notes

WRITING HISTORICAL FICTION about the ancient Mayan culture has its particular challenges. There is a large body of scientific research spanning 150 years, and with continuing discoveries have come fresh interpretations. The predominant archeological view has transitioned from seeing the Mayas as priestly astronomers with ceremonial cities, to thinking they were power-seeking kings conducting endless warfare. In recent years, a more balanced view is emerging that acknowledges the importance of spiritual and worldly concerns in a complex, multi-dimensional culture.

Progress in epigraphy and linguistic study of Maya inscriptions has allowed the ancient Mayas to speak for themselves. Experts are able to read about 80% of the complex hieroglyphs left on walls and monuments in many Maya cities. These expressions have their own point of view, usually regaling the accomplishments of rulers or giving the history of dynasties and ceremonial events. New interpretations of glyphic writing bring forth other possibilities for Mayan culture, such as its cooperative aspects and profound engagement with spirituality through vital and immediate relationships with deities.

Mayan rulers and priests were mystics and shamans. They envisioned and experienced other realities, interacted with otherworldly creatures, communicated with and even became the earthly manifestation of deities. Historical fiction about their experiences, in my view, must include these extraordinary events. Some have questioned whether this belongs in historical fiction, but to me, it is part of Mayan history.

"History is interpretation." I have taken a particular interpretation of dynastic succession at Palenque, based on work of Peter Mathews and Gerardo Aldana. Different successions were proposed by David Stuart, Linda Schele and David

Friedel, Simon Martin and Nicolai Grube. For my focus on the women rulers, succession makes more sense by placing Yohl Ik'nal as the daughter of Kan Bahlam I, Hun Pakal as her husband, Aj Ne Ohl Mat as her son, and Sak K'uk as her daughter and the mother of K'inich Janaab Pakal. Book 1 in the *Mists of Palenque* series tells the story of Yohl Ik'nal, who ruled in her own right for 22 years, the first woman ruler of Lakam Ha.

Sak K'uk is the most elusive among the four "queens" because her times were steeped in turmoil. Lakam Ha suffered a terrible defeat in 611 CE at the hands of Kalakmul (Kan, Uxte'tun) in collusion with Usihwitz (Bonampak). In my story, Sak K'uk plays a decisive role in shepherding her city through this devastation by drawing upon the powers of the Great Primordial Goddess, Progenitor of the B'aakal dynasty, Muwaan Mat. For this fresh and inspiring interpretation, I give thanks to Gerardo Aldana in his 2007 book, *The Apotheosis of Janaab' Pakal: Science, History, and Religion at Classic Maya Palenque* (University Press of Colorado). Sak K'uk became the earthly presence of Muwaan Mat and ruled for three years, until her son Pakal acceded at age twelve. She continued to guide and advise him well into his reign.

The 611 CE attack took place during the rule of Aj Ne Ohl Mat, and it was devastating. The attackers planned to destroy the sacred shrine of Lakam Ha, the portal through which rulers communicated with the Triad Deities. The portal collapsed as the shrine was defiled. Both the ruler Aj Ne Ohl Mat and his father Hun Pakal were taken captive and later killed by Kan. Pakal was eight years old when this happened, and it surely left a deep impression. The glyphs in the Temple of the Inscriptions carved later under the direction of Pakal's oldest son, K'inich Kan Bahlam II, direction tell a plaintive tale about this tragedy.

"On the back of the ninth katun, god was lost; ahau was lost. She could not adorn the Gods of the First Sky; she could not give offerings . . . Muwaan Mat could not give their offerings."

Sak K'uk and her husband Kan Mo' Hix took over leadership during these dark years, but dissention among nobles challenged their position. To consolidate power, Sak K'uk assumed the mantle of Muwaan Mat and held the throne until Pakal acceded. Some Mayanists think Sak K'uk and Muwaan Mat were different names for the same individual; others believe that Muwaan Mat was actually a man. Some believe Sak K'uk was never a ruler. From this maelstrom of disagreement, I selected one stream to follow, the story told in this novel of their extraordinary co-regency.

The life work of Pakal was recreating the portal to the Gods and rebuilding the city, bringing Lakam Ha to its height as the creative, political, and spiritual center of the polity. What most visitors see now when they walk the Great Plaza of Palenque are the structures built by Pakal and his sons and grandson.

Names of ancient Maya cities posed challenges. Spanish explorers or international archeologists assigned most of the commonly used names. Many original city names have been deciphered, however, and I use these whenever they exist. Some cities have conflicting names, so I chose the one that made sense to me. The rivers were even more problematic. Many river names are my own creation, using Mayan words that best describe their characteristics. I provide a list of contemporary names for cities and rivers along with the Mayan names used in the story.

Notes on Orthography (Pronunciation)

ORTHOGRAPHY INVOLVES HOW to spell and pronounce Mayan words in another language such as English or Spanish. The initial approach used English-based alphabets with a romance language sound for vowels:

Hun – Hoon	Ne – Nay	Xoc – Shoke	Ix – Eesh
Ik – Eek	Yohl – Yole	Mat – Maat	May – Maie
Sak – Sahk	Ahau – Ah-how	Yum – Yoom	Ek – Ehk

Consonants of note are:

H – Him	J – Jar	X – "sh"
T – Tz or Dz	Ch – Child	

Mayan glottalized sounds are indicated by an apostrophe, and pronounced with a break in sound made in the back of the throat:

B'aakal   K'uk   Ik'nal   Ka'an   Tz'ak

Later the Spanish pronunciations took precedence. The orthography standardized by the Academia de Lenguas Mayas de Guatemala is used by most current Mayanists. The major difference is how H and J sound:

H – practically silent, only a soft aspiration as in hombre (ombray)
J – soft "h" as in house or Jose (Hosay)

There is some thought among linguists that the ancient Maya had different sounds for "h" and "j" leading to more dilemma. Many places, roads, people's names and other vocabulary have been pronounced for years in the old system.

The Guatemala approach is less used in Mexico, and many words in my book are taken from Yucatek Mayan. So, I've decided to keep the Hun spelling rather than Jun for the soft "h." But for Pakal, I've resorted to Janaab rather than Hanab, the older spelling. I have an intuition that his name was meant by the ancient Mayas to have the harder "j" of English; this gives a more powerful sound.

For the Mayan word Lord —Ahau— I use the older spelling. You will see it written Ahaw and Ajaw in different publications. For English speakers, Ahau leads to natural pronunciation of the soft "h" and encourages a longer ending sound with the "u" rather than "w."

Scholarly tradition uses the word Maya to modify most nouns, such as Maya people and Maya sites, except when referring to language and writing, when Mayan is used instead. Ordinary usage is flexible, however, with Mayan used more broadly as in Mayan civilization or Mayan astronomy. I follow this latter approach in my writing.

Acknowledgements

THE CONTRIBUTIONS OF many people provide a supportive framework for this book. My greatest respect goes to the archeologists who devoted years to uncovering hidden ruins and analyzing the messages communicated through stones, structures, artifacts, and hieroglyphs. Seminal work uncovering Maya civilization was done by Teobert Mahler, Alfred Maudslay, Sylvanus Morley, and J. Eric Thompson. Early decipherment made progress through Ernst Forstemann, Eduard Seler, Joseph T. Goodman, and Juan Martinez. Franz Blom made early maps of Palenque structures and Heinrich Berlin advanced epigraphy by identifying emblem glyphs for cities.

Alberto Ruz Lhuillier made the famous discovery of Janaab Pakal's tomb deep inside the Temple of the Inscriptions. Merle Green Robertson, whose drawings of Palenque structures still captivate researchers, gathered an interdisciplinary team in the Mesas Redondas held near the archeological site. The Palenque Dynasty was identified by the Mesa Redonda teams including Linda Schele, Floyd Lounsbury, Simon Martin, David Stuart, Peter Mathews, Nicolai Grube, and Karl Taube. David Stuart and his father George Stuart continued to advance knowledge of Palenque rulers, while Michael Coe captured the public's interest in books about Maya culture and deciphering the Maya hieroglyphic code.

Two Russian scholars figured large in Maya research. Tatiana Proskouriakoff rendered beautiful reconstructions of cities and uncovered patterns of dates that recorded historical events on monuments. Epigraphy leapt forward with the work of linguist Yuri Knorosov showing that Maya symbols were both syllabic and phonetic. Later scholars added the concept of polyvalence, when a single sign has multiple values and a sound can be symbolized by more than one sign.

Dennis Tedlock translated the *Popol Vuh*, giving us a poetic rendition of Maya creation mythology. Edwin Barnhart oversaw the masterful Palenque Mapping Project, uncovering numerous hidden structures west of the Great Plaza and demonstrating that Palenque was a very large city. Prudence Rice provided fresh and instructive interpretations of Maya social and political organization, including the *may cycle* in which ceremonial and political leadership passed cooperatively among cities.

Gerardo Aldana explored different interpretations of Palenque dynasties, power structures, and astronomy. The amazing intellectual feats of Maya royal courts were exemplified in the 819-day count, a calendric construct used to maintain elite prestige. Aldana's acumen in reading glyphic texts was pure inspiration for me, leading to major ideas for the succession surrounding Sak K'uk and Muwaan Mat, and Pakal's reconstruction of the destroyed portal to the Gods.

Arnoldo Gonzalez Cruz directed the excavations at Palenque that revealed the tomb of the "Red Queen," first uncovered by Fanny Lopez Jimenez. The story of discovering the first Mayan queen's sarcophagus was told in lively fashion by journalist Adriana Malvido in her book *La Reina Roja* (Conaculta, INAH, 2006). Arturo Romano Pacheco determined that the bones were those of a woman, one of the queens in my novels.

The richness of my experiences with indigenous Mayas goes beyond description. I could not write about the ancient Maya without the insights gained in ceremony and study with mentors Hunbatz Men and Aum Rak Sapper, who initiated me into Maya spirituality, and the examples of ancient rituals provided by Tata Pedro Cruz, Don Alejandro Cirilio Oxlaj, Don Pedro Pablo and members of the Grand Maya Itzá Council of Priests and Elders.

Thanks to my beta readers Lisa Jorgensen, Cate Tennyson, Karen Van Tassell, and Ginger Bensman. Each provided significant feedback to help me better hone the story and shape the characters. Endless accolades and many hugs to my husband David Gortner, inveterate web researcher who ferreted out esoteric facts and elusive images, tirelessly re-read chapters, dissected grammar, and always challenged me to get things straight and make them clear. And, my heartfelt appreciation to our wonderful white cats, Takan and Sakah, who were always ready to cheer me with purrs and comfort me with lap-sitting.

Other Works By Leonide Martin

The Visionary Mayan Queen: Yohl Ik'nal of Palenque

Mists of Palenque Series Book 1

Amazon Top 100 Books—Amazon Best Seller Historical Fiction and Historical Fiction Romance—Writer's Digest Award

IN MISTY TROPICAL jungles 1500 years ago, a royal Mayan girl with visionary powers—Yohl Ik'nal—was destined to become the first Mayan woman ruler. Last of her royal lineage, her accession would fulfill her father's ambitions. Yohl Ik'nal put aside personal desires and the comfortable world of palace women to prepare as royal heir. Love for her father steeled her will and sharpened her skills. As she underwent intensive training for rulership, powerful forces allied to overthrow the dynasty and plotted with enemy cities to attack. As the first Queen of Palenque, she built temples to honor her father and her Gods, protected her city and brought prosperity to the people. Her visionary powers foresaw enemy attack and prevented defeat. In the midst of betrayal and revenge, through court intrigues and power struggles, she guided her people wisely and found a love that sustained her. As a seer, she knew times of turmoil were coming and succession to the throne was far from certain. Could she prepare her headstrong daughter for rulership or help her weak son become an effective leader? Her actions would lead to ruin or bring her city to greatness.

Centuries later Francesca, part-Mayan archeologist, helps her team at Palenque excavate the royal burial of a crimson skeleton, possibly the first Mayan queen's tomb ever discovered. She never anticipated how it would impact her life and unravel a web of ancient bonds.

Praise from Reviewers and Readers:

"A story that is fully imagined yet as real as the ancient past that it gives voice to once again. . . The characters here are fully realized, vivid and alive, and often do surprising things. . . that are very human, which can be rare. . . the novel weaves fact with speculation without ever seeming heavy handed. The reader is able to understand the truth of these people's lives and struggles while also welcomed in to a conception of the world that is bigger than anything they might have expected or experienced before." – *Writer's Digest 2nd Annual Self-Published e-Book Awards (2015)*

"Spellbinding, exciting and beautifully paints a picture (of) the world of the ancient royal Mayan Queens." – *S. Malbeouf*

"A page turner. . . draws the reader in with the drama of the era. . . One can smell the incense, feel the tension, share the spirituality, experience the battles, and live the lives of the characters." – *H. and N. Rath*

". . . vibrant storytelling, strong dialogue and authentic characters. . . that ring true to the Mayan culture. . . stunning job of keeping this story fast-paced, compelling, emotional and engaging to the very end." – *S. Gallardo*

The Mayan Red Queen: Tz'aakb'u Ahau of Palenque

Mists of Palenque Series Book 3

Silver Medal in Dan Poynter's Global eBook Awards 2016

THE ANCIENT MAYA city of Lakam Ha has a new, young ruler, K'inich Janaab Pakal. His mother and prior ruler, Sak K'uk, has selected his wife, later known as The Red Queen. Lalak is a shy and homely young woman from a nearby city who relates better to animals than people. She is chosen as Pakal's wife because of her pristine lineage to B'aakal dynasty founders—but also because she is no beauty. She is overwhelmed by the sophisticated and complex society at the polity's dominant city, and the expectations of the royal court. Her mother-in-law Sak K'uk chose Lalak for selfish motives, determined to find a wife who would not displace her in Pakal's affections. She viewed Lalak as a breeder of future rulers and selected her royal name to reflect this: Tz'aakb'u Ahau, the Accumulator of Lords who sets the royal succession.

Lalak struggles to learn her new role and prove her worth, puzzled by her mother-in-law's hostility and her husband's aloofness. She learns he is enamored of a beautiful woman banished from Lakam Ha by his mother. Pakal's esthetic tastes obscure his view of his homely wife. Lalak, however, is fated to play a pivotal role in Pakal's mission to restore the spiritual portal to the Triad Gods that was destroyed in a devastating attack by archenemy Kan. Through learning sexual alchemy, Lalak brings the immense creative force of sacred union to rebuild the portal. But first Pakal must come to view his wife in a new light.

The naive, homely girl flowers into a woman of poise and power, establishes her place in court, and after several miscarriages that bring her marriage to crisis, she has four sons with Pakal to assure dynastic succession. Her dedication supports him in a renaissance of construction, art, and science that transforms Lakam Ha into the most widely sought creative center in the Classic Maya world.

In modern times, ten years after the discovery of the Red Queen's tomb, archeologist Francesca is studying new research about the mysterious royal woman in Mérida, Mexico. She teams up with British linguist Charlie to decipher an ancient manuscript left by her deceased grandmother. It provides clues about her grandmother's secrets that propel them into exploring her family history in a remote Maya village.

Praise from Reviewers and Readers:

"The Mayan world and its underlying influences come alive, making for a thriller highly recommended for readers who also enjoy stories of archaeological wonders. . . The attention to contrasting ancient and modern Mexican settings is also well done and adds depth and meaning to overall events, while Martin takes time to detail the methods of investigation that are involved in archaeological research. . . Oracles and divine visions, priests and priestesses, goddesses and oracles, and ancient medicines that can repel malevolent forces: all these are drawn together in a clear portrait of ancient Mexico and the lush jungles surrounding Palenque." – *The Midwest Book Review, Diane Donovan, Editor and Senior Reviewer*

"The quality of this novel is top notch. . . Lalak is lovely and beautifully written. . . crafting believable yet mythical characters that carry the story almost effortlessly. The plot was interesting and very unique. What a pleasure to read something that is not predictable like so many books on the market these days. . . fans of complex world building will be absorbed by this one—with pleasure! – *Writer's Digest 3rd Annual Self-Published e-Book Awards (2016)*

". . . a fascinating journey into the life of the Mayan Red Queen. . . the story of Lalak, a kind, perceptive—and homely young woman who is whisked away

from everything she knows to an arranged royal marriage. . . the ancient Mayan cities, Mayan art, music, and clothing is exemplified throughout. . . pulses with ritual and sex magic. . . tastefully written with a beautiful weave of historical fact."
– *East County Magazine, January 2015*

"I absolutely loved this book!. . . a story of courage, patience and love. . . Historical fact, Mayan mysticism and the delightful imagination of this incredible author. . . makes me feel as if I had been there. So picturesque and beautiful. It was such a creative and inspiring story and I would encourage anyone to dive into this lovely world! – *Carol Clancy*

"*The Mayan Red Queen* is my favorite of this series so far!. . . an outstanding read, and kept me so engaged that I hardly put it down. . . characters are thoroughly and carefully developed. Their issues are those with which we humans have grappled since the beginning of time. . . love, commitment, jealousy, revenge, duty, responsibility, and conflict resolution. . . Beautifully and affirmatively. . . illustrates the age old process of men and women searching for meaning in their lives. . . "
– *Cheryl Randall*

Dreaming the Maya Fifth Sun: A Novel of Maya Wisdom and the 2012 Shift in Consciousness

The lives of two women, one modern and one an ancient Maya priestess, weave together as the end of the Mayan calendar approaches in 2012. ER nurse Jana Sinclair's recurring dream compels her journey to jungle-shrouded Mayan ruins where she discovers links with ancient priestess Yalucha, who was mandated to hide her people's esoteric wisdom from the Spaniards. Jana's reluctant husband is swept into strange experiences and opposes Jana's quest. Risking everything, Jana follows her inner guidance and returns to Mexico to unravel her dream. In the Maya lands, dark shamanic forces attempt to deter her and threaten her life.

Ten centuries earlier, Yalucha's life unfolds as a healer at Tikal where she faces heartbreak when her beloved, from an enemy city, is captured. Later in another incarnation at Uxmal, she again encounters him but circumstances thwart their relationship. She journeys to Chichén Itzá to join other priests and priestesses in a ritual profoundly important to future times.

As the calendar counts down to December 21, 2012, Jana answers the call across centuries to re-enact the mystical ritual that will birth the new era, confronting shamanic powers and her husband's ultimatum—and activates forces for healing that reach into the past as well as the future.

Fans of historical fiction with adventure and romance will love this story of an ancient Maya Priestess and contemporary woman who unravel secret bonds to fulfill the Maya prophecy that can make the difference for the planet's future.

Praise from Reviewers and Readers:

"Travel through time and space to ancient Maya realms. . . details are accurate, giving insight into Maya magic and mysticism and bringing their message of the new era to come." – *Aum-Rak Sapper, Maya Priestess and Daykeeper*

"Few people have listened to this call and made pilgrimage to ancient Maya centers, but many will follow. . . to serve the planet in the Fifth Solar Cycle." – *Hunbatz Men, Itzá Maya Elder, Daykeeper and Shaman*

". . . power-house historical novel. . . unlocks (Mayan) civilization. . . This well documented book is spellbinding, romantic, thought provoking and gives an insightful look into the spiritual side of ancient Mayas. . . a must read!" – *J. Grimsrud, Maya travel guide*